W9-CNS-165

To Tracy!

Thank you so much

for supporting me in
my writing endeavours.

Best Regards,

(Deb xxx)

Chasing Charlie

D J Sherratt

authorHOUSE®

AuthorHouse™ LLC
1663 Liberty Drive
Bloomington, IN 47403
www.authorhouse.com
Phone: 1-800-839-8640

This is a work of fiction. All of the characters, names, incidents, organizations, and dialogue in this novel are either the products of the author's imagination or are used fictitiously.

© 2014 DJ Sherratt. All rights reserved.

No part of this book may be reproduced, stored in a retrieval system, or transmitted by any means without the written permission of the author.

Published by AuthorHouse 07/03/2014

ISBN: 978-1-4969-2105-5 (sc)
ISBN: 978-1-4969-2104-8 (e)

Any people depicted in stock imagery provided by Thinkstock are models, and such images are being used for illustrative purposes only.
Certain stock imagery © Thinkstock.

This book is printed on acid-free paper.

Because of the dynamic nature of the Internet, any web addresses or links contained in this book may have changed since publication and may no longer be valid. The views expressed in this work are solely those of the author and do not necessarily reflect the views of the publisher, and the publisher hereby disclaims any responsibility for them.

Acknowledgments

There are many friends who have helped, encouraged, listened to, supported and read Chasing Charlie along the way. All of them in some way made it into the pages of this novel. Special mention goes out to James, Jenna, Jim and Melissa for their vast knowledge of all things written and their unending patience with me. Also, a huge thank you to John Bellone's Musical Instruments of London, Ontario who were most gracious and accommodating in helping me capture my cover.

But I would be remiss not to mention my loving family. My sincerest thanks goes especially to Ann for her keen eye and Kevin for "sitting in" and all their love and support. Last but certainly not least to Bailey and Mark. Your support on this project has been humbling. I only hope to inspire and support you in the same way. You've really set the bar high with this one!

All my love,

;Dxx

Table of Contents

If we only look down, there will never be stars.

-Hakuin

Prologue

Present Day

The first light of day struck the left eye of the sleeping man, burning onto the tender eyelid and causing him to stir. Groaning, he cracked the eye open and then hissed air out through his clenched teeth as the sun pierced into his hung over retina. Grabbing a pillow he threw it towards the offending broken blind hanging limply in the window of the bedroom. When in hell was he going to learn to park the bus so that the bedroom window with the broken blind faced west? It had gone on too long. Everything had gone on too long.

He rolled over, relieving his eye of the flaming sun and felt the thud of his head as it fell against the pillow. Oh dear God. This time he had really done it. It truly felt as if his brains were hitting the inside of his skull, the pain was so bad. It was just a hangover but considering his night, this one would take more than the day to recover from. For now, he needed pain relief. He tried swallowing but his mouth was so dry it hurt to swallow. He needed water, water and pain relief. He remembered a blonde body at some point in his bed last night and slowly opened his eyes hoping to find her still asleep, perhaps a willing nurse maid for him. No luck, he was alone. Alone, thirsty as hell with a hangover that could kill a horse and sprawled in the back bedroom of his tour bus in the early morning hours of his 51st birthday. Happy Birthday Charlie Morningstar!

Shit! He slowly sat up, feeling his stomach churn and roil with the movement. It had been years since he drank so much it made him sick to his stomach and he wasn't so sure today wouldn't be a new date to go by. He slid his naked body off the bedside and reached for the doorway.

The door was open, validating the existence and departure of the blonde body; Charlie always slept with his door closed. Grabbing the walls along the hallway, he reached the bathroom stall and pulled at the mirrored cabinet door. Sporting the extra strength Advil he opened the cap, poured three, considered a fourth, but replaced the bottle leaving the cap off. He turned on the cold tap and bent over to drink from the faucet, having the sense to first wet down his mouth and throat. He gulped down the pills and drank for a few more seconds before turning off the tap. God, he felt like complete shit. If he could keep those pills down he might reduce the pounding in his skull. The only thing to do was head back to bed and sleep it off. He retreated back down the hallway and edged himself gently onto the bed, careful not to make any sudden moves that might bring back up the only hope he had of feeling somewhat better.

He lay down and instinctively curled into the fetal position. *Ironic*, he thought, *that I should feel like dying today of all days and be in the same position I was in 51 years ago*. It nagged at him a little. Not wishing to do anything but rest, Charlie tried to erase any thoughts from his head. But his mind wasn't having it. It kept drifting back to the thought of dying. Today. Today of all days – his 51st birthday. *Christ!* His head was pounding, his stomach was rolling and his brain wanted to think about dying… on his birthday. Not a good sign. He vowed there and then to never drink that much again. Never, and Charlie never said never.

As he lay there, his mind continued plaguing him with morbid thoughts. It wasn't that he truly wanted to die physically, he just felt like death. Actually, he felt quite alive which was surprising to him considering. He felt more alive than he expected to be. It dawned on him that he was very much alive in spite of last night's activities. Charlie sat up and regretted the move instantly, but he only grabbed his aching head in his hand to steady himself before launching himself up off the bed. Determined to keep moving he grabbed for his jeans thrown over the dresser and stumbled up the hallway raising his leg to pull up the right side of his jeans. He fell against the hallway wall but managed to brace himself with his back against the wall, all while pulling the left leg through the pant leg. *Fucking Cirque de Soleil move for this poor hung over birthday boy*, he thought as he pulled himself upright and began his trek again up the hallway.

His destination was the kitchen. He managed to make it without hitting the wall, using the handle of his fridge as leverage as he pulled it open. He grabbed the first bottled water he could easily reach, opened the cap and drank the ice cold water letting it soothe his tongue, mouth and throat. He almost drained the bottle and stood leaning against the fridge. The bus looked like a bomb had gone off in it. Glasses, pizza boxes, liquor bottles of all manner were on every visible surface. And the smell... like four days of hard living in a sweat box bar; nasty, stale and stagnant. Suddenly his nostrils were assailed with the smell, forcing his stomach to start churning. He had to get fresh air. He dove for the front of the bus and pushed open the door, almost missing the last step and stumbling onto all fours hitting the ground. He gagged and quickly started breathing in the clean morning air through his nose. In through the nose, out through the mouth, he continued. Using a four beat pace Charlie remained in this position until he believed his stomach had settled some. The new dawn and sounds of the rising day caused him to take pause for a moment as he stayed there. A new day. The dawn of a new day. This day. The day that wouldn't come but did.

Charlie raised his head and squinted at the rise of this new day. For so long no day held promise; now, here it was, the one day he figured wouldn't be his to have and it was here. He pushed his right hand off the ground and stood upright blocking the sun's rays from his eyes with his hand. His pounding head had started to numb and he was glad for the relief. He turned back towards the door he stumbled out of and found a seat on the bottom step needing to take a minute to collect his thoughts.

Where was he? San Francisco? No, that was last week. They had come further south on Friday. No, he was in Carmel. That's right, Carmel, California. And where had they played? The Indigo Palace. Good, he remembered. Now if only last night would return to his memory. There was the singing of "Happy Birthday" before, during and after the show. A cake was presented along with a bottle of Jägermeister, probably the culprit of his near death experience today but he really couldn't recall how he got back to the bus, or with whom. There had to have been more than one person to have made such a mess, surely. He groaned as he brought his head down into his hands and dropped his head between his knees. Once again he was aware of the sun as if it were continuously tapping him on the shoulder, beating down onto him with its warmth. Again with the nagging feeling of life and death and the irony. He looked up and this time looked directly into the blazing circle of light. Of life. On this day. Life on this day. He closed his eyes and raised his face to the welcoming warmth and allowed a few minutes to pass as he basked in the glow of this new day.

Despite his hangover, Charlie felt better. Maybe it was the pills, maybe not, but he truly felt better. He opened his eyes and took stock of himself. Still a hurting unit but there was hope. His right side leaning against the doorway, he wondered if going back to bed and sleeping more would help but for some reason Charlie wanted to be awake. He wanted to be alive. He pulled himself up and turned to head back into the bus.

He left the door open and started opening the windows at the front as much as he could to air the stink out. The morning breeze helped. *No more partying on the bus*, he thought.

With fresh air now slipping through crossways, Charlie sank into the couch near the door and wondered where to go from here. Literally. Last night's gig was a one-off at the Indigo Palace and he hadn't bothered to book past this date. He hadn't thought of anything past this date. Now that it was here, what did he want to do? *Go ahead Birthday Boy, make your wish.* And for the first time in 44 years, Charlie made a birthday wish. There, all alone, hung over on his tour bus on his 51st birthday, Charlie Morningstar wished for the one thing that he had run from all those years ago. He wished to go home. A thought occurred to him that made his heart lurch. An idea. One that could make his wish come true, if only for a little while. He felt around his jeans pocket. *Damn!*

What had he done with it? He looked over the lounge and kitchen area from his seat on the couch. He couldn't see anything but party clutter.

As he was about to raise himself off of the couch to hunt the damn thing down, the muffled ringing located his lost cell phone. He was sitting on it; rather, it was somehow under the cushions of the couch. He pulled the entire cushion out from underneath him, grabbed the phone and looked to see who the caller was. Chase. What an ass, calling him at this hour after a raging party on his 51st birthday. Probably doing it just to piss him off. Charlie rejected the call and placed one of his own. When the operator answered he asked her for help in finding the number for Wade McGrath of Chicago, Illinois. Thankfully, the mid-west was ahead by three hours so he wouldn't be calling at the crack of dawn there. Sure enough, after two rings, the line was answered by a gruff old voice. "Black and Blue, Wade here."

"Wade?" Charlie asked.

"Yeah?" Wade answered.

"Charlie Morningstar."

There was a moment's silence where Charlie wondered if Wade had gotten so old he didn't remember him, but Wade started laughing and said, "Well how the hell are ya, Charlie? Long time no see for these poor old eyes! I half expected to hear from you long before now. Finally ready to bring that band of yours home and treat your hometown to some good old blues?"

"Something like that," Charlie stated.

"Well, how soon are ya coming?" Wade asked.

"You know me, Wade, haven't changed much in 20 years. I'll be driving the bus up. It'll take a good three to four days before we get there but no gigs along the way so it'll make the trip direct."

"Come see me when you get in and we'll talk business then. Good to know you're finally coming home, boy. You'll sure have the town buzzing." Wade said.

"Yeah, the prodigal son returns, huh?"

"Ha!" Wade laughed out loud. "Something like that!"

"I'll see you in a few days, Wade. And thanks for the invite."

"Think nothing of it and, by-the-way, happy birthday." With that, Wade hung the phone up.

Charlie was floored! He didn't even say goodbye, his mouth hung open at a loss for words. It was hard to believe Wade had known his birth date, let alone remembered and had the presence of mind to say so to him. I mean, it's not like Wade was expecting his call. They hadn't spoken in some 20 years and now he was heading back to where it had all begun for him. And for Chase. Charlie Morningstar was headed home. Alive.

Chapter 1

George Morningstar

As the school choir sang for their audience, the choir director, Mr. Morningstar, felt a great sense of pride. These kids were excellent! Their rich, strong voices filled the school auditorium and their harmony was spot on. His daughter Celia was right in the middle of the group giving it her all. George Morningstar had never felt prouder. He had brought these kids together and polished them into quite an excellent choir. He knew it and the people of the small town knew it too. Considering the circumstances, he had done extremely well. After all, it was unheard of that a white man would be inside, let alone teaching, at an all black school.

He held his arms up conducting the last notes, having the singers hold the note for effect. He dropped his arms dramatically and the voices all stopped simultaneously, just as they had practiced it over and over again. The crowd came to their feet and applauded the choir and its director for a job well done. George Morningstar turned and bowed to the audience, held his arm out to the choir and they all bowed in unison. He stood up proud, to his full six feet, two inches, smiled his broad smile and bowed his dark, curly head one more time as the applause continued. Mr. Morningstar was well loved! He had an easy way with the kids often listening to their concerns, angst and fears. His role was sometimes "parent" as well as choir director, more so since his own daughter, Celia, was a key singer in the group. Her range was remarkable and George would feature her as much as possible. As he studied the choir, he looked through all the kids to see her smiling back at him. She always stood out in the crowd! He winked at her and she winked back. Their relationship was solid and strong, something George was most proud of.

He had held back on his dreams to make sure she had the best life a single dad could provide and he had succeeded. He managed to raise her from the age of five to eighteen without much trouble. It hadn't hurt that he had been teaching at her school since before she even started first grade.

The town was just situated a few minutes south of Peoria, Illinois, where George had been born and raised. It didn't have much to offer but George had remained there long after most others would have sought greener pastures. He wanted to raise his daughter amongst the people that he cared for and trusted the most, the people that had accepted him and Meg and Celia when his own had turned away. It was his piano playing at the local Baptist Church each Sunday for years that convinced the administrators to give him the job. Then, when Celia started high school, George applied as the music teacher there. This time the administrators were extremely skeptical until George convinced them otherwise. He came prepared with a lesson plan laid out for the school year and, when that didn't wow them; he offered to also step in as a choir director. They deliberated for over an hour until finally offering him the job. It gave him a great advantage. He could help guide Celia's musical career from infancy, teach her about music both inside and out of school and keep her from straying off the path chosen for her. Oh George Morningstar saw great things for his daughter Celia and it was all very close to coming to fruition! She had graduated high school and was hoping to attend college in the fall, but George had other ideas. Things were in the works and he planned on having everything change this summer. Celia knew nothing of his plans but she'd go along with it, he was sure. She just needed to stay focused and he was going to be sure that happened. After all, they only had each other.

George had been an only child. His parents disowned him after his elopement with Meg and now they were long dead and gone. His father had been a busy lawyer with Peoria's largest firm and had had little time for George. His mother had been involved in everything to do with Peoria's elite, but little to do with his childhood. They were a high society couple who had no time for their only child. He spent many days alone after school with only a nanny for company as friends were not allowed while his parents weren't home and his parents were never home.

At the private boy's school he was enrolled in, he tried to make friends but found the other boys to be just like his father, and he hated his father. The schooling curriculum was geared more towards academia, math and sciences, a schooling factory that spewed out the next generation's lawyers, business moguls and physicists. George was not interested in anything of that nature. When he met Mrs. Preston and her piano he felt as though he'd awoken from a long, lonely, isolated nap. Her daughter Meg was the shot of espresso he wasn't expecting.

The best thing his father had done for him was insist upon George taking piano lessons as a gift for his eleventh birthday. George wanted a bike but his father thought it was important for him to have some diversity in his schooling and the boy's school didn't offer music in its lessons. It had been arranged that George would begin lessons with Mrs. Preston, wife of Rev. Carson Preston, a Baptist Minister who preached in a small church just outside of Peoria. As much as they hated their son taking lessons from a Baptist, George's mother had been assured that Mrs. Preston came highly recommended and was the finest piano teacher around.

George was reluctant and nervous as he was dropped off at the door of the Preston's very modest home for his first lesson. He was told to behave himself and mind his teacher and then the driver pulled away. George considered running for a moment and held his hand before knocking. Just as he was about to make contact with the door, it opened.

George had not spent a lot of time with girls his own age. He stammered to say something to her for he had never seen a girl who looked like her. She was wild and exotic. Her hair was long and sat on her head more like a mane than a head of hair. It was sort of tawny in color with lighter streaks all mixed together. It was extremely thick and fell to the middle of her back. She stood no taller than he and wore a matching short and top set in a green jungle pattern. Her skin was not so much tanned as it was a natural deep honey color. She reminded him of caramel. She did not resemble any of the society women's daughters that he had ever seen. She was an exotic and rare being. Most of all, it was her eyes that mesmerized him. Grass green with flecks of gold trimmed with long, thick lashes. George had never seen anyone like her, although her features seemed more akin to that of his family cook and housekeeper but she was much lighter skinned. Even at the young age of eleven, George was immediately smitten.

She smiled wide, her teeth straight and white. "Hello! You must be George. My mom is expecting you. Come on in!"

George felt at a disadvantage. "What's your name?" he asked.

"Meg," she replied. "I'm Meg Preston." She held out her hand.

George took her hand and shook it. "I'm George Morningstar," he said.

Her smile grew even wider. "Oh, I like your name, George Morningstar. I love the stars, *especially* the Morning Star," she gushed and off she danced, twirling and jumping into a large living room.

Mrs. Preston appeared from around a wall wiping her hands off on a dishtowel. She looked nothing like her daughter, nothing at all and George wondered if Meg looked more like her father.

Vera Preston was reed thin with shoulder length blonde hair and a lean, narrow face which was emphasized by the fact that she always wore her hair in a pony tail. She wore black-rimmed glasses and her eyes were brown and soft. At one time she had been quite a striking woman, but Vera was past that time and looked every moment of her 54 years. She introduced herself and led George over to the piano in the same living room Meg just danced off through. He wondered where she had gone and if she'd be around every time he came for his piano lessons. He'd like to talk more to the girl named Meg Preston with the grass-green eyes, wild exotic look, mane of hair, who also liked his name!

And so it began, a simple exchange that grew into a strong, trusting and caring relationship built upon every Tuesday and Thursday after school for two hours. His parents would have stopped his lessons from the very get-go had they known what it would lead to. Mrs. Preston was an excellent piano teacher and George had a natural musical talent that grew and flourished abundantly under her tutelage. Once George had started lessons he knew he had found his calling. He worked very hard, even learning to read and write music at the same time. He began to beg his parents for a piano that he could practice on at home. His father refused thinking that George only needed to play as a hobby of sorts; it wouldn't be what he studied in University. But George wouldn't let up and his father finally relented. He would never admit to Meg or her mother that his piano at home was worth five times the one he was being taught on. He much preferred the Preston's older, more used and loved piano to the expensive baby grand whose sleek black frame held a prominent position in the Morningstar great room but was seldom heard by anyone other than the hired help.

The world had opened up for George as if, through music, he was learning a new language. George found that he could play entirely by ear and was soon writing his own pieces. It became his way of communicating what he was too shy to say, especially to Meg. He'd often come to lessons with something he'd want to play that had been written just hours before, making sure she was nearby to hear the piano play out his feelings. Mrs. Preston may have taught him a love for the piano but it was Meg that George learned the most from.

He had pinned her correctly from his first sight of her – she was wild. Her mother had schooled her at home refusing to send her to the local public school. She said it was because she could do a much better job teaching her daughter one-on-one but the fact of the matter was that Meg wouldn't be accepted by any white school and Rev. Preston wouldn't allow Meg to attend a black school, not that there was any chance of her being accepted there either. And so, Mrs. Preston had kept her at home and taught Meg about the world around her – a world that couldn't accept her. But then, Mrs. Preston taught Meg to see people rather than color, and that she had a place in this world, contrary to what anyone else said or thought. This, along with very little exposure to the ridicule and ugliness of social views gave Meg such a fiercely independent way of thinking, it infuriated her father. When most girls followed their parent's wishes to the letter, Meg went against everything her Minister Father preached about.

Soon after their initial meeting Meg and George became fast friends. Meg told George how her father's preaching of God was so dark and sinister and controlling, as though he wanted everyone to fear Him. Meg also believed he had a real fear of colored people as well because he had forbid her to go near the west side of town. Her mother was never allowed to take colored students regardless of how much extra money it meant for the household. She thought he was a very cold-hearted man and often felt as though he wanted her in hiding. He would have her sit at the very back of the church so as "not to show favoritism over the more important members of the congregation." But Meg was no fool and she felt his shame.

By the time she was 13, Meg, in complete rebellion, had stopped attending her Father's church and would often spend her Sunday mornings walking through the streets of the "forbidden" west side. She found herself looking through the windows of the houses into the family life of the people living there. They were mostly poor black families with many generations under one roof. Meg was compelled to look in and peer into their lives, if only for a moment. To her, their home life seemed more loving than her parent's home. Her mother tried her best but her father's presence always brought tension along with it.

One Sunday she walked through an area she had never been to and found herself standing at the back of a small A-frame structure, from which she could hear glorious singing. It was a very small church. Peering in through the side door nearest to the altar, she watched in awe as the all-black congregation of approximately 70 people worshiped. It took her breath away how they prayed and sang to their God. The women were dressed in elaborate floral dresses with equally elaborate hats, gloves and their finest jewelry; their handbags held over a wrist.

The men dressed to the nines in the very best suits their meager wages could afford. The entire congregation was held captive by the black-robed man at the altar.

The leader of their Sunday Worship was Rev. Franklin Moore. Rev. Moore was a caring, generous, charismatic, and tolerant man who guided his people through the sermon with loving and touching words. His deep, resonating voice was filled with passion and he spoke about God's love and His desire for all of us to love our fellow man. Meg immediately trusted him. This was completely different from how her father ministered at his church. Rev. Moore would sing to his people and they would sing back to him with everybody clapping their hands and calling out loud during the Reverend's sermon. You wouldn't have been caught dead doing any of those things during her father's sermons. In complete contrast, her father's voice would shriek as he would call out to his congregation on a Sunday morning, almost as if to keep them awake. Rev. Moore's flock didn't need to be kept from nodding off. There was too much energy in the small church for sleeping.

The music was led by the piano player who would move across the keys with such enthusiasm it shook the whole instrument. Her mother was an excellent instructor, but she had never once played her piano with that much passion. Rev. Moore made Meg want to pray and believe in God. She didn't fear God when Reverend Moore spoke of Him. Her dad was always talking about hell and sinning. He made her think that God was just a nasty and vengeful old man ready to smite you for the smallest infraction. But Meg knew better now, thanks to Reverend Moore. He preached about a fair and just God that loved his children and wanted them to follow the examples of his son, Jesus. There was no sinning, rather there was singing. Strong passionate voices raised in glorious harmony. Oh how Meg loved it when the choir sang! Their soulful voices singing for God. There were times that it made her shiver. Her father's church never had that effect on her.

She hid at the side door of the church every Sunday for a number of weeks until she was found by a choir member after a Sunday morning service and brought to Rev. Moore's office as he sat at his desk finishing up some accounting from the donation basket. He was struck by the

7

child's wild hair and eyes. Her exotic look made him wonder where she had come from. She was certainly not from his neighborhood. She could hardly be considered black or white, rather she was like caramel.

"What is it you want child?" he asked her as he turned his chair sideways and held out his hands to her and drew her nearer to him. He guessed her to be about 14 years old. She held her tongue at first, looking deeply into his very dark chocolate-brown eyes. He wondered if she could speak at all, perhaps she wasn't an American.

Then, "I want to be a member of your church. I want to come and sing and pray and dance like you all do. I want *your* God to know me," she blurted out.

Rev. Moore laughed, realizing full well she was an American. "My dear child, God knows everyone! But why do you hide?" he asked her.

"I didn't think you'd want me here. I don't look like all of you," Meg stated matter-of-factly.

Rev. Moore smiled and said, "God created many different faces and colors. Wasn't the rainbow God's creation?"

She nodded and then said, "My father is the other Baptist minister in town, Rev. Carson Preston. My name is Meg and I'm his daughter..." she trailed off the last word and then dropped her eyes as if ashamed.

Without acknowledging his surprise, he nodded his head. *She was Carson Preston's daughter?* he thought. It took a moment and then he understood. He knew of Reverend Preston and his church.

"Does he know you come here?" he asked.

"No," she answered looking him straight in the eye. "He doesn't bother with me. Actually, I don't think he likes me much," she said, looking away.

"Sometimes, our children have to travel far away from us in order to come back home," Rev. Moore said. He squeezed her hands just a little. "You can attend my church any time you like Meg, you are always welcome here. However, you must tell your parents you worship here and next time, you must take a seat and be part of my congregation." He dropped her hands gently and slightly pushed his chair back. She smiled wide. Rev. Moore smiled wide. And they hugged. She wasn't sure about telling her father just yet, but she was thrilled to be invited to sit and join them in worship.

The following Sunday, Meg marched right into the church, bold as you please wearing her very best floral dress with her mother's fancy hat and her head held high. She did her best to make sure she fit in. Everyone in the church stared at her but no one said a word. Rev. Moore came to the altar and smiled broadly at the congregation. He stood there for a moment making sure he had their complete and undivided attention and then said, "My brothers and sisters, we have been blessed with yet another follower of God. Everyone please welcome Miss Meg Preston to our fold," and he acknowledged her with his hand and then spread his arms wide to the rest of the church.

A strange silence hung over the small A-frame church for a split second and then someone said, very quietly, "Bless you Meg." Slowly it started to build with others offering their greetings until finally the room settled again. Rev. Moore stood before his congregation with his wide smile and nodded to his people. He then began his sermon on acceptance and tolerance of others and soon the whole church was singing God's praises for He created us all equal.

From that day forward Meg attended Rev. Moore's Sunday sermon without fail and was accepted by her new congregation with open arms. She stood out in the all-black Sunday service, the only parishioner not from the neighborhood and whose skin was neither white nor black, but her passion for the preacher's words was sincere and how she danced, sang and swayed with the best of them. Meg Preston had found her spiritual home.

Meg's father was not happy. She didn't tell him straight away but when she was questioned by him as to her whereabouts on one particular Sunday morning, she told him the truth. He had yelled and screamed for most of the afternoon. He was not going to have such rebellion living under his roof! How did it look to the town that his daughter wouldn't attend his church? Not only that, but then to choose the black church instead! The shame was too much for him and even though Meg's mother tried to smooth it over, in the end he gave up and became indifferent to his teenage daughter and her choices. It never occurred to him the shame she felt at being told to sit at the back of the church by him and knowing full well why. From that day forward Rev. Preston acted as though she didn't exist.

...

One Sunday after service Rev. Moore was in his office clearing away his desk before leaving for Sunday brunch with his wife and family. He heard a soft tapping on his door and spun around in his chair to see Meg standing in his doorway. She held her hat in front of her in her hands and cleared her voice as she spoke to him.

"Can I speak to you Rev. Moore… please?" She asked quietly.

"Of course child, come on in, come on in," he said, gesturing inside.

Meg smiled briefly as she stepped over the threshold of his doorway and into the office itself. She stood stock still for a moment, then started shifting the brim of the hat in her hands as she spoke.

"I wanted to ask you about dying," she said softly. She looked straight at him with her face like stone. It made Rev. Moore's heart lurch for a moment.

Carefully, he asked her, "Is there a specific reason you're asking me this, Meg? Have you been told that someone you care about is dying?"

She shook her head and looked down. "I don't know her… but, she was my mother. She died. I just wondered if you could tell me about dying," she said.

"Your mother died?" he asked, rather surprised. He hadn't heard that Reverend Preston's wife had died. She knew immediately the mistake he was making.

"Not my mother, Mrs. Preston, my *real* mother." Meg stared at Rev. Moore whose expression had not changed. He wasn't making this easy for her.

She shifted on her feet and then explained to him, "I heard my parents arguing one night. My mother wanted my father to be honest with me about something and was pleading with him to tell me the truth. He just kept saying "NO", screaming it at her. And then he said, "… because I don't want her obsessing over a *dead mother*!" She held Rev. Moore's look.

He slowly shook his head. This poor child. No one should have to find out something so personal in such a manner. He guessed that the Preston's had never told her the truth about her adoption but then, Meg was an extremely smart girl and probably figured it out the moment she saw her own reflection.

He could only imagine what it had been like to be raised in Reverend Carson Preston's house. If he thought for a second he could take Meg into his own household he would, but the church didn't pay much and he already had his wife and three children to feed and clothe. He did, however, make a promise to God in that moment to always watch out for this rare and precious child and to do whatever he could to help guide her along.

He was brought back to the moment by Meg's voice asking him, "So? I *know* my real mother is dead. I want to know what it's like to die," she said frankly.

"Well, that's the thing about dying, Meg," he smiled broadly, "you have to experience it to know what it's about and yet... you can't return to tell others! It's God's little joke on mankind."

She furrowed her brows. "But, what is it about? I mean, what happens to you?" she asked honestly.

Reverend Moore thought about her question as he stared at her face. He wanted to be sure to answer her in a way that would satisfy her inquiry without making her afraid.

"God teaches us that the spirit leaves the physical body to ascend to him." As he said this he gestured with his hands, taking an invisible something from his left palm with his right hand and drawing it upwards. "He gives you *this* body at birth so that you'll be like everyone else on earth, but really it's your spirit, your very essence that's he's interested in." He pressed the fingertips of his right hand into the middle of her chest below her chin.

"But I'm not like everyone else," she said looking at him.

"Yes you are, my child. You are no different from every other human being who walks this earth. What others see as "different" in you, God only sees as what makes you unique. He made *you* that way. He *loves* you that way!"

Meg gave this some thought for a moment and then asked him, "Do spirits live on? Can they see us?"

"Well, there is some argument about that. Some think that spirits exist around us and some think that they don't." He could see she wasn't satisfied with that so he added, "I think that spirits have the opportunity to look down every once in a while and see how we're doing. Sometimes, God allows them to send us a sign, maybe a butterfly flutters around your head just when you're thinking of them or a cloud shaped like their face goes by, something that tells you they're up there."

He finished with that, hoping she'd have enough to think over. He was right. She stood for a moment, watching him closely, nodded her head, spun around on her heels and headed out the door leaving him to the rest of his day. He'd need a spirit of his own after navigating that conversation!

Meg looked for signs of her mother's spirit every day after that. Little did she know it would come many years later when she herself was a mother.

...

As George's first piano lessons began, Meg would remove herself from the room and work on her studies. Once they became friends, Meg began to stay nearer the living room when George was taking his lessons. She'd flip through a magazine or pretend to read a book or even do her studies while she'd listen to her mother teach George how to read music and play the piano. She loved his ability to pick up the lessons so quickly, unlike the other students. Her mother had taught maybe 12 kids over the past few years and not one of them was as good as George Morningstar. After a while, Meg was outright sitting on the couch listening to him, watching as he evolved into an excellent piano player.

Once she started attending, Meg had shared with George her experiences at the small A-frame church. She'd sway as she'd mimic the congregation and sing out like they did with her long limbs up in the air and her hair all in disarray around her, all the while George was her captive audience. She told him about how her father's church did not do for her what Rev. Moore's church did and how much energy the room had when they all got together. George opened up to her and told her of his loneliness, his parent's lack of interest in him and how much he'd love to be able to see the Sunday sermon at Rev. Moore's church.

The next Sunday, Meg Preston walked George Morningstar by the arm into the church. Considering he'd seen the inside of a few high society homes and the uppity functions that his parents attended, George was more excited about this unknown House of God than anything, and it didn't disappoint. After the initial shock of the congregation, and Rev. Moore's obvious expression of surprise and amusement, they once again followed his lead and accepted yet another follower of God. The congregation was soon fully captivated by his interpretation and passionate telling of the gospel.

George wasn't sure what moved him more, the sound of the piano being hammered on and the choir belting out the ode to God with the whole congregation swaying and dancing around him, or watching Meg participate in it all. When Rev. Moore spoke about the love of humanity and helping those in need, George sat in awe. A solo singer came to the altar and sang a Gospel song that spoke to George in a way that no other had before. The song spoke of hardship and loss but also how one's faith in God would bring them into the glory land. A gospel song. Soulful. Meg grabbed his hand and held it tight. Tears were in her eyes. Meg and George were melded together that afternoon and they would always have a love for the soulful gospel music that this church provided. They became regular parishioners together and the church was totally accepting. Of course, George's parents had no idea.

...

By Meg's 16th birthday they were a secret couple with George being just a few months older. George had come over with a small nosegay of posies taken from his mother's garden, more so, his mother's gardener's garden. His present to her was a song he had written just for her. After he played it, she kissed him for the first time and as far as George was concerned, there would never be any other love for him than Meg Preston.

He would come over and play new songs he had written for Meg and her mother. Sometimes, George would perform the gospel songs played at their church and Meg would dance around and sing, her voice strong and soulful, filled with the passion she felt when she was in the church. Her mother didn't quite know what to make of it. She certainly wasn't familiar with the songs or the display of worship as Meg danced about but she tolerated it as she did all things Meg. As long as Rev. Preston didn't come home, it was all fine with her. The minute his car pulled in the driveway, the living room would become Mrs. Preston's piano classroom again with George the respectful, dutiful student and Meg either reading or doing her studies on the couch with Rev. Preston never the wiser.

The first time George saw Rev. Preston, he was sitting behind the piano in the Preston's living room doing his finger exercises listening to Mrs. Preston expound the importance of nimble finger dexterity while playing piano. Rev. Preston entered through the front door, a tall older gentleman, near bald except for the patch of hair framing his cranium like a monk's haircut, all white. He looked 10 years older than Meg's mother. He was long in limb but had a distinct paunch. He was pale, blue-eyed and wore his displeasure on his face – his thin lips drawn into a severe line. He never seemed happy for a man whose occupation was to preach the word of God. It wasn't lost on George that Meg didn't look anything like her parents.

When he'd arrive home after his day, Rev. Preston would grumble and grunt and head off to the basement or his study. After a year of Meg's rebellion he had grown intolerant of Meg altogether and did all he could to not be around her. But George loved her. She had opened up a whole new world to him, first with companionship, then with gospel music and more recently with sex. They weren't actually having sex because Meg believed in marriage first for all her rebellious ways, but they had come close a few times when they managed to steal precious moments away.

George's parents would never condone him marrying Meg, had they known about her. The plan was and had always been to send him off to University out of state in the fall of his 18th year. He was to study law like his father. No choice of his own. No matter how much his love for music or natural talent for it, his father had already made all the arrangements. At the prospect of leaving his Meg in September of that year, an impetuous George asked Meg to elope with him so that they couldn't be separated and she agreed.

So, on a stormy August afternoon, George and Meg went to Rev. Moore and asked him to marry them. It was fitting, they thought. The kind Reverend questioned why their parents and family weren't there to witness the nuptials and they told him the truth. They were eloping because George's family would not approve and hoped to send him off to University separating the star-crossed lovers. "Poor kids," he thought. He knew Meg's father was not supportive of her and now George's family too. Perhaps he would be causing more trouble by marrying them, but Rev. Moore could never deny true love. He had seen the love and respect that had grown between these kids since they started coming to his church two years ago. He could see that they were meant to be together.

Rev. Moore married them with his wife and four ladies from the choir who sang for them and acted as witnesses. Meg knew her mother would be devastated. Her only child and a daughter at that! Eloping! George knew his father and mother would disown him. Their only child failing to live up to their expectations and marrying beneath him. Never mind that Meg would never fit into their idea of what a daughter-in-law should be or look like and with the whole relationship going on without their knowledge. How shameful!

George and Meg spent their wedding night in a small motel along the main road leading into Peoria. They had planned only to spend a few hours and then each go to their respective homes with plans to meet up the next day and speak first with her parents and then his. They made love for the first time that night. It was awkward at first with each of them fumbling and nervous. But soon their kisses became fervent and they began to explore each other as they never had before. It became instinctive to them. They wanted each other and without words, let each other know of the passion they shared. They fit together perfectly and when they climaxed one right after the other, they both held onto each other for dear life. Of all the things they had shared this was, by far, the greatest.

As they lay together in each other's arms, listening to the music of Louis Armstrong, they spoke of their future. George would go to the local college and get his teaching degree so he could teach music. At night he could write songs and maybe on weekends, play at the local club. Meg would also see about taking some courses. She'd had no plans in the fall but after listening to Rev. Moore preach about helping others, she thought she would like to learn about nursing. She could clean houses and her mother had taught her mending which she could advertise at the church. They would school for a few years and work nights and weekends to make ends meet. They could live in a small one bedroom apartment near the church. Rev. Moore had a bulletin published each month and some advertised room and board – perhaps they could board as a couple. Anything was possible as long as they were together. They fell asleep holding on to those dreams and one another.

As the dawn broke the next morning, George woke with a start. They had slept through the night – the entire night. They were supposed to have stayed only a few hours and then back to Meg's home. This was not the plan. Now their parents would be worried as to their whereabouts. But only Meg's mother might suspect they were together. The other three would have no idea where they were.

George woke Meg up immediately. "We have to hurry. Instead of meeting up, we'll go back to your place first and speak with your father. I'd rather face him before my own father," he said.

When they got to Meg's house, her father and mother were in the kitchen. Her mother had been crying and her father looked like thunder. Meg surmised that her mother had told her father about her friendship with George and that he was the one she might be with.

"What the hell is going on?" he spit.

"Carson!" Meg's mother yelled.

"Shut up, Vera!" he spat at her viciously. "This is all your fault! You've *allowed this*," he directed at his wife. "Where the hell have you been?" he questioned Meg.

George stepped forward, a paper in his hand. "I'm here to tell you that your daughter and I were married yesterday," he boldly stated and he thrust the piece of paper towards Rev. Preston. Carson Preston snatched the paper out of George's hand and pulled down his glasses to see what it read. Her mother began openly sobbing into the tea towel she'd been clutching.

"Well, will you look at that...?" Rev Preston looked up from the paper, "they've gone and gotten married. Rev. Moore performed the ceremony, did he?" he snarled as he tossed the paper onto the ground at George's feet. George reached down for it just as Rev. Preston lunged for him. George had seen the slightest movement in Rev. Preston's arm as he bent for the paper and instinctively moved to his right, grabbing the license and moving out of the grasp of Rev. Preston who fell onto the floor face down. George jumped back out of his reach and held his arm out to keep Meg beyond his grasp as well. Rev. Preston looked up from the floor, his face twisted in rage, his thin lips shiny with spit and saliva.

"You!" he shouted pointing at Meg. "You... you've been a source of disgrace and embarrassment to me long enough! I knew it. I knew once we *got* you it would be nothing but trouble. Once you'd get with them you'd never come back. Now you've married in their church with all those blacks! Yelling about and acting crazy! You are all sinners, all of you – going to hell. Those darkies right along with ya!" he screamed. "I suppose I ought to be grateful you've married at all, although I can't imagine *your* family being happy with *your* choice, Boy!" He looked up at them from his crouched position, suddenly seeming troll-like and evil. Both Meg and George stared at him, open mouthed. He was pure rage personified. George half expected him to clutch his heart and drop right there, his face was so red and his temper so high. There would be no reasoning with him, not today anyway.

George folded the marriage license and placed it safely into his pocket. He grabbed Meg by the hand and led her out of the house. Neither spoke a word as the sound of Meg's mother sobbing uncontrollably through the open windows lingered with them as they left.

...

They arrived at George's house to find his father home. He was in his study. George had wanted to speak to his father alone, not wanting Meg to endure his father's type of anger – not violent, like her father, but rather quietly insulting and degrading. She wouldn't let him.

George wasn't sure what he would say about Meg, and in front of her. When he entered the study, George went stiff. His hand became sweaty but held Meg's hand firmly.

"Good morning, Father," George said.

His father looked up from his writing and gazed at George briefly, then to Meg. While still looking at her, he said, "Good morning. What's this then?"

George immediately felt anger. "This is my *wife*," George emphasized the word. "Meg…" George gestured towards her, "and I have married. So I won't be able to go off to University in September because I now have a wife to take care of," he stated boldly.

George's father returned to his writings. Ignoring his son and the girl he said, "Don't be an idiot. You're off to school whether you like it or not. And this… girl… will have nothing more to do with you," he gestured toward Meg with his pen. "We haven't agreed to you marrying anyone and it will certainly not be to her."

"No, Father," George said, "I will not be doing as you say. Meg and I have married. We are starting a new life together and I am not going to school in September and leaving her."

George's father put his pen down and looked directly at his son. "You've lost your mind," he said coldly. "If you think for one moment I'm going to let you throw your life away on this girl and your immature childish dreams, you've got another thing coming. I don't care what you've done or who you've married. I will see to it that it is annulled and you are packed off to school before you can blink an eye." His father dismissed them with his hand as if wiping away a displeasing sight and returned to his writing. George stood there holding Meg's hand for a moment and then turned and left the room taking her with him.

"We need to get some of my things and leave," he said.

They went to his bedroom, Meg silent as he guided her through the house that was at least twice the size of her family home. George's family had some money, oh boy! And he was about to leave it all behind! His room was filled with sheets of music in his handwriting, a desk with papers piled up on it and his bed. He grabbed a bag from underneath the bed and began collecting the papers from the desk and floor next to his bed. Meg glanced about the room and walked over to some of the pictures he had of family. Having never met his father until today, she was struck by how much alike they looked. Both had dark features, brown eyes, strong shoulders and broad smiles, but somehow George made those features seem softer. She could see both younger George and older George in the man that sired him. George had finished grabbing the papers and a few other objects along with some clothes. He motioned for Meg to follow him and left the room. When they got to the front door, they heard George's father call out, "This isn't over! I am not allowing this to happen, George!" They walked out of the house, hand in hand and never looked back. They returned to Rev. Moore who found them lodgings with a host family from the church until they were able to find a place of their own.

. . .

George entered college for teaching in the fall. He also helped by playing the church piano when asked on a Sunday while his adoring wife looked on. Meg found work cleaning with some of the church ladies and working at functions as a server. No communication happened between them and their parents. They not only survived without their families, but thrived. Within a few months, Meg became pregnant. They were overjoyed but realized that they needed to find better accommodations.

Rev. Moore found them a two bedroom apartment for very little rent, complete with furniture and close to the church. They moved in and six months later Celia Grace Morningstar was born. She was the apple of her parent's eye. Meg loved motherhood and doted on her baby and her husband. She would walk Celia everyday in the park in her carriage and show her off to passersby. She secretly hoped that she would one day run into either her mother and father or George's mother and father on one of her outings. She wanted them to see how she and George had found a life and true love despite their upbringings, despite the intolerance that had been shown to them. She would be ready, should it ever happen, but deep down inside she knew it never would.

After three years of going to the park regularly, one afternoon Meg sat down next to an elderly woman on a bench. She and Celia had packed peanut butter and jelly sandwiches in case they became hungry while being out. As Meg sat munching down her sandwich, she happened to look over at the elderly woman. Meg didn't recognize her from the church or the neighborhood. That was odd because Meg had come to know just about everybody who was connected within a five or six block radius. The woman looked a bit frail but her eyes danced as she watched Celia enjoying her sandwich.

For unknown reasons, Meg suddenly asked her, "Are you hungry? We have plenty," and handed the woman a sandwich. As they reached out and the sandwich passed between their hands, the elderly woman let her fingers gently touch Meg. She looked deeply into Meg's eyes and said, "You're a good woman and a good mother to that child. I bet your mother is so extremely proud of you."

Meg smiled gently and said, "She's never seen her," looking towards Celia longingly.

"Oh yes she has! She watches down on you all the time, child." replied the elderly woman.

As she said that, young Celia dropped her sandwich and Meg jumped off the bench to pick it up and see if any damage was done before Celia started with tears. She turned back to explain to the woman that her mother wasn't dead, just estranged, but the woman was gone. Meg stood straight up wondering where on earth she could have gone; she had only turned her back for a moment! She looked around the park and tried to spy her somewhere off in the distance but could not locate her anywhere. *That was strange*, she thought. She sat back down on the bench and was soon distracted by Celia's giggle over something and the moment was gone.

...

George graduated college with a teaching diploma and applied at the local school as a music teacher. He didn't get called right away so he took a job playing piano at a local bar to make some money. From that, he was asked to play with a group of musicians. It wasn't a formal "band," but they played great soulful music together. They made ends meet with Meg taking odd cleaning jobs that could be done while George was home to watch Celia. Often, Meg wondered if George missed living in his opulent world. When she saw him desperately trying to feed them with what little came in from her cleaning jobs and his take from the bar, even with tips, she couldn't help but imagine how different his life could have been.

He was asked to interview for the music teacher's position when Celia was three and a half. He was extremely nervous but Meg had given him a pep talk that morning and he went in with confidence in his ability to teach the kids of the town the gift of music and how to play musical instruments. The Principal and two other school administrators interviewed him. He wowed them with his academia and then blew them away with his ability on the piano. They were sold and that very afternoon they offered him the job. Mr. George Morningstar was the new music teacher at the Camden Street Public School.

This was a major deal for George and the town — the first time the all black school had a white teacher. George knew that being accepted by the church members first off had helped a great deal and he silently said a prayer for Rev. Moore to whose love and tolerance of humanity and caring approach had an extreme influence over his parishioners, neighborhood and most of all George. Of course, it didn't hurt that George was a superb musician and the administrators knew he could bring out the best in their children.

George kept his weekend gig at the bar because he liked it and when tips were good, they were very good. He learned so much from his band mates about the jazz sounds that accompanied his piano. His musical interests were ever expanding, even to the point of taking up the guitar. George's guitar talents were growing steadily. He could hear all the different musical instruments in his head and mimic them easily. His self-taught ability meant an independent flare that no one else had. George wasn't intimidated by any instrument. He understood them, but the piano and guitar were his favorites and he played them excellently with little effort.

The audience loved the bluesy jazz sound of George's musical ensemble and tipped them well to show their appreciation. Within two years, George and Meg had saved enough to move into a house of their own in the neighborhood. Meg also surprised George that year with a piano of his very own for his 21st birthday. She bought it used from an antique market they frequented. It wasn't in great shape and needed tuning but she knew he could make it sing. With some help from a church member and his own elbow grease and tuning ear, the old keyboard came alive under his fingertips and the house once again rang with the sound of the piano. George even let little Celia sit on his lap while he played, her chubby fingers feeling the smooth keys and when pressed, reacting to the sound each key made. *A player in the making*, George thought.

They had never been happier. The three of them, unaccepted by their own and welcomed and accepted by those that weren't accepted. It seemed odd to George that this is how things would turn out but he was more the happier for it. High society was never to his liking; always favoring the simple life with a good foundation of love and trust in those you loved. He knew that was why Rev. Moore has resonated with him on that first day. His tolerance and acceptance of first Meg and then George and teaching his congregation through his own example to love your fellow man, was something he had never seen his father or mother do unless others were watching. His mother would gush to her high society girlfriends about how much she "loved" her gardener Phillipo, but spoke to him like he was dirt when it was just them in the garden. Not an ounce of sincerity in either parent as far as George was concerned.

George, Meg, and Celia lived an idyllic little life. All thriving and growing and learning from one another. Motherhood had consumed Meg's life and she soon started pining for another baby. Although she and George enjoyed a healthy sexual relationship, month after month she would be disappointed by the arrival of her monthly flow. George would do his best to console her by explaining that there was always next month and that if she only stopped worrying about it she would get pregnant in no time. Sure enough when Celia was five years old and had just started school, Meg believed she was pregnant! It had taken four years but finally it happened. She had missed her period two months in a row and was bloated in her abdomen. She had thrown up twice in the last week, although not every morning like with Celia. She felt differently with this baby, more nauseous and maybe a little weak, but this excited her.

She had heard that pregnancies differed when carrying a boy from a girl and she just knew this baby was a boy! Finally she could give George the baby boy to carry on the Morningstar name! Meg had learned shortly after their marriage that his name would only carry on if he were to have a boy child as there were no other male relations that carried the name. She wanted to do that for George. She was thrilled that she felt differently with this pregnancy and made an appointment with her doctor to confirm the results. She didn't divulge anything to George until the morning of the appointment, and only then because she couldn't keep it in any longer.

"I think I'm pregnant!" she blurted out over breakfast. George stopped dead in the middle of drinking his coffee, Celia carefully navigating a spoonful of porridge into her little mouth next to him. "Truly?" he asked astounded. He had almost secretly given up hope that Meg would ever get pregnant again. It had been almost five years with no results whatsoever. He was afraid to get too excited.

"Yup," she nodded enthusiastically, "I've missed my flow twice now, my tummy is slightly swelled and I was sick to my stomach this week." George looked at her for a moment, not sure what to think. "I've made an appointment to see Dr. Swanson and he's going to tell me I'm pregnant. I figure the baby is probably seven months away!" George

24

sat back in his chair still looking at her, disbelief written on his face. "Believe it, George, it's true," she said smiling. "I'm pregnant and I'm carrying your son, the next Mr. Morningstar."

Meg was nodding her head and giggled as she got up from the table, wet a cloth and wiped Celia's face and hands before letting her from the table to play with her toys before leaving for school. George got up from the table and grabbed Meg into a kiss. She laughed as he picked her up into his embrace and spun her around.

"Are you kidding? This is the best news! This is fantastic!! I love you, I love you so much," he said excitedly, allowing the moment to overtake him. They laughed and hugged and kissed each other. They had a fine little existence together and now they were going to add to their family of three with a beautiful baby that Meg was sure was a boy. George was hopeful that she was right.

"What time is your appointment with Dr. Swanson?" he asked.

"3:00 pm," she told him.

"Will you know today?" he asked.

"No, but probably by the end of the week. I'll have a blood test done today and they'll call me with the results after that."

He was satisfied with that, hugged her for an extra long time and kissed her sweetly. He called out to Celia to come and hug her daddy as he needed to get to school earlier than she. George left the house that day feeling like he had the world in the palm of his hand. Life was not what he had expected when he knocked on the Preston's door that day some 12 years ago but he was more grateful for what had transpired than he could have ever known. Life was good!

Meg took Celia to school for 9:00 am and busied her day with cleaning, groceries, dinner and some mending. At 3:00 pm she was in Dr. Swanson's office filling out some paperwork. By 3:10 pm she was in an exam room awaiting Dr. Swanson's arrival. When he came in she was the Cheshire cat, smiling broadly. He sat in the chair opposite her and smiled back.

"Well?" he said, raising his eyebrows at her.

"I'm pregnant," she told him. He nodded his head. She had waited five long years to say that.

"Symptoms?" he asked.

"Two months without a period, my stomach is sickly and I'm feeling tired." Reflecting on the latter, she added, "I believe I'm about 10 weeks along. And, I believe I am carrying a boy," she stated matter-of-factly.

Dr. Swanson chuckled. "Is that so?" he asked. "Why don't we get some blood from you to confirm the pregnancy first, then we'll see what God has to say about the baby's gender."

He smiled at her and patted the exam table as a gesture for her to take a seat upon it. She jumped up and rolled up her sleeve as he reached for the needle to draw her blood. Dr. Swanson looked down into her smiling face as he swabbed her arm. He studied her for a moment and then asked, "Feeling tired are you? Anything else I should know of?"

Celia looked down towards her stomach and said proudly, "He's going to be a big boy Doctor. I'm already showing!"

Dr. Swanson tilted his head as he looked at her. If she was only 10 weeks pregnant as she thought, she shouldn't be showing just yet. Unless there was more than one baby in there, in which case she'd certainly have a small rounding of her abdomen.

"Why don't you lay down flat and let me have a feel of your tummy," he stated.

Meg complied, laying down on the table and pulling down the waistband of her skirt so that the doctor could exam her. He was surprised to see a rise in her abdomen and wondered if she was in fact carrying more than one child. Using his fingertips he lightly pressed down on the area. He moved his hands to the left first and then the right continually pressing down. When he reached the right side Meg winced.

"Does that hurt?" he asked her.

"Not hurt, more like pressure. Maybe a little pain, like a period cramp. Yes, like a period cramp," she replied.

He pressed around a few more times, all the while watching for her reaction. She kept her eyes locked on his and every time he pressed down on the far right side, he could read it in her eyes. When he was finished, he wrote a few things down on his note pad while Meg adjusted her skirt. Undaunted by his actions, Meg sat up smiling and swinging her legs, remaining on the table.

"How soon will we know?" she asked him.

"I'll ask for a rush on this, shall I? Then you won't be kept waiting. I think I'll get some other samples from you too while you're here. Ask the nurse to give you a specimen jar and we'll get a urine sample from you, just in case the blood test is inconclusive," he assured her.

Meg didn't have to do any of this with Celia's pregnancy but she put it down to the advancement of medicine and nothing more. Four days later Dr. Swanson called the house.

"Can you come in and see me tomorrow?" he asked. "I'd like George to be with you, if possible," he said, no trace of answers in his voice.

"Of course. Is this a new policy, Dr. Swanson? Telling the parents together?" she laughed. He stayed quiet for a moment, not sharing the laugh.

"I've asked the nurse to schedule you for noon so that George can be here over the lunch hour," Dr. Swanson told her. "I'll see you then," he said and hung up the phone.

She didn't hear it in his voice, or she denied it. Either way, when George came home that evening, she told him about the appointment and the doctor's request for his presence.

"Oh sure, it's just a new policy thing I think where they have to tell both parents about the pregnancy at the same time," she told him.

He nodded asking, "He said everything's alright?"

...

The next day Meg and George were sitting in the doctor's office waiting for Dr. Swanson. It seemed odd that they would be brought into his office rather than the exam room, but Celia figured there was no reason to examine her. Not after the examination just a few days before and at least not until her fourth month. As it had been with Celia, he would follow her symptoms and as long as she gained the appropriate weight nothing else was of concern.

After a few moments Dr. Swanson came through the door carrying a chart. He apologized for keeping them waiting and sat down at his desk. He looked down at the chart and flipped open the cover page. He read for a moment and looked up at the young couple.

"So?" Meg asked, smiling wide. "Am I right? I'm about 10 weeks along, right?" she questioned.

Dr. Swanson looked back down at the chart. He shook his head and said, "I wanted to run some other tests on the blood we drew because I didn't like the look of the results from the first test we ran. I'm sorry Meg. It's not a baby…" he hesitated, "it's a tumor."

Everything stopped. She didn't hear him correctly. Did he say it was a tumor? What did he mean? Everything was closing in and fuzzy. She suddenly heard George's voice ask, "A tumor? What do you mean? What tumor? I thought she was pregnant?" looking towards Meg in disbelief.

Meg was not hearing this right. What did he mean by a tumor? She couldn't speak. She didn't understand what this meant. He said, *it's not a baby.* How could that be? She'd had the usual symptoms – missing her cycle for two months, queasiness, nausea, fatigue, the bloating in her abdomen. What else could it be other than a baby?

"You have a tumor on your right ovary that we believe is causing your symptoms. We actually believe it is the cause of your inability to get pregnant for the last few years. We hadn't done any kind of examination because you were otherwise healthy and had no symptoms to make me think otherwise. I, too, figured a pregnancy until I examined you the other day. I wondered if you weren't carrying twins actually. But, your blood work shows a high white blood count, which means infection, and nothing points to a pregnancy. The bloating you're experiencing is the tumor itself. We need to remove it surgically as soon as possible before it spreads. There is a chance it already has. I spoke with some of my colleagues and they concur that, given the size of the tumor, it's been growing for some time." He stopped, letting them take in what he had said. They both looked back at him as if he were speaking Greek.

"What kind of tumor do you think it is, Doctor?" George had the presence of mind to ask.

"We won't know that until we do the surgery and run some tests on it," Dr. Swanson said. He sat looking down at the chart and then looked up at Meg's devastated face.

"I know this isn't what you were expecting, Meg. I wish it was a baby."

She stared at him. "I thought it was a baby," she said softly. Her head hung down and she couldn't look up at Dr. Swanson again. It was written on his face, the sorrow.

. . .

The surgery confirmed exactly what Dr. Swanson feared but couldn't say to them that day in his office. The tumor was cancerous and it had indeed spread. The surgeon had removed her uterus and both ovaries.

She would no longer be able to give George his namesake. The surgeon also found cancerous tumors in her liver and lungs. He had closed her up and let Dr. Swanson know that there was nothing they could do. They would keep her medicated to help with the pain but the cancer was too far gone for him to cut it out completely.

Dr. Swanson came and gave them the news while she was still in the recovery room. Although he couldn't give them a time frame, he told them to go home and get their affairs in order. George took Meg home a week later and he and Meg prepared for what was to come. Rev. Moore organized the church ladies and they began filling in as housekeepers, babysitters, nursemaids and cooks for the young struggling family. This allowed George to continue working but also gave him the chance to be with Meg and Celia and not be lost in the hundreds of chores that needing taking care of.

As Meg's health faded, the school was able to give him part time hours and paid him for whatever lessons he would prepare for the substitute teachers. Although he hated leaving her side, he would have a church lady sit with Meg while he worked a few hours, ran errands or took Celia to and from school, trying to keep some small sense of normalcy for the child. One night Meg, struggling to speak from the effects of the medications, held George's hand and spoke to him slowly but succinctly:

"I'm not afraid, you know. I'm okay with this," she said with a groggy but sad smile. "You're going to have to be mom and dad now, George. It isn't fair really but I don't think we get to choose these things. I may not get to raise her but I want you to make me a few promises." George looked at her hard, not knowing if the medications were talking or she was. She continued:

"Number one," she starred, "Make sure she gets her education. She's far too bright to not feed her mind. Keep her in school, George, no matter what!" Meg paused a moment, having weakened herself getting out that last sentence. She licked her lips as her eyes fluttered open and closed.

Then she said, "Number two," holding up two fingers and pausing a moment. "I don't want Celia to ever feel unaccepted or unloved.

Please George, promise me Celia will always be able to make her own decisions, her own mistakes without fear of losing your love. Let her be independent and free spirited. I already see so much of myself in her. My father tried hard to restrict that…"

She stopped a moment and closed her eyes before ending with, "And lastly, she *must* have our love for music. Surround her with it. Feed it to her. She has your gift George, she has your gift."

George held her hands and looked into his dying wife's pleading eyes. Tears filled his own. "I promise," he said. They had both given up all they had known to be together. How could George ever turn his back on Celia after everything he and Meg had been through? It was unthinkable. Celia would always have her father's love and support. Meg smiled dozily, satisfied that he had promised her those things. George watched his wife's face. She suddenly seemed so at peace and serene.

She then smiled widely, her eyes closed. "Rev. Moore was right you know. They do send us signs. That elderly woman in the park that day when Celia was little…" she paused for a moment, "it was her letting me know she had never stopped watching. I'll meet her soon and then I'll know her. Rev. Moore was right." She drifted off to sleep, more peacefully than she had in many nights. What did she mean by that? It puzzled him but after some thought he put it down to the medication kicking in and making her too groggy to be making any sense.

...

George stayed by his dying wife's side day and night for the next few days while she endured the final stages of her life. After a hard fight Meg died with George by her side holding her hand. The cancer had withered her away to a mere shadow of herself. She had died in pain in spite of the pills the doctors said would ease it. A funeral was held and the whole congregation of the small church attended. All were heartbroken at the loss of the free-spirited, wild, exotic, rare girl with the mane of hair that had graced their parish and danced and sang and worshipped with them. Rev. Moore had seen a lot of parishioners die over the years. He struggled with this one the most. Normally he was such a commanding figure on the altar of his small church but on this day, Rev. Moore seemed to decrease in size, as if his grief had reduced him, the weight being so great.

After the burial, the congregation all paid their respects to George and little Celia. Rev. Moore stayed behind to be sure that the father and daughter made their way back to the church for some food and refreshments. As the three were about to leave the cemetery, George spotted a woman's dark figure standing alone under the trees about 30 feet away. At first, George did not recognize her and then he suddenly realized who she was. Vera Preston, Meg's mother. It had been years since he had seen her. Not since the day after he and Meg had eloped. She had aged over those years. Now at 67 years old, she looked closer to 80. Her hair had gone from blonde to completely grey and she looked thinner, if that was possible. Her once soft, brown eyes now looked as if they had lost all life in them. There were dark circles under her eyes and they were red-rimmed and swollen from crying. She held a tissue to her nose and then wiped her eyes as George and Celia made their way to her. She hugged him lightly as he reached her. George introduced Celia to her grandmother and Mrs. Preston knelt down to look at the child for a moment.

"Oh, she's so like Meg," Mrs. Preston said. "She has her eyes and her smile. I can almost picture Meg just like her at five years old." She stood up and looked at George. "I didn't want to intrude. It's just that... she was my only baby." She looked at George hesitantly as her eyes watered and then confessed, "I think you should know Meg's background." She paused and then said, "You *must* be aware that she wasn't our natural child. Meg was never aware of this, but…" she waited a moment, "we adopted her when she was just a year old. Rev. Preston and I couldn't have children of our own and I wanted so badly to have a baby." She said this to George, all the while staring at Celia's face which was cradled in her hand.

"Meg's mother was rather young and had died giving birth to her." Her hand fell away. "She was a black girl and had been taken advantage of by a white man that knew her family." Mrs. Preston looked at George knowing he understood what she meant.

"After her mother's death, Meg was put up for adoption by her mother's family. They didn't want her. We had been trying to adopt for a number of years but kept being denied. They told us we were too old to raise a baby. I learned that it would be easier to adopt a mixed-race baby because no one wanted them. Rev. Preston wasn't interested but I convinced him to at least try and see if it was easier. When we went to the orphanage that day, she was the first child that came to me. We looked through the orphanage at all the children that were there but I kept my eye on her. I couldn't take my eyes off her. She was such a beautiful baby girl with those eyes and that hair. When we went home that night I told my husband that she was the only child I wanted and if we didn't choose her, I wasn't interested in having any other." Mrs. Preston opened her handbag and took out a clean tissue. As she wiped her eyes, she continued, "Carson said that the town probably all knew what had happened, so once the adoption was final, we moved here to have a fresh start with our little family. I knew that he didn't really want Meg like I did, but I think he wanted me to be happy and so he gave in. At first we were happy – really happy, but as she got older and her features changed, Carson's feelings started changing too. He started to refuse to let her be around anyone who was black. I suppose he didn't want her knowing she was half black. As soon as she could see she was different from us, she started asking us questions but Carson refused to let me tell her the truth. By the time she was eight or nine, Carson had become completely cold towards her. He was ashamed to have her in church; made her sit where she wasn't on display for all to see. He wasn't really bothered that she stopped attending his services but when she rebelled against him and started going to the black church, well, he couldn't accept that at all," she finished. She wiped her eyes with the tissue again and blew her nose. She reached into her bag and drew out an envelope and handed it to George.

"It isn't a fortune but I want you to have this. It was given to me by my family and I kept it hoping to spend it on Meg's wedding one day." Mrs. Preston quickly held the tissue to her mouth and wept as she said the last statement. After a moment she gathered herself and tried a smile.

"I know we didn't do right by Meg. I know we made mistakes. I loved that girl with all of my heart but you have to understand, I couldn't fight him anymore after all those years. I was tired. I had to choose. You see, she had a husband and.... I would have lost mine if I didn't choose."

She stopped talking, hung her head and looked away. She then turned her back and simply walked away without another word. George and Celia stood there holding hands, watching Mrs. Preston walk out of the cemetery, never once looking back. George took a deep breath and letting go of his daughter's hand, he opened the envelope. It contained money. George was shocked that Mrs. Preston would hold onto cash for that long, never having used it for food or even giving it to her church. Instead she had kept it all these years. Unable to count it accurately there, he shoved the envelope in his coat pocket, grabbed his daughter's tiny hand and made his way back to the church for Meg's wake.

When he got home that night, he counted out the money. $1,000. There was a time that $1,000 would have been a drop in the bucket to the Morningstar's of Peoria, Illinois, but to George this was a lot of money. He still had some medical bills to cover and Meg's funeral had to be paid for. It would help tremendously towards all of that. He sat on the couch with the money in his hand thinking of what had transpired over the last 12 years. His mind went back to meeting his wild and exotic Meg at the front door of the Preston's house that first day of piano lessons. He could see her so clearly and now 12 years and a lifetime later she was gone. The only thing left of her was the ache and emptiness in his heart, his memories, and her five year old daughter asleep in her bed. The tears in his eyes welled up and all he could do was lie down on the couch and sob himself to sleep.

Chapter 2

George, Celia and Chicago

25 years after they had met and 13 years since Meg's death, George was now smiling and winking at his daughter as tears welled up once again. The choir was milling around their audience, all talking excitedly at the success of their concert. Celia Morningstar undid the ties to her choir frock and stepped out of it to give to the seamstress. She was chatting with her friends when George stepped up beside her.

"My friends are all going for a soda for a little celebration. Can I go with them, Daddy? Do you mind?" she asked, her eyes begging him to let her.

George didn't really like Celia staying out too late, but he couldn't think of a reason to say no. School was days from being done for the summer and she'd never given him any trouble, was always mindful of her manners and didn't get involved with boys, thankfully.

"Sure honey, you can go. Just make sure you're home before dark. If you want, I can come and pick you up later on," he said.

"Oh that's great!" she replied as she threw her arms around his neck and kissed him on the cheek. "Thanks so much Daddy, I promise to call home right after the celebration!" She kissed him on the cheek again and hugged his neck tight for a few seconds and then ran off with two girls in tow towards the exit of the school.

George smiled to himself as he watched her go. She was so like Meg when she was a little girl, but more of George's features had come out as she grew older. Her limbs were long and lean like Meg's and she was about the same height with a few more growing years to go. Her skin was a lighter color than Meg's but still had richness to it and was nothing like George's skin tone. Her hair was the same mane as Meg's in texture but with more of George's dark coloring. But her eyes were all Meg's and when she smiled it would sometimes make him catch his breath. The cross between the two parents had made a very beautiful girl and just like her mother in the small A-frame church that first day, Celia stood out amongst her friends. She'd been accepted from the start just as Meg had been. In an age when blacks, whites and mixed races didn't integrate, Meg had seen to it that she and George had broken through that barrier and not only found family amongst their black community but friendship, acceptance and tolerance for their daughter Celia. In a small town such as theirs, it was really quite an accomplishment considering the rest of the country couldn't seem to figure it out.

George drove home, happy to give Celia some time with her friends and a bit of alone time for himself. He had been so focused on providing a good home for Celia that he didn't think about dating. How could he ever find another woman who could measure up to Meg? She was one-of-a-kind. The only one. George had been lonely at times over the years and had found that distractions like immersing himself in Celia's raising, the choir, playing at the local club each weekend, the church and filling his life full of the music he loved, managed to take away some of the loneliness. Not to mention, he may be accepted by the black community but he doubted that they would allow him to marry one of their women. And now, after living amongst them, worshipping with them, and having his child attend school with them, dating a white woman was not even an option. George really had no choice but to concentrate on his daughter, his music and the students he taught and directed. His life was fulfilled and he was happy. It never occurred to him to move to another city and start anew, or try to find someone that could fill Meg's place – there simply wasn't a woman who could do that.

Celia too had found a happy life amongst her friends and choir mates. She had excelled in her schooling. Although she tried her hand at the piano, her real love was singing. She had started singing at an early age, having been blessed with her mother's soulful voice and was surrounded by all sorts of musical influences thanks to her father. He often played old jazz and blues artists like Rosetta Tharpe, Billie Holiday, Dizzy Gillespie, Nat King Cole, Etta James and other soulful singers in the house on the record player. Celia would listen with her perfect-pitch ear and try to mimic their sound. She was excellent and sang with passion and soul, making the song her own. Her father would play the piano and let her hum along to the rhythm until she found her voice in the songs. They both had such a gifted ear for music and it gave them a strong bond.

Celia was a teenager though, and had been showing signs of wanting more freedom. Lately she had wanted to earn her own money and had been working as a server at social functions in Peoria. Twice she had gone along with the church ladies to serve at the Dumont Estate, a well known rich family in town. She had earned enough to purchase a small leather handbag and a pair of stockings. She secretly hoped that she would be asked back again. The estate was so beautiful. The Dumont's were so beautiful, especially their 18 year old son, Bradley. Celia had spotted him from first visit. She daydreamed of Bradley Dumont.

The Dumont's had big money from way back and the house oozed rich. Every few months Mrs. Dumont would hold a gala to raise funds for some such cause and the elite of the town would be in full attendance. This was Celia's favorite kind of event to work at. The people were so beautiful and wore such fabulous clothing. The women were dripping in jewels. Just one of the stones in one of their necklaces would pay for rent for almost a year, she was sure! She and her dad had never considered themselves poor since her dad started teaching, even though they lived in one of the poorer sections of town, but they certainly weren't considered "well off" either. Celia had always been impressed with the amount of excess that the wealthy took so for granted. Her dad had told her about his and Meg's history and how he had been raised in that kind of opulence but gave it all up to be with her mother. Celia often wondered if her father ever missed having such wealth, but he seemed extremely happy and she couldn't ever recall a time when he complained about not having money.

As George made his way home, Celia and her choir mates walked over to a local soda shop. The concert had been the last in a two-night performance before final exams. Her dad had worked with the students for months getting them ready for their farewell concerts. And it had all gone so well! The students had wanted to mark the occasion with a party amongst themselves. As the group entered the shop they were delighted to find that they would have the place all to themselves. They all clambered into the two booths and surrounding tables waiting for Marla, the waitress, to come and take their orders. As she approached the first table, she asked the small female student what she'd like to order. In perfect unison and harmony they all sang, "17 ice cream sodas, please." She laughed, shook her head and turned away from the group writing on her pad. The group all laughed, clasped hands and congratulated themselves. Spirits were high! Celia sat amongst her friends feeling elated. This group made her feel like anything was possible. She sat laughing and chatting more than two hours before she realized that it was dark. Taking a dime from her purse, she left the booth and made her way to the payphone on the outside of the building. She dialed home and waited for her dad to answer. No answer. It was 9:45 pm. Celia hung the phone back in its cradle and went inside.

"I can't seem to get my dad on the phone," she said.

"That's okay Celia, we're going home ourselves. We'll walk together," said Tess, her best friend.

Celia figured as long as she stayed with the group she'd make it home safely and her dad would not be too upset. A group of seven left all at once including Celia. Walking down the main street and then turning towards the church neighborhood, the group chatted enthusiastically, still enjoying their high from the performance. The street bordered on the party side of town for some of the richer kids. There were soda shops and dance halls and a movie theater that catered to the younger, affluent crowd. These kids didn't have to walk; they were given cars for their 16th birthdays. Their college dreams were secure come the Fall, something that most of her group were still unsure of.

As the group laughed and strolled along they didn't notice the car that had pulled up beside them. Inside, four teenage boys rolled down their windows and started taunting the group. When one of the boys spotted Celia amongst them, he pointed her out to his friends.

"Hey, look at her, the one with the crazy hair," one of them yelled as he pointed towards Celia.

"Which one are you talking about?" laughed another boy, to which they all broke out laughing.

"Her… with the lighter skin. You can't miss her! She doesn't look like she belongs with them. Hey sweetheart, why don't you come and take a ride with us? We'll make sure you get home safely."

The choir group instinctively surrounded Celia as she hung her head and kept moving forward.

"Stop the car!" one boy yelled, to which the car stopped rather abruptly, screeching the tires. The boy jumped out of the car and pushed through Celia's friends to stand right in front of her.

"Hey sweetheart, I ain't gonna hurt ya. Just come for a ride and get out of the middle of all these darkies. You look like you don't belong here – like someone from your past split themselves a dark oak," he said laughingly, turning to his friends in the car.

Celia was about to stand her ground when she heard another boy's voice yell out, "Leave her be, Scott! Get back in the car and get out of here."

She turned and saw Bradley Dumont standing on the opposite sidewalk. He started walking towards the crowd and the car. Celia had never spoken to him. She had only ever seen him at his Mother's events. Secretly, she believed she loved him. He was very handsome, well groomed and had an easy smile. She thought he was beautiful. He had green eyes, deeper than hers. He stood six feet tall at eighteen years old, but seemed much taller and older! His family had money going back to England. He had been raised in opulence much like her father. She thought it ironic that she would find herself pining for a young, rich, white man, much like her mother had done.

Bradley came straight over to her and stood between her and the boy he called Scott. He stood a good six inches taller than Scott.

"Don't be causing trouble with these kids, Scott. They weren't doing anything, just walking down the street," Bradley said.

The group all shuffled away from Scott to stand behind Bradley. The boys in the choir knew better than to fight against these boys. They were known to be bullies and had been abusive to a number of the choir members over the years. Scott stared at Bradley for a moment and then laughed.

"What are you, Brad, a lover of the darkies?" Scott asked. "You wanna protect them from the white man?" he teased and laughed. He threw his hand out at Bradley as if throwing away his respect for him and turned to get back in the car. "You ain't worth it!" Scott yelled from the car and he and his friends laughed uproariously and drove off, tires squealing.

Brad turned to the group of kids. They were all rather shocked at him coming to their defense as he did, and they were unsure what to say.

"Hey," he said to Celia with a smile on his face. "Pay no attention to them, they're all idiots," he said, nodding his head as if to confirm it.

She kept her eyes low and said, "Thank you for helping me and my friends."

Bradley smiled wider and looked around. "It's quite the entourage you travel with," he said jokingly. "Are you sure you're alright?" he asked her.

Celia found her voice, "Yes thank you," she said shyly.

"I'm Brad," he said, holding out his hand to her.

"I'm Celia," she said, taking his hand and looking up into his green eyes. Her heart lurched in her chest and she thought for certain he could hear her heartbeat. He shook her hand gently and held it in place for a moment, while holding her gaze.

The group behind them had stood in silence, mostly in shock at bearing witness to what was going on. One of the most affluent young men in town was coming to her rescue and defending her from his equally affluent friends. They had watched the exchange as if it were a tennis match. Collectively holding their breath, they could all feel the magnetism between the affluent white boy and beautiful coffee-colored girl.

Sensing the audience, Brad asked, "Can we stroll on ahead a little?"

Celia was speechless, taking a step backwards. Thankfully, Tess was there to stabilize her from behind and stop her from falling back completely. Celia opened her mouth to say something but stammered so Tess took her lead.

"It's okay Celia, you walk a little ahead. We'll all be behind you and it isn't that far before we turn off the main road."

As if that was all he needed to hear, Brad gently took Celia's arm and walked on with her beside him. The group fell behind them a respective distance, some snickering quietly and others in disbelief at what had just happened and was continuing to happen in front of them. Brad could feel the group on his heels and decided to pick up the pace slightly so that when he spoke, only Celia would hear him.

"I'm sure you must think this is strange," he started, almost apologetically. "I truly don't mean to frighten you, but I've noticed you at my mother's gala event and Christmas fete and I wanted to know more about you." He smiled at her, genuinely, and she couldn't help but smile back. Again she hung her head and he stopped her a moment and said, "Oh, you should always smile. You look so beautiful when you smile."

Despite the distance that Brad had put between them, the group following overheard most of the exchange and gasps were let our by the girls. This was unheard of!

Brad turned and continued walking with his hand gently guiding Celia forward. She still couldn't find it in herself to say anything more than a few words at a time. She was so fearful of sounding stupid to him or even worse, uneducated. Still, what must he think if she can barely speak for herself?

She cleared her throat, took a deep breath and asked him, "Why?"

He didn't expect the question and it threw him at first. "Well," he said, "frankly, I thought you were, ah... quite... eh... lovely and I... uh, wanted to know who you were," he said as color rose to his cheeks.

She looked directly into his eyes for any kind of sign that he was joking or being cruel in any way. He didn't look anything but sincere and honest to her. She smiled and looked down again as Bradley said, "I realized this is probably not what you ever expected. It surprises me too a little but ever since I saw you at my mother's party, I was determined to find out who you are. I know you know who I am — my mother makes sure everyone does. But I don't know much about you."

"What do you want to know?" she asked him. He smiled. He'd won her over!

"What's your last name?" he asked.

"Morningstar," she answered.

He took this in. "I've heard that name before in a business or something in... Peoria. No, it's a law firm, right?" he said inquisitively.

Of course, Celia knew her family history well and even though her grandparents were dead, the law firm had kept the name, probably because George's father had left everything in his estate to the firm. Shortly after Celia's eighth birthday, George was notified that his mother and father had died. A car accident. They died without having spoken to their only child in almost nine years. George didn't attend the funeral or the reading of the will and he never heard from the family lawyers, ascertaining that he was completely left out.

"Are you related?" Brad asked, sounding almost astonished. Immediately Celia became angry that he sounded so surprised that she could be related to anyone involved with the Morningstar law firm.

"Yes, it happens that my grandfather was William Morningstar, the founder of the firm," she answered with her head jutting high. She wouldn't look down again when she spoke to Brad. She realized that she had a good family name behind her and had nothing to be ashamed of regardless of her father's estrangement from his family.

Brad snapped his fingers and nodded his head, "I remember my mother saying that they died tragically. Something about them attending his 50th birthday party and a car accident. That's sad that you lost your grandparents so early, Celia," he said, sounding truly sincere. "My grandparents are lovely people and I would be very sad if they were gone from my life, especially both at the same time", he continued, hoping she believed his empathy.

"I didn't know them," she said, matter-of-factly. "They disowned my father when he married my mother and they died when I was eight years old, just a few years after my mother," she told him. She wondered why she was explaining this to him. Even though he seemed to be interested, why was she sharing this with him? She'd only really ever told Tess and then she didn't go into the whole truth about her grandmother who was raped and how her mother was adopted. She felt as though Brad really was interested in who she was. Brad looked at her intently as she spoke and waited a minute before asking his next question.

"Why would they disown your dad?" he asked naively. She stopped walking and looked at him, as if it were an obvious answer. Was he teasing her and making fun?

43

"Can't you tell?" she asked him, with her hand on her hip. "I don't think you're being very nice. I think you're poking fun at me," she said rather accusingly.

"No!" he said, panicked. "I didn't mean to be rude. I truly don't understand why they would disown their son." His eyes were wide and he looked at her pleadingly.

"My mother was half black and half white. My father eloped with her at 18 because he knew that his parent's wouldn't allow them to marry and he was about to be sent off to school far away," she said, explaining it to him. She looked at him and tilted her head, as if to say, *now do you get it?*

He nodded at her and this time he lowered his eyes. He was embarrassed by his own faux pas. As they came to the corner where Celia and her friends would turn towards their neighborhood, Brad gently reached out to Celia and said, "I truly didn't mean to be rude to you. I don't understand anyone who would disown their own child. I don't care who they married." She looked at him rather surprised, not saying anything. "My mother is having another event in a week. A Summer Fling or something to raise money for the local library, I think," he said. "I'll look to see if you're there." He smiled a wide smile at her, touched her arm and nodded to the group behind them as he continued strolling on.

Celia stood at the corner in shock. Did that really just happen? Why did she confess all of that to him? She looked at her friends as they all came towards her. They were all silent for a moment until Tess said, rather loud, "Girl! You got a rich man sniffing 'round you!" and the group broke out laughing. Celia smiled and then laughed along with her friends. They turned down her street just as Celia's father's car came into view towards them. He slowed down and rolled down his window, "There you are!" he said smiling. The group gathered around his car all greeting him. Celia went around to the passenger's side, waved and called out goodbyes to her friends and then got into the car.

"Sorry, Daddy, I called and you didn't answer so everyone offered to walk me home!"

"Not to worry," he said happily. "I did drive over to the shop but I must have just missed you by minutes. Time to get home, though. It is getting late."

And off they drove with George none the wiser of the exchange that had just occurred.

. . .

A week later Celia found herself back at the Dumont Estate for the dinner party Brad had spoken of. Her crisp white uniform only accentuated the coffee tone of her skin and the color of her eyes, not to mention her young, supple body. She had tied her hair back as was required, but managed to pull it into a swift chignon instead of just a knot. It looked lovely and even though she was hired help, many men in the room noticed her as she walked past them with her tray of drinks. Celia was unaware of the looks she garnered as she made her way through the grand ballroom with her drinks. She had been at work since 6:00 pm and it was now 7:30 pm with no sign of Brad anywhere. However, dinner had not been served yet and perhaps that was when she would see him.

Almost in answer to her prayers, the dinner bell chimed and the 100 or so guests made their way towards the dining area. The room was set up with several large round tables with 10 chairs around each table. The tables were set in colors of black and silver to simulate the night sky with stars glowing. Mrs. Dumont knew how to throw a dinner party! The guests took their seats each according to the name tag at the head of each plate. Each table had two waiters or waitresses to serve the food and a wine server so that no one went hungry or without a drink for too long.

Celia was working table eight with Tess and a church lady. She waited for her guests to be seated and settled before serving dinner rolls and butter to her side of the table. As she started placing the roll baskets down between the side plates, she heard a voice say, "Excuse me, I'm wondering if you could please bring us some rolls?" She knew immediately that it was Brad who was asking. She turned to look at him. He was seated between two teenage girls, perhaps a couple of years younger than her, both equally blonde and pretty and rich. Celia's heart rose, then dropped within the same moment. One girl looked as though she was leaning in towards Brad and Celia figured it must be a girlfriend.

She felt suddenly very embarrassed and wanted to run from the room, but instead swallowed a deep breath and said, "I know who your waiter is and will ask that they be brought to your table immediately." She smiled awkwardly and moved past his chair turning her back towards him again before he could see the look in her eyes.

"Thanks Celia," he answered.

She wanted to die! Now he's shown he knew it was her! And he's asked her to bring him rolls, just like hired help. She was so stupid to think that he was interested in her that way. He only wanted to show off in front of his pretty, rich, white girlfriends. Oh, she wanted to die! How could she work the rest of the night now?

She managed to find Brad's server and request the rolls for the table and make it through the rest of the dinner without anymore interaction with Brad. But she felt him watching her through the rest of the meal and she was thankful when the dinner was over and the guests returned to the ball room, leaving the help to clear the tables. Celia and Tess cleared away their table quickly so that they could get out to the ball room and serve drinks on trays while watching the beautiful women dance with the handsome men.

Celia didn't want to go back into the ballroom. Tess asked her twice but after the second rejection to her request she stated, "Suit yourself" and walked off to get her tray. Celia hung back from the crowd in hope of getting out to the garden beyond the dining room. She needed some fresh air. She made her way to the garden doors and went through to the patio outside. The estate had pristine gardens and was well known for its boxwoods and hydrangeas. Celia took a very deep breath and closed her eyes, letting the breath release out her mouth slowly. She stood there a moment and then repeated the technique. It was one her dad had taught her, to deal with a jittery stomach just before a performance. She found it served her well during other stressful times as well.

"Sounds as though you have a leak," said Brad.

She starred and spun around. "How did you…?" she trailed off.

"I watched you stay back and then leave once the tables were cleared," he said as he smiled at her.

She was so shocked that he was standing there that once again she couldn't find her voice. *This has to stop happening!* she thought. It angered her that he kept coming up on her when she least expected it and catching her off guard. Just once she'd like to have the upper hand. But then, that was probably never to be in today's society.

"Are you here hiding from someone?" he asked with his eyebrows raised.

She wondered how he could know her so well with having only just met her. She waited to answer, taking a moment to appreciate what a fine specimen of young, adult male he was. Brad Dumont was a serious Adonis. His blonde hair parred on one side had shine and softness to it. He didn't grease it back as was popular with the white boys these days. Instead he left it to do as it wanted, only being tamed by a trim cut and comb. He was dressed in a tuxedo, at his mother's insistence, and it suited him. She imagined he'd look very similar on his wedding day. Hmmmmm. *Another vision to build upon,* she mused.

"I'm not hiding, I'm getting some air," she answered, not willing to give him an inch.

"I was hoping that you would have noticed that I saw you back at the table," he said.

"Oh I noticed," she said rather staunchly. He wondered if her tone meant she was unhappy with him and he couldn't understand why.

"Did it impress your girlfriend that you knew the help by name?" she asked bitterly.

His brow furrowed as he tried to understand her meaning and then his face softened as it came to light. "I didn't do that to impress anyone but you," he said. "Neither of those girls are my girlfriends. One is my younger sister and the other is a cousin."

Celia stared at him once again at a loss for words. "Sorry," she said as she looked away.

"I would never treat you like that Celia," he said as he walked towards her. "It saddens me that you even have to work as a server. I make it a habit never to be rude or demanding of anyone who is working in our house." She wasn't sure what to think of him. He certainly didn't act as though he was raised in an elite family.

"What would your mother think if she found you out here talking to me?" she asked.

"I'd tell her you were a friend and that we were just talking. It's not a lie, is it?" he asked her.

"No, I suppose not," she said. She looked downward. It bothered him and he wanted her to believe what he was saying. Looking down to the end of the garden he found his proof.

"Do you see that little gardener's shed at the back of the garden?" he asked as he pointed to a small cottage lit up by the moonlight.

"Yes," she answered as she turned to follow his pointed finger.

"I used to play in that as a small boy. I pretended it was my house and that my sister was my maid," he chuckled, remembering how much fun it was. "Everything was great until one day, I yelled at Vicky because she broke something. I called her stupid and told her she was fired."

"What did she do?" asked Celia.

"She beat the hell out of me is what she did! Told me I was never to treat her or any other woman, serving help or otherwise, so awfully ever again. And I never forgot it," he said. "It was a very valuable lesson to have learned at such a young age and from someone so much younger than me. But Vicky has always been that way. She's always out to defend the downtrodden or root for the underdog. She constantly reminds us that color means nothing – it's what's inside a person that counts."

"My father would call her an 'old soul'," Celia said as she smiled. "Sounds as though she's walked this earth before and has a better understanding of how to treat people than your average person does."

"She sure does," Brad agreed. He gestured toward the dining room, "She was the young lady with the blonde hair."

"They BOTH had blonde hair, Brad!" Celia emphasized.

"Oh, I guess you're right," he laughed. "Constance, my cousin is also blonde."

Celia looked towards the little shed. "It looks like a beautiful garden to grow up in. I'll bet you had many adventures back here," she said in an almost day-dreamy voice.

"Yes," Brad answered. "I haven't been down the garden or in the shed in many years. Wanna go and have a look?" he asked her, grabbing her hand. Before she could answer him he was off with her in tow leading her down into the back of the yard and towards the shed. It was a lot bigger than a shed when they got close to it and she was amazed that he would refer to it as a "shed." It was almost as big as her house! Brad tried the handle on the door when they reached the porch. It was locked. He knelt down and lifted up the welcome mat to expose a key underneath. He used it to unlock the door and they let themselves in.

"This is a garden shed?" she asked as they got inside. "This looks like someone lived here for years."

"The gardener did, way back when I was little," Brad answered. "But he managed to find a home of his own not too far from us and moved. Mother left the shed up for us to play in as kids. It's not been used since then. Maybe Vicky played in it for a while longer after I stopped but mostly it sat empty."

Celia walked around looking at the contents of the former home and play house. Everything was either cobwebbed or dusty and the windows were shuttered in so no light came through except from the open front door. Brad went around opening a few of the back windows and then went to close the front door. Now Celia could see a little better into the cottage. It was a one-and-a-half story structure. The small fireplace was surrounded by river rock and was the central feature along the left wall. The loft upstairs overlooked the living room and she could see the frame of a bed in the loft area. There were two doorways on the right, one leading to the bathroom and the other to a kitchen she presumed. The furniture had seen many years but was still sturdy. There was a two-seater couch on one side of the fireplace and a wing backed chair on the other. A small table to the side of each seat had oil lamps on them. She imagined what it would have been like to grow up *playing* in a house like this. To have had it all for herself and her friends. She'd have been in heaven!

Brad went around checking into drawers and cupboards, searching for something to light a lamp. Although the windows brought in more light with the shutters removed, they were incredibly dirty and hadn't been cleaned in many years – probably since the gardener lived there.

"Aha!" Brad announced when he came across some matches. He tried twice to light the oil lamp but came to the conclusion that the oil was no good and instead found a candle and holder and lit it easily. As he placed the candle down onto the table he walked over to where Celia was looking at the small collection of books. He came to stand very close behind her, almost reading over her shoulder. She could feel his breath on the back of her neck and she shivered slightly from the excitement his presence gave her. Almost sensing her feelings, he reached up and touched both of her arms softly sliding his hands up and down them.

"I'm glad you came tonight, Celia," he said almost whispering it in her ear. She turned to look at him and he took the chance there and then to kiss her. It started off light and filled with trepidation, but then he took a little more chance and pressed firmly into her soft, supple lips, enjoying the sweet kiss. He moved his hands gently around her waist and kept them there while he kissed her.

Celia's heart hammered in her chest and she thought for sure that Brad could feel it. His lips were soft and he tasted sweet. When he encircled her waist with his hands, she felt like he wanted her to stay forever and this made her just want to swoon. He was so beautiful. She had dreamed of such an occurrence and it was happening… he was kissing her! Celia kissed him back and tried not to let her pounding heart ruin the moment. When the kiss stopped they both look deeply into each other's eyes.

"That was something I have wanted to do from the moment I first saw you," he said. *Me too*, she thought but she didn't say it out loud. She dared not speak just yet for fear of stumbling over her words and ruining the moment. She just smiled shyly and looked down. He placed his finger under her chin and lifted her head up so she would look up at him again.

"I just love your smile," he said. He kissed her forehead and brought her into a hug. This shocked Celia and she held herself a little stiff at first then relaxed once she felt the hug he gave her. It was gentle and tender. He didn't seem to be trying to get at her in a naughty way, he just seemed completely besotted with her. And who was she to argue with that? Her parents had the same kind of love and they did alright. If it weren't for her mom getting sick she knew they'd still be married. So why shouldn't she have that kind of love too? Times were changing. Everywhere things were starting to turn around. She knew there were those who would never agree with Dr. King or the movement that was starting up, just like the boys that teased her and her friends that day she first met Brad, but in this small town things were changing.

"I want to see you more frequently," he said. "Once in a while at my mother's parties is not enough. I'd like it if you'd spend some time with me over this summer. Would you like that?"

"Yes," she answered, not too sure how it was going to happen. He lived across town from her and they didn't really have mutual meeting places in common.

Brad seemed to have given it some thought. "Do you have a close friend that would help cover for you? I thought if we could get Vicky and a friend of yours to cover for us, we could go driving outside of town and spend some time on our own. Do you know someone who would help us out?" he asked, seeming to have it all figured out.

"Perhaps Tess would cover. She seemed happy that you defended me that day and I think she'd be able to tell my dad a fib without giving us away," she said.

It should have bothered her that she needed to fib to her dad about anything but she knew he'd be against her going driving with a boy. Even though this boy was Bradley Dumont! Funny, times might be changing but they both still felt the need to be together in secret, she thought, and then she brushed away anything that deterred her from helping Brad plan out the strategy of their encounters.

"If I can get this place cleaned up, we could even spend some time here!" he suggested. "I'll see if my mom can send out some of the cleaning girls to freshen up the place and I'll say I want to use it for my summer home. I bet she'll think nothing of it!" he stated, pleased with himself for thinking of it.

He didn't notice the change in the look on her face, nor did she say anything to him. Instead, she nodded her head and turned away as if to look around some more. Even though this lovely, rich boy wanted to spend time with her, she couldn't help but feel slightly embarrassed by the fact that she was essentially the hired help. Society may change their views but he still lived in a world where there was hired help to do his every whim and they were generally of a different color than he was. She kept reminding herself that her father came from the exact same background and it didn't have any effect on his view of those who work to serve others, and Brad seemed the same way. Celia smiled to herself. She should stop with the self doubt and nagging thoughts and enjoy this moment.

"We should get back before my mother wonders where I got to," he mused. "I promised I'd dance with her at least once tonight. She loves to show me off to her friends in hopes that I'll make a suitable husband to one of their daughters." Celia's face froze at this sentence and he realized what he'd said.

"Oh, don't worry, none of them interest me. I much prefer to find a rare exotic flower rather than your "garden variety" bloom!" he said, smiling at her and winking. She too broke into a wide smile and he took his fist and punched his chest.

"Oh, that smile will get me right here every time!" he said as he bent over in fake heartsick pain.

They broke out laughing again and made their way towards the door. Brad blew out the candle and closed the door behind them and placed the key back under the mat. He would get right on fixing that little shed up and soon he and Celia would have a place they could spend some time together.

"Where've you been?" asked Tess as she spotted Celia after almost half an hour of looking for her. "I went to get my tray of drinks and you were gone when I got back."

"I know," Celia answered taking Tess's tray from her hands. "I'm sorry I got distracted. Listen, I need to talk to you, but not now," Celia said excitedly.

Tess could tell something was up but she had no idea what Celia was up to. "All I know is, you gonna get fired from serving if you go missing like that again," Tess chided.

"I know, I'm here now. I'll tell you everything on our way home," she said. "I'm going to need you to help me with a plan."

"I hope that plan is to get your ass back into that ball room and serve some of Mrs. Dumont's guests before we get sent home with nothing to show for it," Tess complained. She really needed the money and didn't want Celia messing anything up for her. On the way home Celia confided in Tess all that had happened between her and Brad. Tess was excited for her but also a bit worried.

"You sure you know what you're doing, girl?" Tess asked her after Celia outlined the plan.

"Are you sure you can cover for me once in a while without my dad becoming suspicious?" countered Celia.

"Oh, don't worry 'bout me, Celia. I won't give away your affair with Mr. Moneybags! Now that school is out, our choir practices only happen once a week for church and your dad knows you and I spend a ton of time together over the summers. He won't suspect a thing. I just hope you know what you're doing," she said, like a mother.

Celia laughed at her friend. Sometimes Tess liked to act like a mother to her since Celia didn't have one, even though Celia was actually a few months older than her. She didn't mind though. She knew Tess had her best interests at heart and was really looking out for her.

"So how are you going to meet up? Have you figured that out yet?" Tess asked.

"I gave him my phone number. And I told him that my dad practiced with his group at the club every Tuesday evening and then played there on Saturdays. Now that the summer is here, he may go during the day sometimes too," she explained. "We'll have to work around his schedule. Brad told me that he would pick me up near to where he found us walking that day. It's a good spot. Not too far from home and he can borrow his mom's car for trips for sodas and such. It's all nearby there."

"Well, it sounds as though you've got it all figured out!" Tess exclaimed. "Ain't this gonna be a fun summer!"

"Oh, I sure hope so," Celia said overdramatically dreamily, and both girls giggled as the bus took them and the other servers from the church to their neighborhood.

. . .

The first time they were able to get together after the party was a week later. True to his word Brad had asked his mother if he could have the cottage fixed up. She agreed and had the staff give it a thorough cleaning; he had his things moved from the main house to the "summer cottage" as he had now coined it.

He called Celia on Tuesday evening shortly after dinner. Her dad had already left for the club and she had just finished up doing the dinner dishes. They arranged to meet at their secret spot in 15 minutes and Celia immediately called Tess to tell her she was on her way out and was leaving a note for her dad saying she was going to be with her. Tess agreed to be on guard should her dad call to have her come home, but Celia assured her that she would be home long before that.

Brad picked her up right on time and they drove back to the Dumont Estate. On the way Celia looked in awe at all the large homes that lined the streets in Brad's area of town. One house was so large it had an intimidating wrought-iron gate with a large "M" adorning the middle of it.

"Did you ever go inside?" Brad asked as they slowed down in front of the mansion.

"Inside there?" Celia asked in disbelief pointing towards the gate. "No, never, why would I have? Do you think I've worked there before?"

"No," Brad laughed. "Easy there, I'm not being cruel. Remember, I'm crazy about you!" he said sincerely, grabbing her hand in his.

She smiled easily. "Sorry", she said. "Bit of a soft spot, I guess. I need to be reminded every once in a while. Still not used to this yet," she explained.

"Okay," he smiled. "I'll give you a break this once then. No, the reason I asked you is because this is the Morningstar Mansion. I mean it *was*. I think it was sold years ago but I'm not too sure why the 'M' is still on the gate. Maybe a family named "MacDonald" moved in," he joked.

"Maybe," she said, half lost in thought as she stared at the massive house. *To think that this is where her father was raised.* To see their small modest home now in comparison it was almost hard to believe that her dad ever lived here at all. She wondered why her father had never brought her out here and shown it to her. Perhaps he wasn't very proud of the fact that his very wealthy parents had judged his choice of wife so harshly that they disowned their only son and never spoke to him again. Putting it that way, she could understand why he hadn't.

"It may be large and grand but there isn't a lot of love in that house, I can tell you that!" Celia stated. She folded her arms and looked away from the mansion as if dismissing it completely.

Brad took the signal and understood her indifference. He stepped on the gas pedal and they moved away from the gate. When they got to the Dumont Estate, Brad drove past the main entrance and pulled into a side entrance way that led to a small drive around the back of the summer cottage. This way, no one could see their comings and goings. Brad made it to the back door of the cottage and used his key to gain entrance. He stepped aside the open door making a grand gesture for her to enter. She giggled a little, wanting to curtsy and walked inside.

She could smell the difference right away. The cottage had most definitely been cleaned and scrubbed. Mrs. Dumont had all the furniture given to the local thrift store and had newer furniture from some of the lesser used rooms in the estate brought out to make her son's stay in the summer cottage as comfortable as possible. The windows, having been cleaned with hot water and vinegar, positively shone and when the light hit the pane, it could almost blind you. Nothing of the dusty cobwebbed cottage looked the same. Even the loft upstairs now held a beautifully adorned four poster bed. Mrs. Dumont certainly made sure her baby boy slept in comfort. Celia had never seen such a beautiful bed.

"It was my mother's bed growing up," Brad said, noticing Celia staring at it.

"It's so beautiful," she said.

"She actually wanted Vicky to have it, but my little sister wouldn't have anything to do with it. She said it reminded her of a great big wooden boat," he laughed. He knew Vicky too well. She liked flounce and frilly things, not solid, dark, oak wood.

"Oh, I think it's so beautiful," she exclaimed. "It makes me think of the kind of bed a king or queen might sleep in!"

Brad smiled at her. He liked how she found excitement and wonder in things that most others took for granted. She had a true appreciation for everyday life and he really liked that. She was certainly a breath of fresh air after the numerous silly girls that were paraded in front of him at almost every party. Not only was she nothing like them in her attitude, but her exotic look and those eyes! She was head and shoulders above the best looking girl amongst those available in his social circles.

"My mother made sure I had everything I needed. The kitchen is fully stocked and she's even gone as far as having some ready-made sandwiches in case I'm unable to fend for myself," he laughed. "I guess she thinks I wouldn't have the sense to even go into the main house if I find myself starving to death." Celia laughed too. "Are you hungry?" he asked her.

"No, thanks, I just finished dinner before you picked me up."

"Would you like me to light a fire?" he asked her, gesturing towards the fireplace.

"No, not really. It's a little warm for a fire."

A moment's hesitation, "Can I kiss you again?" he asked.

She stood stock still, holding her breath. "Yes," she said quietly.

They stared at one another briefly and then Brad stepped towards her quickly not wanting to give her a second to change her mind. His hands cupped her face as he bent his head to kiss her. She tilted her head up and closed her eyes. He kissed her tenderly and slowly enjoying everything about her. She smelled wonderful, like the lavender his mother had growing in her garden. Her skin was smooth and had sheen from the warm summer's day. Her hair fell to her waist in long tendrils of multi tawny/brown color. She was exquisite. She had such a peaceful look on her face when her eyes were closed. He liked to keep his open to see her like that.

This time, she leaned her body into him and felt his strong arms hold her tight. He was well built with a strong neck and shoulders and narrow waist. As the kisses became more fervent, their bodies pressed tighter together. Celia could feel a change in her temperature and a warming that she hadn't experienced. She had never kissed any boy before Brad had kissed her the day he first brought her here, at the library fund raiser. She had never had a boyfriend and only dreamed of kissing boys, *especially* Brad Dumont!

He broke the kiss off gently and asked her if she wanted to get more comfortable.

"Sure," she said, half dazed from the kiss.

He led her over to the couch and they sat down together. Brad gently took her legs and swung them over his as he held her closely in a cuddle. He kissed her again, slowly laying her back down on the couch, until she was lying down with Brad nestled beside her and his legs tucked under and hers resting on top of his. Still kissing her, Brad played with her hair and brought his hand down to stroke her neck. Celia was getting very excited by his kisses and the feel of his body in such close proximity. His hands were stroking up and down the side of her torso, just grazing over the side of her breast and she didn't mind it at all!

She had led a pretty sheltered life but every once in a while she and Tess had stolen Tess's dad's naughty magazines and gone hiding in the garage to look through them. The pictures of the women did nothing for her

Chasing Charlie

but the couples were very arousing. Everything she knew about sex she had learned from school, the church and Tess. School taught you to stay clean and virginal. Church taught you to stay pious and virginal. Tess taught you to " …be willing to try everything once, Girl!" As far as she was concerned, "a woman should get something out of sex as well. Not just the man."

She often told Celia of the times she would hear her daddy having sex with her mom and it sounded as though her mom just groaned from it, like it was painful or something. Tess was convinced that she wasn't going to be doing any groaning, instead, " …her man was going to make sure she liked what he was doing! Especially if it was gonna happen every night!"

By now Brad was almost at the point of no return. He could feel his erection jutting into the back of her thighs and figured she could feel it too. He wondered if he should just jump up and stop things right now before they went too far.

It really wasn't his intention to get her into bed immediately. *No, far from it.* He really did just want to enjoy her company and spend time with her. But her lips were so incredibly delicious and she felt lovely in his arms. His mind argued with his heart which argued with his groin. Only one was going to win.

"We could be more comfortable upstairs," he offered. He looked down at her as she opened her eyes at him.

She hesitated a moment and then said, "Okay, maybe for a little bit." She rose up off the couch and swung her legs off him, freeing him to move and get up.

Taking her by the hand, he led her up the open staircase to the loft bedroom. From down below, the bed look grand, but it was much more splendid than Celia first imagined. She instinctively went straight over and slowly lay across the bed stretching her arms above her head, knocking the decorative pillows onto the floor and rolling onto her back as she did so.

59

"Oh, it's so beautiful, Brad!" she exclaimed. "If I slept in this bed every night I'd definitely feel like royalty."

He laughed watching her, his arousal on full display straining against his pants. She looked absolutely gorgeous stretched out before him on his bed. He walked over and lay down slowly beside her, taking her into his arms and kissing her again. Celia was completely lost in his kiss. Many strange sensations started flowing within her and she could feel the want to grind herself up against his hard member. In her mind she knew she needed to make a choice and quickly. Do you go ahead with this or do you draw back now while you still have the chance? As she was trying to decide, Brad moved his hand up under her top and grabbed her breast from underneath her bra. It took her breath away. He took her nipple between his two fingers and twirled it and played with it until it stood hard and firm. Their kisses became even more passionate as Brad encouraged her to open her mouth and allow his tongue access to her sweet tongue. She had never known about kissing in this manner and at first it shocked her until she felt Brad's arousal increase when he kissed her like this. If he liked it, then so did she!

His hand moved down out of her bra and slid brazenly across her body and down to her thighs. He grasped the inside of her right thigh as he continued to kiss her. She could feel a wetness begin to form in her lady parts and she found herself thrusting her pelvis into Brad more and more. His hand slid up her thigh and traced the outline of her privates as she gasped slightly but didn't move away. She knew this was going way too far but she couldn't stop herself. She wanted him to take her virginity. She believed he cared for her honestly, and she wanted him to be the one to own that part of her. Her father had always told her to *check your gut. If something doesn't feel right in your gut, then don't do it.* Another useful piece of advice he had given her. Her gut wasn't saying no! She was so lost in Brad's passion for her that it made her want to give up that part of her to him, and even though they hadn't known each other long, Celia had felt that chemistry immediately. This was exactly how she wanted it to be.

She allowed Brad's hand to linger wherever he wanted it to. And soon, they were discarding her top and bra and his shirt. Bare chest on bare chest their passion rose. Brad had started trying to undo the button on her pants when she stood up quickly, undid them and stripped them off exposing herself fully nude to him. He lay on the bed in awe for a moment taking in her beautiful sight. She was light coffee-colored from head to toe. Her thighs were shaped nicely, complimenting her narrow waist and full, young breasts. She was perfection.

Brad stood up off the bed and removed his pants and underwear all in one move. He stood before her, reaching out his hands so he could stand close. She thought he was beautiful. Strong and lean. He was powerfully built with a strong back and arms but always with a ready smile. His eyes were sincere and deep. His manhood stood erect almost standing up between them. He wanted her.

He had wanted her from the moment he saw her from across the room at a party his mother hosted almost six months ago. He tried hard to find out who she was then, but no one really had an answer. As far as anyone was concerned, she was part of the hired group that had come in for the party. He only learned where she was from by asking the cook to enquire after a party in the spring. Once he found out she lived south of the city and was a member of the small all black church there, he started going to the streets that border it in hopes of seeing her one day. It was a chance shot but until another party occurred, he had no way of seeing her again. It was just before the last day of school when he spotted Scott Niven hassling a group of black kids and then he realized it was her, in the middle of the group, recoiling from the words Scott was saying to her. He couldn't hear what was being said but he could tell by the look on her face that she didn't like it. He felt an urge to walk over to Scott and wallop him a good one, but he refrained from doing that, showing complete restraint. Next time, Scott wouldn't be so lucky.

Brad stepped towards Celia and took her into his arms, naked body on naked body. He was nervous about this because he knew it was completely new territory for her. He wanted her to feel safe and respected. Most of all he wanted her to feel what he felt, heart thumping excitement from head to toe. He hoped she didn't look back on this with regret. He wanted her to know that this was the right time and place. It was not going to work unless they were both on the same page. He stepped towards the bed yanking the covers back and down. He turned to Celia and kissed her again and led her back onto the bed. He lay atop her for a moment suspending himself above her, kissing her body from her neck on down, over her breasts, exploring each nipple as he went. He kissed down her torso while his hands stayed on her breasts. When he got closer to her nether lips, he took his fingers and placed them between them feeling her wetness and arousal. She moaned as he touched her. He played with her little pearl, rubbing it and then letting his finger descend into her wetness and push slightly into her. His other hand remained holding onto her other breast, tweaking the nipple. It was pure heaven to have him explore her body. But she wanted to do the same. She guided her hands down his chest lower to where she could reach his erection. He gasped when she took the head into her hand and instinctively stroked it. It was a magnificent feeling appendage and she allowed her hand to guide itself up and down the shaft, feeling the full length of him.

Brad was trying hard to keep himself from spilling too soon and had to put his hand on hers a number of times to stop her from making that happen. He wanted to have the full experience with her and not get so excited that he lose control. After making sure she was ready for him, he placed himself between her open legs and guided himself inside her slowly, all the while keeping eye contact with her. When he reached her hymen he stopped and looked at her as if to say, *Are you sure?* She raised her head back and her hips forward and pushed herself onto him in an effort to show him her desire. He withdrew slightly and then pushed with full force into her, taking her completely. He then stopped for a moment and held her to make sure she was okay.

Ever so slowly he started moving, in a bit, out a bit, until he was thrusting in and out more rhythmically and she was matching him thrust for thrust. She could feel excitement building from within her and then a sensation of pressure, delightful pressure moving to the top of her body and exploding out around her like a million stars bursting all at once. Her body convulsed over him and she clung onto Brad as she climaxed. He slowed only for a moment to allow her to enjoy her orgasm and as he did, her contractions enclosed over him driving him to climax. He jolted onto her, thrusting hard and staying there as if primeval urges were making sure his seed found its home. Then they both collapsed from the release. For a moment, neither stirred. Her body caught under him, he realized he must be crushing her and tried to lift himself up to give her a chance to breathe.

"Are you okay?" he asked as he kissed her forehead. She smiled with her eyes still closed and nodded her head. "Can you talk?" he asked, hoping she wasn't too hurt.

"Yes," she said quietly. She opened her eyes and looked into his. "I believe this is called "basking in the afterglow" she added, smiling widely.

"Where did you hear that from?" he asked her, laughing.

"One of Tess's dad's magazines," she said, and threw her arm over her eyes in embarrassment.

Brad laughed, kissed her arm and rolled off of her. When he lay beside her, he made sure they were touching and their hands were clasped. They both took a deep breath at the same time and then lay quietly, dozing for a moment.

Celia's voice broke the silence, "Having never done this before, I'm not sure if that was good for you or not," she said.

"I believe that my incredible orgasm is proof positive that it was good for me," he answered with his smile wide and his eyes still closed. She wanted to know if she was as good as what he had had before but she daren't ask that outright. Instead, she lay there with her hand in his and her eyes closed, listening to his breathing and wondering who else had been in this position with him.

As if reading her mind he startled her by saying, "I've only ever done this twice. A girl two years ago who lodged with my family for a short time. She was a year older than me and we only did it two times. She came into my room at night when everyone was asleep." He sounded sad about it somehow.

"Were you forced to by her?" Celia asked wondering why he sounded sad.

"Forced to?" he asked incredulously. "Oh no, nothing like that," he answered her. "She stayed for a month and then traveled to Europe to be with the rest of her family. I haven't seen her since."

"Did you love her?" Celia asked, wondering if this memory could prove to be a problem.

"Not at all," he said with conviction. "But she was very nice to me and taught me a lot. I didn't know how to be with any woman until she came along. I hadn't dated at all through school so I was a klutz around girls. She helped me to feel more confident about myself."

"You needed that?" Celia asked, shocked. "Why would you need to feel more confident around women? You are the most beautiful boy I know. I bet the whole city knows who you are. You could have any woman you want!"

"I only want you," he said, rising up on one elbow and gazing down at her.

She stared at him and shook her head. "It's hard to believe this is all happening. I've daydreamed about you ever since that first party that I worked," she admitted.

"Then it was meant to be," he said as he leaned over and kissed her.

They snuggled for a while longer and spoke of their lives growing up. Brad's family was very philanthropic. Brad had been immersed in helping those in need since he was a young boy. His mother's events were always attached to some fundraising need that she had taken a new interest in. When Beverley Dumont turned her attention to a charity, chances were that they would exceed their fundraising expectations for the year. She was that good and that connected. Despite this, her children were well mannered, humble and *very* generous of heart.

Brad spoke of his mother like she was a Queen. He had great admiration for her and he would do anything she asked of him. Celia listened to his childhood stories in awe. When he asked her to tell him *her* story she hesitated but then decided that he knew most of it already from their encounter on the sidewalk. What he didn't know so much about was her love of music and her father's musical talent. Brad was now the captive audience as she described her father's abilities with a piano and how he could hear a piece of music just once and play it note for note. Brad asked her, "Do you have a musical ear too?"

"Yes, I have a good ear but my ability is more in the singing department. For as long as I can remember I've heard music in my house and no matter what, I sang along. Even if my dad was just tinkering, I would sit beside him and vocalize with his keystrokes."

He leaned over on one elbow and looked at her pleadingly, "Will you sing for me? Now?" he asked.

"Now?" she asked back.

"Yes. Now." He sat up, completely naked and urged her to sit up too. "Please, Celia, I want to hear you sing," he asked again.

She grudgingly sat up and tucked her legs underneath her and leaned on her arm in front of him. *She is just lovely*, he thought as he admired her.

She cleared her throat and keeping her eyes downcast to the left, she began to sing. She chose Etta James' "At Last." She sang this at home regularly with and without the record playing in the background.

Brad was mesmerized by her ability to sing so smoothly with the low notes and the way her voice flowed like liquid through the song. He was being sung to by an exotic, naked goddess and her voice was a Siren leading him astray. She closed her eyes as she sang. Her lips and tongue forming the words were so intoxicating, Brad desperately wanted to kiss her again but wouldn't dare stop her from finishing.

When she did, he hesitated to say anything, trying to catch his breath. She misunderstood his hesitation as rejection and was taken aback for a moment.

"No… no…" he assured her as he reached out to touch her arm. "You have an incredible voice. Truly, you do. I just didn't imagine you were that good. I… you… you sound like a professional," he said honestly. "Do you sing with your dad's band at all?"

"Oh… no," she stammered. "I wouldn't be allowed in there. They serve alcohol there. But I sing with him at home all the time. He plays the guitar and he's really good at that too. He plays whatever he feels like and I sing along," she said proudly.

"You really do sound amazing," he said. He leaned over and kissed her as his hand reached up to cup her breast. She smiled as she accepted his kiss and his hand without reservation. His kisses left her lips and trailed down her neck as she raised her head and gave him access to it.

Just then, Celia caught site of the clock on the wall. It was 9:45 pm. *Shit*, she thought.

"Brad, it's almost 10 o'clock," she said urgently. "My dad will be home in 15 minutes and I should be there. We have to get going if that's going to happen."

She shrugged him off and jumped off the bed looking to the ground for her clothing. As she looked down she noticed the blood between her legs and thought about cleaning herself up. Would it stain through her pants? If so, she could tell her dad that she had had an "accident with her monthly cycle". He'd accept that. She quickly pulled her clothes on and stepped into her sandals. Brad too had jumped up and organized himself. He reached into his jeans pocket and fished out the car keys showing them to her with a broad smile on his beautiful face.

"Your chariot awaits," he said and bowed. She smiled, dipped slightly and turned to go down the stairs and on her way home.

In the car, he stroked her hand as she sat next to him in the seat. He played the radio, set to the latest station out of Chicago and Celia sang along. He could drive forever listening to her singing in his car. When he got near to where he was to drop her off he slowed down to ensure no one around could see them. Once stopped, he pulled her into his arms and kissed her passionately.

"That has to last me a whole week unless we can see each other on Saturday. Do you think you can get away again?" he asked, holding her close to him.

"I'll try. My dad usually leaves for the club around 8:00 pm. I'll talk to Tess and see what she's doing. If she's able to cover for me then I don't see why not," she shrugged. Being with Brad was now the most important thing to her in the world.

"I'd better go before my dad drives by us. I had a wonderful time," she told him shyly. Considering she'd just sung to him while she was completely naked and had sex for the first time, she suddenly felt vulnerable *now*. "Will you call me Saturday?" she asked.

"Yes. 8:10 pm, just after your dad has gone. Then pick you up here 15 minutes later. And home by 10," he said nodding his head.

"Oh no, Saturdays are usually a later night for him. We'll have a bit more time," she told him. He smiled and raised his eyebrows at her in a suggestive manner. She slapped him gently on the arm and kissed him quick on the lips. "Stop! You're going to make me blush!"

"Ha! I haven't yet!" he joked with her.

She laughed again and stepped out of the car. Normally, he'd have jumped out to get the door for her but they both knew that would draw attention and at this point neither wanted that. Celia walked the few minutes towards her front door while Brad sat in the car watching until she went out of sight. It sure was going to be a great summer he thought, as he drove off for home.

As Celia was passing just a few doors down from her own, her father's car pulled up and into her laneway. He spotted her and slowed as he drove beside her and honked once. She turned stiffly, waved her hand at him and kept on walking. He watched her for a moment and decided he should just drive on home, she was only feet from their doorstep. George was just getting out of his car when Celia made her way to their walkway.

...

"Hi Daddy," she said rather excitedly. Recognizing her own fear, she calmed herself using the breathing method he had taught her, only quietly this time.

"Hey, you've been out," he said in a surprised voice. "I didn't know you were planning on going out tonight. You didn't tell me." She knew this was his way of being inquisitive without coming right out and asking.

"Well, I didn't know. Tess called after you left and asked me over for a bit. I left you a note on the table in case I was out much longer but I figured I'd get home by now," she lied. Wow! That was easy! She had practiced and practiced what she would say but she wasn't sure if she could say it convincingly.

George smiled and reached into the back of the car to unload his guitar. "That's fine honey. You are 18 after all. I need to let you have your time with your friends and not be involved in everything you do," he said, laughing good naturedly. "I do have a surprise for you though," he paused, letting her lead the way through the front door.

Celia walked to the kitchen and George waited a moment while he put down the guitar case in the living room near the old piano before continuing. He made his way back to the kitchen and then said, "I... uh... I've asked if you could come and join us on stage to sing along with our group and they... uh... agreed," he smiled at her. "So, do you want to join us Saturday night on stage and sing your heart out like you do at home?" he asked, surprising her completely! "You could sing "Lady Sings the Blues" or whatever you want. We're pretty savvy and can play all the popular stuff. We do have some original pieces too and like to play those from time to time. You could probably do some vocals on those too," he offered casually.

This was the start of his plan. Get her used to the club atmosphere and environment. She had performed in front of audiences that contained mostly church members or parents of school children, but she had never performed to a club audience and he wanted her to start small. The club was the perfect place for Celia to hone her skills before they set out to really make themselves known. He had patiently waited for this. He had kept his promise to Meg and made sure Celia got an education, but now she needed to really focus on her music. This was the summer he'd been waiting for. He wanted her on stage with that voice! George knew perfect pitch when he heard it and Celia had it and then some. He wasn't bothered about her schooling in September, grateful and proud enough that she had excelled in her high school academics. Now was her time to shine and George didn't want her to hold anything back. With his musicality and her voice, they would go far. *He had waited for this!*

Celia stared at her dad for a moment. Was he kidding her? This was amazing! She was just saying to Brad tonight how she wouldn't have been allowed to do that because they served liquor at the club and she was a minor. She wondered that out loud, "Doesn't the fact that I'm only 18 cause a problem?"

"Nope, as long as you don't drink any alcohol. You can have all the soda, tea, coffee or water you want, on the house! I already cleared it with the club owner. All of them have heard you sing with the choir at one time or another. Hell, I practically built the Easter pageant on you alone this year," he laughed.

He had shamelessly flaunted her talent using the holy holiday as a backdrop. Celia had sung every gospel hymn George could find that required her kind of range. The rest of the choir augmented her performance, but Celia was certainly the star of the show and George had orchestrated it that way for this very reason. He knew she could hold her own on stage and he wanted her to have some exposure so that his request for her to sing at the club wouldn't seem ridiculous.

She stood stock still for a moment, trying to understand what he was saying. Oh she had wanted this for so long. She had loved the choir performances but had longed to be in front of a band singing the blues, the songs that inspired her and she'd heard growing up. She knew her dad would eventually let her sing with his band mates but she figured that would be after a few years of college. Not now! Not this soon!

"Uh… honey…" her father's voice broke her thoughts. He looked at her with a troubled face and then motioned his eyes downward towards her waist, a little embarrassed.

She looked down to where he motioned and could see blood staining the inside seam of her left thigh, not a lot but enough to be noticed. *Oh shit!* she thought. And then it hit her. Where she had *really* been tonight and what she'd been doing. *The story with Tess is all a ruse,* she told herself. Her thoughts following the last part of her conversation with her dad, she recalled Saturday night. She was supposed to meet up with Brad again on Saturday night. Now she couldn't go because her dad would expect her to jump at this chance. *Oh, double shit!* Okay, one thing at a time.

"Oh dear… excuse me," she said, appropriately blushing, but not for the reasons George thought. She scurried off to her room, calling over her shoulder, "I'll just take a moment to change and then we'll talk about Saturday, okay?"

"Yup… take your time," George said. He had put away his guitar and had put on a pot of coffee. Sitting down at the small kitchen table he listened to the percolator bubbling away and the smell of the rich dark brew as it began to come alive in the pot. George's favorite drink was a hot cup of coffee. It helped him stay awake at night when he wanted to continue writing his music, and it was easily accessible. No matter what, you could get a cup of coffee in every establishment.

Celia grabbed a change of clothes from her bedroom and went into the bathroom. She wet a facecloth, cleaned herself up, rinsed the cloth out and threw it in the hamper, making a mental note to be sure and wash the laundry by tomorrow morning or her dad would get to it first. When Celia came back out she had changed into a pair of soft, cotton pajamas and had pulled her hair back into a pony tail. It was an impressive sight, the rubber band straining to hold the thick cord of hair in place and bushing out beyond its band. Celia grabbed two coffee cups, the cream, sugar and two spoons and placed them on the table. She then stood near the stove, leaning her hip on the counter waiting for the percolator to finish its job. She didn't say a word.

Her dad looked at her inquisitively. "What's wrong, hon, you alright?"

"Yeah," she answered slightly distracted. "I was just uh… you know, thinking about Saturday night. I should have practiced with your group or something, don'tcha think?" she asked him. Maybe she could get him to agree to do it *next* Saturday night and she could still meet up with Brad to explain everything to him. If she didn't get to call him somehow, she'd not get the chance until next Tuesday, which by then would be four days too late.

"I told them you didn't need it. Listen, we're playing all the same instrumental stuff you've been listening to all your life. And besides, I can accompany you on the guitar or piano for at least three songs alone like we do here. Easy peasey! That will give the guys a chance to take a break, they'd be cool with that," he explained.

Shit, he had it all figured out, didn't he? She really needed one more week, at least to be able to explain to Brad why she couldn't make their date on Saturday. She'd have to think on it. She knew if she hesitated much longer, he'd wonder what was up, so she decided, at least for now, she'd appease her dad and agree to the club for Saturday. After that, she'd have to find a way to reach Brad.

Saturday afternoon came without any chance of contacting him. Celia had spoken to Tess and asked her if she could think of anything. Tess figured calling the main house was crazy since it could raise all sorts of questions for Brad, especially since he had people who answered the phone for them. Besides, he hadn't offered her *his* number, he had taken hers, a fact that wasn't lost on Tess.

"If he doesn't want you calling him, that says something, don'tcha think?"

"He never said he didn't want me calling him," Celia countered.

"Then *why not* call him?" Tess asked.

Celia would much rather have the chance to explain to him in person anyway rather than leave a message with a house staff saying, "Celia can't make it on Saturday" and leave it at that. And how did she explain the phone charge on the bill next month?

It would be more for her to place the call to him than if she were to receive it. After giving it some thought, she realized a pay phone would solve everything. She decided to walk down to the soda shop near to the school and place the call from the phone booth outside. That way it wouldn't give anything away. As she walked, she hoped she wasn't making a mistake. What if his mother asked him all sorts of questions about who she was? Would Brad tell his mother that she was his girlfriend? She wondered that as she reached the phone booth.

Seeing it empty, she walked into the booth and lifted the receiver. She asked the operator for the number and then placed her dime in the slot when the call was put through. It was answered almost immediately giving Celia little time to think of what she would say.

"Dumont residence," a male voiced answered. It wasn't Brad.

"Uh… hello… uh… is Mr. Bradley Dumont at home?"

"I'm sorry Mr. Dumont is not in at the moment. May I take a message for him?"

"Uh… yes… uh… would you mind telling him that… " she hesitated wondering whether she should use her name at all, " …uh, Mr. Dumont had hoped to have reservations on Saturday night and I am afraid they have been canceled. Would you mind letting him know? Thank you so much!" And with that, Celia hung up the phone, her heart pounding in her chest. Best if no names were mentioned. Hopefully, whoever just took that call will let Brad know that some girl phoned saying *his reservations for Saturday night were canceled.* He should be able to piece it together from that and then hopefully, by Tuesday, she can explain herself. This way, she didn't feel like she would be standing him up.

It was hard to have to decide which she'd rather do, sing at the club or spend time alone with Brad. Both held a high level of importance to her. Her dad had always insisted that she stay focused on her school work and her involvement with the choirs at school and church, so there was no time for boys or singing outside of that. Now that the chance had come, God was getting her to make a choice! But, she was satisfied with her decision. Hopefully, she could have her cake and eat it too. She smiled as she made her way home, thinking that this was turning out to be quite the summer! She was less than two hours from her singing debut and she was sleeping with (okay, so far only *slept* with) the most eligible bachelor in Peoria. Quite the summer indeed!

. . .

Celia didn't have anything fancy to wear to a club and she didn't want her father being cross with her for not being dressed appropriately. She did want to look every second of her 18 years, if not closer to 19. She chose a simple summer dress and pulled her hair back off of her with two hair clips at the sides of her head. It managed to keep her face in full view and yet allowed her hair to be loose. The dress was ivory and made her skin seem like it shone. She added a touch of mascara, some soft lip gloss and a touch of pink to her cheeks. In her mirror, she could see her mother's face staring back at her. She wondered what she'd be thinking of her daughter right about now. Set to sing on stage in a club for the first time. She remembered her vaguely, mostly her voice and her loving protective embrace. Celia nodded to herself in the mirror as if in homage to Meg her mother and left the room.

Her dad was waiting in the living room holding his guitar case and smiling broadly. Tonight was the night! He was ready to bust buttons he was so excited. Wait till they heard her sing! Not a church hymn but a Koko Taylor number or some old "Memphis Minnie" like "I'd Rather See Him Dead." George could hardly wait.

The nightclub was dimly lit, smoky, crowded and loud, and the night was still young. Celia had expected a little fancier décor and a larger room but was happy to see the stage was a decent size and the crowd lively and enthusiastic. She walked in behind her dad and stayed near him, feeling eyes on her. George led her to the stage, put his guitar case on a chair and opened it up, taking it out of the case and placing the strap over his shoulder. He then introduced her around to the other four musicians in the group, some she already knew. They spoke with her briefly about what songs she knew when George interrupted, impatiently removing her from their conversation and pushing her towards the microphone.

"Just sing something, honey. Sing "Mona Lisa" by Nat King Cole. Start with that and then we'll ease them into the older stuff," he said excitedly. She nervously stepped to the microphone, peered out into the noisy smoke filled room and tapped the mike to ensure it was on. The feedback screeched and the crowd burst into whistles and boos. Celia stepped back and stopped. George saw her freeze for a moment, removed his guitar and jumped onto the piano. He started playing the intro to the song and Celia looked his way, grateful for the support. And then she closed her eyes and started singing. The crowd went quiet almost immediately as she sang Mr. Cole's hit:

Mona Lisa, Mona Lisa, men have named you,

You're so like the lady with the mystic smile.

Is it only 'cause you're lonely, they have blamed you,

For that Mona Lisa strangeness in your style?

The audience sat spellbound as she sang. George played a brief interlude and she began the frame again. When George hit the last key on the piano, the crowd put their hands together in mad applause and stood up. She had done it beautifully. Perfection. George smiled and began a Billie Holiday number. You could hear a pin drop as Celia began the song, feeling the crowd with her as she belted it out. After that it was Etta James, and then another. She sang for a full 40 minutes before the rest of the band joined George and Celia on stage. Celia had held the audience captive for the entire time and with only the accompaniment of her father's piano. Before the rest of the band could get set up the audience started yelling out names of songs they wanted to hear. The musician's were able to play the requests and Celia would sing as if they had done so every night for years. With each song, the energy in the room was growing. By the time 11:00 pm had come, Celia had sung for nearly two and half hours without a break. Even her dad knew she needed a rest.

He held his hand out to the crowd and stepped to the mike and said, "We're gonna take a minute here to catch our breath and wet our whistle. She could probably keep going…" he motioned to Celia, and laughed, "but us old guys need a break. We'll be back in a bit."

The audience applauded and George took Celia's arm and led her off the stage. He had her sit near the end of the bar and he took the stool next to her. He ordered a soda and a coffee. She was energised and on a high. He could see it in her. This was her calling, George knew it! Her eyes were darting around the room and she kept shifting on the stool until finally she stood up and moved the stool away choosing to lean against the bar facing the crowd.

"That was amazing!" she gushed. "I loved it!" Her eyes were wide.

George looked at her, beaming. "I knew they'd love you. You really are excellent Celia. I am so proud of you. You did beautifully!"

The crowd jostled around them, carrying on conversations, ordering drinks and enjoying their Saturday night out. Celia looked over the room. What an intoxicating feeling they gave her. *Who needed to drink when you could do this?* she thought. Her eye happened to catch sight of a heavyset older man with a cigar butt stuck in the corner of his mouth wearing a shiny grey suit walking towards her. He smiled as he approached her, shifting the butt from one side of his mouth to the other with just his tongue. He turned to George while keeping his eye on her and held out his hand. George took his hand and they shook vigorously.

"George, nice to see you tonight," the man said, smiling, and managing to look George's way for a moment. "Will you introduce me?"

"Of course." Letting go of the man's hand, he gestured towards Celia and brought her towards him. "Celia this is Mr. Samuels. He owns this fine establishment. Mr. Samuels, this is my daughter, Celia." Celia firmly shook his hand, hoping to convey her appreciation.

"Oh, thank you, Mr. Samuels. It's so nice to meet you and I really appreciate you letting me be in here." He smiled even wider and she saw his full set of teeth. Many were yellowed, especially near the corners where the cigar sat wedged between his teeth and lips.

"I should be thanking you, young lady. What a night we've had here. No offense George," he turned to George and patted his back "but you, little lady, have given us a night like I can't remember in a long time. *You* my dear, are going to be a star! That is quite the voice you have." Celia smiled and dipped her head, a little embarrassed. She was used to praise from people in the church community but this was different. She was an *entertainer* tonight!

"You come here whenever you want my dear," Mr. Samuels said, nodding his head. "You are *alllllways* welcome here," he added, emphasizing the word. "George you bring this young lady by whenever you wish. She's certainly got a talent and this crowd loves her."

He slapped George again on the back and laughed aloud, enjoying a profitable and extremely entertaining night. Off he went, giddy in the moment, saying hello to patrons and shaking hands. Mr. Samuels was a very happy man.

Smiling, George turned to Celia, and rubbed her arm. "That was exactly what I hoped would happen," he said excitedly. "You can sing here every weekend now! This is your start, honey! Sing here, polish your style and get some real crowd experience and then we can take it..." he hesitated, "well... who knows where?" She nodded her head. It was all so overwhelming. She wanted back up there, back on the stage. George could see her energy building.

"When can we go on again?" she asked. "Will it be much longer?"

George downed the rest of his coffee having taken only 15 minutes of what should have been a half hour break. He motioned with his head towards the stage and she raced off ahead of him. As she took to the microphone, the crowd erupted before a single note was sung. They were buzzing and energized and waiting for her to begin. A number of "shh's" were heard as they quieted, awaiting her first note. Instead of waiting for George, Celia first hummed in key and then began to sing:

Don't know why, there's no sun up in the sky,

Stormy weather...

As she sang, most of the audience remained standing as if in a trance. Her father had made his way to the stage but, not wanting to take away from the moment; he stood to one side and watched as Celia worked her magic. When she finished, the crowd gave her such applause, it allowed the group a chance to get back on stage and set up. It didn't matter that she was an 18 year old girl – her voice was rich and deep and perfect. She could mimic many of the older blues singers but also had a vast knowledge of contemporary artists. For the remainder of the night, Celia kept them under her spell.

. . .

Brad was starting to worry. He had called Celia's home twice and had received no answer. He looked at his watch. It was now 9:10 pm and there was still no answer! Wasn't the plan for him to call just after 8:00 pm and they would agree to meet up in their usual spot? He didn't know what had happened but for some reason, Celia was not answering her phone. Part of him wanted to drive over to her house and see where she was, but he talked himself out of that at least five times. He decided to drive down to the street that bordered her neighborhood. If she'd gone out for a soda he may be able to spot her and they'd get a chance to talk.

He walked up to the main house to ask for the car keys. On a rare occasion, his parents were home on this particular Saturday night having no social event that required their attendance. Both were lounging outside on the patio enjoying a long summer evening when Brad strolled through the garden. His father looked up from his book and smiled at his look-a-like son.

"Didn't you have plans tonight, Bradley?" his father asked, surprised to see his son home on a Saturday night, especially during the summer.

"I thought I did, but they seem to have fallen through," he said, shrugging his shoulders. "I thought I'd go down to the shops and see what everyone else is up to. Can I borrow the car for a bit?" he asked casually. He had no intention of going around to the shops to see anyone else. He was on the lookout for Celia. His mother looked up from her magazine, smiling at her beautiful boy.

"Do you have money on you, dear?" she asked.

"Yes, I just need the keys," he answered.

She nodded and closed her magazine. She motioned her head towards the house and said, "Come and I'll get them for you." She rose from her lounger and made her way into the house with Brad following her.

Beverly Dumont was a very elegant woman. She practically floated through her home, in her kitten heels, long caftan, head scarf and sunglasses that she had propped on her head more for effect than for function.

As she walked she continued speaking. "You know you haven't really specified any plans for September, Bradley." She always used his full name. "I have something I want to discuss with you," she said secretively. She led him into the office off the main entrance way and closed the door behind them.

"Your Uncle Frank is in London for the summer with a group of his friends. They plan to move to the North Country in a bit and tour up there more and be on the move come the fall. Probably go to Greece and Italy, you know, through Europe. I want you to join him," she said matter-of-factly. She had seated herself down at the giant desk his father had brought home from India during a visit a few years ago. As she spoke, she leaned back into the executive leather chair, staring hard at him. It made him feel uncomfortable. He didn't understand it.

"What? You mean, go to England for the summer?" he asked incredulously.

"And through Europe in the Fall," she added nodding her head.

He hesitated for a moment and then took the seat in front of her. Running his hand through his soft, blonde hair, he looked at her questioningly, "Why do this now?" He wanted to know. Normally, he wouldn't question his mother. Normally, if she said "attend" he showed up. But now, he couldn't help but feel there was something else behind it.

Well... I just think it would be a terrific experience for you in your "in-between" year. I mean, you haven't made any solid decisions for what you're going to do, have you? What would be wrong with a trip abroad for a few weeks?" she said gesturing with her hands as if to make the whole thing very off-the-cuff and casual. But inside, she was seething. She had to get him on that plane to London leaving Monday evening no if and or buts about it. "It's such a wonderful time of year to see Europe and you and Frank get along so well – almost like brothers. He wants you to go and so do I," she said. "So, what do you think, shall I make all the arrangements?"

"I just got settled into the summer cottage, Mother," Brad complained. "I was hoping to have some personal space this summer."

"Then what better way to have space than 5,000 miles of ocean between us?" she countered. Space! Ha! She couldn't agree more. "Besides, it's not like the cottage is going anywhere. It will all still be here when you get back," she said soothingly.

Brad thought for a moment, looking off over her shoulder. It could take her weeks to line this up. That could give him just enough time to spend a few more days with Celia and perhaps explain it to her. He would be gone for a while but back before Christmas and then they could be together. He'd find a small simple ring to give to her in a way to show her he would make a promise to come back. *Good idea*, he thought.

"Bradley, dear, are you going to take all night? I'd like to get back to your father. If I stay away too long he'll nod off on his lounger," she said, irritated.

Brad hesitated for moment and then said, "Yes, Mother" with a sigh. There was no good fighting with her and if he had a bit of time beforehand he could make everything work, he was sure. Even still, he hated how he always gave into her. Sometimes it really did interfere with his plans and she didn't ever seem to take that into consideration.

"Yes? You'll go?" she asked, sitting up in the chair.

"Yes, I'll go. But I'm not spending Christmas there. I want to be home for Christmas," he insisted.

"Alright, home for Christmas! It's a deal. Oh really, darling, you will thank me when you get back. London and Europe are fantastic and Frank will make sure you see every part of it!" she gushed.

Her brother Frank Spencer was only 12 years older than Brad and Brad very much looked up to Frank. Beverley had called upon Frank once or twice in the past to help navigate him through the teen years, especially when it came to women. Frank Spencer was a 30 year old rich bachelor from a wealthy family who had made his own fortune as a shrewd businessman. He liked to parry and jet set around the world, impressing one woman after another but never committing to any of them. He had helped Beverly with a delicate situation that happened a few years back and had never let on to anyone that he had. She knew he'd be the perfect person to take Brad away this summer and guide him through London and Europe.

80

Beverly motioned to her son to come and give her a hug. He made his way around the large desk as she rose to hug him. They embraced for a moment and she kissed his cheek.

"Now there's a good boy," she gushed at him. "Leave all the arrangements to me," she assured him.

As he stepped away to leave he realized he'd forgotten his purpose for coming in. "Uh, the keys, Mom. Remember? I came in for the keys… for the car?" he looked at her with his hand outstretched.

"Oh, quite right!" She glanced half-heartedly around on the desk a moment and then said, "Oh, of course, silly me! The car isn't here, I had Duncan take it in for a cleaning. We should get it back sometime on Monday. If you want, I can call for a driver for you?" she asked him, lifting the receiver off of its cradle.

He sighed. "No, never mind." He dropped his head and turned to leave. He figured he wouldn't be able to find Celia tonight now anyway. He'd have to call her on Tuesday once her dad left for the club. He walked out of the office leaving his mother sitting at the desk.

Beverly sat for a moment and then rang for her house butler, Duncan. He was an elderly black man that had served their family for years. He was Beverly's eyes and ears for the staff as well as her children and Beverly paid him handsomely for it.

"Operator, can you please connect me to London, England at 44 77 657 8819. Yes, I'll hold," she spoke into the receiver. Duncan came into the office as she was waiting.

"Yes ma'am?" he asked her.

"Duncan, I need you to go up into the attic and pull down the largest travel case we have," she said, as she covered the receiver end of the phone with her hand. "As soon as Bradley has sat down to breakfast on Monday morning I want you to go into the cottage and pack all of his clothing, shoes and coats. Whatever he doesn't have, I'm sure Frank can figure out for him," she said, thinking out loud. "You and he are going by train to O'Hare Monday morning and see that he gets on *this* flight." As she held on the phone, she cradled the receiver between her neck and shoulder, and grabbed a pen from its holder on the desk, jotting down a number and words on a piece of paper. Before she had finished writing, she began talking into the receiver again, "Hello? Hello Frank?" She tore the paper from the pad and thrust it towards Duncan waving it impatiently. He stepped forward taking the paper and left the room.

"Frank is that you? Yes, I know honey, I know it's late where you are but I had to call. He's agreed to come. I have everything already arranged. He's on the flight leaving Monday mid-afternoon and will arrive Tuesday early morning your time". She paused listening to him grumble. "Yes, I'm sorry about that dear but it couldn't be helped. It's the first flight I could get him on. I have his flight number so you'll have to check on it from your end." She listened to Frank speak for a moment and then said, "No, he has no idea. I'd like it to stay that way too, Frank. Oh, and for God's sake keep him away from dark-skinned foreigners! He seems to have a thing for them." With that she hung up the phone, then raised it back up to place one more call.

"Hannah? Hannah, its Beverly. Are you sure all bookings are confirmed?" she asked. "Excellent. I owe you one honey! Thanks so much!" And again, without a goodbye, Beverly hung up the phone.

Quite satisfied with her maneuvering, she left the office area and went back outside to sit with her husband. By now the sun had gone down completely and they were washed in the soft garden lights that were strung about the pergola. She found her husband, Geoffrey, snoring softly with his book in his lap and glasses on his head.

Geoffrey was a business mogul from another wealthy background. He left the running of the household to his wife and did his best to stay out of her way when she was on a mission. She had been on a mission all week from the sounds of it and he was trying to keep a low profile. She kissed his head and removed his glasses and put them in his lap.

"Saving the world again, dear," he asked her as he yawned and rubbed his face.

"One situation at a time my love," she smiled back at him. The less he knew the better.

. . .

On Monday morning, Brad walked into the breakfast room to find his parents at the table. He was surprised to find them both there – usually his mother was in the office organizing some fund raiser or event and his father would be on his way to his city office to wheel and deal his millions. Today, rather, they were both present and welcomed him into the room as he entered.

"Good morning, Son," Geoffrey Dumont said to his boy.

"Good morning, darling," said Beverly, with a smile.

He walked over to the table and kissed them both. "This is a surprise. You're both sitting down to breakfast on a Monday morning."

"Well, it's a special occasion," his father said. Without filling him in too much, Beverly had explained that Bradley was leaving first thing in the morning to spend the summer in London with Frank. Geoffrey knew not to ask. The less he knew the better.

"Yes, my dear. We wanted to be certain to be here before you left," his mother said.

"Left? Well, I can't go anywhere until the car is back. Is it back?" he asked her.

Geoffrey gave his wife a confused look but she just shook her head and focused her attention back on Brad. "My dear, we aren't going to see you for at least 5 months after today. We'd like to spend some time with you before you're off," she said rather casually.

"Today?" Brad nearly yelled. His raised his voice this time, "You made arrangements for me to leave TODAY?"

"Bradley, lower your voice when you're speaking to your mother," his father admonished. He bit his tongue and clenched his fists. Damn! Why had she done this?

"Bradley, darling," she said as she rose. She held both his arms with her hands as she looked at him pleadingly. "Now please don't be upset with me, I told you, darling, that your Uncle Frank was leaving for the North Country soon and it would have been too difficult to line you two up after that. Besides, he's only in London for a few days more and I want you to experience it too." She ended with a puppy-dog look on her face almost begging his forgiveness.

Damn! Now how was he supposed to get in touch with Celia? It wouldn't be safe for him to call the house until tomorrow night. He sat through the rest of breakfast listening to his mother and father reminisce about their time in London and throughout Europe. He didn't really pay much attention and just made the appropriate noises when asked. When he'd finished his meal he excused himself.

"I suppose I'd better get packing," he said, anxious to get away from them and think of something he could do to contact Celia.

"Oh, I've already had Duncan pack your things. If you need anything else, I'm sure your Uncle Frank will get it for you," she said quite satisfied. She had planned it down to the last moment.

"You and Duncan are leaving for the train station right away," she told him. "I've asked Duncan to travel with you and see to it you are safely aboard the plane. It leaves at 4:00 this afternoon."

Brad stared at his mother for a moment. If he didn't know better, he'd think she had had this in the works for some time. She didn't seem the least bit upset or concerned that he was leaving for months on end, which was in complete contrast to his mother's personality. Her kids never went to boarding school; she would have missed them far too much. And yet, here she was practically pushing Brad out the door without so much as a tear shed. He felt slightly manipulated but wasn't sure what was going on. Besides, he had greater concerns to think about. He had no choice now but to try and call Celia's house in hopes she would pick up the phone. He had to try to let her know what was happening so she didn't think that everything they had shared had meant nothing to him. He had to tell her... he loved her.

"Excuse me won't you? I... uh... this is all so overwhelming. I... uh... just need a few moments," and he quickly left the room exiting towards the bathroom. He didn't go to the bathroom however, he went left down the hallway and entered his parent's office and quietly shut the door. Making his way over to the phone he lifted the receiver and dialed Celia's number. He knew it was a rash decision but he didn't know what else to do. It took a moment for the line to connect, but it felt like an hour. His heart was pounding so hard. If her dad answered, what would he say? If his mom walked in, what would he say? Trying to think of something, he listened to the phone ringing in his ear... third ring... fourth ring... hmmmm, maybe no one is...

"Hello?" the man asked.

Pause, he held his breath trying to think of what to say.

"Hello?" the man asked again, a little louder this time.

Again Brad held his tongue, and tried to think of what to say. Suddenly the line went dead as George Morningstar hung the phone up in disgust.

Celia hadn't heard from Brad for weeks. He hadn't called her on the first Tuesday after she missed their Saturday date. He hadn't called at all during the following Saturday and she spent the night singing at the club again. He still hadn't called after the next three Tuesday nights. She had started to feel foolish. She had believed him and she had given him the most precious thing she had to offer a boy and he didn't care. He was off to find another conquest. Oh, he hadn't said that, but his actions spoke loud and clear. She'd been a fool. In an ironic twist, it only made her performances at the club that much better. Her soulful songs of love and loss were belted out like someone who knew what she was singing about.

George had noticed a difference in her singing mood over the last few weeks, choosing a sad love song over a rousing rendition of Lizzie Miles' "Salty Dog". When he asked her if everything was alright, she would only shrug her shoulders and walk away.

There had not been any more events at the Dumont house for her church group to serve at. Actually, for the summertime, the serving jobs had been quite scarce. She had counted on it for a few dollars here and there, although she was making some pretty good tips at the club. So when Tess called her to tell her they had a function to serve at, she was in. The Ladies of Peoria Auxiliary were holding their end of the summer luncheon at the Grand Gazebo in Peoria's Victoria Park. The group would have to set up for 80 women, serve them and clean up within an afternoon. This was a tremendous amount of work but her church ladies were up to the task.

The afternoon of the luncheon, Tess and Celia were given tasks of setting tables, wiping stemware and cutlery down with clean cloths and folding napkins. Once the Ladies of Peoria had all arrived, the hustling and bustling behind the scene quieted so as not to disturb or intrude on the ladies celebration. Celia was set up behind a large banquet table and a narrow wall polishing cutlery and folding napkins. She was within earshot of one table of ladies in particular and she could hear their conversation quite well. She became increasingly interested when she recognized the voice of Brad's mother, Beverly Dumont. Just to be sure she was right, she poked her head out from behind the wall to see firsthand. Sure enough, Brad's mother was sitting directly on the other side of the wall from her! Celia stopped her activity to be sure she could hear every word that was said.

"Beverly, I am surprised you haven't been able to Chair this committee this time. I would have thought you would have jumped at the chance," said a woman with a nasally voice.

"Oh, I would have, Sue-Ann, but I had my hands full with a bit of a situation at home, dear," Beverly said smiling. She loved being dramatic.

"Oh, I do hope it wasn't anything too horrible," one lady said.

"No," said Beverly, "I managed to get it taken care of pretty quickly but I'm still monitoring the situation," she whispered, as if in code.

"Oh for goodness sakes, quit talking around it and tell us what's happened," remarked Sue-Ann. Celia heard the other ladies cajole her on until, finally, Beverly relented.

"Well," she sighed. "I'll only tell you this as a cautionary tale. But, you mustn't breathe a word of it past this table. I know some of you have sons and it's important you learn from my mistakes and my conquests," she added proudly. She took in a deep breath and let it out as she began her story.

"A few weeks ago my darling Bradley asked if he could clean up the old gardener's shed at the back of our yard. You've seen it, right? Juan-Carlos lived in it for a few years until he married. Anyway, Bradley had said he wanted to spend the summer in the cottage and I didn't think anything of it. I actually thought it would be a nice place for him to spread his wings, have his friends over and socialize with them. I got the house staff to go in and clean it all up and we made it quite cozy." She paused a moment then continued.

"Well, he hadn't been in there two weeks when Duncan came to me. He said that one of the house girls had told him that she thought Bradley had hurt himself because she found blood all over his bed sheets. She was concerned and thought Duncan should know. He went into the shed and found the bed sheets and then brought them to me."

"Was he hurt?" one lady asked, worry on her face.

"No!" she said sternly, *"Far from it!"* She leaned into the table and whispered to the other three women, "He'd taken a virgin to his bed." She then leaned back and gave them all a knowing look, nodding her head. Celia heard gasps as she herself covered her hand over her own mouth. Oh my God! His mother knew!

"Oh, boys will be boys!" Sue-Ann's nasal voice piped as she laughed.

There was silence for a moment. Celia imagined that the last statement wasn't appreciated by the other ladies.

"What on earth did you do?" asked another ladies' voice.

"First thing I did was ask Duncan to grill the staff so see if he could find out who she was," Beverly explained.

Celia's heart went into her throat. Her stomach started rolling slightly and she felt weak but she refused to go anywhere until she heard the rest of Beverly Dumont's story.

"Duncan said that Bradley had asked the cook about the servers we used for a few recent events I had hosted at the estate," she said in a lowered voice.

"You think it was a server?" one lady spat out.

"A darkie?" another asked with disgust.

"Well, I haven't had it confirmed yet but just to be safe I have canceled the group I was using and will be looking for another group for my next event. I don't mind them serving me but I won't have them mixing with my Spencer bloodline or the Dumont's for that matter!" she said haughtily.

The ladies all made agreeable noises as Celia's eyes widened and she gasped into her hand. So there it was! For all her refinement and charity work, she was an intolerant, two-faced bitch! Celia shook her head in disbelief. But then, Beverly continued.

"The best however, my dear ladies, is that I managed to have my son on a plane flying to London, England within four days of finding out!"

she said proudly. All the ladies laughed out loud understanding the mother's conquest.

"And how did you manage that, darling?" asked nasal-voiced Sue-Ann.

"I simply called my brother, Frank, who was right then touring London with friends. I explained the situation and asked for Bradley to join them. Frank agreed wholeheartedly. After all, he too has a vested interest. My family name is as well known as the Dumont name. We can't have either sullied by a cry of rape from a black serving girl or worse, an illegitimate child. My Bradley was packed up and flying to London before he even realized what had hit him. He'll spend the next few months under Frank's tutelage on the finer art of romancing women and not paying a heavy price for it," she emphasized.

"And if that should happen?" asked a shrill voiced lady.

"Well, I doubt any black girl in that situation would have the gall to come to the door holding a baby. We'd deny it was our son's and send her on her way. She's probably slept with dozens of the town boys," she paused, looking questioningly at the group of women. "And I will not have Bradley Spencer Dumont become a father to some baby who is not even his! Who is going to believe her story over ours?" she asked the ladies. "Besides," she continued, "we have the best lawyers in town. She'd be foolish to try and force us into anything."

"Which firm do you use, Beverly?" she was asked.

"Oh, Morningstar's, of course!" she answered, head held high. "They're the best and were a very reputable family."

Celia was nearly faint. She was trying hard to take in all that she had heard. Mrs. Dumont knew that her son had slept with *someone* in his bed. She had tried to find out who it was and found out enough to know it was her church group. That explains the lack of work over the last few weeks. And then, she had Brad shipped off to London for the next six months! No wonder she hadn't heard from him. Celia wondered if he ever got the message she had left for him that first missed Saturday. It was all starting to make sense now. His mother had manipulated him into going away to keep him from Celia, although his mother didn't know who she was. But, could she find out?

Celia's stomach was churning at this point and she started feeling sweaty and cold. She kept her back to the wall so the ladies on the other side would remain unaware of her presence and then rested her head on the table for a bit. She couldn't be seen by anyone where she was and it gave her chance to gather her thoughts and settle her stomach. She started the breathing technique her dad had taught her, the four paced beat, in through the nose, out through the mouth. It helped get her stomach to feel a bit better but she was still quite shaken.

The luncheon ended just a little while later and once the ladies had left, Celia came out from behind her walled spot. She looked around for Tess and found her in the make-shift kitchens drying up the larger pots that had been used.

"I need to leave," she said shakily.

"Oh my God, are you alright? You look terrible!" Tess asked.

Celia was pale and shaking and her eyes were as wide as can be. She looked like she'd just seen a ghost. Celia grabbed the pot Tess was in the middle of drying and heaved her stomach contents into it. At first, Tess was revolted but quickly her mood changed to sympathy for her friend.

"Oh, girl, you eat somethin' bad or are you worryin' something bad?" she asked Celia, who continued to retch and heave.

Tess found her a chair to sit in. She waited until Celia's stomach had settled a little, took the pot from her and rinsed it out as best she could. She then returned the pot to the kitchen area and said to no one in particular, "This one ain't been cleaned, only rinsed." She said pointing to the pot she had just placed amongst the bunch. "It needs a good cleaning, okay?" She caught the eye of one of the workers who nodded his acknowledgement, happy with that, she made her way back to Celia sitting in the chair. When she got there, Celia was pale and breathing funny.

"C'mon, Celia girl," Tess said as she hoisted Celia from the chair. "I'm gonna take you home to your bed." Celia leaned on her friend as they walked to the bus stop.

Celia spent the next three days in her bed. She managed to make her way out of bed on the fourth day and went about with little change to how she felt. When she was still queasy by the third week, George was extremely worried and insisted that Celia go to see the doctor. Celia knew it was a waste of time – all her vomiting, all her weakness and her fatigue could be summed up in two words: heart break. Her performances of soulful, sorry, blues songs were knock outs. She had a bit more insight into loss and was able to convey that even more in her performances. The sadder she was, the better she performed.

George had made an appointment for Celia to visit the doctor and had wanted to drive her to the appointment but Celia insisted she go on her own. It wouldn't take her very long and she would have time to think about Brad and what had happened.

. . .

As Celia was making her way to the doctor's office, Beverly Dumont was sitting at her large East Indian desk reading documents and enjoying her morning cup of tea. Within a few minutes, Duncan entered the room carrying a silver tray containing the Dumont's daily mail delivery.

A longstanding routine then played out, with Duncan bringing Mrs. Dumont the mail on a silver tray and Beverly going through it to sort its importance. Today's delivery had just a few invitations to evening soirees, a letter from family overseas and a few household bills. Beverly opened each one and scrutinized it before going onto the next. She gave each one her full attention. The phone bill was her last bill to open. She cut through the envelope's paper lid with the silver letter opener from the silver desk set that Geoffrey had given her along with the desk. Before she had completely unfolded the paper something tweaked her curiosity. She snapped the invoice to have it in full view and spied it with an eagle's eye.

The bill covered the last 90 days. A few of the outgoing calls she herself had made to acquire the black church group as servers at the events she had organized and she could see the dates and numbers corresponded. But then, there was a different phone number that she didn't recognize from the same area that was called four times. She stared at it for a moment wondering if Bradley could have been so careless as to use their household phone to call the girl! She contemplated calling for about five minutes and then impulsively picked up the receiver and dialed the number. She put on her "work demeanor" and set her back straight. She would think of something to say – this was her forte. She was excellent at fundraising because she could talk an Eskimo into ice cubes! She'd work her liquid smooth approach and maybe get some information. She listened intently as the phone rang.

"Hello?" a man's voice answered.

"This is George Morningstar. May I ask to whom I am speaking?" he asked right back.

"Uh, hello," she said, already dripping with charm. "I think I may have called the wrong number..." she lied hesitantly. "Could you please tell me to whom I am speaking?" she asked.

Morningstar? Hmmm. That was interesting. She couldn't remember hearing of a lesser relation to the Morningstar's of Peoria! William Morningstar and his wife had died in the accident many years ago, as the story goes. She didn't recall there being children or siblings that might have carried on the name. Beverly wondered about going through with her mission. It may be a mistake. It may not lead to anything.

She hesitated for a moment and then asked quickly, "Sir, do you have a daughter? About 18 years of age or so?" George immediately became excited. This woman was calling about Celia. More than likely about her singing! This was the phone call he had hoped for. This woman had probably seen Celia at the club at some point in the past few weeks and now wanted to talk about her talent and how to market it. Get her out there and get her some more exposure! He listened intently as she began speaking.

"Sir, my name is Beverly Dumont. I believe your daughter has worked in my home as a server for a number of events I have hosted." She let that sink in for a moment and then continued. "Sir, I believe your daughter has had intimate relations with my son, within the past six to eight weeks," she stated bluntly.

. . .

Celia was in the doctor's exam room awaiting the doctor's arrival. Around her were paper posters or advertisements of various creams, medications or procedures that heralded a new life for those suffering from various afflictions. Celia read each poster three times, counted the ceiling tiles, (67 if you included the edges) and stared at her shoes for a good 10 minutes. Finally the kindly old doctor walked into her room carrying a paper folder.

"Hello Celia. What brings you in to see me today?" he asked with his kindly eyes. Boy, she reminded him of her mother!

Celia smiled at him. "I've been sickly, Dr. Swanson," she sighed. She thought a moment and then said, "My stomach hasn't been good for weeks, I am constantly feeling tired, I cry at every little thing and I don't want to eat," she confessed.

Dr. Swanson looked at her for a moment and lifted her chin up with his index finger. He looked into her eyes with a light he grabbed from his lab coat pocket. After flashing it into her eyes and moving it from side to side, he checked the glands along her throat to see if they were inflamed. No inflammation whatsoever. She did look pale and her eyes were slightly darkened underneath, but not alarmingly so.

"Have you been vomiting at all, Celia?" he asked as he sat and started writing in the chart.

"Yes, actually, I've been sick to my stomach on and off for the last few weeks," she answered him.

He stopped writing and looked at her for a moment. Then he looked back down at the chart as he asked, "Normal periods?" He stopped writing as he waited her response.

"Uh, well... I... uh..." she hesitated a moment, "I am not sure that I've had normal periods. My last one was about 6 weeks ago and it was spotty. Then about a month before that... it was probably okay. I haven't had my period yet this month but I'm expecting it at any time."

"And prior to this your cycle was fairly regular, is that correct?" Dr. Swanson asked her, nodding his head.

"Yes," she agreed. "...fairly normal." He lifted her chin up, looked up her nostrils with his light then had her open her mouth as he told her to say "Ahhhh" and looked down her throat.

"Well, we'll take some blood and urine and see what we get back. I can't see anything obvious but we'll see what these tests say," he said, assuring her of his decision. He continued to write on the chart for a moment and then looked up at her with questioning eyes and asked, "You haven't, by chance, been having sexual relations, have you?"

He knew by her reaction alone that she had. *This girl should never play cards for money*, he thought, as he looked at her face. It was written all over her expression. She had colored a deep rose color, easily seen even with her skin tone.

"Do you want to tell me what's been going on, Celia? You know, I can't repeat any of it to your father under the law," he assured her.

She hesitated for a moment and then confessed, "I did have sexual relations about seven weeks ago, Doctor." She couldn't look at him at that point. She only stared down.

"I see," he said knowingly.

He turned his attention to the needle to draw the blood. He wrote out her name and what tests he'd like to have administered on the few vials he was collecting. The silence in the room hung heavily. The good doctor was trying his best to be optimistic and non-judgmental.

"Well," he rubbed her arm, "let's take some blood and run some tests and see what we're dealing with after that, shall we? I'll get you to leave a urine sample with the nurse on your way out. I'll call you with any news," he said.

He nodded to her, and tied off her upper arm in order to draw some blood as she closed her eyes and sat back in the chair. Dr. Swanson couldn't shake the déjà vu feeling he was experiencing.

. . .

"Did you hear me, Mr. Morningstar?" Beverley questioned.

"Is this a joke?" George asked into the phone, disgusted.

"No, sir, I assure you that this is no joke!" Beverly emphasized. She continued on, hoping she wasn't moving too fast for him. "My son and your daughter had been secretly seeing one another for a little while about six weeks ago." She paused a moment then she said, "I'm concerned that your daughter will want to spread hurtful gossip should anything come from their... relations..." she paused again.

She didn't want to come right out and say the word "baby" or "pregnancy" because she felt it would give power to the suggestion. As if by saying it, could make it happen. Rather she skirted the issue with double entendres and suggestive words. It was annoying George. He knew exactly what she was saying and he wanted to tell this snobby bitch to go to hell and leave him alone.

"Mrs. Dumont, I can assure you my daughter has not been seeing, let alone sleeping with, your son. She has only just graduated high school and has spent the summer serving at various functions with her church group. I doubt she's had time to herself or time to spend alone with someone else. I don't know where you get your information from my dear, but you're wrong."

Beverly's lips drew into a thin line. Who was this little weasel to tell her she was wrong! She was the one with the facts. He obviously had no idea what his daughter had been up to. She tried to control the anger in her voice so as not to ruin any chances of obtaining information that may be useful to her later.

"Mr. Morningstar, I know this must be an extremely difficult conversation to have. Especially if you are not aware of what... uh, I'm sorry, I don't know your daughter's name?" she asked hoping he'd give it to her.

George wasn't buying it. "Oh, you're so sure it's my daughter and you don't even know her damn name? Go to hell!" and with that, George slammed the phone down in Beverly's ear.

...

Celia took the bus home after visiting with the doctor. She had no answers as yet and still felt rotten. All she wanted to do was go back home and curl up into a ball and cry her eyes out. She had a few days before she was back on stage Saturday night and she hoped to be feeling better by then. As she came through the front door of her home, she found her father pacing in the kitchen. He was in a foul mood. This was not typical for him.

"Is everything alright, daddy?" she asked him.

He stopped pacing and looked at her. Oh, she looked so sick!

"You need to get back to bed," he grumbled to her. "Did the doctor say anything?" he added.

"No. He took some blood and stuff and will call me in a few days. S'probably just a stomach bug. I can't seem to keep anything down." Her last sentence made George stop dead in his tracks. Beverly Dumont's words came back in his mind: "...should anything come from their...

relations…" He looked at Celia hard as she slumped down in the kitchen chair and rested her head on her hand.

"I feel very tired too. All I want to do is sleep," she yawned as if on cue. He didn't believe Beverly Dumont but he couldn't help but think something was going on with Celia. She certainly hadn't been herself lately. She seemed emotionally preoccupied with something but any time George asked she just shrugged it off. Now, George was starting to want some answers.

"Celia, is there anything you want to tell me?" he asked softly. "I want you to know you can tell me anything…" he paused slightly, "anything at all. If something is troubling you, please share it with me and maybe I can help you figure it out."

Celia raised her head and looked at her father. She took a moment to imagine what it would be like for her to tell him all about Brad and what had happened. She visualized the range of emotions that her father would go through. First, surprise at her actions, then anger at her promiscuity and lastly, disappointment in her for doing all this behind his back. Nope, Celia decided, that wasn't something she wanted to endure. After all, Brad was gone now and she just had to learn to live with it. Her broken heart would slowly mend and she'd have learned a very valuable lesson. She smiled a tired smile at him. She rose up out of the chair and kissed his cheek.

"Thanks daddy. I'm fine, I'm just sick is all. I'm going to bed." And off she went to her room. He didn't feel like he'd found out the truth from her and for the first time in her life, Celia's father didn't trust his daughter's words, and he didn't like how that made him feel.

…

Dr. Swanson called the house on Friday morning. George answered but the doctor asked to speak to Celia.

"Can you come in and see me?" he asked her. "Alone," he added, pointedly.

"Sure," Celia replied. "I can get in this afternoon if you like."

"Yes, that would be fine. I'll see you then," the good doctor hung up the phone without giving Celia any kind of indication as to what was up. For a moment he drummed his fingers on his desk and thought of a day long ago when he had to tell Celia's mother some very bad news. And now, he had to do it again.

. . .

"You're pregnant," he told Celia, as she sat in the examination room.

"I'm WHAT?" she yelled out! Oh dear God. "Are you sure?" she asked him.

"Yes, I'm afraid so, 100% sure. And judging from your reaction, this was the last thing you expected, wasn't it?" Without speaking she stared at him in shock and nodded her head.

"But surely you knew what you were doing when you had sexual relations, didn't you?" he asked incredulously. She shouldn't be this surprised. She should be old enough to know how it all works.

"But, Dr. Swanson, I swear, we only did it the one time. I swear it," she insisted to him.

Dr. Swanson shook his head and said with a sigh, "That's all it takes my dear, just one time. The only way to prevent pregnancy for certain is to abstain from sexual relations all together. At least until you're ready to deal with the consequences," he lectured her. She hung her head. Now what? What was her father going to say? Never mind that she hadn't told him about seeing Brad, but now she was pregnant. She'd have to confess everything to him and he'd know that she'd being lying to him for weeks.

Dr. Swanson gave her some instructions, things to watch for, had her weighed and measured her and told her she was about six weeks along and calculated that the baby would be born in March of next year.

He had the nurse set up appointments for the next few months, gave her some reading materials and left her alone in the exam room for a moment for her to gather her thoughts. Pregnant. With Brad Dumont's baby! Holy shit! Holy shit indeed!

She cried all the way home on the bus. All the other passengers tried their best to look away and give her the privacy that she needed, although a difficult task on a public bus! Celia had chosen a seat with no one beside her but after one stop an elderly woman took the seat next to her. Celia tried to calm her crying but it wasn't working very well. Very quickly she was having a tissue offered by the kindly old woman. When she passed the tissue, the elderly woman touched her hand and looked into Celia's tearful eyes and said, "Not to worry my dear. All will work out just fine. Everything happens for a reason and this is exactly how things were meant to be."

She smiled at Celia and Celia smiled back weakly. She accepted the tissue and wiped her eyes and blew her nose. Celia sat for a moment lost in her woes, looking forlornly out of the bus window. Then she turned to the old woman to ask for another tissue but she was gone. It gave Celia pause for a moment. She shrugged and figured the kind lady had gotten off at the last stop and Celia had not been paying attention. She turned her thoughts back to the window, the baby and her life.

. . .

George Morningstar waited anxiously for his daughter's return from her appointment. Part of him was scared to death that it was a tumor much like Meg had. He couldn't deal with going through that with his daughter. It would kill him too! Another part of him hoped she'd caught a nasty cold and just needed some bed rest and fatherly love, which he'd happily dole out to her. But there was a nasty, deep-seeded, nagging thought that it was something else. Something he couldn't even think about. How could it be? He'd have known if Celia was seeing a boy – surely she would have told him that much.

As he sat there pondering the different scenarios, Celia walked through the door. Her face was still pale but now she looked as though she'd been crying. *Oh no*, George thought, *bad news!* His heart fell to his stomach with the look on her face. Obviously, Dr. Swanson's news was grim. He grabbed a chair for her to sit down on and took the bag she was carrying out of her hands and set it on the ground.

"What is it, sweetie?" he asked her gently. *Oh dear God, please, please*, he prayed secretly. "Tell me honey – what did the doctor say?"

"He said... that... I'm pregnant, daddy," she sobbed out and dropped her head onto her arms and rested there sobbing uncontrollably. She couldn't look at him to see his reaction. He'd be just floored, she was sure.

George looked in shock at his daughter's head. Pregnant? Pregnant! His worst fears confirmed. How on earth did it happen? He couldn't speak. He was slowly burning from within and the rage he felt building was about to burst.

"How in the hell did you become pregnant? Who have you been seeing?" he demanded of her, but he already knew. He knew that snobby bitch, Dumont, was right.

Celia kept her head down, tucked into her arms, not telling him anything. George was furious with her. He must look like a fool to everyone, not even knowing she was seeing a boy. He boasted about her and what a good girl she was, meanwhile, she's laughing at him behind his back and doing God only knows what! George's anger continued to rise as Celia's sobbing increased. He wanted to pick her up out of the chair and shake some sense into her – get some answers out of her. How would he ever trust her again? Pregnant! Now what? She'd be the gossip all over the city. Mr. Samuels will not want her on stage – especially pregnant! She may be able to perform for a couple more weeks but after that, she'd have to stay in the house. What will the church think? And Rev. Moore?

This ruined everything. All the time he patiently waited for Celia to get through her education so that he could get her on stage and have her performing, it was all for nothing now. She couldn't be out at night with a tiny baby, nor could they afford a babysitter, let alone a baby! Not to mention the stigma that would be attached to her for being wanton. George's anger and disappointment overtook him. He should have let her be but he lost all control.

"You stupid, stupid girl," he said viciously. "This has ruined everything. Everything we've worked towards! How are we going to make a name for ourselves now? Are we supposed to travel to other cities to perform with a baby hanging around our necks like a millstone? The thing will need to be fed and washed and it'll cry all the time," he complained, as he paced around the kitchen.

Celia continued her crying, but she sat up and was watching her father's animated lament in shock. She figured he'd be angry, but she had never seen him like this. She was scared to say anything to him and kept in her seat while he blamed and barked at her for more than an hour. Her tears had dried up but she had crying hiccups and had difficulty staying quiet. Her noises annoyed George and he finally dismissed her to her bedroom. "...so I don't have to see your face or hear you cry anymore," he said cruelly. He'd never been so angry or disappointed.

...

Beverly Dumont's phone rang just before 4:00 pm. She'd take this one last call and then go off to her hairdressers for her 4:30 pm appointment.

"Beverly Dumont speaking," she answered, full of confidence.

"Uh... Mrs. Dumont... this is George Morningstar," said the voice quietly. He sounded... wounded.

Beverly sat up and stared straight ahead at the mention of his name. "Yes, Mr. Morningstar?" a pause... silence... "Are you alright?" she asked, concerned for a moment.

"Yes... eh... no, I mean... I uh... I need to talk to you about our previous conversation," he said. "I've been given some information that would confirm what you had discussed with me. I uh... think it would be to both our advantages if we came about with a solution together. I'm not happy about this either and would like to see if the whole thing could just be, say… given away… if you get my meaning."

Beverly Dumont held her breath. It took her a moment to grasp exactly what George was saying. It seemed that he now knew for sure that their children were together and if she understood correctly, the girl was, in fact, pregnant! Shit!

"Mr. Morningstar, let me ask you straight so that I know we are speaking about the same thing. Your daughter has come home pregnant?" she first asked. She was very shrewd.

"Yes, that is correct?" George confirmed.

"And she's telling you that it's my Bradley's baby, is that correct?" she asked.

"Uh… well, no, not exactly. I, uh, haven't managed to find out who the father is," he admitted.

"Well Mr. Morningstar, I don't see why we've bothered to have this conversation then," she told him. "She hasn't stated that Bradley is the father and it could certainly be any one of the young lads that your girl fell down with," she told him smugly. She ended with, "I take it from your *meaning*," emphasizing the word "…that you would rather the baby be given up for adoption than be kept, am I correct?" she asked him. George, still seething from her last comments, managed to answer her with a curt and tight, "Yes."

"Well, then, I suggest you send the girl away to one of those medical homes in Chicago. Manning House I think it's called. They set her up for the next few months while she gets further into her pregnancy, they are there while the baby is born and then they find the baby a loving and caring home that it can go to and the girl will return to you with no one the wiser and no harm done," she told him bluntly.

She certainly has all the answers, thought George. She had it all wrapped up in a fancy little package and presented it to him with a bow on top. And that's how good she was!

At first George hated the idea, but only for about five minutes. It really would be the answer to everything! A few months setback for them, sure, but once she was home again Celia could continue back at the club and then they'd be back on track.

For Beverly it was a well laid plan. By showing him the indifference to the news, he now knew that she'd fight him for proof that her son was the father, making it hell for Celia living with the mockery and shame she was sure to suffer. So it was unlikely that George would create a fuss. If he sent her away to have the child, then the news is kept to just between them. Even Bradley doesn't have to be told! My goodness it was easy to manipulate these people! It was so damn easy she should feel badly, she admonished herself, but she didn't.

. . .

George contacted the house in Chicago that took in young pregnant girls and took away their newborn babies. "Manning House" was set on the east side of Chicago and its boarders were mostly young black girls. George had told Celia that this was going to happen and Celia conceded. She hadn't the will to fight him. He was not acting like her father anymore. He was incredibly rude to her, made her feel unwanted and she spent her days hiding in her room. She did two more shows at the club and then George would not allow her to go anymore. He had come up with a lie that she had to go and take care of a sickly aunt but would be back as soon as she could. He put her on the train to Chicago, gave her the directions to Manning House and pushed her up the train steps, not even a kiss goodbye. She stood there, with her face long and sad, looking at her utterly disappointed father.

"I'm sorry, daddy," she said quietly as the train started to pull away. For a moment, George broke from the black-cloud mood that had hung over him for the past few weeks and looked at his daughter. She looked like she was five years old and he remembered a time when she and he

103

were all they had and she was only five. A huge lump welled up in his throat as he watched her ride away on the train steps, waving at him and crying softly. *It will all be over soon*, he told himself. Pretty soon, it will all be behind them. The train pulled away and George stood watching until it was completely out of his sight.

. . .

Manning house was a large manor house whose rooms had been broken down into dorm-like quarters for the girls that stayed there. There was a small nursery that could hold up to 10 babies at a time. When Celia arrived she was taken to a room on the third floor and told to get her things unpacked and then come back downstairs to the main entrance way. Her room was pretty starkly decorated. It had two beds so she assumed she'd be sharing her space with someone. A cross hung over the head of each bed. She chose the bed to the right of the window and started unpacking her things. She had her back to the door when she was startled by someone entering the room with a loud crash.

"Oh, I'm sorry," the young girl said breathlessly. "I was hoping to get up here before you!" she said, and thrust her hand out. "I'm Anita."

Celia turned to look upon a very dark skinned young woman with jet-black hair in braids close to her head and large chocolate-brown eyes. Her smile was brilliant white and wide and contagious. She shook her hand.

"Hey Anita," Celia smiled back, I'm Celia," she said, rather quietly.

"Uh. . . I hate to be a problem on our first day but you are setting up on my bed. See, I've been here for a few months now," she said, pointing to her engorged belly. "I'm needing this bed," she gestured to it, "because I'm in there," she gestured towards the doorway to the left of the room, "every five minutes through the night." Celia looked at her blankly.

"It's the bathroom," Anita explained. "I pee constantly through the night!" she laughed. "You okay with that?" Another infectious smile.

Celia nodded, smiled and moved her things off the bed and went to put them on the other bed. At least she had a room-mate who could smile. Her father had been irritable and moody ever since she had told him about her pregnancy. It was actually nice to be around someone who was happy and smiley again. It helped Celia to feel a little better.

She took to life in Manning House rather easily. Anita provided all the inside scoop on each and every person there. From the oldest nurse who lost two husbands during the war, to the young doctor who wasn't married yet and helped when deliveries were tough. Anita had spent four months there already and she knew the drill. The girls were treated with kid gloves while they awaited the baby's birth. Once the baby was born though, it was a different matter. They would be manipulated and forced to sign papers to give the baby up and then basically discarded a day or two later with nothing to show for their months of stay or for the baby they carried. Not even a picture of the child. Perhaps that was what the girls coming here and their families wanted, but Anita had told Celia that she wasn't going to be giving her baby up for adoption.

"There is no way in hell I am signing any damn papers to give away my baby. Tucker and me made this baby in love and there ain't nobody who is gonna take him away." Anita was hell bent and determined that once she left here with her child, she'd head back to her hometown and demand that Tucker marry her.

"And he will, you watch!" she insisted. "He said so himself. He was yellin' that at me when they was pulling me into the car to come here. I put up a good fight but they got me in the car and drove me straight here but I could still hear him yell after me, "I'll marry you, "Nita, I'll find you and we'll marry!" Oh, I came in here like a hell cat, but I soon settled down." She smiled, laughing to herself at the hell she had raised upon entering the house.

"I figured I could stay at home and have my father beat on me day and night for getting pregnant or I could come and be here and be safe from him. Then, when my baby is born and I marry Tucker, I don't have to go back to that mean old bastard."

Anita hated her father. Celia's father had said some very cruel and hurtful things to her in the past few weeks, and had even made her feel unwanted in her own home, but at least he never beat her. Celia had never known George to raise his hand in temper.

As time went on Celia started thinking a lot about her mother. She wondered if she could see her now if she, too, would feel disappointed in her like George did. Celia confided in Anita about her thoughts on her mother amongst other things.

...

"Yes," Celia answered. She wondered where Anita was going with this.

"You don't think that the baby you have growing inside of you is alive? That's who you should be worrying about — that little miracle, right there," she said, pointing to Celia's growing belly.

"Oh, CC, (her nickname for Celia) you can't be worried about what she's thinking, girl. She's dead! But you're alive, right?" she asked Celia, as she held her hands and sat on her bed, pulling Celia down beside her.

"This here is a miracle you know, the miracle of life. Do you know what it takes for that poor old sperm to swim his way through that giant obstacle course and break through the egg's shell in order for a baby to be conceived?" she asked, her voice going higher with intensity. Celia laughed at her animation and dramatics. "Don't you laugh at me, CC, its true! Not only all of that but he's got millions of other sperms in competition with him every time..." she shook her head, "poor bastard doesn't stand a chance!" She broke out laughing as did Celia. Anita really was good for Celia's spirits.

"I'm telling you, you stop thinking about dead mothers and fathers who force us to do things we don't want to do and start thinking about that baby and the life you are bringing into the world. Can you really be telling me you'd be happy giving up that child?" she asked Celia rather bluntly.

Celia stared at Anita wide-eyed. She had confessed the whole Brad story to Anita when she first came to Manning House and Anita had made her see and agree that the baby she carried was also made in love. At least, she knew she loved Brad. She wasn't exactly sure about his feelings for her. But knowing his mother like she did and overhearing the conversation at the luncheon, Celia was convinced that Brad stood about as much chance of winning against his mother as she did with her father; utterly hopeless. It was from the very beginning really. How on earth did they think they could have pulled off a romantic relationship? She longed to see Brad and tell him everything. She daydreamed of how great it would be if he found out where she was and came to rescue her. But the reality was that he was jet-setting around Europe and by the time he got home she'd be three months from giving birth. No one would tell him she was here because no one knew. As far as everyone at home was concerned, she was helping an ailing aunt and would be back at an undetermined date.

"I... uhh... I don't know, Anita. I don't know," she moaned. If she kept the baby how would she manage? Her father had already told her that it wouldn't work.

"Listen to me girl," she said, holding Celia's hand hard and looking her straight in the face. "You are this child's *mother*," emphasizing the word strongly. "No one, not anyone can force you to give that child up. Not anyone *including your father*. If you want to keep the baby you and Brad made during your one and only time of love making, then do it and don't let anyone try and stop you!" Celia stared into Anita's eyes. She was so powerful with her words. For effect, Anita added, "And do you honestly think that your mother would be happy with you giving that baby up for adoption? Didn't you tell me that *she was adopted* and she didn't enjoy her childhood at all?" There it was – the final nail driven home to seal the deal for Celia.

. . .

Anita was now in her final days of pregnancy and was in a lot of discomfort. Her belly extended far out and had dropped low with the baby's preparation of its arrival. She was moody and irritable and had bitten off the head of everyone around her at least twice. She sat with her feet raised in an easy chair in the living area of Manning House, watching as the cold, early January day promised only frost bite to those who might be adventurous enough to go outdoors. Well, Anita wasn't, she knew that. She was happy just staying put right where she was. This baby was getting too damn big for her to carry around like this anymore and she was going to take matters into her own hands if he didn't get himself born right damn soon!

Anita adjusted her back some to ease a pain when she felt a gush of water flow out of her and soak herself, the chair and the carpeted floor beneath her.

"Oh Shit!" she yelled. "I think my damn water just broke!" She tried to get herself up out of the chair but was not successful on her first attempt. Before making another, Celia had come into the room and reached under her arms to help her up.

"Easy there, Anita. Take it easy," she reassured her. "I'll walk you down to the infirmary and you can see the nurses there. They'll probably get you ready for birthing this baby of yours huh?" Celia said joyfully.

It was anything but a joyful time though. She had yet to see a girl who was happy and danced out of here after giving the child up. Most cried their eyes out and left looking lost and alone, even if they were lucky enough to have family pick them up. Anita had said she would never let them take her baby away, but Celia doubted that she'd win. Most girls caved. In the months she'd been a border there, she'd seen six girls come in pregnant and not one left holding her baby. Chances are, Anita and she would have quite a fight on their hands. Celia brought Anita to the infirmary and let the nurses clean her up and get her set. Anita asked if Celia could stay with her and they allowed her to. Celia sat by Anita's side the whole time, holding her hand and encouraging her as the contractions started to increase in intensity. She labored for 10 long hours, soaked through four night dresses and pissed off most of the nursing staff, but by 3:15 am the cries of her baby boy could be heard.

She laughed as she heard him cry out, telling him, "That's right, "TJ", you cry out loud as you please so your daddy will hear you and come runnin!" She and Celia laughed out loud. When the baby was cleaned up, the nurses went to take him from the room, but Anita wasn't having it. As exhausted as she was, she demanded that they bring the baby over to her so she could hold him. When they handed him to her, her eyes filled with tears as she studied the tiny face and counted the five fingers on the little hand thrust upwards while in the middle of a yawn.

"Oh my God, he's so beautiful, Anita," Celia cried, her eyes also filled with tears.

"He's my "TJ", my Tucker Junior! He's gonna be as big as his daddy is!" she said proudly. "Look, CC, look at his hand!" she exclaimed excitedly. "It's like a paw for God's sake." They laughed as they admired Anita's beautiful baby boy.

"Now you pay attention, girl and you do everything I do. You be watching when I leave here in a few days. I promise you on my baby's soul that I will be carrying him out of here," she insisted as she held tightly to her little bundle. "They've put him in my arms and they'll be hard pressed to take him off of me now." Celia knew she meant it. *I feel sorry for the poor person who tries to come and start that conversation with you*, she thought.

By 4:00 am, all three were exhausted. Anita tried nursing TJ and it worked to settle him down but she knew her milk wasn't in yet and he'd want to be fed again soon. The nurses would probably want to come and take him to bottle feed him and that would be her next fight. Celia kissed the baby on his little forehead and whispered something in his little ear. She smiled at Anita and said, "Secrets!" She kissed Anita on the forehead, who then mouthed "thanks" to her and returned her attention to her new baby boy.

Celia left the infirmary and walked back to her room. As she got herself ready to sleep she thought about the day and how it had gone for Anita. She'd shown tremendous courage and, except for calling the one nurse a "stupid fat cow", she'd managed to come through it fairly well. TJ was a good weight and size and both mother and son were fine. She could only hope it would go as well for her.

True to her word, four days later Anita came busting into their room, holding TJ wrapped in a blanket to gather her things.

"I told ya so!! They ain't gonna fight me!" she said excitedly, "They ain't even asked me about signing anything!" she added. Celia was shocked! Was it really that easy?

"Tucker came last night and he told them there was nobody going to give away his son!" she gushed.

Celia's heart leapt for her friend as Anita gently placed TJ onto the bed.

"Oh, I am so happy for you, Anita! Just as you said, right? You promise to send me word and pictures of when you marry, right?" she asked her, hugging as Anita finished packing up the small bag that held her belongings.

"It's all yours now, girl. You can have the bed next to the bathroom. I don't need it anymore." Anita hugged Celia once again, picked up the bag and gingerly lifted TJ into her arms. Celia raised the soft blanket covering his little head and kissed him tenderly.

"Look after your mom, little man…" she said, "and don't forget our secret!"

Anita smiled and was out the door in a split second. "Don't let them talk you into anything," she called out as she left the room and went off down the hallway.

Celia smiled to herself and watched from the window in her room. She could see a car outside, pulled up near the front doorway with a tall, black man standing in front of it. He had a huge smile on his face. *Must be Tucker*, Celia thought. Just then Anita came out from the building and rushed over to the man. He grabbed her and kissed her and then held her back to look at the baby. They both stared at the child smiling and gushing. It was such a lovely scene and so different from the other times she had watched girls leave. She captured that picture of the three of them, Tucker, Anita and baby TJ in her mind's eye and would refer back to it many times in the years to come.

. . .

By mid-February the snow had trapped all boarders in the house for yet another day. But, as the saying goes, "Neither snow nor rain nor heat nor gloom of night stays these couriers from the swift completion of their appointed rounds…" and today was no exception. The mail had arrived and as Celia sat in her room quietly reading and enjoying her privacy (no one had come to share the room with her since Anita's departure), there was a tiny knock at her door.

"Come in," she called out.

"It's just Lucy," was the reply, as the old housemaid opened her door. She walked over to her on the bed and handed her an envelope. Celia took the envelope and recognized the handwriting immediately. It was from her father. He had written her once before and sent a card at Christmastime but otherwise, he had been silent. She quickly opened the letter as Lucy left her to her reading.

Dear Celia,

I know it has been a long time since we saw one another. I hope you are doing well. There have been some changes around here and I have some news for you. I have decided to sell the house and move to Chicago! I figured it would be best if we both have a new chance in a new place once you are finished there. I have a few things more to finalize but will write with the new address and information. Perhaps you can take the train that stops nearby the new house and I can pick you up there when you are ready to come home.

I am looking forward to seeing you, honey, and putting this all behind us.

I will write again when I have more information.

Take care,

Dad

Celia held the note and re-read it, stone stiff. He didn't even once mention anything about the baby, his obvious shame coming through loud and clear. And now, for whatever reason, he was moving them to Chicago. She could only imagine that he didn't want her coming back to town where people might talk. Celia could feel the anger rising in her. He had acted like she was a pariah, as though having a baby was the worst thing in the world that could happen! Well, wouldn't the worst thing in the world that could happen be that his wife would think she was pregnant only to find out she was dying and then to die, leaving him with a five year old? Wasn't that worse than anything else? Her father had suffered a terrible ordeal but still lacked perspective. Anita was right, there was no way her mother would have wanted her to give this baby up and she was just going to have to make her dad see that.

. . .

George faced the blustery, cold morning with his head down. Not just for protection but it was also fitting for his mood. He was going to speak to Rev. Moore one last time. He felt he owed the kindly Baptist minister that much. Rev. Moore had been the catalyst for the town's acceptance of Meg and him and Celia. George entered the old A-frame church and made his way to the Reverend's office. He tapped lightly on the door and heard the man's deep voice call, "Come on in!" George entered the office and removed his hat.

"Hello there, Reverend," George said, shifting from one foot to the other.

"Well hello, George," he said. "Come take a seat. What brings you in today?" the kindly Reverend asked. He already knew – news was buzzing about and he had been told of George's plans.

"I... uh... that is, me and Celia... we've decided to move to... uh... Chicago," George stammered out.

"Oh, I see," said Rev. Moore, as he brought his chair in closer to the desk and rested his arms on the top of it. "May I ask why, George? You and Celia have been members of our church for many years. What makes it that you have to leave everything you love, George?" he asked, hoping George would tell him outright.

"Well... uh... see, I sent Celia to take care of a sickly aunt..."

George's voice trailed off as Rev. Moore's head dropped slightly. He was disappointed George felt he couldn't be truthful and his disappointment was clear to George. He hesitated to continue. He thought about all that the dear old man had done for him especially when he and Meg were first married and needed his help and guidance, and then again during Meg's illness and death. George knew that Rev. Moore knew the truth but, even so, he deserved to hear it straight from him.

"Celia got herself in trouble a while back, Reverend. She became pregnant. I sent her to Chicago to have the baby. She's due in March and will give the baby up for adoption and then we'll start a new life somewhere in the city." He blurted out the whole story like purging a disease. He felt relief afterward and gave a heavy sigh. Reverend Moore just looked at George with sad eyes. He had very much enjoyed George and his family and the difference they had made to his church and to himself.

"I learned an awful lot from you and Meg, George," Rev Moore confessed. "You changed the culture of our church with your color blindness!" The good Reverend sat back in his chair and smiled.

George just looked at him, astonished. "Reverend Moore, I respectfully disagree with you. It was your tolerance, you showing the rest of the "congregation how to love his fellow man that brought us here!" George gushed out, his eyes near to tears.

Rev. Moore laughed out loud and stood to shake George's hand.

"Then I suppose it was God's intervention, wasn't it George? And neither of us should take credit for His work," he chuckled as he pointed up. George laughed too. Who was he to argue with that reasoning? The two men shook hands warmly.

"I shall miss *you*, George Morningstar," the kindly old Reverend said solemnly as George left his office.

"I shall miss you Rev. Moore," George said gratefully.

. . .

As March was ending like a lamb, Celia enjoyed watching things come back to life in the gardens that surrounded Manning House. She could see birds coming back from their winter break down south and the noises of life beginning anew in the dawn of the early spring. She had awoken that morning to a new pain in her back and wondered if this child was ever going to come into the world or if it was happy as a lark right where it was. The date was March 31st, the last day of the month. A Saturday. Dr. Swanson said that the baby would be born in March and she had seen the whole month through without as much as a stir from her womb. Now, a new pain in her back. Dear God, how much longer would this go on for?

She got up from her bed to use the bathroom, her third time in the last hour and noticed that she was wet. She wondered what it was from. She hadn't washed yet and she hadn't anything to drink. She used the facilities, cleaned herself up and was just about to leave the bathroom when, there it was again! She was wet again. And the pain in her back started again. Hmmmm. The nurses had told her that her labor could start any day and didn't always start with her water breaking; perhaps that was what was happening with her. She thought she had best get herself down to the infirmary and they could answer her questions.

Walking was a little cumbersome at this point and she took her time in getting down to the medical area. As the nurse on site saw Celia waddling towards her, she could tell she was in some discomfort.

"What's wrong honey, you in pain?" she asked, her kind smile making Celia feel better.

"I sure am. I keep leaking or peeing or something, I'm not sure," Celia said with a pleading face.

"Okay, okay… let's get you up on a bed and have a look. Come here honey and I'll help you up," the pretty nurse said as she patted the bed she was standing next to.

Celia waddled her way over and together, they hoisted Celia up onto the bed. She then lay back looking embarrassed at the wet stain that now covered her night dress. The nurse raised Celia's dress up over her hips and put her feet into the stirrups that were mounted on either side of the bed. She peered between Celia's outstretched legs and her eyes grew wide.

"Oh my!" the nurse said, "Your baby is just about coming my dear. I can see the little head. That is one impatient baby," she laughed as she busied herself about the room gathering instruments, and placing items on trays near to the bed.

"You hang on and I'm going to get the doctor. While I'm out of the room, if you have a contraction, *don't push*! No one is here to catch that baby if it comes flying out so hold tight until I'm back here, you got that?" she told Celia sternly. Celia nodded her head, using her father's breathing technique to absorb the pain of every contraction. The nurse left the room and Celia did all she could to endure the pain and not push when a contraction would hit. At one point, the pain was so great that she groaned out loud just as the nurse came back into the room with the doctor behind her.

"No sense wasting time in groaning my dear, that breathing thing you were doing is the best thing you can do. Focus on something clear across

115

the room and when the doctor tells you to, push with all your might. Okay?" she instructed Celia. Celia nodded and continued breathing her four beat pace as she focused on the clock on the wall across the room. The young doctor sat on a stool between her legs and kept his head bent low. She felt the pressure of another contraction coming, the pain in her back a dead giveaway. She felt herself bear down and the doctor yelled, "Push! Push hard!"

She pushed with all her might, feeling sweat forming on her body. This baby had done a lot of the labor through the night, quietly, but had now come awake and wanted out in a hurry. Poor Celia went from hardly any labor pains to full on labor inside an hour.

"Push again, Celia!" the doctor ordered and again she bore down with all her might. The pretty nurse took the pillow behind her head and lifted it against her back to give her comfort and leverage as she pushed.

"One more time, Celia," the young doctor said. "Just one more time for me and this baby will be out." Celia was trying to catch her breath and gain the strength for that next time. She hoped the doctor was right.

"Now!" he yelled at her. "Push hard, Celia!"

Celia squeezed together every lower muscle she had and felt a surge of pressure release from her body. She heard the nurse gasp and clap her hands and the doctor laugh as her child was born. A mighty cry was heard throughout the infirmary and Celia smiled exhausted.

"That's a singing voice for certain," she said smiling.

"It's a boy" the doctor said. "A fine looking boy with a full head of hair."

That would explain all the heartburn she'd felt. She heard that hair was the culprit during pregnancy. The doctor and nurse started moving almost robotically, cleaning her and the baby and setting things in order. They didn't bring the baby over to Celia and she remembered that they didn't do it with Anita either. Anita had to insist, and so would she.

"I'd like to hold my baby, please," she said.

"Well, now, we don't believe that it's a good thing for you to form an attachment to him. Best if we let the nurses take care of him," the doctor said condescendingly.

"I want to hold my baby, please," Celia hissed. "Bring him to me please." She stared down the doctor who looked at the nurse. Neither was willing to face another confrontation like the one they'd had with Anita. Rather than argue, the doctor turned away. The nurse turned towards the baby, shook her head as if to disagree with the whole thing and handed the baby boy to Celia. Her arms were not even around the blanket and she was in love. His hair poking out in little blonde tufts was enough to make her melt. He was such a beautiful baby, *definitely a Dumont child*, she thought. He had no coloring from her side of the family at all. No George, Meg or Celia in this child. And then he opened his eyes! Green! A beautiful shade of green but not grass-green like hers, *his own green*, a deep forest green. He definitely got his eye color from the Morningstar's. Mostly, he looked a lot like his father, Brad. Yes, it would probably be a good thing that they moved to Chicago!

. . .

George was excited as he got up that Friday morning. He had received word that Celia was due in by train for 9:00 am. Rush hour time. There would be a lot of people at the train station at that time and he wanted to get there early so he could get in, pick her up and get home. He was excited to show her the new house. He was mostly excited to show her Chicago! This was the place to be! He and Celia were going to get things started again. Granted, he'd left behind his band mates but the move was a necessity. Rumors were flourishing back in town that Celia had run into some trouble and was not away with the sick auntie. Some even managed to put her and Bradley Dumont together but nothing was ever confirmed. Even Celia had never confessed to him who the baby's father was, but George had his suspicions that the snobby bitch, Dumont, was right.

None of that mattered now because today was their new beginning. A new life going forward and Chicago was going to bring them the fame and success George had so longed for. Music had been a huge influence in his life since his early days with Meg and her mother's piano. He had always wanted to be a professional musician but needed to provide for his family, and then his daughter. But now, she too was able to bring in some money and together, with their combined talent, George saw great things in their future! There were dozens of blues clubs in the city core and even the outlying areas had well known places for blues/soul/gospel singers and musicians. *I should have moved to Chicago years ago!* he thought. *Probably would have saved Celia from all of this trouble.*

As he parked his car in the station's parking lot, he noticed the train pulling in. He got out of his car and ran up to the platform to find his daughter. He hadn't seen her in almost eight months and a lot of things got said before she left – things that he couldn't take back. He was sorry for saying them now and hoped that all was forgiven.

There were a lot of people both inside and outside of the small train station. *This must be the popular train for commuters going into the main city core,* George thought. He looked about at each and every young woman who walked past or came into focus but he couldn't see her. Finally, he thought he spotted the back of her. He wasn't sure, as she was wearing a hat covering that wonderful hair of hers, but he thought it was her. He could only make out her head as the rest of her was blocked from sight. She looked as if she too were looking around for him and it made his heart leap. Oh, how he had missed her! Things would be much different now. He'd show her that they could move past this.

He continued walking towards her as the crowd pushed into him moving in all directions. She turned slightly towards him and he caught her profile. Yes, it was her! She looked good, maybe a little older and had put on a bit of weight but that was to be expected considering.

The crowd parted as George finally got closer to her. She stood there looking away. He studied her for a moment. She reminded him so much like his Meg. Oh, how he missed Meg. He thought about the time he had spent with her, both before her illness and during. And in the last few weeks of her life, he remembered her dying requests and promises she asked of him. He thought about how things had transpired over the last year. He hadn't really held to those promises, had he? He hadn't done as he promised he would. He felt pangs of guilt rush through him now, standing there, watching his daughter.

She turned towards him giving him a full view of her. Her face lit up briefly as they caught each other's eye. He raised his hand to signal he had seen her and started walking her way. She wore a long, grey coat with a small, woolen, grey hat, still needing the warmth in the cool early April weather. She was holding a blanket or something. No…. a bundle. George stopped. No, she was holding a baby! He got up to her and before he could even say a word she held his stare and spoke evenly.

"Hello, Father, I hope you are as happy to see me as I am to see you," she said blankly. "This has been an extremely difficult time and it has given me a lot to think about. So here is what I've come up with." She paused only a moment but held up a finger to stop him from speaking.

"Number one," she counted off, "I remember you telling me stories of my mother's childhood with her nasty father who had made her feel unwanted. You have spent the last few months making me feel exactly the same way. If you decide that you can't live with me or my child, then leave us here and I'll find my own way from here on in. I won't have my child feel unwanted in his own home and you and I can continue the family history of estrangement from one another as both you and my mother were forced to do," she added smartly.

His eyes lost some of their intensity. He looked into her eyes as tears began to form in his.

"Number two," she continued, "I'm old enough to make my own decisions and be my own person. The actions I took that got me into this situation, I fully accept. I will take on the responsibility of raising this child and I am not asking for your help, only for your love and support." She waited to see his reaction, but he only stood before her listening as tears rolled down his face.

"And finally," she finished, "How dare you ask me to give up a child for adoption when your own true love suffered the same and was miserable with her adoptive parents? Shame on you!" She paused, letting that hit home. Then she added, "My mother was desperate to give you a child that would carry on the family name and sadly, that never came to pass. And so, I will have to do it. May I introduce you to Mr. Charlie Spencer Morningstar, your grandson?" She turned the baby so that he could look into the forest green eyes of his new baby grandson.

"Now please, take us home."

Chapter 3

Charlie Morningstar

The young, blonde boy ran home from school as soon as the bell rang and raced into the kitchen hoping to see his Papa immediately. He was 7 years old today and Papa had promised him a guitar!

"Papa?" he cried out. "I'm home now!" He looked around the main floor of the house for his grandfather but couldn't find him anywhere. He continued calling out to him until he reached the back door to their yard. He opened the door calling "Papa?" as he did so. The eruption of "Surprise!" scared him backwards for a moment and he broke out into a glorious smile when he realized what had happened. Before him stood 20 of his closest friends and family all in honor of his seventh birthday. His mother had gone to unbelievable lengths to not allow him even an inkling of an idea that he was going to have a surprise party. And on a Monday afternoon at the end of March. Unheard of! But Charlie's mother was not going to allow his birthday to happen without some kind of celebration. It had been like that each year since he was born. His birthday was always a time of huge celebration because his mother and grandfather saw Charlie as their little godsend. Everything revolved around him, everything centered on him and they were all the happier for it. Charlie was not ill-affected by their attention either. He thrived from it. They spent hours teaching him music and singing, filling his young little mind full of everything musical they could and, like a sponge, he soaked it up. He had a vast knowledge of blues and soul singers from way, way back. He learned piano from an early age on his Papa's knee and now Papa was going to give him a guitar and teach him how to play. Charlie was thrilled!

George Morningstar laughed at his grandson's reaction to his surprise party! What an enormous amount of joy the little boy brought him! And to think he had wanted Celia to give him up for adoption. He had even been slightly furious at first when he had seen her at the train station and realized she was holding the baby. But once Celia set him straight, in complete Meg style, George took one look at the little face that bore his last name and fell in love. He had not anticipated a baby when he had set the house up prior to Celia joining him, so little Charlie had to sleep in the second drawer of his mom's dresser for his first few months. By Charlie's third month, George had been given a crib and some wood that he had managed to botch together into a cradle. Charlie thrived in his makeshift world. George and Celia were so in love with their new family member that their upset with one another was soon forgotten. George found the grace to apologize to her for his words and his actions, and Celia apologized for being so careless. But oh! how they loved the results!

George had begun playing almost immediately in many of the clubs that scattered Chicago's night life. He had played with B.B. King and all sorts of famous and locally famous blues/jazz artists within Chicago's city limits. He had managed to make enough so that Celia could stay at home for Charlie's first few years and although he wasn't living his dream, it was pretty damn close. When Charlie was old enough that George could watch him for a few hours during the day, Celia did take a job, although it was more in the serving industry rather than as a singer. Celia had put that on the back burner until Charlie would be old enough for her to enter back into the nightclub world. It broke George's heart for her to step back when she had just begun to break out, but he couldn't fault her for her reason. If George and Celia were considered gifted, then Charlie was a master!

True to his word, his grandfather, better known as "Papa", had given him his first guitar for his seventh birthday in hopes that Charlie's talent would only expand with a guitar in his hands. George planned to spend his daytime on weekends one-on-one with Charlie teaching him how to play the blues. George now believed all the hardships and setbacks he had faced were so Charlie could come along and be the reason that the "Morningstar" name was no longer associated with some hard-assed lawyer who died on his 50th birthday. Charlie would be the one to take the family name farther, and with music! George had long ago given up his dream of making it as a famous musician, happy as he was to back up some of the best there were in his time. He had hoped Celia might have gone far – she still could, but should she ever marry she wouldn't be able to keep her name, and surely someday she would marry. Charlie was the shining hope now, and his incredible musical talent had George hoping it would take him places!

Amongst the group gathered to enjoy Charlie's birthday was a band mate of George's, a trumpet player named Wade McGrath. Wade was 34 with sandy-blonde hair that covered his head in curls. He had an outrageous sandy-blonde mustache that reached far beyond the corners of his mouth. Wade stood six foot, three inches tall and had a very lean frame. He was ten years younger than George but the two had formed a strong bond over the seven years George had lived in Chicago. Wade's family home, which he now owned, was just down the street from George's and when they realized they were neighbors after playing together one night, they started hanging out and jamming together all the time. Wade introduced George to his younger sister Jean and her large husband, Marco Pelos, who was of Greek decent. They had been married just a few years and were expecting their first child. Marco was an excellent drummer who would perform with them sometimes. They had met through Wade and all three of them had a strong love for music. Knowing Celia would welcome new friends, George introduced Jean to Celia and Charlie. Jean and Celia became close friends despite being years apart in age. Marco had purchased a house a few doors down because Jean loved the neighborhood and wanted to stay close. She was a much prettier version of her older brother but the family resemblance was strong. Jean carried the McGrath curly hair trait to a new extreme. Her hair was a mass of blonde curls that obviously had their own ideas. Jean too loved singing and she and Celia often harmonized on songs at home, with Charlie being their only audience.

Wade, Jean and Marco were taken into the Morningstar's household as if they were long lost family. They shared many meals together. They spent Thanksgiving and Christmas together and regularly had late dinners when the three men would finish a set at a club and would end up back at the Morningstar's to share with Celia and Jean the night they had missed. The three made quite the trio and were asked to sit in on some pretty famous blues musicians' jam sessions. George was actually able to earn a decent living playing his music. No more teaching, no more choir direction. He would be lying if he said he didn't miss the kids but his heart really was in performing his music.

With Charlie's party in full swing, the atmosphere was electric! Although the party had started outdoors in order to surprise Charlie, it quickly moved indoors as Chicago's cold March winds weren't favorable for an outdoor event. The house was small and 20 people quickly packed into the kitchen and living room area while Jean helped Celia serve hotdogs and hamburgers to the guests. Once everyone had eaten, it was time to open Charlie's presents. All the guests gathered around the living room couch where Charlie sat centre of attention surrounded by packages. Some were very large, some smaller but it was one in particular that Charlie was anxious to open. Charlie looked through the assorted gifts with his eyes trying to spy his obvious choice. He couldn't see it! George caught Celia's eye as if to say, let him open it first and Celia agreed. She reached behind the couch to bring out a guitar case with a huge red bow on it. She handed it carefully to Charlie overtop of the heads of the other children. An audible "Ahhhh" was heard from children and adults alike. Charlie's eyes widened as large as the case itself. He struggled to hold it up as it was handed over, but Papa was beside Charlie helping him hold the case safely.

"Sit down, Charlie and I'll put it in your lap," said Papa, always coming to Charlie's rescue.

Charlie sat immediately and his Papa placed the case so that the latches faced him. His mother stood back with the camera ready to capture his reaction when he opened the case. As if opening the lid to the lost treasures of the Incas, Charlie slowly opened the lid and his face registered the awe that was before him just as Celia snapped the picture and a flash lit the room up momentarily. The case held a Gibson Les Paul electric guitar with a solid body and set-in neck joint. It was made of mahogany with the neck having some maple in it too. The wood was stained to a caramel color that spread to a red tone, the design was called "Sunburst". Charlie examined it closely. He gently touched the wood thinking it looked like the color of caramel. The fret board was rosewood and ebony and the black parts of it shone like the ebony keys on the piano. It was absolutely beautiful. Charlie's little frame would have a difficult time holding the exquisite piece but he wanted to give it a try. Once again, Papa helped by removing the case and helping Charlie put the strap over his head and rest the guitar on his knees. Charlie instinctively put his left hand along the fret board and ran his fingers across the 22 frets, gingerly stroking them. His right hand went immediately into place as if he was about to start playing. Although Papa had shown him a few chords, Charlie hadn't learned enough yet to play it to its full potential, *but it's just a matter of time*, the guests in attendance thought collectively!

"Whoa! Papa, it's a Gibson Les Paul. She's soooo beautiful! Should I name her?" Charlie asked excitedly. The room broke out laughing. It made Charlie stop for a moment. "No… you know, like B.B. King has "Lucille", Charlie explained to the group.

"If you want to name her Charlie, you go right ahead. I think a musician has a much closer relationship with his instrument if it has a name. It personalizes it," Papa said, meaning the double entendre for the mixed age group and winking to no one in particular.

"I want to call her Meg," Charlie said proudly. George's face froze for a moment and he looked to Celia who also had the same look. Both father and daughter smiled at each other and nodded their heads.

"Meg, she is then!" said Papa, clearing his throat just a little.

Charlie looked over the guitar with awe as he touched the shiny body.

"Well, I know that was a tough act to follow but if we don't get on with these presents, we'll be serving breakfast to everyone and sending the kids off to school!" Celia laughed.

Papa helped Charlie pack away the guitar into its case and Charlie continued opening his gifts. There were Lego blocks and toy cars and clothes. All sorts of gifts to keep a seven year old boy happy, but Charlie's eyes kept looking over at "Meg".

When Celia announced that it was cake cutting time, the crowd moved into the kitchen to watch Charlie make his wish and blow out the candles. But before Charlie went over to the kitchen he stopped his Papa and asked him. "When can you start teaching me, Papa? I want to learn how to play?" he asked his grandfather excitedly.

George looked into his beautiful grandson's face. Charlie was a green-eyed blonde with a face like an angel. His smile spread from ear to ear and his features were strong and striking. George could see this child growing into a very handsome man indeed!

"Papa can't teach you until we have some time during the day. You must not bring "Meg" out of her case unless I'm here, Charlie," using the child's name for his new guitar knowing it would please the boy. "She's very special, much like my "Meg", your grandmother was. So promise me that you'll wait until I'm home before you ever try playing her, okay?" he asked Charlie gesturing with a pointed finger to bring the point home.

This did not please Charlie one bit. Papa was hardly ever home at night and when he was home during the day, Charlie was in school. That meant only weekends for George to be able to teach him! Charlie was not pleased at all. Some gift it was if it took him forever to learn how to play it. Charlie's heart sank. His Papa guided Charlie over to the kitchen table and in front of his birthday cake as the guests sang "Happy Birthday" to him. The cake was a large slab of chocolate cake with chocolate icing, Charlie's favorite. "Happy 7th Birthday Charlie" had been written in blue icing and the cake had little musical notes drawn all over it in all different colors. There were seven candles strategically placed upon the cake, flickering and waving their tiny flame, awaiting Charlie's wish.

George stood behind him with his hands on his shoulders and leaned in to whisper, "Okay Charlie, now's time. Make your wish and make it a good one!"

"Yes, but… be careful what you wish for!" Celia said wisely.

Charlie thought for a moment. One wish… what did he want most of all? Well, it wasn't a toy or money or anything. Charlie closed his eyes and raised his head making the wish to himself. *I wish my Papa was home more with me to teach me to play "Meg"*, he wished and opened his eyes and blew out the candles in one go. Everyone clapped and congratulated him, and his Papa squeezed his shoulders proudly. His mother started to cut the cake and serve it first to the children in attendance and then the adults.

By 9:00 pm everyone had cleared the Morningstar's home except for Wade, Marco and Jean who remained behind. Jean chattered while she gave Celia a hand clearing away all the party mess and Wade, Marco, Charlie and George sat in the living room. George had lifted "Meg" out of her case and was showing Charlie how to hold her while he was still so young.

"Play something for us, Papa, please?" Charlie asked, his large green eyes looking pleadingly at his grandfather.

George smiled and thought a moment. "Well, you know Charlie, a musician never lets another play his most prized possession. But, just this once, I will play a little something, shall I? And then, she's all yours after that!"

Charlie smiled and gently handed over "Meg" to his Papa and George stood to accept the guitar. As he stood, George froze and suddenly started swaying slightly. His face went pale and his eyes rolled back into his head. He fell back on the couch with "Meg" in his hands, knocking

Charlie over with him. George's right arm went limp and he struggled to speak.

"Gg… get… Mom… Cc… Cel…ya!" he managed to sputter.

Wade jumped up immediately and shouted to the kitchen, "Girls, get in here. George is in trouble." He grabbed the guitar off George and Charlie and put it to one side as he undid George's button on his shirt to give him some air.

"Hang on there, Georgie-boy," Wade said close to him. "We're going to get you to the hospital. Celia, call an ambulance!" he bellowed.

· · ·

George's limp body lay in the hospital bed with tubes and machines and whirring sounds filling the room. He was breathing on his own; his heart rate was slow but stable. The right side of his face was drooping slightly and he rested with his eyes closed. Celia sat in a chair at the end of the bed, eyes swollen from crying, head hung down, dozing slightly herself. Wade entered the room backside first carrying two coffees in large paper cups. He tried being quiet so as not to disturb the sleeping pair but Celia's head rose quickly as he came in.

"Is he alright?" she asked Wade, as he handed her a paper cup of the hot drink, its heady smell filling the room.

"Yeah, he's fine." He said. "He's a little shaken up, poor kid. Right on his birthday too! Jean says he keeps sayin' *it's all his fault!* Poor little guy," he said, shaking his head. "She says she'll keep him overnight and get him to school in the morning, if you still want him to go." Celia nodded absent mindedly at Wade's words. He caught her look and gave a thought over the day's events. "I tell you, it's not a birthday I'll soon forget," Wade whispered as he sipped his coffee.

"Me either," Celia said as she blew onto the steaming liquid before taking a sip.

"Any more information?" Wade asked. He had stepped out to make a quick call to Jean and pass along the news they had so far and to check in on Charlie. He found a vending machine by pure luck and bought the two coffees on his way back to George's room.

"The doctors believe he stroked on the left side of his brain which is why his right side looks so droopy," she started softly. "He hasn't spoken yet so they don't know how much his speech has been affected. They also can't tell me if he's got any brain damage or not." She looked over at Wade as the tears welled up in her eyes and gently rolled down her face.

"Do they know *when* they'll know?" Wade asked her as he looked back over at George. He noticed George's eye flickering and heard Celia begin to answer in the negative when he interrupted her. "His eyelid just moved," Wade said, pointing to George. He stood up and went over to George. "Hey Georgie-boy, you wake up for us now," he said gently. Wade continued drinking his coffee over George as he studied his friend's face for any sign of movement. George's eyelids fluttered briefly and excitedly, Wade pointed again at George and shouted, "There it is again! Hey Georgie-boy, you come on and wake up now so we can talk with you, okay?" Wade urged as Celia came and stood by the other side. They watched in shock as George's eyes continued fluttering until finally he slowly opened them. He couldn't move his arm and he was hardly able to speak. He blinked a few times making out Wade's figure first and then, able to turn his head, he saw Celia.

"Oh Daddy!" Celia cried as she came to hug his head on the pillow. "You had us so worried!" she said as she pulled back from her hug and looked into his eyes.

He struggled to speak, stammering his first words to her, "Cc… ccof… eee," was what he got out.

Wade and Celia looked across the bed at one another and broke out laughing and crying at the same time. He wanted coffee! Typical George! A great sign as far as Wade and Celia were concerned. George was still in there and with some strong love and support they would see to it that he would recover to his fullest potential. Over George's body they toasted to him, quite appropriately with their coffees.

...

While in Jean's care, Charlie came and asked sadly, "When do you think my Papa might be able to teach me on my new guitar?" As he leaned into her for some comfort, Jean hugged the boy with her arm and kept him close while she said gently, "Oh honey, your Papa is very ill right now and will have to spend many days at home recovering before he's able to play music again."

Charlie spent the whole next day with his head hung low and his heart in his shoes. He had almost killed his Papa with his birthday wish! How would he ever be able to live with that? It was a *birthday wish* not a spell or a curse! He didn't expect it to go *that* way. He had wished for many things over the years and they hadn't come true. Why this one? His mother had said, "...*be careful what you wish for!*" and it stuck in his memory that day. It would be 45 years before Charlie would ever make a birthday wish again.

George's recuperation at home was daunting. Celia had her hands full with both Charlie and George but, thankfully, his stroke was not so severe that he was completely unable to fend for himself. The right side of his body was still weak and he now walked with a cane but he was able to move pretty well on his own which made things a lot easier. His arm was better having been only mildly affected but George still struggled with his speech. It seemed that it was to be the one major lasting effect. He stammered and sputtered to get words out and although Celia would practice with him, it was still very difficult for him to say the simplest things. Charlie would help his Papa by speaking for him at times which would get him into trouble from his mother.

"Don't speak for him, Charlie, he has to learn to use his tongue and form the words!" his mother would admonish.

130

"But he's struggling, Mom!" Charlie would plea.

"I know sweetie, but he won't ever learn it if you keep doing it for him," she would say. Then she'd ask her father again what he wanted and George would sputter and stammer but finally get out his request, whatever it may be. This would cause mother and son to catch the other's eye and each thinking they knew better, would roll their eyes at one another. Like mother, like son. They both loved George Morningstar very much. The hardest thing for George was that his mind was as quick as a whip. He was now trapped inside a body that didn't work for him while his mind was speaking sentences and conversing full on with those around him. It was just all in his head and was extremely frustrating for George.

During his recovery, Charlie would race home from school, happy to have his Papa around to chat at and entertain. Charlie didn't ask his Papa to teach him on the guitar. He knew that wouldn't happen for a while; Papa was still so weak and couldn't really teach him without speaking. One day Charlie sat watching TV, while his Papa watched him intently. Charlie sensed his Papa's gaze and broke his attention from the TV to look over at George. George motioned to the boy to come over to him. When Charlie reached him, George slowly leaned forward and said quietly into Charlie's ear, "MMMeg!" Charlie looked back in astonishment at his grandfather to be sure he understood the request. The pair locked eyes and Charlie instinctively knew what his Papa wanted. He ran from the room into his bedroom and reached under his bed for the precious case that contained the beautiful guitar. He had only looked at it once or twice since his birthday, never taking it from its red velvet form. He carefully carried the case into the living room and placed it on his grandfather's lap. But George shook his head and pointed to Charlie and then to the floor. At first, Charlie didn't understand his motions so George sputtered, "Yyou… p… play."

Charlie nodded his head, took the case from his Grandfather's knee and placed it on the floor. He got the neck out first and let his grandfather hold it while he pulled out the body so that the whole instrument was free from its case. He leaned against his Papa's chair for support as he put the strap around his shoulders and gently let the guitar hang, Oh, it was soooo beautiful! The strap hung too low and needed adjusting and George managed as best he could. At least the guitar didn't sit on the floor! It was far too big for a seven year old boy but Charlie's smile lit up the room and he held his stance as if he'd been playing for years.

George beamed! *Charlie is going to be a star!* he thought. George showed Charlie how to hold his fingers on the frets and would then sputter out the chord name. He continued to go through the entire neck of the guitar holding Charlie's fingers in place as he told him all of the basic chords. He then sat back and watched as Charlie repositioned his fingers into exactly the correct placement and would tell his Papa the name of the chord. They did this all afternoon until Charlie could do it backwards.

The next day, when Charlie came home from school, instead of going to the TV, he went under his bed and brought Meg out to the living room. He then went to his Papa's bed and pulled out the guitar case hidden underneath the bed. He marched back into the living room and without saying a word, put the guitar case on George's lap. He helped open up the case and together they removed his grandfather's guitar, all the while, George watched the young boy with a grateful look. It wasn't a Les Paul, but it was years old and well played. Charlie helped put the strap around his Papa's head and made sure George had it in his hands safely. He then struggled to get Meg safely strapped around him and the two of them smiled at one another when they were both ready. George would play a chord then Charlie would do the same. George would play a riff and Charlie would do the same. Whatever George would do, Charlie would mimic. It didn't help George's speech worth a damn but his dexterity progressed by leaps and bounds which improved his mood. He looked forward to every afternoon teaching his grandson how to make Meg sing!

Charlie would tell his grandfather, "If you can't use your words, say it with your music, Papa. I'll understand you." "Together, they created a musical language that only the two of them understood. Music began to flow through the Morningstar house again.

···

Wade, Jean and Marco had remained close to the Morningstar's. Jean gave birth to a baby girl, "Georgina", named after Marco's grandmother, but they called her "Georgie" for short. This made George Morningstar smile. He liked to see the young baby girl with the shock of thick, black hair and dark brown saucer-sized eyes play on the blanketed floor in front of him. Wade and Marco would help with hard work around the house and would have Charlie help them so the boy might learn a bit himself and be able to help out a little from time to time. Jean would come over and bake with Celia for companionship and to be sure they had a full pantry. They all managed to make it work. George's progress improved and he and Charlie made fast work with his guitar lessons. George was right – Charlie was a master! He grew up in the company of all adults who eat, breathed and drank music. The house was rarely without it. Even Wade and Marco had started coming over to jam with George a bit and get him back into playing his music again. Celia warned Wade to start him slow, so Wade would only stop by once or twice a week and they would play music for a little while. At first it would exhaust him but George's strength slowly returned. His speech however, did not.

. . .

Within five years George was almost back to his old self. He was nearing his 50th birthday and Celia had asked Wade to arrange to have George play at one of the clubs in town. George had moved around to all the clubs, never favoring one, always wanting to make a name for himself with his music. Wade had gone to a friend of his who owned a Blues/Jazz Bar called "Black and Blue". He had insisted that George was worth it and explained the back story. His friend, the owner, gave Wade the go ahead and arrangements were made to bring George out on his 50th birthday for him to perform in front of an audience for the first time in years.

On the night of his performance, he stood before a mirror in his bedroom practicing the words "thank you" so that he said them cleanly. He watched as his lips formed the words but his tongue wouldn't quite make the proper movements to make the words crisp. Charlie, now a boy of 13 years stood watching him. He leaned his tall body against his grandfather's doorway and felt sorry for the poor guy. He sure had struggled these past few years and it had aged him. His dark hair had greyed and the stroke had caused the right side of his face to permanently sag which didn't help. But Charlie knew he had worked hard for this night and was anxious about how he would seem to people. Oh sure, he could be around some of the neighbors without feeling vulnerable but this was an audience of people who didn't know George Morningstar or that he had suffered a stroke some years back. They were expecting an entertaining evening and Charlie didn't want anyone to be disappointed, especially his grandfather. More than anything, Charlie wished he could go with his grandfather and the rest of them to see his performance, but he was too young and he wasn't allowed. He would be satisfied seeing him walk through the door after his night and sit and listen as everyone would tell him excitedly how great he did, all the while his Papa would be sitting in the middle of it all proud as a peacock!

. . .

Charlie awoke to a strange sound. In his groggy state, he forced his brain to become aware. The sound was a ringing phone, constantly ringing. He got himself up out of bed and stumbled into the hallway where the phone hung on the wall. He sighed, leaned against the wall with his right arm as a resting pillow for his head as he grabbed the receiver off the cradle with his left hand.

"Hello?" he said with his eyes closed.

"Charlie?" Wade asked.

"Yeah?" Charlie yawned. "What the hell time is it?

"Never mind that buddy, listen to me. Get dressed, I'll be there to get you in 15 minutes," Wade said quickly.

He sounded anxious and it gave Charlie reason to ask, "What's goin' on, Wade? S'everythin' alright?"

"Just be ready to go when I come and get you okay? I'll see you soon," and with that Wade hung up the phone.

Charlie stood for a moment holding the receiver in his hand thinking about what had just happened. What the hell was going on? He still didn't know what time it was. He went back into his bedroom and turned on the light, squinting his eyes against the offending brightness. His clock said 3:15 am! What the hell?! Where was everybody? They were supposed to be back by 11:30 pm, maybe 12:00 am tops. He shook his head starting to feel a nagging worry enter into his heart. He didn't like this – not at all. Why wouldn't they have been home by now? And why was Wade on his way over at 3:15 in the morning to pick him up? To take him where? Charlie knew enough to know that this was not good. He quickly got himself dressed and was just pulling on his shoes when Wade's car pulled up in front of the house. He honked once and Charlie grabbed a coat and ran out the door. He jumped into Wade's car as Wade sped away in the middle of the night.

"What's going on, Wade?" Charlie asked as he got in.

"It's your grandfather, Charlie. He's had another stroke. It's bad buddy, real bad. Your mom wants you there," he said, speeding the car towards the hospital.

Charlie was speechless. How could this be? He worked so hard at this, it was his night! Just a few hours ago, he was standing in his bedroom doorway watching him practice for his moment. Now he was possibly fighting for his life, again.

Wade made it to the hospital in record time. He led Charlie into the Emergency area and through the doors that had a large "STOP" plastered across it. Apparently, it wasn't meant for everyone! Charlie followed Wade into a pod of curtained cubicles and watched as Wade threw back the curtains on cubicle number "3". There stood Celia and Jean with George lying pale in the bed. Celia was holding his hand and crying. Jean was also crying. George was still, his breathing shallow. Charlie entered the room hesitantly and was waved over by Celia. She

135

took her father's hand and put it into Charlie's hand and let him take her place at the head of George's bed.

"Speak to him Charlie. He can hear you. He hasn't said anything at all but we've been saying a few words to him," she said softly.

Charlie held his grandfather's hand. A huge lump formed in his throat and he felt his eyes well up immediately. How he longed to put a guitar in his hand and have his grandfather play what was on his mind. George was not coherent. His face looked fallen and kind of grey. Charlie could hear his breathing and it sounded strained. Charlie leaned close to his ear and said softly, "Hey there Papa. It's me Charlie. I want you to get better okay? We need to continue with our guitar conversations."

He choked off the last part of his sentence, his tears hitting his grandfather's pillow. Charlie squeezed his hand tightly but George didn't squeeze it back. Charlie wiped his face off on his sleeve and looked into Wade's eyes. Wade shook his head at him as if to say, "there's nothing we can do," to which Charlie started crying harder. He got close to his ear again and said to his grandfather, "I promise to make you proud of me, Papa. I promise to keep "Meg" alive with your music and all you've taught me." Those were the last words George was left with. His "Meg" would sure be singing when she saw him! He was finally going to see her again – his wild, exotic, rare girl with the mane of hair.

George Morningstar died a little while later. He slipped away peacefully with his hand held by his beloved grandson and surrounded by his daughter and good friends. He started life out with incredible wealth and had given it all up for far greater riches. He had exceptional love, had seen the best in humanity, had been forgiven his flaws and most importantly, he did better than just passing on a name – he was able to pass along his passion for music and the gifts he had been blessed with.

His funeral was held a week later. The church was filled with his family, his small circle of friends, blues artists, mourning fans and even some of the school children, now adults, whom he had taught years before. Some Celia remembered, some she didn't. They all spoke of how much of an influence George Morningstar was on their lives and how, because of him, they were now doing something musically to earn a living.

As Charlie listened he was astonished to hear how many people his grandfather had influenced musically and how much he must have loved that last night he performed. His 50th birthday.

Wade gave his eulogy, nervously unfolding a piece of paper on the podium and clearing his voice. Not wanting to break down or lose his cool he spoke of the last night of George's life. Wade told the group how the crowd that came was filled with former fans of the musically gifted Mr. George Morningstar, surprising him.

"He didn't know it but he'd had his own little following," Wade said proudly as he choked back tears. "When they heard of his return performance, they all showed up making the night even more special. And he played his heart out that night," he paused as the mourners timidly applauded. Lastly Wade told them, not reading from his paper, "George has done more than just be an excellent friend to me, he truly touched my life. George Morningstar may have lived for only 50 years but his talent will live on longer than plenty of us who walk the earth for many years more than that. He shared his blessings with me and I am the better man for it." He nodded his head, looked down and left the altar.

They buried George in the only cemetery in town that was near a blues bar. It had cost a pretty penny so Celia went cheap on his casket. She figured her father wasn't worried about his trappings; he'd want to be close to hear the city at night when it was alive with music.

Charlie was given George's old guitar and pick. Out of respect, he didn't play it once, his grandfather's words in his ear, "…*a musician never lets another play his most prized possession.*" It took prime real estate in his room on grand display.

. . .

Charlie lost himself in his guitar playing to ease his grief. He took the loss of his grandfather heavily. The house seemed like a tomb, it was so quiet. Celia couldn't bring herself to clean out his room so it sat, exactly as it had that last day as he had prepared for his final performance, like a shrine. Charlie would often find himself leaning in his grandfather's bedroom doorway staring at himself in the mirror and picture his Papa there practicing his "thank you".

He had mourned his grandfather for 18 months when he happened to have a strange encounter that helped bring Charlie out of his grief. Charlie had taken to visiting a local record shop on his way home from his high school. He spent hours in there looking through the various old recordings of some of the music his grandfather had taught him about. One day while flipping through the archived albums, he happened to look up and see an elderly woman standing opposite him also flipping through the albums. They looked right at one another and Charlie smiled before returning to his records. He was scanning over an old Louis Armstrong recording when the elderly woman spoke up.

"Nice to see someone your age appreciates the music from my time," she smiled at him. Her eyes were shining bright and she had a cheery smile with full, rounded cheeks.

Charlie nodded his head and said to her, "My family has always loved this music."

The elderly woman nodded back at him appreciatively. "Music can help you through so many things. It has a funny way of touching certain times in our lives." She motioned her head towards the album he was holding, "Louis Armstrong always makes me think of my husband," she said smiling sadly. Charlie passed the album to her for her to see and as she reached to take it from him she touched his hand.

"He makes me think of my grandfather," Charlie answered. She nodded her head again, looked at the album and then handed it back, watching him closely.

"Sometimes people who leave us too soon, leave the most lasting impression," she said to Charlie. "It's up to you to pass his memory on to those who didn't know him, be they stranger or kin!" she admonished, holding up a finger. "What was his name?" she asked Charlie.

"George Morningstar," he replied proudly.

"Oh, what a fine name," she said. "I do love the stars…" dreamily looking up, "*especially* the Morning Star! It shines so brightly for such a short time, but while it does, it outshines all others."

Charlie smiled at the elderly woman and looked back to the Louis Armstrong album. He read the names of the songs on the album and wanted to ask her if she had ever heard any of them. When he looked up to ask her, she was gone. He looked around the store in hope of seeing her down the opposite isle or even near the cashier, but she was nowhere to be found. Charlie stood there for a moment looking around and thinking, *"Huh!"*

. . .

Celia had also been mourning her father's loss. Now that Charlie was older, she had been going to the blues bars with Wade and Marco and sometimes singing along at their jam sessions to try and lift her spirits. She still had a voice that could rival any of the well known blues artists out there and Celia had dreams of spending her nights using her voice to make money singing in the clubs. More and more she would feed Charlie his dinner and see that he was doing his schoolwork and then race off to whatever club she was a guest singer at that night to belt out her best Billie or, for the more contemporary crowd, Janis. On such a night, Celia, Wade and Marco played and sang with a group of musicians that called themselves "Cobalt Blue." The piano player was a jolly 37 year old pot-smoking musician nicknamed "Campbell" because he liked the soup a lot. He was always in a good mood and could do accents and tell jokes like a pro. His easy manner and clever comebacks usually had the group laughing and the audience at the club liked his quips between songs. He let his hair grow shaggy and walked with a cool ease that had most women in the club swooning over him, including

Celia. She, Marco and Wade had performed with Cobalt Blue for the third week in a row and Celia was starting to flirt with the glassy-eyed piano man. He noticed the beautiful singer with her gorgeous hair, mesmerizing eyes and interesting last name.

Celia hadn't lost her looks at all despite the years of being a caregiver to George and a mom to Charlie. Her body may have thickened in the waist and her bust line might have swelled some, but it only added to her beauty. No longer an innocent of 18, but now a woman of 33, she had maintained a lovely figure and she still attracted a man's eye, including Campbell's. He had reciprocated her flirtatious advances and had hoped that he might find an opportunity to get her alone. As the band took a break half way through the gig, Celia remained behind on the stage. She went over and sat next to Campbell on his piano bench. She smiled at him suggestively and said, "You should think of something that you and I could do together," her hand stroking the smooth piano keys as she said it.

"Do you mean musically or otherwise?" Campbell asked her back, just as suggestively.

"Yes!" was all she said as she smiled ever wider, got up and walked off the stage.

Campbell was left sitting there, staring straight ahead as her retreating backside sashayed its way to the bar. He could barely swallow. Wow, he liked the way that girl moved! After the gig that night, Celia hung back, not heading out to Wade's car immediately. Campbell caught her eye and nodded to her. She went out to Wade and Marco waiting in the car and said, "Hey guys. Why don't you go on ahead? I'm gonna stay and work on some stuff with Campbell," she gestured her head towards the club and patted the window frame of Wade's door.

Right away, Wade was worried. He tilted his head at her and asked, "Is he gonna get you home safe?"

"Oh, yup," she answered straight away, nodding her head.

Marco, sitting in the passenger side of the front seat didn't seem the least bothered and waved her off. "Have a good night then, Celia," he said, eager to get home to Jean and Georgie.

Wade looked at her with a bold look. "You sure you're okay? You don't want me to stick around?" he asked her.

"Nope. No, I... uh... I'm sure we won't be here much longer and then I'll get a lift with him," she told Wade. She smiled and stepped back from the vehicle and waved them on. Wade drove off, squealing the tires slightly but Celia didn't notice. She was too busy planning her next move.

As she entered back into the club, Celia noticed that the room had cleared of most of the smoke and some of the patrons. She could easily see Campbell still on stage, sitting at the piano, tinkering with the keys. His mike wasn't on so she could barely hear the keystrokes as he lightly played his tune. Celia sat down beside him on the bench and listened to his melody for a time. He seemed to have played the same 16 bars over and over again. It was very pretty and soon Celia was vocalizing to Campbell's music. When they had gone through it eight times, they instinctively stopped at the same time.

Campbell was very impressed. He had never met this kind of singer with the kind of perfect pitch and musicality tossed together and an incredible vocal range as well. Celia was the real deal! Not to mention, she was gorgeous. Campbell loved to watch her lips and tongue as they formed the words or sounds she sang. What a turn on! He stared intently at her face for a few moments and then whispered heavily to her, "Let's get out of here!"

They gathered up their few belongings and made their way to the parking lot. Campbell's car was an old model Cadillac with large bench seats. He was parked to the furthest side of the lot. They threw their things into the front seat and both climbed into the car quickly. Before Campbell could reach for her, she was kissing him. They were crazed in their desire. Campbell couldn't get his hands on her quick enough and Celia was desperate to get across his lap and be dry humping with him as they kissed. It soon became obvious that their love making would be much better served if they were in the back seat. "In the back," Campbell motioned with his head, between kisses.

Celia, her top half up her body and her skirt lifted high, climbed up off Campbell's lap and hurled herself into the back seat giggling and laughing as Campbell followed. She managed to remove her top but left everything else on as Campbell succeeded in navigating his climb over the front seat and landed purposefully between her spread legs. He smiled down upon her and she raised her hips up to him. Resting on his arms, he held himself above her and began to kiss her passionately, his tongue searching her mouth, her tongue, her teeth. She felt ravaged by him and it was an incredible turn on! She had allowed herself few sexual encounters over the years and usually they left her feeling unsatisfied and wishing she hadn't bothered. Her first time with Brad had set the standard for what she expected love making to be like and her experience had taught her that most didn't live up to that. Add to that a baby to raise and then an ailing father for the past few years, Celia had invested very little into her sex life. Charlie turning 15 and her dad having passed, now gave Celia new found freedom she hadn't had for many years. She felt young and vibrant and in Campbell's passionate embrace she let her inhibitions go.

Campbell had removed her bra and hiked her skirt as far up her waist as it would go. He'd worked her panties to one side and was using his thumb to stimulate her as he kissed her deeply. She moaned at the pleasure he was giving her and unbuttoned his shirt, finally tearing away the last three to open him up to her. His erection was straining against his jeans and he pulled back a moment to drop them down. Efficiently, Campbell wore no underwear to impede the progress of their act and holding aside her panties he thrust himself into her in one quick motion. She cried out as the impact hit her but the pain felt good! He pistoned her quickly, feeling his arousal growing and warning her with a quick blurt, "I'm not going to take too long at this sweetheart. Hope you're close," he said, as his orgasm began to overtake him. She was and as he began to thrust madly and shoot his seed into her, she thrust back onto him exploding all around him with orgasmic contractions. It was quick but totally mind blowing! They lay there panting for a full minute before Campbell shifted his weight so that she was able to move into a more comfortable position. He then rolled off of her and sat up in the bench pulling his jeans back on.

"That was amazing", he said to her.

She had straightened her panties and skirt and was leaning forward to do up the clasp on the back of her bra.

"I'll say," she agreed, smiling. "Imagine how good it would be if we had a proper bed underneath us," she laughed.

"Is that an invitation?" he asked her. He could do this with her all night if she let him.

"Oh, I'm sorry Campbell, but I can't have you come home. Not just yet anyway. See, I have a boy who is 15. It would be wrong if I started bringing you home and taking you into my bedroom. He's old enough to know what would be going on. I couldn't do that to him," she said, hoping it wouldn't change how Campbell felt about her. He couldn't care less. She could have 15 one-year-olds at home and as long as she was willing to raise her skirt in the back of his car, he was fine with that. Sex was sex, no matter where it happened. She got herself put back together and waited until he had done the same. When he saw the buttons ripped off of the bottom of his shirt he looked at her and raised an eyebrow.

She smiled at him, "Don't worry. I can sew them back on."

"Forget it. Next time I'll know better and wear a T-shirt," he joked. He got out of the car and got into the front seat. She followed his lead. He possessively kept his hand on her upper thigh as he pulled out of the parking lot to take her home. Campbell pulled up in front of her house and turned off the car. No lights were on in the house and she hoped Charlie was fast asleep. They kissed for a few minutes and basked in the afterglow of their frantic lovemaking.

"I'm back on Thursday," she said to him.

"That's too long," he said, biting her luscious lips and groping at her breasts.

"I know but I can't sing until Thursday. I can't be out every night, not with my son," she explained.

He stopped kissing her and tried to catch his breath. God she was so intoxicating. "Make sure you come in Thursday then. I'll be anxious to see you. I'll drive you home again that night, if you want," he said, hoping she'd understand and agree. She nodded her head. He smiled and kissed her tenderly trying to keep his control in check. He could drag her into the back seat and screw her right here in front of her house and not give a damn about her kid or the neighbors.

"I gotta go," she whispered. She kissed him once more and hopped out of the car.

He watched her as she headed up her walkway to the front door. She turned and waved at him as she unlocked the door and stepped into the house. Campbell started the engine, turned the steering wheel hard and pulled a u-turn in the middle of the street. Off he drove from the same direction that he had come.

Neither one of them noticed Wade's car sitting in the dark on the opposite street corner. He had dropped off Marco safely to Jean and had made his way back to the club, parking in a darkened lot adjacent to the club's parking lot all in an effort to catch Campbell and Celia's second performance after the stage show. When they left the lot he followed shortly behind and stayed to watch them kiss good night. He had no right to feel so possessive of her — it's not like they had ever even come close to having a relationship past being good friends. But Wade felt a special closeness to Celia and wanted to be sure she was taken care of. He owed it to George. He drove away thinking he'd start by talking to Campbell. Maybe there was something more there than just a quick act of sex in the parking lot behind the club. Celia surely deserved better than that!

Thursday came and Celia had been anxious all day! What was it with her? There had only be two times in her life when she'd been careless sexually, her first and only time with Brad and then again on Tuesday night with Campbell. Both times she felt an *instant* sexual attraction and connection that made her do things she otherwise wouldn't do. She had some past experiences but all of them were within respectable time frames of meeting her beau. After all, she didn't go around loose. She wouldn't want Charlie ever thinking that she did. There hadn't been a long parade of men through the house; there hadn't been many nights out on a date. There had been only a handful, and of those she'd only slept with three of them. None of them were earth shattering experiences and for a while it honestly made her wonder if the memory she had of making love with Brad was blown way out of proportion now, almost 15 years later. How was anyone to measure up to that kind of a standard?

But Campbell gave Brad a run for his money! She couldn't quite put her finger on it, but there was something about him that made her feel sexy. This was new to her. Celia had felt wonderful in Brad's arms, but thinking back on it, she didn't *feel* sexy. Maybe she was too young then. Maybe now she'd lived a few more years and had a different perspective of what made her feel sexy. She decided not to analyze it too deeply and just enjoy the feeling. Although, she was still pissed at herself! She had sex without protection the first time and she ended up pregnant. Not that she'd change anything at all – she was blessed with Charlie! But since then she had made sure that the man she was bedding down with had a condom with him and thank God they had all worked. Until the night with Campbell. He hadn't stopped to put on a condom and she hadn't bothered to ask. And, she had sex in the back of a car! Regardless of how he made her feel, she had to control her urges better next time and insist on both a decent place to go to and a condom (at the very least!) She was hoping she hadn't already given a trashy first impression but figured she'd set him straight before the next time.

Celia drove in with Marco and Wade on Thursday night. As she pondered all her differing emotions in the front seat, her thoughts were interrupted by Wade.

"So, didja work on some new stuff for tonight, you and Campbell? Are you going to show us what you did?" he asked, knowing full well that he was goading her.

"What we did?" she asked him back, a bit of a shocked look on her face.

"Yeah, can ya show us what you worked on?" he pushed her.

"Oh, well, we didn't get too far along. He has some ideas about some older songs but we didn't actually talk about specific pieces," she lied. Wade sat quiet for a moment and wondered if he should just come right out and ask her what was going on, but he knew she'd only get annoyed at him and he didn't need her going on stage pissy with him. He really needed to talk to Campbell and see where his thoughts were. He decided to leave it until they got to the club. He'd feel out the situation first and then see if Campbell was willing to talk.

The club wasn't busy. In fact, there were only about four tables full in the whole place. Celia walked right over to the bar and ordered a cup of coffee, her favorite drink. Another thing she had learned from George, coffee kept you energized. She waited until the coffee came and then took the cup up onto the stage with her and took a seat at the piano. Campbell was nowhere to be seen. Celia tinkered with the keys, trying to recall a little tune that George had taught her when she was very young. The rest of the musicians had gathered on stage and prepared for their first set to start. They warmed up for just a moment and then all held their positions looking at Celia to get up to the mike.

"We're going to do this without Campbell?" she asked, her hand held palm up to the sky in question.

"He's not coming tonight, Celia," said Sam, the bass player. "He called and said he had something he had to take care of and couldn't sit in tonight. Didn't figure it would matter if we had no piano. We can cover just about everything with what we got here," he said casually.

Celia sat there in shock for a moment. Wade watched her reaction closely. He didn't know what Campbell thought but he was pretty sure that Celia put a lot more meaning into their intimacy than Campbell had. He knew guys like Campbell, so free and easy. It had its good points and it's bad. It was usually pretty rare to see these guys lose their cool, but the down side was that they really didn't give a shit about anything, including women and their feelings. Every girl was a *darling*, but then *every* girl was a darling! Wade worried that Celia had just fallen for the one guy on this stage that would treat her like that. He didn't get the attraction, but then, he wasn't a woman either.

"So? Let's do this without our piano, shall we?" suggested Sam. Marco twirled his drumsticks in the air and as they came down he began to drum a beat that all the other musicians followed. Celia stepped up to the mike, took a deep breath and started vocalizing with the music, a smooth jazzy improvised number that the small audience appreciated. Her mood served her well that night. Having Campbell not show up was like having Brad not call her all over again, only this time she didn't think there was a manipulative mother behind the scenes. Her singing was stellar, her confidence was not. She didn't disappoint the small Thursday night crowd but when the night was over she was grateful to be going home.

Wade dropped Marco off first and then drove over to Celia's.

"You okay, Celia? You seemed a little off tonight – not your singing but more your mood," he asked her, hoping she'd open up to him.

She turned her head away from his gaze so that he couldn't see the tear in her eye. "You know," she said forlornly, "I don't seem to have much luck in the love department, Wade."

"Love?" he blurted out, "…you're in love?" he asked her incredulously. He'd seen Celia and Campbell flirting but he didn't think there had been time to have fallen in love! She smiled. She didn't expect Wade to understand. In all the years she'd known Wade, she couldn't remember seeing him with a woman. Now as he got closer to middle age, she figured he'd probably spend his life alone.

147

"No, Wade I'm not in love," she said, reassuring him. "But I thought I was in a pretty good amount of *like*. And I led myself to believe that the feelings were reciprocated but I'm starting to think I was wrong."

"Well, then he's a fool," said Wade. "You deserve so much better than that, Celia. You deserve to be loved, properly. And admired, thoroughly, and adored completely. I know that your dad would say the same thing if he were here."

She smiled sadly at him. "Thanks Wade," she said. "That's very sweet of you." She sat for a moment and then said, "Do me a favor would you? Please don't mention this to Marco. He'll tell Jean and she'll give me hell. I don't need to feel any crappier than I already do."

With that, she parted his leg and got out of the car. Wade watched her get into her house and then sat out front for a moment longer. He wondered what it would take to get Celia to look at him romantically.

. . .

Once again, Campbell had not shown up for the night's gig. This was the third show he had missed in a row. His band mates were starting to get fed up and had brought along a different piano player named Eddie who smelled like Aqua Velva and made Celia's skin crawl. He could play the piano but had *slime ball* written all over him. Celia didn't like him, but then, she didn't have to, she only had to sing along with his playing. When he tried flirting with her she gave him a dead pan look and told him, "Don't bother, Eddie. I'm out of your league." And when Eddie hammered on the keyboard to show his displeasure she only matched it with her glorious voice. They may not have been well matched in any other way but they sure made great music together.

. . .

Five weeks had passed without a word from Campbell. Celia could only assume that he did not want to face her again and had decided to take his musical talents on to another club. It was difficult for her to believe that he'd let down the rest of his band mates just because he was reluctant to be around her, but then he had that free and easy thing going on so perhaps it didn't faze him much if he let them down. Celia had written him off and put it down to a lesson learned. When she came to the club now, she came to sing to the audience and perform, *not to flirt or find a man*, she'd admonished herself. Wade and Marco pulled up to her house one Saturday and honked once. It was the usual sign to notify her they were waiting for her and ready to go. This time, Celia didn't come out right away. Wade sighed heavily thinking they would be late if they took any longer and leaned on the horn to bring Celia out. Instead, Charlie emerged from the door and came running out to the car.

"She can't come guys, she's in there puking her guts out. Says her stomach is real queasy," he said, shrugging his shoulders.

"Does she have a fever?" Marco asked. "Did you feel her head?"

"No, I don't know what to do," Charlie said indignantly.

Both Wade and Marco rolled their eyes and got out of the car at the same time.

"For Christ's sake, Charlie, she's your mom," Wade lectured. "You gotta take care of her too, ya know." He led Marco into the house with Charlie following the two men, his head hung.

"Celia? Honey? Are you okay?" Wade called out as he entered.

"I'm in here," she called back weakly. She was sitting on the bathroom floor, looking terribly pale and sweaty. She was dressed in a black sequined dress that came to her knees and a matching headband, dressed for the stage. Her high heeled shoes were off to the side of the toilet and she had rested one arm on the seat and the other on the bathtub, wedged between the two. Her head was also hung.

"Aww… honey," Wade said as he knelt in front of her. "You got a bug?" he asked innocently.

She slowly lifted her head and looked him in the eye, a bit of a snarl on her face and sarcasm in her voice. "No, Wade," she said with a heavy sigh. "I don't believe I do." By then Marco and Charlie had also reached the bathroom and were both standing on the outside of the door frame peering in at her and Wade. All three men were confused by her statement.

"What do you think it is then, food poisoning?" he asked her, the aroma of dinner still fresh throughout the house. "Maybe you ate something that didn't agree?" he suggested.

"No, Wade," she repeated, "I don't believe I did."

"Then what do you think it is? Something more serious?" Wade asked her, trying to keep calm in case it was really bad news.

"I do believe that I'll feel much better in approximately six and a half months time," she said. She looked at the three pairs of eyes on her, all of them blank.

It was Marco, already a father to seven year old Georgie who finally clued in. "No shit, really?" he said excitedly. "I mean, is this okay, will you be able to manage?" he asked her.

"I'm going to have to, aren't I?" she said weakly.

Looking at the two of them she could tell that Wade and Charlie had no idea what they were talking about. She realized that she'd be better telling Charlie alone. She owed him that. It might embarrass him to find out his mom is pregnant in front of these men.

"Uh… Marco, why don't you and Wade go on without me tonight? Please send my regrets," she said nodding her head. Wade nodded, patted her on the knee and left the bathroom.

"Marco?" Celia called out to him. "Fill him in on the way, will you?" she asked him. He smiled very wide. Marco was a good man.

"Sure thing, doll. You take care, okay?" He winked at Celia and patted Charlie on the back as the two men left the house.

She sat between the two bathroom fixtures with her head drooping for a moment, taking pause before she confessed to Charlie the truth.

"You okay, mom?" Charlie asked her.

"Oh sure, just got a queasy stomach. Help me up will you?" she asked him as she reached out an arm.

He stepped into the room and pulled her up. She walked to the sink and rinsed her mouth taking a moment to sip some of the cool water. She wiped her hands and walked out towards the kitchen with Charlie following her. When she reached the kitchen she pulled out a chair and sat with a thump.

Charlie came into the kitchen and stood against the counter staring at her. He didn't know what was wrong, he just knew that she'd been sick on and off for a bit now. She seemed to eat nothing at all as everything put her off. He remembered stories that Papa used to tell him of when his grandmother Meg was very ill and he worried that his mother had the same thing. He braced himself for whatever she was going to say.

"Oh, Charlie," she sighed. "I have something to tell you."

She hesitated wondering what he was going to think. Her boy had grown into a fine young man. He reminded her of Brad so much. His hair was Brad's right down to the way it fell across his forehead when he leaned forward. He had his mannerisms and his gentle nature. How was it possible that the boy hadn't spent five minutes in his presence and yet sometimes when Charlie told a story or chatted easily with her on a Sunday morning, she couldn't help but think it was Brad sitting before her?

Celia had never really told Charlie much about his father. She'd been vague when he'd asked her at age five, enough so that he was led to believe she didn't know who he was. It didn't bother him so much then, but now Charlie was older and it bothered him that his mother didn't know who had fathered her only child. If Celia had known this was what he was thinking, she'd have set him straight, but it had never come up past their conversation when he was little and she was thankful for that. When he was very young, Celia's house had always been full of men, be it Marco or Wade or her father. And since George's death, Wade and Marco had really stepped up, both filling in, both feeling slightly fatherly towards him as neither had a son. Charlie had plenty of male role models to turn to and never felt the void of not having his father in his life. It was Anita who made Celia realize that she had loved Brad when she stayed at Manning House and she wasn't ashamed of having Charlie — not at all. But she was worried that, with Brad's mother being the super bitch that she was, Charlie would only get hurt by the rejection and she couldn't have him go through that. She really wanted to protect him from that. So, what Charlie didn't ask, didn't get answered and didn't hurt him.

Celia's stomach had settled somewhat and she was feeling a bit better. She found some saltine crackers and sat eating them slowly as she spoke to Charlie. She decided to tell him straight out, like ripping off the band aid.

"I'm pregnant, Charlie. Your mom is going to have a baby," she stated matter-of-factly between bites of a cracker.

He looked at her for a moment and then smiled a huge smile, relief washing over his face. His body dropped and he leaned onto the counter with his elbow to act as if he was near faint with reaction.

"Is that all?" he asked her, throwing his hands up in the air. "God, mom, I've been worried sick since you started throwing up every day. All I could think of was Papa's stories of Grandma Meg and how sick she got," he admitted.

"Oh, you poor dear," she said. "I'm sorry, honey, I didn't mean to worry you. I wasn't sure until a few days ago and I was hoping to wait until I got a little further along but Marco knows now and that means Jean will know as soon as he gets home tonight and..." she trailed off. "I thought you should be told before anyone else knew. And since you're the man of the house since Papa died," she said, "it's up to you to pass his memory onto those that didn't know him and *you're going to have to be the one to teach him all about being a Morningstar.*"

Charlie had heard those words before. He couldn't remember where or when but he had a strange sense of déjà vu.

Celia smiled at him feeling very proud. He had taken the news really well and seemed supportive and never once asked her the question she dreaded most, *who?* Charlie felt a heavy weight lift off his shoulders at his mom's beautiful smile and he pushed himself off the counter and came over to hug her around the neck. *Such a sweet boy,* she thought, *such a sweet, sweet boy.*

. . .

Once Wade found out about Celia's pregnancy he made it his mission to hunt down Campbell for an explanation. He might be playing busybody but he felt the man should know he'd impregnated a woman. He thought he should do right by her in some fashion. Maybe he was from a different age but when he grew up, you didn't treat women like that and you would never have disrespected them so much as to have had your way with them in the back of a car! He had seen a lot of musicians take advantage of their fame with the women that came to their performances. Times had changed a lot since the olden days when he and George would play together, but he thought Celia was owed an explanation and Wade wanted to get that for her.

He started by asking around the city to see who had seen Campbell recently. Wade spent a Thursday and Friday night going from club to club, seeing if he was either there himself or had been spotted. He had no luck from any of his contacts. His band mates hadn't heard anything from him in five weeks so Wade had to rely on his network of musicians and they didn't know anything.

He had sat down at the bar at the "Black and Blue" club and asked for a whiskey straight. The bartender, well known to Wade, put a glass in front of him and poured two fingers high of the amber nectar. Wade drank a generous gulp and put the glass down on the bar. He swallowed and braced for the breath to be taken from, and then come back to, his body. He wasn't a huge drinker but he'd needed that. The bartender went to put another shot into his glass but Wade covered his glass and shook his head.

"I still gotta find my buddy," he said.

"You looking for a friend are ya?" the bartender asked.

"Yeah, I'm not sure if he's left town completely or what. Do you know him?" Wade asked. "He's a piano player named Campbell." The bartender looked at him for a moment and thought for a second and then said, "You really a friend?" as he tilted his head in question. This raised Wade's attention. This guy knew something! Wade removed his hand and let the bartender give him a small shot more.

"Yeah, he's been AWOL for about five weeks now. Used to play with us all the time and suddenly he says he can't play one night and next thing you know we haven't heard from him. Do you know where I can find him?" Wade asked him. The bartender shook his head as he wiped down the bar in front of Wade. He looked over Wade's shoulders, out into the room, to see who was in there. He checked over the full length of the bar and then brought his eyes back to Wade.

"I don't know where you'll find him, but I doubt you will. I heard that he owed someone money for his smoking habit and he neglected to pay accordingly," the bartender said in a very low voice. He made direct eye contact with Wade and said, "I'd leave it the hell alone if I were you buddy. I wouldn't go digging any deeper than this."

With that the bartender stepped back from Wade's earshot and turned his attention to a patron down at the other end of the bar. Wade sat there contemplating his next move, nodded his head as if in agreement with himself and shot back the rest of the whiskey. He threw $50 on the bar and left. Money well spent.

Chapter 4

The Red Trunk

As Celia's belly grew, Charlie became fascinated with all things baby. He and Celia finally packed up George's room, cleaned it and painted it for the new baby coming. When Charlie asked her what color she wanted to paint the room, Celia replied *happy*, so he painted it bright orange. *Next time*, she thought, *I'll be more specific!* Wade brought over his father's old rocking chair at Jean's insistence; it hadn't been used in years. Jean and Marco had kept Georgie's crib just in case they had another child and now found that Celia needed it. They gave it to Charlie who surprised his mom by giving it a fresh coat of paint. They purchased a new mattress and bedding to complete it.

A lot of Georgie Pelos' old things were given to Celia to become cleaned up or refurbished in time for the new baby's arrival. And for his part, Wade would pull up with boxes of bottle liners or diapers for one year olds; things that weren't going to be needed right away, but his heart was in the right place.

He'd done far better as an Uncle when Georgie was born. She absolutely had him wrapped around her little finger. She only had to look at him with those large chocolate-brown eyes and her dark brown, loosely curled hair and he was a goner. Now, as she was seven, he was all but mush in her hands and with Celia's announcement, the word "baby" practically had him giddy.

Even Georgie herself was getting excited for the baby. She had been the youngest amongst all of them for her whole life and she was looking forward to passing on the baton! And a real baby to play with! She happened to be playing in the front yard of her home one day when Charlie came walking up.

"Hi Georgie!" he waved at her. She really was a cutie. He could understand why Wade became a giggly-goof whenever she started giggling around him. Her laugh was infectious and her smile could melt your heart.

"Hi Charlie!" she waved back at him. She really liked Charlie. He was always so nice to her and sometimes he played snakes and ladders with her and he would let her win. She was clever enough to know he did it and it made her like him more, even though he was a boy. He was very good at playing the guitar and when she visited at Celia's with her mom she would ask to use the bathroom and sneak into the hallway near his bedroom to spy on him using the reflection of a tall narrow mirror in his room. She could clearly see him sitting on his bed with his guitar in his lap plucking away at it with his eyes closed and biting his bottom lip. Sometimes, even his tongue would hang out and he'd bite it when he was really concentrating. She didn't always like the music but she liked how he concentrated on it. He was very cool.

"How's your mom?" she asked, hoping the baby was coming soon.

"She's doing good today, Georgie. Your mom and I are going to carry over some boxes of your things from when *you* were a baby, for us to go through. Wanna help?" he asked her.

"Oh sure!" she said and led Charlie into the house. She loved doing things for the new baby. "Mommy! Charlie's here to help with the boxes!" she called out to her mother.

"They're in Georgie's bedroom, Charlie," she called back from somewhere inside the house. "I'll just be a second."

Georgie showed Charlie where her room was and he saw the boxes piled up on top of a red steamer trunk.

"It's very nice of you to give up some of your things so my mom's new baby has stuff to play with," he told the chocolate-eyed little girl.

She smiled wide at him and she danced around her room. Jean came through her bedroom door and stopped to point out the boxes to Charlie.

"There's these here, Charlie," she motioned towards the boxes on the trunk.

"The trunk too?" Charlie asked.

"Oh no... that's a family heirloom, believe it or not. That trunk has traveled more miles than we'll ever know. It brought the original McGrath's from Ireland almost 100 years ago. It's been every McGrath's toy trunk for as far back as I can recall. Georgie's favorite dolls are in there."

As she said that she handed Charlie two of the boxes and took two, herself. Georgie took that moment to open the trunk and show Charlie her treasure trove of dolls.

"Wow!" he nodded approvingly. "I keep my favorite thing in a very safe case too, and it's in red as well!" Charlie said, making a fuss of the little girl.

She beamed at him, closed the trunk and followed her mother and Charlie out the door. She loved to help to do anything for Celia, Charlie and the new baby and maybe if she was really good, Celia would let her babysit from time to time!

157

Chapter 5

The Letter

Celia was starting to feel like the size of a house. She was in the last few days before the baby was due and she was ready and a half to have this child! Her pregnancy had gone very well and she was excited about welcoming a new person into her and Charlie's life. She wasn't concerned about how Charlie would manage with a new baby in the house; he had shown such love and support through the pregnancy that she felt like he was fully prepared to be an excellent big brother.

What she *was* concerned about was money. Things were very tight these days. Thank God for Marco, Jean and Wade who had all been so giving and generous of not only their food but also their time. Her father had willed the house to her and a small inheritance, but very small and it was long gone within a number of months of his death. Celia had been able to make a decent living with her performances, tips included. She had managed to keep up her performances throughout the city for some time but had to stop in the last month because she was too uncomfortable. She had never been in this situation before and it frightened her. She was even thinking that before long, she and Charlie would have to seek out Social Assistance for help with keeping food in the house. Now Celia faced having an additional mouth to feed.

This played upon Celia's mind as she sat outside in the warm summer's day. She could hear Charlie calling for her from the front of the house and she called out to let him know where she was. Charlie soon came bounding out of the back door with envelopes in his hand.

"Here, the mail's come," he said handing her the envelopes and returning straight indoors.

She dreaded the mail these days. The mailman never brought any answers, just bills. She needed answers and in a hurry! As she was flipping through the envelopes she happened to see one addressed to her from a law office called Birbaum & Gutfreund, LLP, in Peoria, Illinois. *Oh no!* she thought, *what's this about?* She tore open the letter and quickly caught a loose piece of paper as it fell out separately from the crisply folded letter, which read:

August 19, 1977

Dear Miss Celia Morningstar:

We are writing to you in representation of an anonymous client who recently purchased all shareholdings of the Morningstar Law Firm of Peoria, Illinois on or about the date of June 26, 1977.

Our client requested a thorough audit of the bookkeeping and an investigation into practices of the Morningstar Law Firm. The audit conducted found and reported errors regarding the execution of the Estate of Mr. & Mrs. William G. Morningstar. Upon this investigation it was determined that Mr. Wm. Morningstar (b. April 10th, 1902 : d. April 10th, 1952) had revised his will to leave his estate to the Morningstar Law Firm of Peoria, Illinois; however, his wife Mrs. Sharon Morningstar (b. January 3, 1906 : d. April 10th, 1952) died leaving no will.

An investigation into the car accident that claimed Mr. & Mrs. Morningstar's lives was required and it was further determined that Mr. Morningstar was found dead at the scene while Mrs. Morningstar died a short time later that night at the hospital. Mrs. Sharon Morningstar passed away after Mr. Wm. Morningstar making her the sole owner of the estate. This was overlooked in the initial declaration and the estate of Mr. Morningstar was, in the findings, wrongfully administered to the Morningstar Law Firm and its shareholders. As per the law of the State of Illinois, the estate of Mrs. Sharon Morningstar therefore goes to the State Treasury's Office for their determination as to who is the legal inheritor of the estate.

The State of Illinois researched the registrar's office and found Mrs. Sharon Morningstar had a son, Mr. George William Morningstar (b. March 13, 1925 : d. March 14, 1975). The registrar's office listed Ms. Celia Grace Morningstar (b. February 2, 1944) as the daughter of Mr. George Wm. and Meg Morningstar (b. January 2, 1925 : d. April 12, 1949). It is therefore deemed that Miss Celia Morningstar be the sole recipient of the estate of Mrs. Sharon Morningstar, by the laws of the State of Illinois and from Peoria District Court Office £39.

Our client has retained this firm to locate Miss Celia Morningstar and deliver the notification and inheritance. The State has retained all applicable fees and taxes having to do with this case (#545718). Please find enclosed a cashier's check in the amount of $279,226.12 from the State of Illinois. Further enclosed please find a detailed accounting of the disbursements of the estate of Mrs. Sharon Morningstar.

If you have any questions or concerns, please don't hesitate to contact our offices.

Yours sincerely,

Mr. R. Gutfreund, LLP

Birbaum & Gutfreund, LLP

Legal Associates

Celia read the letter three times. Her right hand, holding the check, began to shake. She daren't look at it in case it was a joke and the check was blank. *Was this for real?* she wondered. *Was she seeing things?* She carefully looked over the letterhead, closely examining the signature, the address, the letter completely. She then turned her attention to the check. It was made out to *Miss Celia Grace Morningstar.* On the *memo* line, it read:

Estate: #545718 Morningstar, S D.O.D: 4/10/1952

It certainly looked authentic. And she wasn't sure about the dates for her grandparents, but she knew her father's birth date and when he died and *her* birth date *for certain*, and they were all correct. She read the check again: Two hundred and seventy-nine thousand, two hundred and twenty-six dollars and twelve cents. Celia began shaking. She suddenly burst up out of her chair and starting whooping and yelling.

Charlie came running back out to see what was wrong with her. He figured it was the baby and he ran to her side as she was jumping about with her huge belly and yelling so that it was heard throughout the neighborhood.

"Mom… mom…" Charlie tried to help her. "Calm down mom… is it the baby?" he asked, wondering what on earth was wrong with her.

She had tears streaming down her face and a huge wide grin and she was hugging Charlie one minute and jumping up and down the next. She finally stopped to explain and catch her breath when she felt a *whoosh* from her insides and looked down to see the puddle of water at her feet.

"Oh, Charlie," she said looking up at him, giddy with joy, "we are going to remember *this* day!"

Chapter 6

Chase and Charlie

Charlie raced around the back yard with the sandy-blonde haired toddler in close pursuit. Charlie wasn't really trying to run away, rather just get the little guy worn out so that they'd have a good night's sleep for a change. His baby brother was wearing both he and his mother out with his unending energy and he wanted that remedied fast!

Nicholas Morningstar was already two and a half years old and was the apple of both his mother's and his older brother's eye. When he was first born, Celia struggled with a name. She had just finished reading a novel on the Russian Tsar Nicholas and she thought it was a strong name, despite his ending. But Charlie had been insistent that Nicholas carry his biological father's *last* name, which angered Celia when he suggested it. It didn't seem as if he thought Chase was any different, he just thought it was important that Chase not be a "Morningstar."

"Why would I do that?" she asked him with a temper on. "He's a "Morningstar" no different than you or I or your Papa and if he were standing here today, he'd say so himself," she told him angrily.

She didn't want to admit to Charlie that she wasn't even sure of Campbell's real first name, let alone his last name. It just made her seem without morals and although it may look that way, it wasn't like that at all.

163

"Why is it so important to you, Charlie?" Charlie just shrugged his shoulders and lowered his head. "I don't know," was his reply.

"No" she told him flatly, he's *Nicholas Morningstar,* end of discussion."

Except, he was never really called that. Oh sure, his birth certificate read "Nicholas Morningstar" but Charlie referred to him as *the smile with motorized legs* and Celia referred to him as *Chase* because all he ever did was *"chase"* after Charlie.

Soon, everyone started calling him that and after a while it just stuck. Everyone in his world called him *Chase* and so Nicholas became Chase. *It suited him more,* his mother thought as she watched her nearly 18 year old boy run around with her two and half year old baby chasing him. Things just didn't turn out as you'd think!

Just when she thought she was going to make her way as a blues and jazz singer in Chicago's city clubs she became pregnant. And just when she was down and out needing some kind of luck to come her way, a windfall from an inheritance she had no idea she was entitled to, had arrived in the mail! Life became so much easier after that check was delivered and just in time too. Quite literally! Its arrival brought on her labor with Chase. In all the commotion she had misplaced the check in one of the many bags she took with her to the hospital and there was a nervous few days before she found it and had it safely deposited into her bank account. She had paid off all debt, put a lump sum in her checking account, a lump sum into some investments through the bank and took a few thousand home with her to share the wealth with Wade, Marco and Jean. She bought Jean a new dishwasher and took her on a shopping spree. For Marco she bought a new drum kit. For Wade she bought a new case for his beloved trumpet and a few dress shirts for when he performed. She also bought a used car and she and Charlie took driving lessons so that if they needed to get about, neither had to depend on anyone else. This wasn't Wade's favorite decision and in some ways he cursed her getting the money because it meant she didn't depend on him for things as much anymore. Lastly, she took them all out to the best club/restaurant in the city that would allow Charlie and had a grand old time.

Yes, that letter could not have arrived sooner! It had made such a difference in their lives. Charlie was able to attend to his schooling, not needing to take an after school job to help out. Once his home work was completed his would sit and play his guitar for hours on end, breaking only for Chase, food and bathroom visits.

Celia could stay at home to raise Chase, filling his world with the music she and Charlie loved. She was worried their windfall would change their world too much, so she kept the same house that George had willed to her, staying close to the friends that now completed her family and she made sure that the three Morningstar's sat around the dinner table each and every night and thanked God for their blessings. She gave up singing in the clubs while she stayed home to mother Chase, he now becoming her captive audience. On days when Jean would visit, Chase would have front row seats to some of the best blues singing in the city, and his appreciation was so genuine. He would clap his hands and squeal with delight and yell "Nuther," to his mommy and Jean. He was their #1 fan!

Charlie, on the other hand, did not need hands on mothering anymore. Charlie was becoming a man and started showing signs that he needed some space. Celia had noticed a change in Charlie since Chase's arrival, his mood had become quieter, distant. He would often take to his room, not saying anything to anyone for hours. He was a huge help in the household but he and Celia often butted heads about how things should be done or how late he could stay out. He even started having an opinion on how Chase should be raised which didn't go over very well with her. He would borrow the car and go for long drives by himself, out to the more rural areas that outlay Chicago. His mother had her concerns. Charlie had his reasons.

He'd drive under the stars and sing to the radio or the tape that was playing in the cassette. He had never sung for anyone before having only found his voice a few months previously but now when he wasn't in his room playing beautiful music on his guitar "Meg", he loved to drive alone and sing to his heart's content with no one else as audience, trying hard not to think about what worried him most.

Celia wanted to keep Charlie from the bar scene until he was of age but he met some older boys who were able to get him into bars and clubs with a fake I.D. He hadn't been irresponsible in any way but she found him drunk on the front step one early spring morning at 5:30 am.

"What are ya doing out here, Charlie?" She asked him, bleary eyed. She'd only a few minutes more before Chase would be up and going at 100 miles an hour and she was hoping to spend every moment in her bed.

"Waiting," he said, his head drooping and his eyes heavy.

"Waiting for what, honey?" she asked him gently. It was cold and she wanted to get him inside.

"The Morning Star," he said as he yawned loudly, and then he continued. "Someone once told me they loved the Morning Star and I realized that I had never been up early enough to look at it," he told her sloppily. "Of all the millions of stars in the sky, she chose that one to love the most…" He shrugged his shoulders. "I just wanted to see what all her fuss was about."

"Was she a girl you liked?" Celia asked, unaware of his encounter with the elderly woman all those years ago.

"No, mom," he shook his head and hung it in frustration. "She was… like… like… one minute she was there saying that she loved the stars and the next she was gone." He snapped his fingers for effect.

She smiled at him and pulled her housecoat closer, waiting for the Morning Star to make its appearance. She wasn't really sure what Charlie was talking about but she knew him to be a very talented sweet boy with a dark worry that he carried and drinking it away with the older boys he had started hanging out with was not going to help or further his career. As they sat there waiting, Charlie started humming. Before she knew it, he was singing to no one in particular. . .

Amazing Grace, how sweet the sound,
That saved a wretch, like me.
I was once lost, but now am found.
Was blind, but now I see.

She had never heard Charlie sing before. For a moment, she thought about joining with him, harmonizing to his singing, but she stopped herself, wanting to hear him. His rich, deep voice was beautiful, filled with passion and heart. He had great range and hit every note spot on. Celia sat thinking how incredible it was that he was blessed to have George's musicality and her wonderful voice – talk about passing down familial traits! The three of them looked nothing alike. You wouldn't have taken them as blood relations if you were to meet them all together on the street and yet there was no mistaking where Charlie got his talents from. He could go out into the world and really make something of his life. Much like George had wanted, much like she had wanted. *Now it's Charlie's turn,* she thought, *I have to help make this happen for him.*

They sat silent for a long time until Charlie suddenly pointed into the sky and said, "Look Mom! There it is." He studied it for a moment and then said, "It's so bright."

Celia looked where he pointed and could see a small bright dot standing proud against a blue and coral morning sky. Wispy, thin clouds completed the picture perfectly. Silence fell over them again until finally Charlie said quietly, "I get it now." He nodded his head and stood up. He turned around on the front step and held his hand out to his mother, helping her up and into the house. *Such a sweet, sweet boy.*

. . .

Celia had decided that it was time to talk to Wade about Charlie's career. Wade could get him into the clubs and keep an eye on him. Wade could keep Charlie safe and maybe introduce him to the right people – people who would know what to do with that kind of talent. The next time he came over for a visit, she spoke to him in private.

"I have a favor to ask of you, Wade," she began. "And I realize I have no right to ask any favor of you for all that you've done for me and the boys. But this one is kind of special."

She smiled at him and he smiled back. He'd have gone to the moon for this woman. She had no idea how he felt but over the course of the years he had come to realize that she was the only woman for him. If he couldn't have her, then he was going to be satisfied with being her friend and helping her and her kids in any way he could. Wade sat waiting for the request wanting to say *yes*, even before she had asked.

"I think Charlie is ready to get out there and start performing. He's good Wade, he's very good. And, he's got a great voice. I mean beautiful... great tone, nice resonance, perfect pitch, he's the real deal Wade," she bragged, rightfully so. "I would prefer it if *you* could introduce him to the nightclub world. Maybe see if one of the owners would let him sit in for a night or two, get his feet wet?" she stopped. She wanted to hear what he had to say, but she was ready to sell him more to Wade if she had to.

"You're preaching to the choir here, Celia," he smiled, nodding his head. "I've wanted Charlie out there for a while now but I didn't want to overstep. I mean, I can't just walk into your house and start this ball rolling without your consent," Wade said sincerely. "But I'll tell you what I've been thinking. I think Charlie is good enough that he could start anywhere and I've been hoping that you would allow me to take him on a little tour with me? I have some gigs lined up over the next few months and they go all over the southern states. His kind of blues and jazz guitar playing would be a huge success down there, you know?"

He paused expecting to hear her stop him and shut down the deal. When she didn't he continued, "I mean, we could start around here, see what he does in front of a crowd, but really, I don't think it'll be long before he's out past state lines playing for larger crowds than what the "Black and Blue" can hold."

There, he'd said it to her straight. Charlie needed to be traveling and touring and Wade wanted to make sure that she understood it meant he'd be gone from home. They stared at each other, neither knowing what the other was thinking. Celia looked down to the ground as if contemplating something and then said, "Charlie won't want to stay in a hotel every night. He likes his own bed. And besides, if you have to pay for rooms everywhere you play, there won't be much money to keep."

Oh here it comes, thought Wade, *she won't want him to be away, she'll want him home every night. Damn!* Her next sentence shocked the hell out of Wade and nearly had him fall out of his chair.

"I'll buy you a bus!" she exclaimed, clapping her hands together at her revelation. This was a brilliant idea, they could travel on the bus, have a home anywhere they parked and Charlie would have the same bed every night. This would be the best way for him to feel comfortable and able to be away from home. She loved it!

"A bus?!" Wade said, astonishment written all over his face. "What the hell for?" he asked her.

"Wade, it'll be like a trailer home, you know? It'll have beds on it and a kitchen and a bathroom. I've seen them advertised for people who like to travel and camp, only you guys will travel and play! Apparently, all the rock stars travel in buses so why can't you?" she asked him, palms up in the air, shoulders shrugged.

He didn't have any answer for her. He knew she still had some money from her inheritance and he wasn't so sure he wanted her spending it frivolously on a bus tour that may only last a few months.

"A bus is gonna cost, Celia," he warned her, tilting his head to one side.

"Well I ain't gonna buy you a top o' the line, friggin' Greyhound!" she admonished him jokingly with her hand on her hip. "We could go and look and see what they have and what the price is. We'll make sure that it has all the features you two will need. It'll be perfect," she gushed. "I only wanted you to take him to the clubs around town so trust me, if you want me to be okay with my baby leaving my house and touring, this is the *only* way we are going to agree," she told him straight.

He nodded and understood. Agreed!'

...

After a few weeks of searching, Celia and Wade found a suitable camper-bus. It was a school bus that had been excellently converted into a camper by a family that once loved to travel. They went all over the U.S., Canada and into parts of Mexico with it. They painted it navy blue with white accents around the windows and the inside was just like a little home away from home. The traveling family was all grown up now and the bus wasn't in use as much so they decided to sell it. It was perfect for what Wade and Charlie needed.

Celia had Wade drive it to a car wash where she marched inside it with a bucket of bleachy soapy water, a pair of rubber gloves and half dozen cloths and wiped every surface down twice, then rinsed it twice as well. She stripped all the bedding and bought new mattresses and bedding for the three beds. She raided her own kitchen for unused pots, pans, cutlery, dishes, condiments and other useful kitchen items. Wade did the same recognizing that he didn't need to have a fully stocked house when he'd be on the road for the next little while. Between the two of them they managed to completely outfit the inside of the bus without spending a dime. They even brought in a small color TV set for entertainment.

Wade made some calls and spoke to most of the owners of the places he'd already lined gigs up for himself. He asked that they give Charlie a chance, even just a quick tryout during the day, before a night's performance and see what the kid had. He promised them on his mother's soul that Charlie would not drink a drop of liquor and wouldn't be a problem during his entire time in the club.

Celia had waited to tell Charlie of her plans until everything was set in place. She wanted him to *want* this too. She wanted him to envision his life performing for others. But Charlie was shy and reserved and carried some kind of weight on his shoulders. He didn't give away any secrets and Celia found it hard to break through the protective outer shell he had created. The only time he seemed to feel at ease was the few times he'd play for her. He didn't do it often but if she goaded him enough he would bring out Meg and play a little something for Celia and the rest of their makeshift family. *He was so damn good!* And she could see it in his face. Charlie's face would become soft and it would light up from within. He'd lift his face to the heavens as if being channeled by a higher force. When it came to his music, Charlie went into another realm, but he didn't do very well with people – always staying back from crowds, singing with his eyes closed. He didn't do very well with girls either although they all fawned over him. He seemed to lack the self confidence needed to be on the stage and Celia knew it. It worried her because she could easily buy him a bus, outfit the thing to the nines and pay to gas it until they starred making a bit of cash, but she couldn't buy Charlie self confidence. He had to gain that for himself. How could he not be self-confident? She didn't get it. He was handsome, looking just like Brad at age 18. Although, Charlie was not as tall as Brad and nowhere near as muscular. Brad had been a sports player in high school; Charlie played music, mostly the guitar. But just as the girls had crushed over Brad, Charlie also had girls that went dreamy when he was near. Celia had seen it with her own eyes when she picked him up from school once or twice. When she inquired as to who they were and suggested, "...why don't you ask one of them over. You could play your guitar for them," Charlie would only blush and hang his head. So she wasn't sure how this whole, "you're going to go on tour with Wade and perform on stage and be hugely famous," idea was going to be taken. She only hoped he'd be willing to at least try.

. . .

Celia decided to let Charlie know on his last day of school. He graduated from High School with honors. He didn't attend his prom nor did he apply to college out of state because he wanted to stay near to his mom and Chase. It was Charlie's intention to see about teaching music like his grandfather did and his mom needed him around now more than ever. He really wanted to be there to help raise little Chase and do his grandfather's memory proud.

He came home on his last day of school. Having cleaned out his locker, he was carrying many books and binders and school paraphernalia. He came through the kitchen and dropped all of it on the kitchen table.

"And that sums up my 12 years of education," he said triumphantly. "Go ahead... ask me anything," he said jokingly with a huge smile on his beautiful face.

"Okay," said Celia as she sipped her coffee, leaning against the counter. She eyed him closely wondering what his reaction would be and then asked, "What would you say to going on tour with Wade for the summer?" She dropped it on him like a bomb.

"What?" he stopped cold. The smile dropped from his face and he looked at her blankly.

"Wade has some gigs lined up all over the lower states for the next two months, maybe more, and he wants to take you with him," she explained, a tentative smile on her face. When he didn't say anything she continued. "Charlie, I think you're ready for this, honey. I think you should get out there and play your ass off. The audiences will eat you up!" She started getting excited as she tried convincing him. "Now, I know it's probably a bit worrisome for you but Chase and I will be fine here. Marco and Jean and little Georgie are just down the road and money isn't a worry anymore," she assured him. "We'll be fine here, honey," she paused and then grabbed his wrist with her hand and held it tightly to emphasize her words, "I want you to do this. I want you to have this kind of life!" she said, staring at him hard. She then dropped her hand and backed away giving him the time and space to process it all.

Charlie's mind was reeling! She wanted him to go on tour? *What for?* Charlie dreaded the thought of playing in front of others, having only ever done it for the four adults and two children that filled his life and that was only once or twice. His friends had never *really* heard him play although he had done guitar work at school. It wasn't blues or jazz though, it was more for school band and he played in the orchestra pit for a production of "Guys and Dolls." Otherwise, Charlie was an unknown. He didn't want to be up there, the centre of attention with all eyes on him. He loved playing music but wasn't sure he wanted to be a *performer*, per se.

"I didn't really want to go on stage, mom," he tried explaining. "I want to teach like Papa did, you know?"

"Really Charlie?" she asked him, incredulously. "You have such God-given talent, such a blessing in your ability to play instruments and your singing voice… why on earth would you not want to share that?"

"What about teaching it to others, Mom, what about that?" he fought back. This was starting to piss him off. He hadn't wanted to ever be a huge famous *anything*, he only wanted to pass along his grandfather's teachings, as he'd been told. It was up to him after all. He was happy just to be Charlie Morningstar who played the guitar and taught music.

"Charlie, honey, I am trying to help you, honestly I am," she said. "You have to believe me when I tell you that you are gifted, *truly* gifted. You've been doubly blessed. God doesn't want you to hold that in to yourself. He wants you to share that with the rest of the world," she told him. Charlie shook his head knowing he wasn't going to win this fight. But he didn't want his mother to have the final say.

"I'll do it until the end of the summer. If I'm not happy, then I'm coming home and going to college for teaching," he said firmly. "It isn't *my* dream to be on the stage, Mom, that was yours and Papa's but it's *never* been mine," he said grudgingly and walked out of the kitchen without saying another word, his head hung down. Last day of school, first day of a long dreaded summer. Charlie wasn't happy.

Celia let Charlie have his mood for a little while. He'd see she was right in the end. She hadn't bothered to tell him about the bus, she'd wait to tell him that when the time was right. At least she'd got him to agree to tour for the summer. At least he was willing to give it a try. She was sure that by the time he'd get out there and get the high from the audience, he wouldn't think twice about returning for college in the fall.

That night she prepared his favorite lasagna dinner and made a nice fresh strawberry pie to sweeten his mood. She called the boys to the table and waited for them to come to the kitchen. Chase entered first from the back yard. He was covered in grass stains and dirt and had been pulling up some of the dandelions that spotted the yard.

"Look, mommy," he said proudly, "I brought you some flowers!" His chubby hand produced a bunch of the weeds complete with ants crawling on some of the yellow heads.

"Oh, thank you, Chase! Mommy just loves them and I'll put them in some water while you clean up for dinner," she fussed. "Remember to wash your hands," she called after him as he ran towards the bathroom.

She threw out the dandelions that had ants, keeping three or four for her bouquet. She dropped them into her water glass sitting at her place, moved it to the centre of the table and waited for either of her boys to come into the kitchen. Chase came running back and boosted himself up and knelt on the chair to reach his dinner. His mother served him a small portion of lasagna and passed him the rolls. He took one and bit into the roll right away. She shook her head at him. "Don't fill up on bread Chase, eat your dinner too." She mussed his hair and put the roll basket back on the table.

"Charlie?" she called out. "Dinner is on the table and getting cold!" He came walking in a short time later with a long face and a hung head.

"Oh, come on now, Charlie, it won't be that bad. Wade'll take care of you and he won't put you into any situation that you don't want to be in," she assured him. "And I haven't even told you the best part," she said, deciding now she would tell him about the bus. "I've bought a bus that you and Wade can tour around in. It's all decked out like a mini home with a kitchen and a bathroom and your *own bedroom!*" she emphasized. "That way you won't be in a different hotel room every night and wanting for your bed. Wait till you try the mattress, it's pretty cushy." She bent close to his ear and whispered, "I spared no expense!"

Lastly, she dished out a huge piece of lasagna onto his plate and sat down with a sweet smile on her face and leaned towards him with her chin in her hand and her elbow resting on the table and gushed, "I also made a fresh strawberry pie!" Just to sweeten the deal!

. . .

Charlie loaded the bus up with his clothes, Meg and some personal things he wanted to bring along. As much as he was pissed at Celia for pushing him in to this, he couldn't fault her for making sure that he lived in comfort while he was gone. The bus was pretty cool! His mattress on the bus was better than the one he had at home and he made a note to do something about that when he got back in the fall. He loved the kitchen area. Although he didn't really know how to cook, he figured he and Wade would botch it out together while they were gone, and his mom had filled the freezer part of the half-sized fridge with portion sized frozen meals like lasagna, meatloaf and shepherd's pie. She had even written instructions for cooking each one on a piece of paper and taped it to the top of the frozen item. The rest of the fridge was stocked too. He had to admit, if he was going to have to do this, she sure knew him well enough to know that *this* is how he'd want to do it. Charlie liked his privacy.

After Celia had found him outside on the front steps that night, she found him out there regularly, but not drunk. Sometimes, he'd get up in the wee hours and sit outside listening to the night as it crept by, cricket by cricket, star by star, until at last he would see the Morning Star and then, satisfied, he'd crawl off to bed. His bedroom was his sanctuary and although he was ever indulging of Chase, he forbid him to enter his bedroom without Charlie being in there at the same time. He also moved his grandfather's guitar into his room since Chase began to walk, hiding it away under his bed so that Chase wouldn't get into it.

Celia believed more than ever that Charlie needed this time away. He carried something, something she couldn't put her finger on but it had changed her son from an easy going child with a natural love for music into a troubled teen who turned to music to ease his tortured soul. *Typical teen angst?* Celia didn't think so. There was something more going on. She secretly hoped that some time with Wade might coax it out of him and Wade would be able to talk him through it. At the very least, he could inform her of her son's troubles and maybe she could be of help to him. Regardless, it was apparent to her that Charlie had changed over the last little while and she didn't know why.

Charlie and Wade were set to get going. The bus was packed up and all ready. They enjoyed a good luck celebratory dinner the night before with Wade, Celia, Charlie, Marco, Jean, Georgie and Chase all in attendance. Wade even made a little "speech" thanking Celia for the bus, Marco and Jean for looking after his house in his absence, Chase for allowing his brother to be gone for a while (to which Chase began to cry) and offering praise to Charlie for his willingness and integrity to do something so monumental. Charlie blushed when he said it because it didn't feel that way to him – rather he couldn't wait for it to be all over and done with. At the end of Wade's impromptu speech, the small gathering of seven raised their glasses to toast the touring musicians, wish them much success and pray for their safe return.

Chapter 7

Chase and Georgie

Once Charlie and Wade left, it created a huge void in Chase's life. His older brother was his favorite play toy and he wasn't around to occupy him or exhaust him, as Celia soon came to realize. She was grateful when Jean came over and brought Georgie with her. Georgie was a terrific distraction for Chase and she seemed to love bossing him about and mothering him. *She'll make a fine mother one day*, Celia thought, as her youngest son picked up after himself with Georgie nipping at his heels about not making messes and keeping his things tidy. The two ladies agreed that when the time came, Georgie would be the perfect babysitter for Chase and she was already trying it on for size.

Chase adored Georgie. She certainly did help fill in Charlie's absence. When he first began speaking, he couldn't quite get her name right as she was "Dordie" to him. He called her that for a long time until she sat down with him one day and patiently taught him how to say it properly. He was so proud of himself he called everything "Georgie" for about an hour afterwards. He liked the way it sounded when he said it.

Sometimes they sat and watched a movie or TV show together and if he got tired, she'd cuddle up into a blanket with him and they'd snooze while the show played on. It was Chase's favorite thing to do. Georgie smelled so nice and he'd play with a strand of her dark hair as his eyes got heavy and within minutes he'd be sound asleep. The mothers would peek in to the living room and see Georgie and Chase all snuggled up and fast asleep in front of the TV and smile to each other. Jean knew her daughter well and she was a loving and caring little girl. At 10 years old, Georgie was already showing maturity far beyond her years, probably due to the fact that she spent the majority of her time around adults. She had a few friends from school and she would sometimes be invited over to their houses to play or for a sleepover, but mostly she stayed close to home and looked forward to visits at Celia's house. When she visited and Charlie was at home, Georgie hung on his every word. He had a serious side and he was a thinker. Charlie was very smart and Georgie hoped that one day he would think that she, too, was very smart. She purposely sought him out when she had a problem and he would listen patiently to her and then provide an answer that she had already thought of. They thought the same way and she liked that. Georgie thought Charlie was wonderful and as she got older, it only intensified.

With Charlie gone for the summer, Georgie got to know Chase a lot more. She thought he was very creative and funny and he always had a smile on his face with the energy enough to power his million watt smile. Whenever Georgie taught Chase to do something, he'd always go beyond expectations. She taught him his numbers and letters and pretty soon he was not only spelling his name, he was spelling hers as well. She taught him how to made sand castles, only Chase made such a grand castle that Georgie called Celia and her mom out to show them his creation. It was beautiful; he even used discarded soda caps as the castle's dentil molding capped walls. When they colored together, he didn't just color, he outlined, he shaded, he stayed well within the lines and when it was complete he'd put a small scribbly "CM" in the corner as if it were a work of art. Georgie was always impressed when he'd show her whatever new little project he finished. For a three year old boy, Chase had definite creative talent. *It was nice that Georgie had a different relationship with each of Celia's boys,* thought Jean. *Hopefully they'll know each other all throughout their lives and be able to appreciate the other as they grow into adults.*

As the summer stretched into the long, hot days of August, their playtime activities generally included water. Celia would set up the sprinkler in the backyard and Georgie and Chase would run through it for the better part of the day, happily occupied and kept cool. If it was too hot, Celia brought everyone into the living room and turned on the air conditioning (another splurge) and they'd sing and dance to music on the radio. Celia didn't mind the music that was coming out these days. Artists were more versatile now, and since Elvis and the British Invasion, people's attitudes had changed toward the way artists performed. It seemed the more outrageous they were, the happier their audience was. Celia preferred her older blues and jazz to what was out there, but she was able to find herself singing along to Michael Jackson, Prince and even Eric Clapton. She and Jean would dance around the room with Georgie and Chase trying to copy their moves and giggling the whole time. *It had been such a fun summer*, thought Celia. She only hoped it was going as well for Wade and Charlie. She had heard from them just a few times. It was hard to make long distance calls at a pay phone and although she'd told them to call "collect" they never did. Celia was hoping to hear from them in the next few weeks to find out if Charlie was still headstrong about teaching. If he was, then she'd move on to plan B, whatever that was.

Chapter 8

The Summer Tour

Wade and Charlie first set out to play some of the smaller clubs that dotted the outside of Chicago's city limits Wade set them up for a night playing at a tucked away little gem called "The Blues House". It was very small with an intimate crowd and Wade thought Charlie might do better there than a bigger club with a jumping audience. The owners name was Tim Plat, a tall dark haired man who seemed to like Wade a lot. When they met up, Tim was vigorously shaking his hand and telling him it had been too long.

"This is Charlie Morningstar, the kid I was telling you about," Wade said, introducing Charlie to Tim.

"Hey Charlie," said Tim, shaking his hand in a firm grip. "I understand you've got quite the gift with the guitar. Wanna show me?" he asked. Charlie's head dropped, instinctively shy about his playing but he knew the deal and had to at least try.

"Uh… sure," he responded, not looking Tim in the eye. Charlie brought his guitar case up onto the nearest table and opened it up, revealing Meg to Tim.

"Wow!" he said and then whistled a wolf whistle. "That's a Gibson Les Paul. And she's a beauty! Where'd you get her from?" Tim asked, as

181

he bent over to inspect the guitar still in its case. "I mean look at the work here," Tim continued without waiting for Charlie's answer, as he pointed to the frets and the detailed inlay of wood. Charlie waited a moment letting the man have a good look at it, happy knowing that his grandfather's fine gift was also appreciated by others.

"It was a gift from my grandfather for my seventh birthday," Charlie said proudly.

"Seventh!" exclaimed Tim. "It was probably bigger than you then!" he laughed. "How long did it take before you could actually play it?" Tim asked him, standing straight up and now giving Charlie his full attention.

"Well... uh... within a few months my grandfather was teaching me and I was using it. I had to sit most of the time and I had the strap adjusted so much that the unused part almost hit the floor."

Charlie smiled as he recalled his stroke-riddled grandfather helping him put Meg on and how they'd converse back and forth using their guitars. He didn't tell Tim that part but it made him feel better thinking about his grandfather when he was about to play for this guy. *Whoever he is, I like him,* thought Tim. Someone who plays the blues and jazz ought to have some kind of mentor from the past to draw from – some kind of story that gives them the passion and the soul to be able to play the music from the heart. *Otherwise it's just shit, it ain't real,* he thought.

"Well, come on and show me what you got," Tim said, motioning Charlie towards the stage. Charlie hesitated a moment. He had never stepped foot on a stage before and especially not with Meg in his hand. This was his secret he was about to share. This was the place he went to that no one else could and now he was about to open it all up and let the world in. *I need to calm the hell down!* he thought. What was that technique his grandfather had taught him so many years ago? It was a breathing technique he showed him after Charlie fell off a cement wall he was trying to walk along. He hadn't fallen far but landed badly and sprained his ankle. "Breathe, Charlie... breathe, in through the nose, out through the mouth in a four beat pace. It will help bring down your heart rate and get you steady again," his Papa told him. He had used it many times throughout his childhood. Now, as he was about to take his first step into a new world, he was hearing his grandfather's words once again ringing in his ear.

Continuing with his breathing, Charlie took Meg from her case and carried her to the stage. He preferred to sit when he played, just from having done it for so long. He grabbed the nearby piano bench and dragged it over to centre stage. There were only three or four people in there and Charlie was sure two of them were wait staff which meant he was only really playing for Tim and Wade, and he knew Wade. *How the hell am I going to do this when the room is full?* he thought. He decided to concentrate on his breathing, think of his grandfather, look down not up and go for it. He cleared his throat and began.

Charlie started with an old but well known Muddy Waters blues song called, "I Feel Like Going Home." The intent wasn't lost on Wade and he smiled at the boy's unspoken message. Charlie closed his eyes as he performed. Maybe if he could perform like this, not seeing the audience, he could get through it. That way he could manipulate what he saw. He could picture anything in his mind's eye. His voice was excellent and Wade was so impressed with his singing ability, never having heard it before. *Celia knew what she was talking about,* he thought to himself. *This kid really is the real deal.* When he finished his song he sat there with his eyes closed. Applause was heard from very small pockets about the club and he felt glad to have heard it. He opened his eyes and saw Wade and Tim standing near to the back of the club, both clapping and both smiling wide.

"Do you know any Lynyrd Skynyrd?" someone called out from the bar. Right away, Charlie started the first chords of "Sweet Home Alabama" and the bar guy whooped his approval! Charlie performed the full song, again with his eyes closed. Tim came bounding up to the stage when Charlie had finished his second song.

"Well, you're a hit boy! Now don't go giving the whole show up. You come back tonight with Wade and we'll let you jam with the rest of the guys. Good job, son," he said to Charlie, shaking his hand more firmly and vigorously this time. "You sure have a hell of a gift there," he said. He waved to Wade at the back of the club and jumped off the stage. Wade walked over and leaned against the stage smiling. He motioned Charlie over and Charlie knelt down to hear him.

"You gotta make a connection with the audience Charlie. You really need to open your eyes more," he advised.

"My music is the connection, Wade. If I open my eyes, the connection gets broken for me. If I see them all out there I lose my cool," he explained. "If you're gonna make me do this, I have to do it my way," he said firmly and stood up to come down from the stage.

"So, how was it otherwise?" Wade asked as he followed Charlie back to the table with his guitar case still on it.

Charlie shrugged his shoulders. "S'alright," he answered noncommittally. "I liked when they clapped. And I like that the guy asked me to play something afterwards. That felt good."

Wade could tell Charlie wasn't quite sold yet. It was going to take a few more performances and a lot more audience to feel swept away by it but he was sure once Charlie did, it would make all the difference. At least his first "audition" went well and he got the job.

. . .

That night, Charlie jammed with Wade and five other musicians and brought the house down. For a small little gem of a club, The Blues House had a very select patronage. These people knew their blues and weren't going to be happy with just the run of the mill play list or musicians. They wanted these guys to improvise when it came to jazz and the blues had to be from way back. The kind of stuff they all grew up on, listening to their parents play, just as George and Celia had done with Charlie. So Charlie fit right in. He didn't mind the jam sessions at all. Playing amongst the group, Charlie felt hidden. But when Charlie was given the centre stage for one or two songs, he fell back into his own world, closing his eyes and feeling through the song with his finger work. He had the whole crowd in awe of his ability at such a young age and they generously applauded him when he finished. He sighed a heavy sigh and opened his eyes shooting a look at Wade. Wade smiled back at him with a "thumbs up" and a wink.

There now, that wasn't so bad, was it? Charlie thought to himself. *I might be able to do this after all if I do what makes me feel comfortable.* The night ended with many patrons clapping Charlie on the back and congratulating him for his excellence. He took all their praise with a continual blush and his head lowered. Next time, Wade would make sure he'd get him out of there before anyone could corner him. Charlie hated crowds and didn't do well with praise, Wade noticed, and until he could try helping Charlie figure out a way to be able to accept those things, Wade would have him leave before last call and meet up with him on the bus. There was no need to make it painful for the kid, especially if he was only doing this to make his mother happy. Wade hoped that Charlie would accept these things more easily along the way and Charlie would find it in himself to deal with his fears and enjoy what he was doing. The audience was certainly enjoying what he was giving them! They were reacting exactly like Celia and he had thought; they loved him. He was practically a blues virtuoso and his ability to jam was phenomenal. It was as if his fingers started on fire when they got anywhere near a guitar and Wade was impressed with how much Charlie was able to play and cover. He had George's gift, an ear with perfect pitch. . . .

And so their summer of touring began. It was the same almost anywhere they went. They'd drop by in the afternoon for Charlie to meet and audition for the owner and that night the club would erupt with applause, mostly for Charlie. He played with the group members easily and even smiled and laughed with the guys during their improvised set. But once he got out on his own, he withdrew into the song and would only allow the audience in at the end. There was never a time that Charlie wasn't praised immensely, although he seldom heard it, often opting to head to the bus early before the crowd let out. Wade heard it all and was often questioned as to the boy's ability and his reserved nature. Wade would just explain that he was a very introverted, gifted, guitar player who liked his privacy and it made Charlie seem even more mysterious and untouchable.

After traveling through lower Illinois and then moving into Montana, they made their way south east. Then they moved west. Charlie loved the south. He found the people were friendly and warm and he loved the food, and the south sure loved Charlie. They played in 5 states and 47 clubs in just under 60 days. When they toured through Oklahoma City they were fortunate enough to be jamming with Fenton Robinson, a Texas blues guitarist who was doing a few shows on his way up to play in the Chicago clubs. He had heard that Wade and Charlie were from that very area and he wanted to check them out – see what their style and sound was like. He wasn't disappointed. He thought Wade was an excellent trumpet player but it was Charlie who blew him away.

"I foresee great things for you, Mr. Morningstar. Great things indeed," he told Charlie.

Charlie nodded his head in appreciation of his words and then thought to ask him, "Do you think it matters if I keep my eyes closed when I play?"

Mr. Robinson looked at him very hard and said, "I think it matters that you use all your *other* senses to play with the kind of passion that you play with," he said to Charlie, pointing at his chest. "When your eyes are closed you play to assuage *your need* to play; it isn't for the audience. But it's when you play with the most purity. It's a gift that you let us in at all," he said and smiled a big warm smile at him.

If Mr. Fenton Robinson understood, then it was just fine as far as Charlie was concerned. From that day on, whenever Charlie was on centre stage, he closed his eyes during his performances, regardless of Wade's advice.

The summer was days from drawing to an end and neither Wade nor Charlie had spoken up about going home. Wade was wondering how to approach the subject with Charlie because if he wasn't thinking about it, Wade didn't want to remind him and set him back on his original plan. Charlie had been on fire with every performance and seemed to be getting used to the praise, even being able to stay after some of the shows and hear the audience's comments to him. One night after a show, some of the musicians had stayed and were all sitting around drinking and talking. Charlie and Wade were amongst them, Charlie drinking a soda and Wade drinking a beer.

"So what's next for you two? Have anything lined up through the next few months?" asked Ron Panchaud, a piano player from Louisiana.

Wade held his breath for a moment, hoping it wouldn't trigger anything in Charlie. He looked over at Charlie and he and Charlie locked eyes.

"I was thinking about going home to attend college. I want to become a teacher," Charlie said taking a sip of his pop.

Wade looked away. *Damn!* he thought.

"Teacher?" asked Ron. "What the hell for? You can *teach* by playing on stage, boy!" he insisted. "Do you have any idea how much we all learned from you tonight? Do you know how much you can pass on to the other musicians, not to mention audiences when you play? You got it wrong boy, *that stage"*, he said, emphasizing it by pointing at it hard, "is your classroom." And there it was — what Wade and Celia *couldn't* say to him, someone else did and he had *heard it.*

Charlie pondered this. He had never looked at it that way at all. He always thought that by being in the classroom he'd be passing on his grandfather's teachings. But maybe Ron was right. Maybe he could teach just by being on the stage. Charlie knew it wasn't the same thing but he knew what Ron meant. Another guitarist said that he learned something from watching Charlie play, and that it helped him to improve his own playing. Wasn't that even better in some ways? To be teaching other guitarists how to be better? And for reward, Charlie also learned a great deal from them. His playing only improved with every gig, playing off some of the best the southern blues had to offer. It really was a perfect symbiotic relationship for the musicians and Charlie was starting to think of himself as a musician. He'd certainly been called that since the start of their summer tour.

When he looked back over the last 60 days, he realized he hadn't hated it at all. He had quite enjoyed himself despite the constant nagging thought that darkened Charlie's mood on a daily basis. He tried very hard to push it to the back of his mind during these summer months and had done a pretty good job of it. Perhaps he could do this for a while. Perhaps he could travel around with Wade on the bus and keep a somewhat lower profile and he could run away from his nagging thought. He came out of his reverie to find Ron, Wade and the rest of the guys staring at him. He remembered where the conversation had dropped off.

"I guess I didn't think of it that way, Ron. I can't say I enjoy the spotlight, but I sure like the jamming sessions and the audiences that go crazy for the music," Charlie said smiling.

Wade smiled too and let his breath out. *Maybe Charlie will change his mind*, Wade thought, but he didn't speak a word. When they were back on the bus and alone again, Charlie brought up the subject of their next move.

"I think we should see what's further West from here, huh Wade? Maybe try going to California and up the western sea board. Can't hurt," Charlie said, shrugging and not looking up.

Wade smiled a knowing smile and nodded his head to Charlie in agreement. "Sure thing, Charlie. I think that sounds like a great idea. We should… uh… maybe call Celia and let her know just so she doesn't worry. She's probably wondering what you'll do," he said casually.

Yeah, Charlie thought. *Shit! I hate it when she's right.*

. . .

'Oh! I *love* it when I'm right," Celia gushed into the phone.

Wade rolled his eyes at the other end. He called Celia the next day to advise her of their plans and she bragged to him that she had known all along. The thing was, Celia didn't understand how hard it had been for Charlie to admit this. He had come to have a strong bond with Charlie during their summer tour and, although he loved his mother, Wade would not push Charlie if his heart wasn't in it. Charlie made this decision for himself and Wade respected him all the more for it. Charlie knew Wade had his back and they worked like a team, both inside the bus and on stage. They switched off driving to give the other some much needed rest when they had back to back gigs at opposite ends of the state and had to get there overnight. When they were on stage, Wade and Charlie would lock eyes and follow one another through an improvisational piece that would have the crowd standing in applause. Charlie thought of Wade as his Uncle; Wade thought of Charlie as his nephew.

"Yeah, well, he's really making the crowds go nuts down here and he wants to see what California has to offer," Wade explained to her.

"I think he's right," she said excitedly. "Take him there and see what happens. Bet you anything they love him. I bet you anything out there, he'll get a record deal or something, Wade," she said, secretly hoping that was the case. She'd love to see her boy's name and beautiful face on an album cover.

"Let's not get ahead of ourselves now, Celia," Wade laughed.

He did see where Charlie felt pushed into this by her. *The poor kid has to fight for his own desires because his mom is truly a force to be reckoned with*, thought Wade.

"I'll take him there and we'll do our thing and see what happens," he said calmly. "How's Chase?" he asked, changing the subject.

"Oh, he's lonely without Charlie but Georgie spends a lot of her time with him. Once she starts back at school, I'll be back on full time Mommy duty. This summer has been so nice to let Georgie take care of him from time to time. Even if it's just while Jean and I have a visit, y'know?" she said.

Chase could be very exhausting. Wade knew that and he felt for Celia. It was tough work keeping up with him and he knew Charlie had been a great help with that. He had to respect the lady for not wanting Charlie to stay behind if only to help her with Chase, but she wanted better for her child. Wade loved that about her — that, and her fantastic green eyes. Wade was brought back to reality by Charlie tapping him on the shoulder and motioning for them to get going. Wade nodded his head to Charlie and then spoke into the phone.

"Okay sugar, listen, I gotta go here. You take care and we'll try calling again once we've had a chance to get settled in California. I'm not sure where we're headed next. Gotta make a few phone calls when we get there. Bye for now," he said sweetly.

"Bye Wade and give Charlie my love and a hug and kiss from his mom. Thanks for everything, Wade, I mean it," she said sincerely.

"Yeah, it's not a problem little lady. You take good care now," and he hung up the phone.

He gave himself a moment and a bit of a heavy sigh. Sometimes he wished she knew how he felt. Sometimes he wanted to tell her so badly but he was afraid it would scare her away and then he wouldn't have her at all. And look at his relationship with Charlie now. How would it be changed if he was to confess to Charlie that he loved his mother? Probably wouldn't go over well. Wade decided to keep his little secret to himself and cherish it always.

As Celia hung up the phone she could see Chase standing in the doorway.

"What's the matter, little man?" she asked her youngest son.

"Charlie?" he asked her, pointing to the phone. He looked at her with hope on his face. He sure missed Charlie.

"No, honey, Charlie isn't on the phone now. He's not done touring with Wade. He'll be home in a few months or so. You'll see, before you know it, he'll be walking through that door!" she promised the young child and mussed his hair with her hand as she walked past him into the living room.

Chase looked around after her and started walking back to his bedroom. As he passed Charlie's bedroom door, he paused. Charlie had asked that the room stay closed to Chase while he was gone and Celia enforced that rule. Chase stared at the door hard, wishing his older brother would return so he could go back in there and spend time with him. He continued walking to his bedroom hoping his mother was right and that before he knew it Charlie would be walking through the door. Little did they know that it would be a lot longer than anyone thought before Charlie would make it home again.

Chapter 9

Charlie and Wade Come Home

Days before Chase's seventh birthday, Charlie phoned home. He had great success out on the West coast and he and Wade had spent the first 18 months traveling up and down and playing in the clubs out there. Charlie was applauded greatly everywhere he went and one gig usually lead to another then to another. Before they knew it Charlie and Wade were earning a fair living at touring together and hooking up some old blues artists and some contemporary artists, provided they played the smaller more intimate clubs. Charlie didn't want to play to large audiences, just those small, select groups that chose a more intimate setting and he was known for his little "eye closing" quirk, along with his unbelievable guitar playing and his amazing voice. The traveling also taught Charlie a lot about the history of his genre. When they were in Mississippi, they stopped in to see the "Center for the Study of Southern Culture" at the University of Mississippi. Charlie read that in January of 1982, B.B. King had donated his personal record collection, which included nearly 7,000 rare blues records. It was a fantastic sight for both Wade and Charlie and they spent the whole day listening to some of the rarest blues recordings known.

He and Wade made it home just a few times since they left that early July morning more than four years ago. They missed all but one Christmas, surprised Celia once for Mother's Day (she cried the whole time) and had pre-arranged visits only twice after that. Charlie loved how being on tour and playing his music made him forget his little nagging thought. Each time he found his way home it brought it all back to him. Charlie had started setting up some of their shows too, so that it made it impossible to take much time off. For four years he and Wade worked solid, mostly for Charlie's career. Wade would always be in the background and didn't pretend to himself that his fame and fortune would skyrocket. He was doing this to help Charlie along and he knew it meant the world to Celia.

Every once in a while Wade would fly home to take care of something with his house, which he had started renting out, and he and Celia would talk for a bit while he was home. But mostly, Marco and Jean kept up with things while Wade and Charlie toured the states making a living at doing what they loved. Wade had Charlie open a savings account and Charlie was taught to save what he earned. Wade too saved and when it came to gas, maintenance or food they split everything 50/50. This meant that by the time four years had gone by, they each had a nice little nest egg. Both agreed that it was time to put the old bus out to pasture and each chip in to buy a much better, more modern bus. Upon the purchase Wade made a suggestion to Charlie.

"Hey, whaddya say we book a gig up in Chicago, drive up there and surprise everyone with this and take them out to see the show? We haven't played in the north in a long time and I'd bet they'd love to have us back and show them how they do it down here *in the south*," he said with an exaggerated Southern drawl.

Charlie thought a moment; he knew he couldn't really say no. It had been quite a while since they'd been back and it would be nice to see everyone again. Chase would turn seven in a few days and if he could line up a gig it wouldn't be just a vacation.

"Sure," he agreed. "Why not? Maybe we can play the "Black and Blue" if it's someone we know who's playing." Wade nodded and threw Charlie the keys. "Here, you get to drive her first, Charlie-boy," he said endearingly. He made a grand gesture of stepping aside to let Charlie climb onto the bus first and jump into the driver's seat.

"Right on!" he said enthusiastically. "Now let me show you how it's done!" he bragged to Wade, smiling wide. *I couldn't be closer to him if he were my own son,* Wade thought.

. . .

Celia hung the phone up and hooped and hollered about the house. Wade and Charlie were coming home for a visit! They were to be here on Chase's birthday and had a gig to play that night. It had been hard not seeing them for all this time. She'd gone over to Jean and Marco's for Christmas and New Year's Eve each year because she missed Charlie so bad. But she knew he was doing exactly what he should be and she would only be selfish to want to keep him home all to herself. But now he was coming home and he was going to go get them all together to go out and see him and Wade perform! She could hardly wait.

When Chase asked her what all the fuss was about she gushed to him, "Charlie's coming home and he's going to play at the club and we're going to see him play!" she danced about, holding the boy's hands as she did.

He began to laugh and dance with her as he asked her, "Do I get to come and see him play too Mom?"

"Oh, no honey. I'm sorry but you aren't old enough to be allowed into these places. These places are for adults only," she explained.

The little boy's face dropped and he stopped dancing immediately. She knew he was devastated. He missed Charlie so badly and when he hadn't returned shortly after that first summer, Chase stopped asking her when he was coming home. On the rare occasion when he was home, Chase had no chance of getting him alone at all. He always had to share him with everyone else. They'd all visit together as a family of seven so he and Charlie were never able to be one on one. Chase walked off thinking to himself, *I miss chasing Charlie in the back yard.*

When the bus pulled onto the street where they lived, Charlie was driving it and honking the horn from way down before where the three houses were located. As he approached Marco and Jean's house Charlie leaned on the horn and paused outside for a few moments before heading down to Celia's house. He stopped completely outside the house and did a "shave and a haircut" honk to bring them outside. The bus looked like an elephant on a tiny garden path. It took up a lot of room and cars had to go one at a time around it into the oncoming lane to be able to pass. Charlie opened the door and walked out with a huge smile as his mother came running out of the house and threw herself into his open arms.

"Oh my God, it's good to see you again, Charlie," she cried. "I feel like I never see you anymore."

"Oh, that's not true at all," he said softly to her as they hugged tightly. Charlie took the word "never" very seriously. It was one he didn't use lightly. He was *never* going to perform on stage and look how that turned out!

"I'll admit I haven't been back as much as I should have but I have truly been working my ass off. Isn't that what you told me to do?" he asked her, as he pulled away and flashed her with a crooked smile on his beautiful face. His soft blonde hair was a lot longer these days, in *keeping with the times of today's musician*, she figured. He'd been in the sun, which was also apparent from the deep golden hue to his skin. *Dear God if Brad could see him, he'd swallow his tongue*, she thought. Her son was now a man at 22 years of age. She could enjoy a drink with him at the club tonight for the first time! And she could watch him perform and see him entertain a room full of people who will applaud and praise him, her son. Oh, what a glorious night!

Charlie let go of his mother and walked her towards the house. Chase rose up off of the couch and over to the door. He tried to remain cool as a cucumber but inside he was so excited to see Charlie his heart was in his throat. As Charlie approached the door he could see Chase standing there watching him. He smiled to his little brother and motioned for him to come towards him. Chase needed no other encouragement and burst through the door at Charlie who took off running away, and there they were again with him chasing Charlie, giggling as they ran around the yard.

. . .

They spent about a half hour touring through the new bus and testing every drawer and closet to see what secrets they held. All of them agreed that the men had made an excellent purchase and left the bus to sit around Celia's kitchen table and enjoy their time together. Celia made an enormous dinner for the group. It was Chase's seventh birthday but it may as well have been Christmas. Georgie would be arriving later from a friend's place as she was designated babysitter so Celia could go out. Everyone brought Chase a present and Celia made sure that he got cake. Celia made Chase's favorite meal which was chicken with roasted potatoes and salad. They all sang "Happy Birthday" to him and chatted excitedly about getting to see Charlie and Wade sit in with Willie Dixon and his crew at the "Black and Blue" later that night.

Chase opened up his gifts and the cake was served. He hoped for something really special from Charlie for his birthday, after all, he'd missed all the others in the last four years. Instead, Charlie gave him a car model. He had to admit, the model was cool but he hoped for something more personal from Charlie – something he might have wanted to hand down to him. Maybe something from his room. Chase had longed to go into his room and peek through the forbidden things in there but he had long been *forbidden* to enter unless Charlie was in there with him. And so, he didn't get his birthday wish either that year. Chase was starting to think that the whole birthday wish thing was just bull crap like the kids at school said. He was never again going to waste his time on making a birthday wish if that was the case!

As the crowd prepared for the night out, Chase stayed in the living room, out of the way. Marco and Jean went back to their house to get ready while Wade stepped out onto the bus to get showered and change. Charlie walked into his bedroom after his shower and Chase quickly got off the couch and went and stood near the door watching Charlie get ready in the mirror. He was wearing boxer underpants and parting his very blonde hair while crouching to see himself in the reflection.

Charlie caught sight of Chase and said, "Hey there little birthday man! Come on in and take a seat on the bed." "Chase shot into the room like a bullet and sat on the bed straight as a pin. He took the chance to examine the room meticulously while Charlie chatted with him and got ready for his performance. His room was filled with blues posters, music sheets, guitar magazines and some knick-knacks he'd acquired while he lived there.

"You excited for me tonight, Chase?" Charlie asked. Chase nodded his head enthusiastically but said nothing. "Yeah?" Charlie asked him as he caught his eye in the mirror.

He spun around to look directly at Chase who sat on his bed intrigued by every move that his older brother made. Charlie came over to the bed and sat down beside his little brother. They looked somewhat alike, both having lighter coloring than their mother and both with blonde hair. But Chase's features were more refined than Charlie's. His nose was thinner and he had higher cheekbones. His eyes were deeper set and were a hazel color. Nothing like Celia's or Charlie's with their unique shade of green. Chase was his own individual person just like Charlie was; just like their mother was. Their only familial trait seemed to be a musical one and it was too early to tell if Chase had that in him or not.

"What's the matter little buddy?" he asked the young boy. "Aren't you happy with the model I brought for you?"

Instinctively, Charlie knew something was wrong with Chase. He normally had a smile that was so wide and bright that you couldn't look directly at him. But tonight, he seemed very melancholy and crestfallen.

"I like it sure enough," the little boy shrugged one shoulder, "it's just that I was hoping you'd give me something so that when you're on the road I'd have something of yours to remember you by," he told Charlie honestly.

For only seven years of age today, you've aged many years in my eyes, thought Charlie. He sat there on the bed in his boxer's thinking about what Chase had said. On his seventh birthday he received his Gibson Les

Paul guitar from his Papa. He'd never forget that. Perhaps he should have carried on that tradition and introduced Chase to music by gifting him with a guitar. But it was too late now, he only had an hour before he was to be on stage and there wasn't anywhere he could get a guitar at this hour.

Looking into the small boy's face, he had a thought. He jumped up off the bed and climbed underneath to pull out a guitar case that had seen better days. George's guitar case was now more than 30 odd years old and had been hidden under Charlie's bed for at least the last six years. It was rough at the edges and the latch wasn't great but when Charlie lifted it from underneath the bed, Chase's jaw dropped, astonished. Charlie blew on it to take some of the dust off it and rubbed it down a bit before placing it on top of his bed. Chase scooted off the bed making room for the case and they both knelt before it as if praying to a higher God. Charlie undid the latch and opened up the top to reveal the guitar pictured in every picture of their grandfather that dotted the walls and in curio cabinets throughout the house. It was well used and worn and loved. Charlie had carefully placed three of his grandfather's picks that he had used the night of his final performance into the strings on the neck. Chase was afraid to go near it. He had seen this guitar in the pictures and often wondered what happened to it. It was the most beautiful thing he had ever seen and although it was miles too large for him to play right away, he was surprised that Charlie brought it out to show him.

"Papa George would want you to have this, Chase," he said to the little boy. "It was his guitar for years and he played incredible music on it. When he couldn't speak to me, he used it to communicate with me and I understood him," Charlie said softly, remembering the days when he and his Papa played back and forth with one another. "It's not right that it sits under my bed and gathers dust. I think you should have it and learn how to play it," Charlie said with conviction.

Chase was overwhelmed! He never dreamed that he'd be given such a gift from Charlie; all he was hoping for was a special T-shirt or a picture from his room.

"Thank you, Charlie. I promise to take good care of it and to learn how to play it properly," he said sincerely.

Charlie wondered how that was going to happen without him himself teaching the boy, and that wasn't possible because he and Wade were back on the road in less than a day.

"When you're ready I think you should ask Marco if he knows of anyone who could teach you Chase, at least the basics and then you could practice on your own. I'll cover the cost so mom doesn't have to pay. Count it as part of your birthday present," Charlie said as he thought of it on the spot.

Why hadn't he thought of this earlier? It was a perfect gift to give his little brother on his seventh birthday. As he was given a guitar and the love for music, Charlie should pass it along to Chase, just as he was told to by the elderly woman.

"Maybe by the time I come back, you'll have some songs down that you can play and I'll listen to you and tell you what I think," Charlie said, his little brother's face lighting up.

"I'd love that Charlie," Chase answered excitedly.

This was way better than he expected. Now he had his own guitar and some day he was going to be as big as his big brother was — just everyone wait and see! He bounded off the bed, dragged the guitar case close to the edge, closed it carefully and slowly dragged it entirely off the bed to carry it to his room. Charlie knew that he would take very good care of the guitar. And he had no doubt that Chase was smart enough to use the gift to its highest potential.

Georgie was late as she rushed from her friend's house down the street to Celia's. She had promised to be there by 8:00 pm so that the group could leave for the club and get seated before Charlie and Wade had to be on stage for 9:00 pm. She came bounding up the front steps and knocked twice before opening the door and coming straight in. As she did, Charlie walked through the living room in only his underwear, carrying his shirt for his mother to iron for him.

"Hey!" he stopped where he stood. He was shocked to see her. Almost 4 years had passed since the last time he'd seen the little girl and she now stood before him almost half way through her teen years. Georgie had grown over the last few years. She shot up in height, her hair became long and thick and her body started blossoming into a young woman. Her chocolate brown eyes were more almond shaped than Charlie remembered and her face had narrowed. She was a beautiful young girl and Charlie could imagine what 10 more years would do for her.

"Hey," she said back, laughing, "You always greet people in only your underwear, Charlie?" she asked him, confident with herself.

"Uh… no…" he answered and blushed. "Sorry… I was just going to see abou…" he trailed off, realizing the explanation wasn't necessary. He nodded to her, smiled and dropped his head and left the room quickly.

Georgie smiled to herself, *not a bad thing to have happen, to catch Charlie in his underwear!* she thought.

"Chase!" she called out. "Chase I'm here!" she called out again and went on the search for the little boy. He came running around the corner and collided into her legs in the hallway.

"Hey, happy birthday, little man!" she said to him, endearingly rubbing his back.

"Thanks Georgie," he said. "Charlie gave me Papa's guitar," he gushed proudly, hardly able to keep it in.

"He did?" she said, surprised.

She remembered Charlie's Papa's guitar. She was very young but she remembered watching he and Charlie play together repeating each other's finger strokes. She hadn't known what had happened to the guitar after the old man's death but it didn't surprise her that Charlie had kept it safe and sound. He'd do something like that.

"You must be very special to receive such a treasured gift, Chase. Be sure to take good care of it just like Charlie did to keep it all these years to give to you," she told the young boy.

Charlie overheard the exchange and smiled to himself. She was just lovely to Chase. They had obviously spent a lot of time together to have such an exchange and judging from how Chase looked at her, Charlie figured his little heart had already fallen for the young family friend. And why not? She was going to grow up to be a very beautiful woman, Charlie figured. And she had such a tender way about her; she'd make an excellent mother. He smiled to himself at that thought.

As everyone finished their final preparations, they gathered in the living room for a picture to be taken of this momentous occasion. Georgie and Chase joined the group and the camera was set up and all seven of them posing as the camera took the picture of the smiling, makeshift family. Chase's seventh birthday caught on film with all in attendance. Truly a momentous occasion.

The group all piled into the car and backed out of the driveway with Georgie and Chase standing on the front steps, he only reaching up to just past her waist and hugging her right leg as he stood there watching. Georgie waved too hoping they all had a great night.

Once they pulled out of sight she turned to her little charge and asked, "Well little man, what book do you want me to read to you tonight?"

He shrugged his shoulders. Nothing appealed to him right now. All he wanted to do was learn how to play Papa's guitar. After exhausting his small library Georgie suggested, "Why don't I take you to the library tomorrow and you can pick the next book I read to you, okay?" she asked him indulgently.

"Okay," he answered. He wasn't interested in a story book – he wanted an instructional book.

...

It had been a long time since Celia, Wade, Marco and Jean all went out together and they had never all gone to see Charlie and Wade sit in on a session. Willie Dixon was said to be fantastic and Celia was excited that her son was to play alongside him. The car was charged with excitement as it pulled into the "Black and Blue" parking lot and came to a stop. En masse the group piled out, the trunk popped open and Charlie and Wade got their instruments out. The music could be heard from outside and Celia smiled to herself as she heard someone singing "Mona Lisa" on stage. Whoever it was, she was good. The song took her back all those years to her first night singing in the club with her father at the piano. *How fitting,* she thought, *that I should hear that song again on the first night I see Charlie perform.* When she walked into the entrance, she straightened her shoulders, held her head high and clutched Charlie's arm as if he were escorting her in for a royal event. Celia Grace Morningstar had come a long way from the small town and her school choir. She had brought two wonderful children into the world and tonight her eldest was going to entertain this crowd and knock their socks off. She was so very proud!

Charlie escorted his mother to a table, got her seated with a drink in front of her and then went to the stage to get ready for his set. They were to go on at 9:00 pm and he only had a few moments to grab Meg and get his head in the right place. He still had difficulty being centre stage and for the most part avoided it at all costs, but there were a few classics that audiences always asked for and Charlie couldn't disappoint them. Willie took care of introductions to the rest of his band and they quickly discussed the night's playlist and their type of rhythm and blues. Charlie listened carefully with his head down as if in a huddle. With everyone in agreement as to how the night would go, Charlie took his seat and waited for the announcer to come on stage. He could see Celia, Jean and Marco at their table chatting away to one another. He felt a few butterflies knowing they were out there and he wanted to be sure that they, most of all, enjoyed the evening.

"Good evening, ladies and gentlemen!" called out the announcer. "Welcome to this evening's entertainment at the Black and Blue," his voice dropping extremely low as he said the latter. "We have a special evening for you with Willie Dixon and the band making their final appearance here tonight, and also a veteran of Black and Blue, Mr. Wade McGrath on trumpet and Mr. Charlie Morningstar on electric guitar." He threw his hand out to the group of musicians gathered on stage behind him and walked off clapping his hands.

Immediately, Charlie started the evening off with "Sultans of Swing." The crowd was hypnotized by his ability to make his Gibson Les Paul sing. They whistled, they applauded and they called out all throughout the performance. For the most part, Charlie kept his eyes completely closed, as was his thing. As Celia watched him she thought about Brad and wondered what he'd think of the seed he had planted 22 years ago. She felt a lump in her throat and couldn't hold back tears as she watched Charlie have such an effect on the crowd that they responded to his every riff and when the song was over they rewarded all with a thunderous cheer and applause. Celia had never felt anything like it. As much as she had enjoyed the crowd's reaction to her, to see them react to Charlie with even more gusto was incredible. She rose with the crowd as the final notes ended, clutching at her heart with her fist and all but sobbing as she stood there. Charlie was the *real deal*.

By the time 1:00 am rolled around, the Black and Blue patrons were thoroughly worn out. Their excitement and enthusiasm for the musicians only enhanced the electricity that the music created. The night was filled with such a cornucopia of blues, jazz and improvised moments that each time they ended the audience would acknowledge with deafening applause and heavy anticipation for the next song. Charlie dazzled the crowd and set the bar high for any other performer who would grace that stage for a long time. It was staggering to think he was so young given his ability, and still Charlie became anxious at performances and much preferred to be in the background rather than out front for all to see.

The chatter home in the car was all in agreement that it had been a long time since they experienced such a night. The makeshift family drove home for the last few miles in silence, all of them taking a moment to appreciate the complexity of the forces that had come together to make tonight a possibility. All five of them knowing full well they were family, bloodlines be damned!

The car pulled into Celia's driveway and everyone emerged and made their way into the house. Georgie was lying down but still awake and watching TV as the now reserved group entered. Quickly, Celia went straight to the kitchen to lay out snacks and drinks she had prepared for Charlie's big night. Charlie walked directly into the living room to put his guitar case down as Georgie sat up and greeted him.

"Oh, hey," she said shyly as she dragged her fingers through her hair and pulled a decorative pillow in front of her to hold.

"Hey Georgie, are…you awake?" Charlie asked good-naturedly, as he gently placed his guitar case down.

Georgie yawned and rubbed her eyes. She definitely took after her Mediterranean father's side and her features had matured so that anyone looking at her was lost in her dark chocolate almond eyes and how the eyebrow framed it before it edged its way downward in a sultry slant. Her skin was flawless and she had inherited her father's full mouth. Georgie was a beautiful girl even at her young age and it struck Charlie as he stood before her. "Yup" she smiled back at him, her face lighting up as she was inwardly thrilled by his attention. It had been many years that she carried a torch for Charlie Morningstar and any time that he spent acknowledging her existence was monumental to the love-struck teen.

Charlie smiled back at her. She had always been such a nice girl.

"Yeah?" Charlie asked. "So, it's been a long time, huh? Four years," he said as he sat in the lazy chair next to the couch.

"I know, right? I'm going into high school this fall and I'm really looking forward to it," she stated, nodding her head. She and Charlie had always had a good relationship. Although he was the age of a much older brother, he tried not to treat her that way. He could see that, as a teen, she was much more confident and he admired her for that. He still didn't have that at 22.

"Oh yeah? Any idea what you want to do when your days are 9 to 5?" he asked, smiling as he leaned forward and rested his elbows on his knees. He was quite interested in her answer, wondering what this young girl on the edge of blossoming might predict for her future.

"I'd like to do live theater," she told him, sitting up proud. "I've taken dance classes for years and I want to get involved in the school theater program and see if I can't use it towards a degree out of state, like maybe New York?"

Her eyes light up as she laid out her plan and all Charlie could think of was how incredible she looked when she smiled. For a moment he was lost and when he finally gathered his thoughts, he caught her looking at him quizzically.

"Uh... hello?" she said, one eyebrow raised.

"Sorry, I'm here. I was just imagining you doing a great Maria in West Side Story. Do you sing?" he asked her, truly interested in her abilities. After all, she was Marco and Jean's daughter; she came from a musical background.

Georgie was astonished that he asked her. *He knew Broadway musicals as well!* She held her breath for a moment. Maria in West Side Story was the equivalent to Juliet in "Romeo & Juliet." That he thought of her that way only made her heartbeat soar. That he chose to sit only feet away in the easy chair rather than go to the kitchen for food and drinks after a night's performance made her feel wonderful!

"I actually *do* sing," she gushed. "My mom and I have been working on some pieces for the auditions when school starts. I'm auditioning for our school's production of Sound of Music."

Charlie whistled. "That's excellent," he said encouragingly. "Another Maria" he said, nodding as he acknowledged the similarity. She smiled at him and blushed a little. She was actually auditioning for the part of Liesl, the eldest daughter, but didn't want him to know that.

"I bet the whole football team lines up to play any part they can, right?" he asked her honestly. He could imagine she turned most male heads over the age of 15.

"I can't imagine I'd be interested in anyone on the football team. I'd think none of them has the sense God gave a false penny," Georgie said with disgust. "I figure if those boys want to run around bashing into each other over a pig's skin, especially when they get hit in the head, then I'm not interested in them. I'd rather have someone who uses their brains than wastes them on injuries."

She raised her lip in pure Elvis fashion to emphasize how disgusted she was in the whole sportsman persona. It made Charlie laugh! He wasn't sure if she was being funny and charming, or serious and full of herself, but he didn't care. Georgie always made him smile.

"Well, it's their loss, Georgie," he said. "They'll wake up in a few years and realize what they overlooked and you'll be long gone on the arm of someone they can't even think of competing with. Mark my words, you'll break many hearts over the years," Charlie predicted. They sat staring at one another for a brief moment, their eyes locked on one another's, sharing that moment before it was broken by Celia walking into the room.

"I've put food out if you're hungry," she told them, realizing instantly that she had interrupted a private conversation. She halted, finger pointing in the direction of the kitchen and smiled. They both looked at her after a moment and nodded as she held her gaze at them and then spun around and left the room. *That was weird*, she thought. As she continued to cut up cheese and place crackers and grapes on a plate for more edibles for the group, she wondered what had taken place between the two and considered how much things had changed in the past years. Celia was certain that the next four years would certainly bring about huge changes for both Georgie and Charlie!

. . .

True to her word, the next day after Charlie's debut performance at the Black and Blue club, Georgie held Chase's little hand as she guided him through the library seeking their next book.

"What kind of story do you want Chase?" she asked the intrigued young boy. "Do you want fantasy, true stories or maybe something with animals?"

Chase thought for a moment and then said, "I want a book that will teach me how to play the guitar. But I need pictures too. Charlie gave me Papa's old guitar for my birthday but he can't teach me. I thought there might be a book I can learn from," he stated matter-of-factly.

He had certainly given it some thought, Georgie mused. *Resourceful little guy*, she thought. "Okay," she answered easily. "What if we look for a book that will show you the basic chords and then maybe we can go from there."

She made a mental note to talk to her dad about Chase's request. He must know someone who could teach Chase better than any book could. Chase was relieved at her encouragement and held her hand tightly as she led the way into the "Informative/Instructional" area of the library. Once they found the correct isle, Georgie wandered down one side reading book spines looking for something suitable and left Chase standing on the other side doing the same. Just then Chase noticed an elderly woman also looking sideways at the books names. She happened to glance over at him and then smile. He returned her smile and felt as though he had seen her before but couldn't quite place her.

"This is an interesting isle for a young lad like you to be in. Are you trying to learn something?" she asked him inquisitively.

"I'm trying to learn how to play the guitar," he answered, without hesitation.

"Ah," she replied understandingly. "There is more to playing the guitar than just what can be learned in books my dear young man."

She admonished him with a pointed finger to emphasize her meaning. As she continued reading the books names she reached up and plucked one from the shelf, read its title briefly, and then handed it to Chase. As the young boy reached out to take the book from the elderly woman, their hands touched momentarily.

She smiled sweetly at him and said, "You should also utilize all that God gave you when you play. Use your entire spirit," she said, holding his gaze. "That can only come from within, not from a book," she smiled at him. "You are already a very bright light. Use that when you play and you'll outshine all others."

Chase took the book from her and read its title: Beginner's Guitar Lessons Learned Easy. He flipped through the pages and found instructional photos of how to hold your fingers for each chord. He studied it for a moment and then looked back to the elderly woman to thank her, but she was gone. He looked around and down the other isle to see where she had gone, but she wasn't anywhere to be seen. He directed his gaze back to the book, grateful for her help and advice.

Chase spent the next few days leafing through the book and trying his best to hold his fingers exactly how the book displayed. The following Saturday night, Celia joined Jean for a movie night while Marco was out working. Georgie stayed with Chase and the two of them tried to figure out the different chords together while watching TV. Chase had his Papa's guitar slung across his midsection and was near to biting his tongue off with concentration. Georgie had changed channels for the third time looking for something they could enjoy when she happened upon an Elvis Presley movie. Chase's attention was captured as he watched Elvis shake his hips on the beaches of Hawaii, kicking sand and singing as everyone smiled and swooned around him. It made such an impression on the little boy. He heard a voice in his head say,… *you should also utilize all that God gave you when you play. Use your entire spirit.* At the time he had no idea what it meant, but now, just a few days later, watching Elvis create magic on the TV screen, Chase knew exactly what he had to do. He would be the brightest star of them all!

...

Chase renewed the instructional book several times and kept it for over five weeks. He practiced hard every day but it wasn't very easy for him. After watching him struggle while she sat with him one night, Georgie approached her dad about finding him a guitar teacher.

"I can think of a few nearby," Marco said to her query. "I'll talk to Celia about it... see what we can line up."

Within days Chase was meeting with Peter Schmidt, a blues guitarist that Marco knew from way back. He gave lessons in his basement and lived only a few doors down. Chase was able to stop by on his way home from school a few times a week and Peter would instruct him for an hour or so. Chase also had a natural ability, although it wasn't like Charlie's; rather, Chase's ability was more in his performance. His musicality was definitely genetic but the way he moved, even with his Papa's oversized guitar hanging around his waistline, was something else again. This kid had "Star Quality" written all over him. Peter knew his guitar playing would only improve with time but no one had to teach the child how to draw focus on stage – Chase had that in spades! He'd stand holding the guitar and shake his whole body as he belted out James Brown as if he were the Godfather of Soul himself.

After many months, Peter convinced Marco to watch his young protégé as he performed the hell out of Jail House Rock and Marco's jaw dropped. *How was it possible that one family could have so much talent?* he wondered. *Charlie had better watch out,* he mused *because soon he won't be chasing Charlie, he'll have caught him!*

Chapter 10

Celia's 50th Birthday

It had been 10 years since Charlie's debut at the Black and Blue club. He and Wade spent those years mostly touring and getting quite the loyal following throughout the blues and jazz circuit that dotted the cities of America, mostly in the south. But so far, Charlie kept a low profile with the recording industry, remaining a performance artist who wouldn't do interviews. It infuriated the main stream media who constantly vied for his opinion on anything. He became known for his elusive nature and his ability to dodge an audience as well as a photographer. He had been able to keep his anonymity for the most part while entertaining all over the States. It sure beat the hell out of ending up on the cover of People Magazine!

Charlie had few relationships in that 10 year period, opting not to date women who frequented the clubs he played in. He did have a one year relationship with a waitress named Rita from Albuquerque but it ended up being too long distance for Rita and she phoned him to tell him they were through. He then met a nice lady at the reception desk of a motor home dealership that he and Wade had gone in to see. Sharon was a small Texan woman with a huge attitude. Charlie liked her nerve. She liked Charlie, for about eight months, and then she left him for a guy who owned his own home and had a nice car. *No accounting for taste, I guess* thought Charlie.

He only just finished a brief affair with a nice girl by the name of Penny. He met her at a guitar shop in Charleston and while he played the area, she stayed the night. He enjoyed the hell out of her and Penny taught Charlie a thing or two he hadn't known before, but the relationship ended when Charlie left town. He'd always be grateful to Penny for their time together. She really was an incredible woman, but she wasn't *the one*.

Through it all – the relationships, the hundreds of gigs, thousand of musicians and tens of thousands of audiences, Charlie still carried a nagging thought. Now, as he approached his 32nd year, the nagging thought was heavy on his mind. He needed to go home.

...

Chase spent those 10 years under Peter Schmidt's instruction and had become an excellent guitarist. He liked blues and soul but his favorite was good old rock and roll. It was more his generation and he watched current artists perform on stage and thought about doing that himself. As he matured, it became apparent to Celia that Chase was definitely more Campbell's offspring than hers. He had such an easy going nature (not pot induced) and his smile and energy level could light up all of Chicago.

He had the same personality as Campbell and chatted easily with anyone, telling jokes with such a clever sense of humor. Chase was a true entertainer. He had a nice singing voice, excellent stage presence and knew how to work a crowd, even if they were only the cashiers at the local grocery store. Chase performed wherever he went. Celia loved to go places with him and watch him work the room. It was so impressive. He was now 17 years of age, another handsome boy with soft brown eyes and sandy blonde hair. He had a crooked smile that exposed white straight teeth. He smiled often and when he did, the lines at the sides of his eyes created little sunbursts that fanned out into his face. This made the girls swoon and his social calendar was pretty hectic. Girls called the house constantly asking for him to the point that Celia stopped answering the phone. The only trouble was Chase loved only one girl... Georgie.

Georgie attended the local high school and left her mark on the theater program there. She starred in each year's production, singing, dancing and generally being the school's strongest leading actress for those four years. She also started honing her skills by doing Community Theater and was known as one of the best amateur actresses the town had ever seen. Often, Celia and Chase would join Marco and Jean out for a night at the theater courtesy of Georgie's latest show. They always left feeling amazed at Georgie's acting talent and convinced she was headed to New York.

By age 18 she had grown into a lovely young woman, with dark chocolate almond shaped eyes, long thick dark hair that was left loose unless on stage in character. She was 5', 4", with a toned dancer's body, Georgie Pelos was a stunner!

When it came time for Georgie to pick college's she opted to apply to The New York Conservatory for the Dramatic Arts. Georgie had no interest in doing film work; she loved the energy of a live audience and the instantaneous feedback they gave. She dreamed of seeing her name on Broadway!

She *only* applied to the Conservatory because she believed so strongly that she'd be accepted and had no interest in attending anywhere else. She was accepted, and as Jean and Marco packed up the car to take Georgie to New York for her first semester, Celia and Chase dropped by to wish her well. Chase had a difficult time saying goodbye to Georgie and in the end, hugged her quickly, wished her luck and made his way back home ahead of Celia. It was the first time that any of their little group had seen Chase at a loss for words. Jean guessed what was wrong, but there was nothing she could do to help. She had known for years that Chase carried a crush for Georgie, and why wouldn't he? He had known her all his life and spent more time with her than he did with his own brother, Charlie. He and Georgie had more memories of Christmas mornings, Thanksgivings and Fourth of July picnics than Charlie was ever present for. They were practically siblings, but Chase didn't see it that way. Georgie was his love.

She spent four years at the conservatory and landed her first role in an off-Broadway production of "The Apple Tree." She played the three-role musical piece to rave reviews and Marco and Jean were able to come out for a weekend and catch a performance, beaming at their incredibly talented and beautiful daughter. Georgie was living the dream!

She seemed very close to her fellow actor who played opposite her in the male three-role, a man by the name of Carter Banting. Carter was from Florida and had a permanent tan. He was a match for Georgie in the talent department, could sing like a nightingale and had been on and off Broadway for a few years. Carter was five years older than Georgie and she was infatuated with him. They had rehearsed together for three months and had played the parts for over a year before Carter made any kind of move on her. It all started with a simple kiss, off stage. With that, their relationship grew and pretty soon they were sharing a one bedroom apartment just off 63rd street and enjoying their very New York life. Georgie was now 22 years of age, in a serious relationship with a man named Carter and making her living on the stage in New York, but her heart was truly elsewhere.

. . .

As Celia's 50th birthday drew near, Charlie called the house more frequently. He started having difficulty sleeping. He wanted to be sure that he was home for the celebration and although she had originally planned on a party out at the club, Charlie convinced her that a big old house party would be a better fit.

"If we go to a club," he had told her, "then it's us celebrating with a lot of other people we don't know. If I spend the night on stage, then I won't get the chance to enjoy the evening with you."

She listened to him and agreed to hold a house party with practically the entire neighborhood invited. The house was decorated with streamers, banners and balloons that all proudly displayed "Happy 50th Birthday" on them. Jean spent the entire week cooking and baking in preparation. Celia bought a new CD player and was loading it with some of the best blues and jazz that she could find. She wondered why her son didn't have a record yet and thought about asking Wade that very question when he and Charlie arrived.

On the night of his mother's 50th birthday, Charlie was anxious as hell. He practically shoved Wade aside and insisted that he drive the last 200 miles to get home before the party was to start. When he did get home he followed his mother around like a puppy and watched her like a hawk. When Chase tried desperately to get his older brother's attention to show him his latest rendition of "I'm a Soul Man", Charlie was easily distracted and constantly looking past Chase to see what was going on within the house. It pissed Chase off to no end and he sulked for part of the night in his bedroom thinking, *you watch, Charlie. One day it'll be me on the stage that everyone will be looking at, and then you'll notice.*

To a rousing rendition of "Happy Birthday", Celia blew out 50 candles on a huge slab of chocolate on chocolate cake. When asked, "What did you wish for," she answered "a long and happy life." She smiled to the crowd that had gathered to celebrate with her. As she looked around the room she was astonished that so many people had come out in her honor. At the back of the room, on opposite sides of the doorway, stood her two boys. They were 15 years apart in age and even farther apart in personalities. Charlie, standing proud, arms crossed with a bit of a furrowed brow, always a thinker. She remembered he used to smile a lot more when he was younger. He hadn't smile like that in a long time. Then she looked at Chase, leaning against the doorway with a forever smile on his face, her eyes drawn to him just as he stood there. He had presence that lit up even when he was simply leaning against a doorway. They each had had their own personalities, each their own way about them. One carried a heavy burden and the other had no burdens at all, but thankfully each one gifted with something that would serve them well. She had done her best with them and felt a great sense of pride.

Charlie watched as Celia enjoyed her party and celebrated with friends. As much fun as it was to watch her have a great night he couldn't help but feel a terrible sense of foreboding. He had asked Wade if they could stay for a few days before heading off again and Wade made sure that they were not due to perform for at least a week, giving them a couple of days to travel should they need it. Even with the extra day's vacation,

215

Charlie couldn't settle. He would get up in the middle of the night and wander through the house, sometimes flicking on the TV for company. He'd sit outside on the front step waiting for the morning star, greet it and then go back inside to put on hot coffee and wait for Celia to rise. When she did, he'd kiss her and head off to bed for the next few hours.

After five days, Wade and Charlie were packed up and ready to go. Charlie hugged his mother in her kitchen and gave her a listing of his performance itinerary for the next few weeks – something he had only started doing.

"...and don't forget to call me. Now that we each have a cell phone, you can call me anytime and I'll hopefully be able to get it. If not, at least you can leave me a message, okay?" he said as he hugged her tight. "I love you, Mom," he said as he looked at her intently.

"Oh, you're such a sweet, boy," she gushed at him. "Thanks so much for coming home this week, Charlie. I so appreciated you doing that for me. I know how busy you and Wade are," she said, throwing a wink to Wade at the door.

He winked right back and smiled wide. *One day, he was going to have to tell that woman how he truly felt!*

"Take good care of her, okay little bro?" Charlie directed towards Chase who stood in the hallway watching the farewell. He walked over to his brother with his huge grin and hugged him briefly.

"Not to worry, man," Chase said. "I got it all under control."

"I know you do and I'm counting on it," said Charlie as he clapped Chase on the back and grabbed his shoulder, squeezing playfully. "And you keep on practicing and doing those incredible moves, you *Soul Man*." One day you'll be front and centre with all the girls screaming for you."

Chase smiled at him and laughed as Charlie pushed him gently into the wall and smiled back. *He had noticed*, Chase thought. *Well I'll be damned!* Celia and Chase stood on the front steps as Wade and Charlie waved goodbye from the bus and it pulled away. So many years had passed since they had started touring. Now it seemed as though they had been at it longer than they had ever been at home. *So much had changed,* Celia thought as she watched the bus drive out of sight. As she turned to make her way into the house, she was sure the best was yet to come!

For the next little while Charlie asked Wade to book them within a day's drive of home. Wade wasn't sure what was going on with Charlie and Charlie wasn't telling. He called home more often now than he ever had and was anxious to find out how Celia was doing, and she'd always tell him she was doing fine. She even divulged that she was thinking of going back to singing in the clubs and was going to see if Marco could set her up with a show or two. Charlie was always relieved to hear her voice and after a few months he started to relax more and more with every answered phone call, to the point where Wade saw a turnaround in his mood. Charlie was actually light hearted these days and was connecting with his audience more often. He was jovial, quipping with the band and the audience, even staying afterwards to celebrate the night. There was a real difference in Charlie Morningstar in the last few months and Wade was watching it all closely.

Chapter 11

Celia, Marco and the Fire

As the buzzing persisted, Charlie was awakened by the noise. He was flat on his stomach, with his left arm raised above his head, his head stuffed into a king size pillow. His right leg was thrown over Carmen, or Carla or something like that. They met at a Wal-Mart when Charlie had gone shopping for supplies. She commented on his laundry detergent choice and ended up in his bed. Wal-Mart was great for cheap purchases!

Charlie's left arm awkwardly reached for his cell phone on the bed side table and he gruffly answered as he lifted himself up on his elbow.

"Hello?" He cleared his throat and tried to clear his blurred vision.

"Charlie?" Chase's voice called out, hoarsely. Charlie's heart froze.

"What is it Chase. Is it mom?" he asked, suddenly awake.

"You gotta come home," Chase cried. "You gotta come home!"

. . .

The day had started out as many other hot late-August days. Chase just celebrated his 18ᵗʰ birthday a week earlier and Celia had surprised him with a microphone stand and speakers of his very own. She had her sights set on doing a duo with him on stage and wanted to be sure that he was comfortable with his equipment. She and Chase practiced "Proud Mary" amongst other great bluesy rock and roll songs and she just knew in her heart that Chase was the one who would be famous. He would be more famous than Charlie, more famous than her father, George. Chase Morningstar was going to rock the world and she had every intention of helping him do that.

Now Celia sat on Saturday, the 26th of August, enjoying her back yard, some lemonade and her Billie Holiday CD, fanning herself with a small handheld oriental fan. She had no idea that the power had gone out in her area thanks to everyone running their air conditioning. As she sat with her feet in a cool water bath, in the shade of an umbrella, sitting at a patio set, Chase came out of the back door.

"Hey, there's no power on in the house at all, Mom. I think the whole street is out," he said, as she sat back in her chair and closed her eyes.

"There's nuthin' we can do about it then," she said, shrugging her shoulders. "If it isn't a blown fuse downstairs then it's beyond my abilities and I certainly have no control over the *powers that be*," she said laughingly, keeping her eyes closed as she fanned herself double duty. Chase scoffed at her and went back inside the house. Celia continued to sit outside enjoying the day as she sat thinking of her boys and how far things had come. She remembered her father, George and, vaguely, her mother Meg. She remembered Meg singing church hymns to her and George playing the piano with her on his lap.

She remembered introducing Charlie to her father at the train station and the look of thunder in his eyes until she told him her demands and then introduced him to his beautiful grandson who carried the Morningstar name. She remembered her father giving Charlie his first guitar and how he used that to help George to communicate and how this became Charlie's guitar lessons. She remembered how Chase had been conceived, welcomed and then how he flourished within the home she had created. She had done herself proud and Celia spent the day in peaceful bliss, enjoying her reminiscing with her lemonade and her fan.

As suppertime came, they ate cold leftovers and salad. Neither Chase nor Celia were hungry and both filled up on whatever the fridge offered from previous dinners. As dusk descended into night, Chase and Celia lit candles and played cards at the kitchen table. They were joined by Marco and Jean shortly after dinner and the four of them enjoyed a night of simple conversation over a few hands of euchre. By 10:30 pm Marco and Jean made their way back to their home and Celia and Chase went off to their own bedrooms each with a candle to light the way.

The still night was augmented by the chirp of crickets and the buzz of cicadas chanting endlessly. Without power, Celia had no air conditioning and was as victim to the heat as everyone else. She opened her bedroom window hoping for a slight breeze but none was to be had. She poured herself a small sip of whiskey to help her nod off and sat reading for a while as she sipped the drink. Eventually Celia fell fast asleep with her book in her lap, dreaming of an elderly woman on a park bench long ago. She must have been three of four years of age but she remembered her mother Meg handing the woman a sandwich. Her dreams then jumped to seeing herself sitting on a bus, crying, and the same elderly woman sitting next to her, handing her a tissue as she wondered how she would tell her father of her pregnancy. She had a sense of being compelled forward as she looked back through images of her life. She had never dreamed like this before and as she did she was aware of a feeling of lightness and peace.

The candle next to Celia burned down to the small holder and sat precariously in it. When the weight of its own wax building up in the top cavity forced the skinny candle to topple over, the orange flame quickly caught the silken rust-red drapes at the side of Celia's bed and soon the entire curtain was ablaze.

Celia remained completely lost in her dreams, watching in fondness as loving memories from the past were once again before her; her mother, her father, and her children when they were small. As the drapes burned away, their remnants fell onto Celia's bed clothes and pillows surrounding her sleeping form. It took only moments for the bedding to ignite and yet she remained oblivious.

Chase was too lost in his guitar playing to have known what was happening. He had practiced and practiced the opening riff of "Money" by Pink Floyd, because he wanted to use it in an audition he was going to ask Marco to help arrange. His plan was to have Marco introduce him around and help him get his first gig, much the way Charlie had started. He sat concentrating on his finger technique and trying different ways of playing the opening when he suddenly had a sense of something not being quite right. He first tilted his head as if in question and then it hit his senses, his olfactory senses, to be more precise. He could smell it from his first floor bedroom. Smoke. Something was burning! Chase threw open his bedroom door and ran upstairs calling out to his mother.

...

"Mom!" he screamed, as he climbed the stairs two at a time to the second floor. He got to the door of Celia's room and reached for the handle with his right hand as he spread his left hand out onto the door to feel it.

"Mom!" he screamed again as he pulled both hands away. The door knob *and the door were hot!* He ran into the bathroom down the hallway and grabbed a towel, wrapping it around his hand. He ran back to Celia's bedroom door and, using the towel as protection, turned the door knob to gain entry into his mother's room. When he did a back draft was created that blew him back several feet and down the stairs, leaving him shaken and dizzy. The wind was knocked out of him and he had a few moments of panic when he couldn't breathe. The roar of the fire had intensified greatly and Chase knew his mother was in trouble. He could hear someone yelling "Celia" from out of the back of the house. It sounded like Marco. Chase was aware of breaking glass and a commotion as someone came through the back door with force, came over to him and took him over their shoulder and carried him as such outside to fresh air. He was placed on the ground and left quickly as he heard Marco's voice say, "Stay here and breathe deeply Chase. I'm going to get your mom."

Celia's room was now engulfed in an inferno that swallowed the second story quickly. Chase lay on the backyard grass trying to get a deep breath of air and coughing and choking on each breath. He could hear Marco screaming his mother's name and the sound of the fire popping and cracking as it licked at the contents of his house. He couldn't move – he couldn't help and he couldn't look. He lay with his arm over his eyes crying out as the house was destroyed by the fire started by a single candle. He could hear the distant sound of the fire trucks as they made their way to the house. He did the only thing he could think of and reaching into his pocket for his cell phone, he called Charlie.

. . .

The Fire Department arrived within a few minutes of Jean's call. She and Marco had smelled smoke and heard someone on the street calling "Fire." They looked out to see the back of Celia's house fully engulfed and thick, black smoke rising from its centre. Marco took off running in his underwear and a T-shirt telling Jean to "…call 911!" She called them immediately and as soon as she was confident they had the information she, too, ran towards her best friend's house in hopes that Celia and Chase had made it out safely.

As Marco came upon the house he could see the flames and smoke billowing from the back upper floor. He ran to the gate and opened it up to gain entry into the backyard. Celia's screen door was unlocked but she had locked the back door itself. Marco saw the umbrella tied up into her patio table and thought it would be the best bet the break the window on the back door. Using it as a battering ram, he broke through the window and was able to gain access to the house. He found Chase at the bottom of the stairs choking, crumbled and disoriented. His face was slightly burned and he mumbled something about his mother. Marco hiked him up over his shoulder and carried him out to the back yard and placed him on his back, giving him strict instructions to *stay here and breathe deeply* before returning into the house.

Marco took a deep breath and made his way to the stairwell and up the stairs. The flames were all around him and as he reached the top of the stairwell, he turned to the room that was once Celia's bedroom. The flames were all-encompassing as Marco took a step into her room. He heard a loud crack as the floor gave way and he dropped through to the first floor with Celia's bed, her body and the entire second floor with him. The implosion happened as many neighbors had gathered in the street including Jean who watched in horror as the house collapsed into flames with her best friend, her best friend's son and her own husband nowhere in sight.

...

Charlie drove like mad through the night as if hell was on his tail. He hadn't heard from Chase since the initial phone call and all he was able to get out of him was that he needed to come home right away. He could feel that something was wrong and grew angry at himself for getting off his guard. He had become complacent. He didn't think there was any more danger but he was wrong.

Wade was calling Jean's house and her cell phone every few minutes with no answer. *What the hell was going on?* he wondered. *Why was no one available now?* He didn't question Charlie's speed of 85 mph in a bus, down a dark Illinois highway headed towards Chicago. He just hoped they got there in time.

The bus pulled up about a half mile down the road from the house. Two fire trucks, an ambulance, police cars and all sorts of other traffic littered the area and Charlie wasn't able to get his bus any closer. He parked and flew out of the doors, running full speed down to where Celia's house was. The smell of acrid smoke hung thick in the air and Charlie was feeling its effects as he drew close to the house. A large crowd had gathered and was blocking the way, but Charlie could see that his mother's house was burned. Gone. Burned to the ground. The house that stood next to it on either side each sustained major damage and it was pure luck that there wasn't a breeze on that hot August night or else the entire street could have gone up. Charlie ran frantically around to each side of the house calling for Chase and his mother. It was Jean that spotted him and came over to him in a panic.

"Charlie... we have to get to the hospital. They've taken them to the hospital. I need you to drive me," she begged him as they stood before the burned out wreckage of Celia's home.

Charlie managed to take stock of her. She was wearing a thin muscle shirt and shorts, sweating from the heat of the night and the fire. Her hair was badly mussed and most of her curls were flattened to her head. She had glasses sitting on the end of her nose and nothing on her feet. Jean had literally come running from her bed, Charlie surmised. But it was her eyes that impacted Charlie most. They were wide with fright and almost unblinking. He could tell she was terrified by what had taken place and she hadn't found anyone that could help get her to the hospital to get some answers.

Wade joined them shortly after. He led Jean to her car and got the keys to take her and Charlie to the hospital. On the way, Jean relayed all she knew. The power went out earlier in the day. She and Marco played cards with Celia and Chase until around 10:30 or so, then left to go home and to bed. About an hour later, Marco woke her saying he could smell fire and hear someone calling "fire" down the road. He looked out the window and said he could see smoke and flames coming from Celia's house and to call 911, which she did. She was shaking with fear and sat staring straight ahead, her lips trembling. She sat quietly as Wade drove to the hospital and parked near the Emergency centre. The three rushed into the Emergency room. Wade got to the nurse at the reception counter first.

"We are family to Celia and Chase Morningstar and Marco Pelos who were brought in about an hour or so ago. They were in a fire… " his voice trailed off.

The nurse typed something into the computer. Keeping her eyes on the screen she said to Wade, "Mr. Morningstar is in Pod B, bed four." Her hand hit a large silver button on the wall next to her desk and the doors leading into the emergency bays opened up.

Wade, Jean and Charlie headed through the doors looking for a sign saying Pod B. When they found the pod, they looked for bed four and pushed back the curtain to reveal Chase lying on a bed with his eyes closed and an oxygen mask covering his nose and mouth. His hair was singed slightly around his face, as were his eyebrows. The right side of his face looked sunburned and his lips were swollen. He was wearing a hospital gown with his jeans. All three stood there for a moment, taking in the sight and smell of him.

"Chase?" Charlie said quietly as he approached the head of the bed. "Buddy, it's me, Charlie."

Chase opened his eyes and smiled slightly. Charlie felt a wave of relief wash over him.

"How you doin'?" he asked Chase.

"I feel like shit," Chase answered, his voice light and weak.

"Yeah, well you don't look much better, buddy," Charlie said and ruffled his brother's singed hair.

Chase smiled slightly again but Charlie could tell he was hurting.

"I am going to try and find a doctor," Charlie said as he watched his brother's eyes close, as he drifted off. Wade turned immediately and said to Charlie, "You stay here and be with Chase. Jean, have a seat next to the bed and I'll go and see about a doctor. I'll also see if I can find out where they've taken Celia and Marco."

With that he turned from the curtain and was gone from sight. Jean took the chair next to Chase's bed and sat like she was told. *I'll bet she's in shock*, Charlie thought wondering what had happened and what she had seen. Instead of questioning her, he let her be. She seemed quite fragile and ready to break at a moment's notice. Charlie would have to keep his eye on her as he didn't have a good feeling about this. Not at all. *Where were Celia and Marco? Why hadn't the nurse at the reception told Wade where they could be found? What the hell was going on?*

Wade came back through the curtain with a middle aged man wearing a blue shirt, navy tie and navy pants with a white lab coat. He looked like he had seen better days.

"This is Dr. Davis. He's Chase's doctor. He can answer questions," he said to Charlie.

"So, how is he?" Charlie asked right away.

"He's experienced second degree burns on his face and hands. He broke a couple of ribs and has a concussion. He also has some smoke inhalation, but all in all I'd say he was very lucky. I want to keep him overnight, just for observation, and make sure his lung function is okay and then let him go tomorrow morning," said the doctor. Charlie watched Chase intently as the doctor told him his prognosis. He nodded his head when the doctor finished and shifted his gaze to the middle aged man.

"My mother Celia Morningstar and our friend Marco Pelos and Jean's husband," he motioned to Jean in the chair, "were also brought in at the same time. Is there any way you could find out where they are and if we can see them?" Charlie asked.

The doctor nodded a moment and then left them. They looked across at one another and then all three turned their attention to the sleeping Chase. He seemed settled for the most part. There was nothing more they could do for him but let him rest peacefully. Charlie would make sure that they got him into a room for the night so he wouldn't have to spend the night in the Emergency department. He'd get no rest here with nothing but thin curtains separating each patient. Dr. Davis returned a moment later.

"Mr. Morningstar here is fine. Why don't you come with me and we'll see about getting you some information on your mother and friend's husband," he said, with his arm directing them out of Chase's room. Dr. Davis took them into a room with "quiet room" labeling the doorway. It was painted in cream with subdued lighting, two vinyl tan couches, a vinyl tan chair and indiscriminate paintings on two of the walls. It was a small room but had two very large Kleenex boxes on tables next to one couch and the chair. Charlie didn't like this.

"I have a colleague that I'd like to have join us, if you don't mind. Her name is Jenna and she's a social worker." He looked to the three for approval and they all agreed with a nod of the head.

Dr. Davis left the room closing the door behind him. They sat there quietly, Jean in a state of shock, still trembling, with Wade sitting next to her rubbing her back. He was very concerned for his sister. She didn't look like she was coping very well at all. Wade surmised from her story in the car that Marco had entered the house but never came out. They all had a bad feeling. When the door opened, a young woman with copper-colored hair cut in a bob to her shoulders, wearing glasses and a concerned look on her face, entered into the room carrying a chart and a pen. Dr. Davis followed shortly behind her. She and Dr. Davis both sat on the other couch opposite Wade and Jean. Charlie took the chair.

"Jenna, this is Mr. Wade McGrath, Mrs. Jean Pelos and Mr. Charlie Morningstar. They are the family of Chase and Celia Morningstar and Marco Pelos." The three all nodded to Jenna and she said hello to each back.

"I'm afraid that we have some rather difficult news to share with you," Dr. Davis said with his head down and his hands clasped.

"The fire that occurred has unfortunately claimed the lives of your mother Celia," he looked at Charlie, "and your husband, Marco," and he looked to Jean. "We are very sorry to have to tell you this. There was simply nothing that could be done. They died at the house before the fire trucks even got there," he finished, his face crinkled at the eyes as if in question as to what their reaction would be. "Jenna," he continued, "is well trained in grief counseling and can help you with what steps to take next." He looked to Jenna and got up and left the room.

The room sat silent for a moment. It was Jean's anguished cry that broke the silence. Sitting on the couch next to Wade she sobbed aloud and then fell into her brother's arms and cried heavily while he stroked her head and held her. He too was crying. He too had suffered loss. His beloved and talented brother-in-law of 30 odd years was dead in a tragic fire. His heart was already broken but then he thought about Celia. His

Celia. He had been in love with her since she started coming out to sing with George at the clubs. He never got the chance to let her know that he loved her. He had waited too long and now it was too late. As he sat holding his sobbing sister, his own tears streaming down his face he realized his loss was far more than he had originally thought. His heart was shattered.

. . .

Charlie sat stiff in the chair. He was so fucking angry! *Why had he allowed himself to stop being careful? Why had he been so stupid as to not keep watch over her? He knew* this was going to happen! She was 50! He knew what happened to the Morningstar's when they became 50 – death was coming soon! Wasn't that what the letter from the lawyer's office telling Celia about her inheritance clearly showed? Charlie had kept that letter hidden away for years, but he could recite it verbatim. All the dates were listed for the Morningstar family going back to his great-grandparents. The dates they were born and the dates of their death and so far, it was 4 for 4, including Celia! He didn't consider Meg – who still died *under* the age of 50! He had since recalled the elderly woman who, after his grandfather had died had said to him, " ... *especially* the Morning Star! It shines so brightly *for such a short time* but while it does, it outshines all others." Those words were stuck in his head like glue. *That* was why he didn't want Chase named "Morningstar." He had hoped to prevent the same outcome that would take them all – death before age 51. Charlie hung his head, drawing his hands through his hair. His heart was aching for the loss of his mother, the loss of his friend Marco and Chase who he had to tell this news to. Charlie felt as though he had been punched in the chest. He held his breath to try and keep his tears in but they came anyway. He had lost his beautiful mother Celia in a tragic fire. He could only hope that she felt no pain and was dead before the fire overtook the room.

. . .

The funeral for Celia was held a week later. Much to Charlie's surprise, she had arranged a burial plot next to George's nearest the blues club. She also left very detailed instructions for her service and had requested that Charlie sing Amazing Grace, Wade give her eulogy and Chase be made head pallbearer. Although he was overwhelmed with grief, Charlie sang Amazing Grace a cappella, for his mother, before all in attendance, with his eyes closed. *She would understand*, he thought, *especially now*.

After a reading from the bible chosen by Celia, Wade came to the altar and stood before the mourners. He took a deep breath and brought his head up to address the group.

"Celia was the finest woman I have ever known," he said quietly into the microphone. "She was strong and vibrant and extremely talented and she passed that along to her boys, Charlie and Chase." He struggled for a moment, looking to the front row where the aforementioned men were sitting. Chase with bandages still covering the right side of his face and sunglasses on; Charlie next to him also with sunglasses on. Both men nodded at Wade briefly as he struggled and it helped Wade get by the moment.

"Celia Grace Morningstar was the definition of class and she loved her boys most of all. For the past 20 some odd years I have watched as she raised Charlie first and then Chase, giving both unconditional love and guidance. She lit up every room she walked into as far as I'm concerned and I'll miss her every single day for the rest of my life."

Wade hung his head and left the stage. It was more a confession than a eulogy but no one questioned him. It was amazing the man could speak at all. He was also giving Marco's eulogy in two days as Jean had asked him to, stating that she couldn't possibly address a group of people at this time.

Wade also did Marco proud in his kind words. He spoke about how playing together had brought Marco into Jean's world and what a beautiful daughter they had produced in Georgie. He talked about how Marco and he had found a brotherhood because of their desire to make a living doing what they loved, playing music. They both loved Jean and they both loved Georgie. Wade figured he and Marco were kindred spirits, always finding satisfaction in the same things. Jean and Georgie sat staring straight ahead, holding each other's hand.

Georgie had flown in immediately after her uncle's call and took care of a lot of details while her mother was completely lost in her grief. She had attended Celia's funeral and now sat in attendance at her father's. *So like him*, she thought, *died trying to save someone else.* She wanted to be angry at him but she just couldn't. He spent his life showing her the gentle and kind side of a man's love and never once raised his voice or his hand to either Georgie or Jean. He had been completely supportive of everything either of his ladies requested and if he had an affair on Jean, it was with his drum kit and only when he played for the crowds. Marco was a stellar man with integrity. His daughter knew that and although her heart was broken, she sat with her head held high in honor of her father, Marco Pelos.

After Marco's funeral the mourners gathered in the basement of the church for refreshments and food. Georgie had seen Charlie and Chase at Celia's funeral but her mother was so at a loss that she hadn't time to talk to either one of them, having to take her mother home and put her to bed immediately afterward. When the ceremony was over, Wade offered to take Jean home and Georgie agreed. She could do with the break and it would be easier to take on everyone's condolences when her mother wasn't there under a drug-induced spell or sobbing uncontrollably.

She managed to get through the first half hour just fine but it started to take its toll on her. Charlie watched as Georgie paled at the approach of another musician to tell her about their experiences with her father. It wasn't that she wasn't appreciative, she was just overwhelmed.

Georgie had been living in New York for the past seven years and barring a few visits home, had not seen most of the people before her in many, many years. Her mother's inability to be present left Georgie in a very difficult and vulnerable position. She was only 25 years old. She hadn't even married yet although Carter was bound to propose very shortly. Now she faced a wedding without her father walking her down the aisle, and the possibility of grandchildren being born, with no grandfather to play with. Her mother widowed at the early age of 56. *That sucks! All of it just sucks*, she thought, as she fought back tears. *If one more person comes to tell me how sorry they are, I'm going to scream!* she thought, as she stood in the church basement. Georgie plastered a smile on her face and kept her eyes lowered, hoping she could soon leave.

"Hey," said Charlie as he approached her. "How're you doing?" he asked, briefly smiling while rubbing her arm. His touch set off electrical bolts through her skin and she almost jumped. Even now, with her and Carter in a serious relationship, she still thought that Charlie Morningstar was a dream.

"I don't know how much more of this I can take," she replied through smiling, gritted teeth.

Charlie hadn't seen Georgie for many years. Some things about her had changed dramatically, but deep down inside she was still the same sweet girl he remembered from long ago, playing on her front door step, dancing in her room.

"If you want we can get you out of here pretty damn quick," Charlie said, smiling gently as he looked around the room.

His dark suit, the second time she'd seen it in less than a week, looked good on him. For a blues guitarist, Charlie liked his clothes. He made sure he was always dressed well and knew how to dress for an occasion. Today he wore a black suit with black tie and shirt — he felt that sad.

Georgie looked him in the eye and asked, "How are you still standing? Between Chase coming out of hospital and your mom's funeral to take care of, you probably haven't had much time for rest. Besides," she smiled for the first time in a week, "you live on a bus." Oh, he liked it when she smiled! Even now, under a tremendous amount of grief and loss, Georgie still had a smile to show him. Charlie would be forever grateful to her for that.

...

Chase was sitting by himself at a table not far from where Georgie and Charlie stood talking. His face hurt and he needed more pain killers. He felt like shit and wanted to get out of there. He had been told about his mother's death and then Marco's death shortly after Charlie picked him up to take him to his bus parked in Jean's driveway. There was nowhere else for them to go immediately, although Charlie would eventually get a hotel room for a short time. Chase sat with his elbow on the table and his aching head in his hand. It had been the worst week of his life and all he wanted to do was find a place to hide. For the first time he could remember he didn't want to be out front and centre, he wanted to be away from any spotlight and cry his guts out like a three year old. He had witnessed his mother die in a horrific, tragic event and he was useless to help. He himself had to be rescued and it played upon his mind. What kind of man was he if he couldn't save his own mother? Georgie and Charlie made their way over to Chase who sat alone at the table.

"C'mon, little brother, we're going to go and take this lady home," Charlie said, as he helped Chase to his feet. The three of them walked out of the church basement all bearing the weight of their sadness on their shoulders and in their expressions. As the two men donned each side of Georgie, many turned to watch them as they ascended the church steps towards the main level. They made a memorable silhouette.

. . .

In the living room of the Pelos home, Wade, Charlie, Chase and Georgie sat discussing the future.

"I know you'll understand my decision Charlie, but I can't go anywhere for the next while. Jean... she needs me here," Wade said, his voice trembling. Charlie knew Wade would be staying. He couldn't bear the loss of both Marco and Celia and go back on the road. He, too, was going to need to heal and he would do that better helping Jean, for right now. Georgie was relieved to hear that. Carter had tried to get time off but couldn't seem to get his understudy to cover so he wasn't able to be there for her; even still, he had tried. She had been granted 10 days bereavement but she needed to be back in New York in a matter of days and couldn't leave her mother in the state she was in. Knowing Wade would be staying with Jean to keep his eye on her was a huge relief.

"Yeah, I know that Wade. I figured you'd want to stay here and watch over Jean, especially with Georgie being away," Charlie said, looking at Georgie as she sat next to her uncle. He shook his head and paused before saying his next sentence. "Thing is, I can't say I have much reason to stick around here, Wade. The house is gone and burned to the ground with almost everything precious to me in it, my only blood relative lives with me now and I'd rather put this fucking town behind me and not look back," he said bitterly.

Chase stared at Charlie. *Really?* he thought, *You really want to drive away from Chicago and not look back?* He sat wondering if his mother was looking down and shaking her head in frustration at them. His mother's desire was always for one of her children to make it big with their inherent musical gifts. What better place to do that than Chicago? But, at 18 years old, Chase didn't feel as though he had any say. Besides, he needed to heal first in more ways than one and didn't want to go throwing out his opinions when he wasn't able to live by them.

"I understand," was all Wade said. There was silence in the room as the four sat thinking of the enormity of their decisions and where their lives would take them. 20 years would pass before they would all be in same room together again.

Chapter 12

Present Day: Chase's Call

Charlie put his cell phone down and looked around at the mess before him. His hangover continued to ease and he figured he'd better get the bus cleaned up before he did anything else. He also needed to let Chase and the band know where they were going next. Some might choose to ride with him, but most usually flew if the gig was that far enough away. No one was as fond of living on the bus as Charlie. Realizing he needed a place to throw all the garbage, Charlie left the bus and went outside to where a steel garbage bin lined with a bag was just feet away from the back of the bus. Charlie grabbed it and rolled it to the front door and then proceeded to get inside and throw anything he could into it. It almost became a bit of a game to him and by the time he was finished he had scored 51 points, by his reckoning. *Fitting,* he thought smiling.

He filled the kitchen sink with hot, soapy water and wiped down the bus counters, cabinets and anything that looked or felt sticky. It must have been one hell of a party – too bad he couldn't really remember it all. He did remember the two encounters that he hadn't expected that changed everything for him. Charlie had spent 20 years running away from his fears. Now he was going home to face them.

His cell phone rang, breaking into his thoughts. It was Chase, again. He answered the phone and sat down on the couch.

"Hello?" he said.

"Happy birthday you old fart!" said Chase. Charlie laughed good-naturedly. "You still alive?" Chase asked him.

"Yeah", thinking of the irony of his question. "I'm feeling it today after last night! Who the hell was here? The bus looks like we partied for a month," he asked Chase.

"Oh, let's see, there was me, Rosa, Stilts, Simon, some girl he'd met, the blonde you were with and Frank, the guy who was on the bar last night. And you, of course." Charlie counted them off in his head; that was eight. Eight people partying in his bus. Jesus Christ, no wonder it looked like it did. Charlie was surprised it survived at all.

"Any idea what the blonde's name was?" Charlie asked. Chase started laughing and it made Charlie laugh too.

"You sorry old fool! You didn't even get her name?" Chase admonished.
"That's bad Charlie, really bad."

"I know," he said. "I don't usually do that – guess I was in a partying mood. 51 is a big number," he said to Chase, with more meaning than Chase understood.

"So, wanna grab some breakfast, birthday boy?" Chase asked him.

"Yeah, sure." Charlie would tell him over breakfast that they were headed home, although Chase wouldn't believe him.

Chapter 13

1994: The 20 Year Tour Begins

Chase and Charlie were to head straight out of town once they got on the bus. But Chase had asked if they could stop by their mother's and grandfather's graves one more time before they left. Chase wasn't sure how long it would be before he could gaze upon those sites again and wanted to let their spirits know that they were leaving.

When they got to the grave site, the earth was still fresh where Celia's remains were buried. No marker adorned her grave. George's headstone was simple; it read: *George Morningstar 1925 – 1975, Beloved Husband, Father and Papa.* Charlie had asked Wade to be sure and purchase a headstone for his mother's grave within the year. He left some money and instructions for her epitaph to read: *Celia Morningstar 1944 – 1994, "Lady sings the Blues."* Charlie thought it was fitting. Wade wept when he read it.

The men stood over their families graves, lost in their own thoughts. They didn't notice the elderly woman standing nearest to George's grave. When Charlie looked up, she was smiling gently at him. He smiled back and politely said, "Hello." Chase looked up to see who Charlie was talking to.

"Hello, I am so very sorry for your losses, boys," she said kindly. "I hope you find peace in your travels." She motioned her head towards the bus they had come out of and they nodded their understanding.

She moved past George's head stone and Charlie and Chase felt compelled to ask her, "Is this your husband?" as he pointed to a headstone with the name "Mitchell" written across it.

"Oh, no… I have loved ones nearby here, but I'm farther away you see. As she walked past Chase, she reached out and touched his arm as if she was bracing herself. Chase reached up to steady her as she passed on the grass and she happened to turn to him and smile. "You've done your work, now it's time to make your mark. You'll find family makes you stronger," she said as she patted his hand.

Chase smiled at her quizzically and asked, "Did you know our mother, Celia?"

"I'm not from around here," she said sweetly, shaking her head. She bent over to read George's headstone. "Such a shame to die so young. I do hope his memory lives long with you," she said to Charlie, as she shook his hand and offered her condolences. "It's good you boys have one another. Perhaps one day you'll find more family to surround yourself with."

She turned to walk away and Charlie and Chase watched after her a moment and then turned to look at one another in a "*that was weird*" way. They both looked back to see her leave but she was already gone.

. . .

Charlie and Chase left the cemetery that afternoon and kept on going. The first order of business was to get Chase a new guitar. Shortly after he had been released from hospital he realized to Charlie, "Papa's guitar was in my room. It was lost in the fire too, wasn't it?"

"Yes," Charlie confessed. "I didn't want to tell you yet but it was burned too badly to save," he said gently to Chase.

"Oh, damn!" Chase cried. "It's all my fault. If I hadn't left it in the room, I'd still have it," he said to Charlie, a look of anguish on his face.

"No, Chase, that's not true at all. That guitar saved your life, don'tcha get it? If you hadn't been awake and playing it... if you had been asleep in your bed, the second floor would have come down with you underneath it. Because you were awake and playing Papa's guitar, you smelled the fire and ran to try and help," Charlie explained. Chase thought about it a moment and seemed to accept this. He was grateful for Charlie's understanding, having felt guilty for not being able to save his mother. Charlie always put his mind to ease as if he had known it would happen and was out of their control.

Charlie drove them to a guitar store in Paducah, Kentucky, to meet a man named Ray St. Clair. This man had the best vintage guitars that Charlie had ever seen. He introduced his brother to the Willie Nelson look-a-like salesman and asked him about a replica to their grandfather's guitar. Ray scratched at his beard a moment and then his face lit up as he went into the back room mumbling to himself. He emerged a while later carrying a near twin to George Morningstar's beloved guitar. When Chase saw it he raised his eyebrows as if believing this actually might be okay. He took the piece from the salesman and studied it closely. It was pretty damn exact to his grandfather's except there were less markings and scuffs on it. The one he held had been used far less than George's had.

Chase looked up at Charlie and said, "It's near perfect. I can't believe it." His eyes were wide as if he was holding a golden statue.

"Sold," Charlie said simply to Mr. St. Clair and the men shook hands.

The boys left the shop with a smile and a bit of a lump in their throats. That was a hell of a find!

Now that they spent all their time together, they were finally able to jam and Charlie could see that Peter Schmidt had done an excellent job. Chase was a fine guitarist. His finger work was impressive and he could match the contemporary artists easily. It wasn't until he got Chase up on stage that he saw his brother's true calling. Where Charlie wanted nothing to do with being the front man, Chase was meant to be there. He had charisma and charm. He sang with animation and a style that made his performance utterly spellbinding. Charlie could happily sit back and play his guitar using his voice as only a backdrop to Chase's performance. This made Charlie very happy.

"I've been thinking about something," Charlie confessed to Chase one day while driving to Charlie's next gig. "I want us to form a band," he said carefully. "I want to start vetting drummers, piano players, trumpet players and backup singers and get a band together," he paused a moment, "and I want you to be the lead singer," he finished, looking over at Chase.

Chase's face burst into a huge smile. "Really?" he asked Charlie, incredulously.

"Yes, really," Charlie said. "You got what it takes, Chase, I'm telling you. You got what it takes," Charlie said, smiling too as they drove along. "But here's the thing, Chase. I'm not looking for fame and fortune here. I don't care about making it big in the music industry and playing to audiences that fill football stadiums. That doesn't interest me in the least. So, if your head is full of that, then we need to not do this," Charlie said sternly. At 18 years of age, Chase didn't know for certain what he wanted yet. But the damn sure wanted to give performing a try, and he had always thought that he and Charlie would be great together.

"No, I'm fine with that, Charlie," Chase agreed. "I'm not all into "Hollyweird" or anything. I just want to entertain like all the Morningstars have done for the past three generations. It's what I'm born to do," he said honestly.

"Amen to that," Charlie said as they crept along the highway.

Chapter 14

Present Day: Birthday Breakfast

When Chase found out they were going back to Chicago he almost fainted. At first, just as Charlie thought, he didn't believe him. But when Charlie told him about the conversation with Wade, Chase knew it was real.

"Holy shit, Charlie. I didn't think you'd ever want to go back. I actually bet Rosa one night a few years back that you wouldn't. Now I owe her a hundred bucks," he said shaking his head.

"Yeah, well, it's about time I think. Wade is family and it's been too long. Besides, we can help him out. Times are tough everywhere," Charlie said knowingly.

"Yeah, no shit," said Chase. They had toured for 20 years, making a decent living, a name for themselves, and having a good time. But these past few years had been hard on the country and the effects had been felt right down to the musicians that toured and played their hearts out to their audiences. Rooms that once were crowded were now not quite filled. Bookings were now sometimes more than a few days apart rather than back-to-back. Many club owners couldn't afford to pay the band for several nights and only booked for Friday and Saturday which really cut down on the band's revenue. The economy was killing the nightclub industry. But Chase and Charlie continued to do what they loved and always managed to find gigs that paid decently. They didn't need to let anyone in the band go and all were able to have some dollars in their pockets at the end of a night.

As he wiped his mouth from his breakfast, Chase sat back, sipped his steaming coffee and asked Charlie, "So, when do we leave? And more importantly, can we ride along or do you want to do the drive alone?"

"We leave as soon as breakfast is paid for and we can organize the crew. And yes, company would be nice," Charlie said, simply, and left it at that.

Chapter 15

1994: Chasing Charlie

Chase and Charlie auditioned for several weeks before choosing Rosa, a 28 year old backup singer of Latino decent. She wore her hair pulled back very tightly but it didn't take away from her dark looks and sultry smile. She was sexy as hell but more importantly her voice was excellent and she had an instinctual singing sense about her that Chase played off beautifully. They played off one another and matched note for note. They were electric when they sang together and Rosa's harmonizing worked well on some of the more bluesy pieces that Chase and Charlie created or improvised on.

They found their drummer Eric in Fort Worth, Texas. He was a 6', 3" tall, lean drink of water that was mostly legs, as Charlie described him. Eric was 24 years old and liked his food. Charlie had never seen anyone put food away like Eric could, but he played his drums with such passion and power that he was soaking wet by the end of each gig. Charlie figured he must drum away all his calories. By the time he was hired, Chase and Charlie were calling him "Stilts" and it stuck.

Their piano player was found one night in a small club outside of Atlanta, Georgia. It happened by chance that the group weren't playing and just stopped for a bite to eat. They watched a small group of musicians performing and all of them thought that the piano player

243

was excellent. Charlie approached him after the show and introduced himself.

"Oh, I know who you are," Simon smiled as he shook Charlie's hand. "I once caught your show outside of Austin, Texas, a few years back. Had me one hell of a night!" Simon gushed.

"Really?" Charlie asked as he smiled. "I wonder if you'd be interested in sitting with my group and me for a while and talking with us. I think we have an idea you might be interested in," Charlie said as he led Simon over to a table where Rosa, Chase and Stilts were sitting. He introduced Simon to everyone at the table and then ordered two more beers and brought a chair over for the man to take a seat. Within an hour, Simon was toasted as the new member of the group. Drinks were raised in honor, but as they toasted the group they were at a loss as to what to call themselves. Several suggestions were thrown out and even argued over but finally Chase spoke up with his suggestion.

"I think we should call us," "Chasing Charlie," he said. "And here's my reasoning:

Number one," he stuck up his index finger, "he's the oldest so we're all chasing him in age. Number two," two fingers shot up to emphasize his point, "it's what I remember best was chasing Charlie in the yard. And lastly, well it contains both our names, you know? Chase - ing Charlie... get it?" he said with his shoulders shrugged up, hoping they would.

A silence hung over the table for a moment and then Stilts piped up. "I like it," he said honestly. "I like your reasoning, Chase, but I also like that the audience can come up with their own reasoning for it. It can have its own mystery like, *What's chasing Charlie?* you know?" He looked around the group for agreement. He was greeted with mostly positive looks, except from Charlie himself who stared back at Stilts as if he'd just spooked him pale.

"I like Chase's thinking on it better," Charlie said grumpily and shot back the rest of his drink.

He raised his hand to the waitress and did a circle with his hand and then a shot motion in a request to get a fresh round and a shot for each at the table. Once everyone had their fresh drink and shot of whiskey in their hand Charlie raised his glass and said, "I hereby name this band "Chasing Charlie."

The collective group raised their shot glasses and repeated, "*to Chasing Charlie,*" downed their shot, and then each had a sip of their fresh drink. And so the band was formed and christened.

Chapter 16

Present Day: The Boys Come Home

Charlie pulled into the parking lot of the Black and Blue club and parked the bus.

"You guys can go in and get a drink if you want. I need to chat with Wade for a bit," he said.

He gave Chase a knowing look which told Chase that the two men needed to talk life before they talked business. After all, Charlie left Chicago 20 years ago, and other than a handful of phone calls for a short time after, he had completely lost touch with Wade. They shared more than 15 years together touring and playing their music, living in close quarters on a bus that Celia bought for them. *Had it really been almost 20 years?* Even though his phone call to Wade had gone well, he wanted some privacy to talk to his old friend and make sure that any hard feelings were completely set aside.

Charlie entered the bar through the back door. It was early afternoon so he knew that the cook and a few wait staff would be in setting up, but for the most part the bar would be empty. He walked into the front area and asked a person cleaning the griddle where Wade's office was. The man motioned to the stairwell to the left of the kitchens and Charlie headed up the stairs. He walked down a narrow hallway and looked into each open door until he came upon one that had "Wade McGrath" on it. He knocked lightly and walked into the room. Two large desks sat in the room on either side. One with a banker's lamp, very neat and organized with a pen holder and papers neatly stacked to one side. The other was a complete mess with papers strewn all over it and a curly, grey-haired, older gentleman sitting in the chair. He had a phone to his ear and was smiling as he spoke. When his eyes rose he spotted Charlie at the door. He motioned him to come towards him and quickly said into the phone "...well, gotta go Jim. You take care now and we'll talk real soon. (a pause) Yup, we'll do that. Alright now, bye-bye... Yup." And he hung up the phone. He rose from behind the desk and made his way toward Charlie with his arms wide open. "Charlie-boy, how the hell are you? It's so damn good to see you, my eyes hurt," he said sincerely. Charlie smiled as his old friend took him into a long embrace. Wade hugged him hard.

"Good to see you again, Wade. Been a long time, huh?" Charlie said, almost embarrassed for the time that had passed. He had kept in touch with Wade briefly in the beginning, had approved the purchase of the headstone for his mother's grave, had heard that Georgie had married and was expecting a baby and that Jean had gone to college for two years to study and earn a business degree. Once she graduated, she and Wade purchased the Black and Blue club with the life insurance that Marco left and some money Wade had saved up. They were equal partners; Jean running the business side and Wade running the talent side. It was a money maker from the very get go and the brother and sister team had flourished from their grief. Charlie had been informed of Jean's battle with cancer and that she had succumbed many years ago. He sent flowers to the funeral but he and Chase had not shown up, unable to bring himself back to that area at the time.

Wade brought Charlie to a chair in front of his desk to sit in and once again sat behind his desk. His smile hadn't changed or his curly hair, although it was now grey, but he had aged over 20 years and at almost 77 years of age, Wade McGrath was feeling tired. Charlie could see it in his eyes. Wade was always kind of thin, but he looked thinner and drawn and slightly pale. Charlie even wondered if Wade's health was in check or not. He had a paunch and he tended to keep his hand resting on it, like a bit of a shelf.

"Christ, Wade, aren't you ever gonna take a break from this?" Charlie asked as if no time had passed at all.

Wade laughed at his honesty. "Ahhh… I know," he said, resting his head back against the office chair he sat in. "There are times that I wonder who the hell is on stage and then I look at the next few weeks playbill and I'm excited to see the bands coming through. It tells me I'm an old fart that needs to retire from this," he said, cautiously looking at Charlie. "Thank God Gina is here to take the business side over. When Jean died I wasn't sure what the hell I was gonna do, but Gina knew enough business to be able to pick it up and we've done great," he gushed. Charlie didn't know who "Gina" was and wondered who had been able to take Jean's place in Wade's eyes. Whoever she is, she must be a hell of a business woman for Wade to approve of her.

"Oh, I know what you mean, my friend. I've been on the road some 30 odd years, living out of a bus and not really living a real life. I think it's about time that I find myself a place to settle and be at peace with," Charlie admitted to Wade.

The two men stared at each other for a moment and then Wade made a suggestion. "How 'bout you and I come to an agreement?" he said, moving some papers around on his messy desk. "Why don't you agree that *"Chasing Charlie"* plays for an indefinite period of time, perhaps even becomes the house band at Black and Blue for the next little while, and you find some settling here and quit your running away?"

He nodded at Charlie with drilling eyes and Charlie nodded back, but he didn't agree or disagree. The two men understood one another quite well. As they sat in a moment of agreement, a shadow passed by the doorway and caught Wade's attention.

"Gina," he called out. "C'mon in here," he told her.

Charlie could hear her saying something about "giving her a second while she found the papers for the liquor order" and then she walked into Wade's office and dumped her belongings into the chair at the tidy desk. Her long, dark, chocolate brown hair reached well past the middle of her torso and she kept her back towards Charlie as she unpacked her arm full of things and then turned to Charlie as she admonished Wade for "not keeping invoices straight."

Their eyes met at the same time and Charlie's breath was taken. It was Georgie... *his* Georgie! *How old would she be now?* he wondered. He remembered that she was exactly half way between he and Chase in age and they were 15 years apart. Charlie did some quick calculations to realize she was 43, almost turning 44. She had maintained her dancer's figure. Although Charlie couldn't imagine it was from dancing anymore, she was still in great shape. She was wearing a black turtleneck sweater dress that clung to her figure until just past the hips where it flared slightly out. She had black high-heeled boots on and all silver accessories.

"Charlie, you remember Gina, don'tcha?" he asked Charlie. *Gina?* Charlie thought.

His expression said everything and before he could speak, she said, "Of course he remembers me, don'tcha Charlie?" she said confidently. "Uncle Wade started calling me "Gina" after mom died," Georgie explained. "He thinks it sounds like Jean. He hasn't grown into a dementia-ridden old fool, Wade!" she joked with her elderly uncle. "Not like *some* people around here."

She smiled wide and walked towards Charlie to hug him. His heart leapt in his chest. He could hardly breathe, let alone speak and he was grateful for the moment it took for them to embrace and let go so that he could find his voice again. She felt good and smelled wonderful.

"Hello, Georgie," was all he could manage, but he was smiling at least. He couldn't stop smiling.

"Hello, Charlie," she said shyly, as she too smiled.

"S'bin a long time, huh?" Charlie asked the same thing she was thinking. "How are you?"

"Good," she said, nodding at him. "Real good."

"How'dya end up here with this old dog?," Charlie asked, pointing his thumb at Wade.

"I moved back to Chicago after my divorce. Mom took ill soon after so it was good that I was here. She died a few years later. Wade asked me to take over mom's side of the business and thankfully, I knew what to do, so it worked out. That was about 13 or 14 years ago now," she said, leaning against her tidy desk.

To Charlie she was perfection personified. Georgie would have been a damn good reason to come back to Chicago alone, but Charlie had no idea she was here. The fact that she was and was working in the Black and Blue was definitely a sign that he was on the right path. And she said *divorce!* He wondered if he was already too late and if she was in a serious relationship now.

"Are you here to play for a while?" she asked him, with her eyebrows raised. "Didn't think we'd ever see you back here," she admitted. Charlie hung his head — he did feel bad. He literally dropped off the face of the earth to them, he supposed.

As if almost reading his mind, she added, "Good thing most of the musicians we've had come through here have heard of you, jammed with you or seen you, so we were able to keep track of you. And you must have been doing the same 'cause we saw your flowers at mom's funeral." She didn't say any of it with sarcasm or attitude; she truly meant it just as it was said. Life had gone on for all and that was okay. Shit, she wasn't going to make this easy on him at all, was she? The more understanding she seemed, the worse he felt.

"Yeah, I really did need to be away from here for a while," he explained. "I thought that maybe this place had it in for us Morningstars"

"*Geez*, can't imagine why?" Georgie said, now with full sarcasm. "With me having divorced and mom taking ill, I think I'd be feeling the same way. It's not like Chicago has given you fond memories," she said understandingly, folding her arms across her chest. Charlie took a moment to study her. She had aged but only into a more beautiful version of her younger self. She had wisdom in her eyes, and a sense of self that Charlie found extremely refreshing. Her travels and life experiences had taught her well and not seemed to have done her any harm. He was glad for that. Georgie had always had a wonderful outlook and an easy disposition. Charlie was lost in thought when Wade broke in letting Georgie in on Charlie's plans.

"Charlie's decided to come and play for a while here, sort of like an honorary house band," he explained. Charlie nodded his head in agreement to what Wade was saying.

"What?" Georgie asked, surprised. She dropped the smile from her face and asked Charlie directly. "Thinking about giving up touring?" *Christ! She could read that deeply into something that was said so casually? Is it possible that she knew him that well?*

"Uh… that may be what's behind it," Charlie smiled at her and looked her directly in the eye. "I think I want to be static for a while. Touring's been great but I have nothing to show for it – it doesn't allow for much of the American Dream. Not unless you consider the bus to be the charming little house and white picket fence," he laughed. Georgie was still studying his face. He looked good to her. He may have lived a musician's life but he sure didn't seem to have paid the usual price that most musicians paid. Charlie was a class act, didn't do a lot of drinking, didn't smoke and stayed clear of drugs. Because of all that, he didn't look close to his 51 years. Georgie was impressed with how well he looked. She had wondered if, after he and Chase left Chicago, he would become a different man and fall into the hard life, but that never seemed to be the draw for Charlie. He was happy just making his music without all the trappings.

"Anyway, I haven't really explained it all to Chase and the group. I'd like to say that we're helping you out for a while until I figure out what I'm going to do," Charlie said. "I'm not lying to them, but I didn't book anything beyond last week, so the work will be great. It's just that the length of time might make them wonder what the hell is going on," he explained.

"Hey, they're *musicians!* Any work is good! I doubt they'll even care as long as they're getting paid," Wade said honestly, slapping Charlie on the back. *Too bad what the band thinks*, Wade thought. If Charlie wants to settle, then Wade was going to help his old friend do just that. Oh, Wade had ideas in mind and now that Charlie was here he could see them all falling into place.

The three of them made their way down the stairs and into the main club area. Charlie could see the group, including Chase, sitting in a booth across the room. Chase was mouthing off about waiting for service, or something. Charlie sighed heavily. Sometimes Chase's ego got the better of him. Again, as if reading his mind, Georgie turned to Charlie and said, "Oh, let me take care of Mr. Nicholas Morningstar!" with a huge smile on her face. *Uh-oh, this should be good*, thought Charlie. He hung back and let Georgie head straight over to the booth, carrying menus in her hands and lifting them to slightly cover her face.

"Wanna start with drinks first?" she asked, as she handed out the menus and gave the last to Chase, exposing her face to him.

"A person could die of thirst and starvation in here," Chase bitched, without looking up. He grabbed the menu from Georgie's hand and paid her no attention as he looked it over and told her in an off-the-cuff manner, "I'll have a beer," he ordered, completely ignoring her. Georgie stood stock still, staring at him with a blank look on her face. Seemed like Chase had changed – what a piece of work. She'd soon sort him and put him back in his place.

"Is that so, Nicholas? So life on the road has given you ego and taken away all the good manners your dear mother, Celia, instilled in you?" she asked him, in a stern voice.

Chase shot a look up at her as if he was about to explode, but then he heard what she had said. She called him *Nicholas*. It took a nanosecond for him to realize who she was and then he jumped up out of the booth and grabbed her in a huge hug and spun her around.

253

"Georgie Pelos, I don't believe it!" he gushed as he swung her around once more before putting her down. "My God, I so didn't expect for you to be here. What the hell? Are you working here or what?" he asked her, completely taken by surprise.

"I own half with Wade. I run the business side, he takes care of the talent," she said proudly. Chase looked good too, still a handsome man with sandy blonde hair and that million watt smile. He was a bit taller than she remembered and had filled out into a man with strong arms and a thick chest. He was strong enough to pick her up and spin her around without so much as breaking a sweat. She remembered the boy, but now saw the man. He stood back to give her a good look too. He whistled a wolf whistle, always the charmer.

"You sure have done well Georgie, you're a beautiful woman," he said honestly. Chase had no problem speaking his mind to women. He exuded confidence and sex appeal and you could literally watch a woman melt right before him. As if on cue, Georgie blushed slightly.

Charlie watched the entire interaction. He knew Chase had feelings for Georgie when he was younger and wondered if they still existed. It would be interesting to see how Georgie now responded to a mature, confident, charismatic front man of Chasing Charlie and not the younger boy she once babysat.

"Thanks, Chase," Georgie said sweetly. "And it looks like you've been eating your Wheaties," she joked with him. Charlie wasn't getting any sense of anything between them. Maybe he didn't have to worry about Chase's feelings 'cause they no longer existed.

"Well, I hope you see some change. Hell it's been almost 20 years! I'm a grown ass man now!" he laughed. "It would have been a sad day if the puny weakling of a 17 year old showed back up, wouldn't it?" Chase joked, acting out his stature and behavior when he was young and the booth all broke up laughing, even Georgie. It had been a long-lived joke about how young and puny Chase was when he started out, nothing like he was now.

"I remember you being a bundle of energy like the road runner!" Wade piped in as he walked toward the group, giving Chase a big hug. "It's been so long that you actually grew a neck," and the booth collapsed into fits of laughter again.

Chase could take the jokes and give them just as well. Charlie remained in the background, taking it all in. They were all together again; the four of them, and watching Georgie and Wade smiling and interacting with Chase and the rest of the group made Charlie feel more complete than he had in years. Charlie then entered into the circle and made formal introductions of his group to Wade and Georgie.

"Where are you staying?" Georgie asked the group. No one had thought of looking for a hotel or anything as they had driven straight in from California.

"Well, I can house the boys at my place. I have the room," Wade motioned to Chase, Stilts and Simon. "Charlie, I don't imagine you'll want to crash with us, huh?" he asked, knowing full well that Charlie would stay on his beloved bus.

"Nope, I'm good where I am Wade. Just as long as you're okay with me parking it at the back of the club," Charlie asked his old friend.

"Oh sure, that works fine. And listen, I drive a truck that you can borrow whenever you like. Don't be driving that thing around town like it's your damn vehicle. You'll have a bitch of a time finding parking for it!" he said as the group had a good laugh at Charlie's expense.

Another long running joke amongst the group was Charlie's penchant for his bus. They couldn't figure it out!

"Thanks Wade, I appreciate that," he said smiling.

"But that leaves Rosa all on her own, so I guess you'll bunk in with me then," Georgie said to her.

When Jean passed, Georgie was given the house. It was more than she and her daughter Hailey needed and since she'd be working at the Black and Blue, Georgie wanted to be closer to the club. She put her mother's house up for sale, much to Wade's chagrin, and found a red brick home with windows lining the one side of the house so that if you pulled into the driveway you were visible to the occupant and she could follow your arrival from inside the house by just walking from room to room. The driveway ended at a back door with a covered porch. It had a lot of natural lighting, bright rooms and a cozy, quaint feel to it. Georgie loved it immediately and found a school that Hailey could start attending. She could walk to the club in less than five minutes and she still had a yard, a neighborhood that was friendly and a decent school nearby. Georgie now felt at home, more so than she had in the past few years.

And so it was settled; Rosa would stay with Georgie and Chase, Stilts and Simon would stay with Wade, Charlie would be on his own aboard the bus.

Chapter 17

1995: Georgie

She left Chicago for New York many years before and when she and Carter married and Hailey was born not quite a year later, Georgie assumed that she would live her life there. But she came home one afternoon, earlier than expected, to find Carter instructing an understudy from the stage production of "Beauty and the Beast", on the finer points of fellatio. He was lucky his protégé didn't bite his damn cock off when she realized that they'd been caught. Georgie secretly wished she had! She took her half of everything, grabbed her one year old daughter from daycare and came straight back to Chicago, staying with her mother temporarily. Jean soon took ill after Georgie arrived and she never left. She stayed and took care of her mother until her death.

Carter didn't fight her in the least, which spoke volumes about the level of caring and commitment he had for her and Hailey. He contacted Hailey a few times over the years but the girl and her father didn't really have much of a relationship. Even when Hailey went back to New York to study theater herself, she didn't contact her father to let him know. He had certainly let her know that she didn't mean much to him so she wasn't about to give him any kind of importance in her life.

. . .

Georgie had concentrated so much on taking care of the business and her daughter that there was little time for anything else. What spare time she did have was spent helping as an assistant instructor at a ballet school which she had enrolled Hailey in. It was a great way to keep Hailey focused and gave Georgie a chance to dance again, if only for instruction of others. She found a happy life back in Chicago and was not sorry for how things had ended up. But she was lonely.

There had been very few options for her to date outside of musicians and Georgie really didn't want to date band members from the club. That was a policy that she stuck to. So, it was difficult for her to meet men her age with similar interests that weren't playing that week and gone the next.

She dated Michael Heslop on and off for a while. He was a single father of a boy at Hailey's school but it fizzled out when she became too tied up in her mother's health and then the club. In waiting for her to make time for him, he met Daisy Heaton and the two were married within six months. She wasn't even heartbroken about it; she was truly happy Michael had found someone. He deserved happiness.

She stayed single for a few years before she met Kevin Learmonth, a self employed entrepreneur who made big bucks in the stock market and watched his investments wisely. Just before the markets began to fail, Kevin sold his higher risk portfolios and settled nicely into careful markets where his losses weren't so great. He knew everything there was to know about investing and gave great advice, but knew nothing about romance. He had all the personality of a side door and after only a year and a half of dating him, she ended it. She'd heard enough about investments to last her an entire lifetime.

After that she had a series of dinner dates and one or two that maybe could have gone somewhere had Georgie shown more interest, but she just didn't try hard enough. She allowed the club to overrun her life and used it as an excuse to keep her from getting attached to anyone. She thought it was because of Carter's betrayal, or at least that's what she said, that she didn't trust men like she used to, but Wade thought there was a lot more going on. He didn't speak to her about it, but he had his own theory as to why she was otherwise engaged. Her reputation around town was nil. Known for her extraordinary beauty but also for being elusive and unapproachable, Georgie lived her days out in the tranquility of her home raising her daughter, and her nights at the club, watching the patrons, enjoying the music and counting the money. She rarely met with the band, if only to write their checks or count cash, depending on what deal Wade made with them. Sometimes, it was a cut of the intake at the door and so she would sit counting out the dollars while the show went on. Regardless of how she spent her time there, every night you could find her at the club, so she hadn't been dating for a while and since Hailey had left for college the year previous, she found herself at the club now more and more.

Chapter 18

Present Day: Chasing Charlie is Black and Blue

Signs went up all over town that Chasing Charlie would be playing at the Black and Blue starting Friday. Tickets were selling like mad and Wade knew the first few weeks they played would be sell outs. Good for business, good for Charlie. The more Wade could get Charlie to settle, the more his plan would fall in his favor. He wanted Charlie to be sure that his touring days were behind him and no better way to do that than to give him a stable footing right on a home base. If he could do that, he might be able to get him out of that damn bus and into a house; now *that* would be a triumph!

The stage had been prepared during the week for Chasing Charlie's set up. They did a sound check during the early evening to ensure everything was a go and were enjoying a meal in the club before the show, as was their ritual. The Chasing Charlie group was a close bunch. Although Chase and Charlie were the only two related by blood, they had welcomed each member with open arms and now had made lifelong friendships with them. Much like Charlie and Wade had, where after 20 years of not being in touch they could pick up right where they had left off, Charlie in turn gave the same kind of offering to Rosa, Stilts and Simon.

"Crowd will be in shortly," said Stilts, looking around as he picked up his second burger. "Bet you it's going to be jumping in here tonight," he said, just before taking a huge bite.

Charlie looked on in awe. "I can sure tell you're not even worried about your colon there, are ya, Stilts?" he teased laughingly. Stilts just smiled and chewed. He couldn't talk if he tried but it wouldn't have mattered 'cause he knew Charlie was right.

"Are you guys nervous at all?" Rose asked, looking from Charlie to Chase.

"Naw," said Chase confidently. "They'll be like any other audience and I'll have them eating outta the palm of my hand in no time."

He was sometimes a little too confident for Charlie, but he was also right. Chase was able to manipulate an audience into doing whatever he wanted. Where Charlie worked his magic with the guitar, Chase's real forte was with his audience. *They* were his instrument and he played them masterfully which always made for a memorable evening. And all the band members knew it. As they sat finishing up their meal, Georgie walked into the club. She was once again dressed in all black, which really suited her. Charlie watched her as she made her way over to the bartender, had a few words with him and then grabbed some books from under the bar, poured herself a water and lime and glanced through the entries in the bar log as she sipped her drink.

He couldn't take his eyes off of her as she studied the information intently. Damn! Even the way she sipped her drink was incredibly lovely. She let her tongue dance with the straw as she concentrated on the book. Charlie sat mesmerized by her and didn't hear Rosa's question until she finally had to say his name loud.

"Yoo-hoo," she said in a sing-song voice, "Oh Charlie. Earth to Charlie, come in please... ".

He broke free of his thoughts and looked at Rosa not knowing what she had said.

"What, sorry… What did you say? I missed it," he said apologetically.

Rosa stared at him for a moment, with a knowing look and said, "I asked if you were expecting to see anyone in the audience from the old days," she repeated, thinking that Charlie was more interested in the books and who was keeping them than he was in tonight's show or who would be in attendance.

"No, no one that I can think of," he answered honestly. "Once I started touring with Wade, we weren't home too many times. You've been with us for all these years – you know how many times we've been back," he said, as he made a big "zero" sign with his thumb and index finger.

"Yeah, but I bet they know of us. Chasing Charlie has got a following despite your efforts to not go into the main stream music industry. Always just a live performance group, right?" Chase said almost mockingly.

It had bothered him for some time that Charlie wouldn't even record with other artists when they asked. He remembered the deal he and Charlie made so many years ago, but he almost felt as if it were a deal with the Devil. Chase had been approached so many times over the years to "break free" and do his own thing but he felt a great sense of loyalty to Charlie for all he had done for him and didn't want to break up the band.

Charlie looked across at Chase wondering if he was reading Chase right. He could hear it in his voice that, for a while now, Chase was tired of not being a much bigger celebrity than Charlie would allow. Perhaps things would work themselves out in the next little while and they would both get what they wanted.

As the group left the booth ready to do last minute adjustments before taking the stage, Chase caught sight of Georgie at the bar. He whistled upon seeing her and walked right over to her.

"Hello, gorgeous Georgie," he said to her, all swagger and charm. He smiled his brilliant smile and Georgie couldn't help but smile back. He really was a lady killer.

"How is it a woman as fine as you remains single when you're surrounded by men all the time. Are they all blind?" he asked her, his arms outstretched as he took the bar stool opposite her and sat, leaning his elbows on the bar and giving her his complete attention.

"It's partly because I'm not swayed by a pretty smile and empty promises and partly because I make it a rule not to date the staff, including the musicians," she said with an equally dazzling smile. And with that she closed the book in front of him and left the bar. "I may not be able to call you "little man" anymore but don't forget, I taught you to stop sucking your thumb and used to change your poopy diapers," she threw back at him, with a cheeky smile on her face as she left the main room.

Charlie's face broke into his own million watt smile as he lowered his head, enjoying the zinger that was just thrown at his overly confident baby brother. He had listened intently to what Georgie replied and, although it meant that he might not have a chance with her, it definitely meant that Chase didn't, especially the poopy diapers comment. Once again, unbeknownst to Charlie, Rosa was watching him intently and now she knew for certain what had been going on all along; Chase loved Georgie and Charlie loved Georgie. *Oh shit!* she thought, *this could get either really interesting or become a disastrous mess.*

...

Their first show was a huge success. The crowd was catapulted into a night of hard core rhythm and blues by a band known for their captivating front man and stellar sound. Charlie watched as Chase carried the audience through his manic sets, his energy going higher than the ceiling, only to bring it back down when the song called for it. Their playlist was eclectic, spanning some 50 years of jazz and blues. They even improvised from time to time and the crowd loved it. Chasing Charlie would be a hard act to follow at the Black and Blue, that is, if they ever left at all.

After the show, as was another ritual for them, the band would sit around a table, have some drinks and talk about what worked and what didn't, amongst other things. It was at this time that the most interesting discussions would come up. As they all sat around the table this night, the atmosphere was still electric. Each of them was on a natural high from the energy the audience gave them. Wade sat next to Charlie, joining the group with Georgie at the bar, close enough to hear but far enough away to work on her books with an electric calculator. She was forever punching numbers and making the paper move forward as she figured the total earnings for the night. The room, once filled with loud and enthusiastic patrons, was now empty except for the group of seven. It made them feel like a family.

Funny, Charlie thought as he looked about the room and counted the heads of those round him. Seven again – I have seven family members just like when we were younger. As he looked over at Georgie at the bar, she looked up and caught his gaze. They shared a moment just taking in the other, then she looked at him and smiled and went back to her books. Charlie continued to watch her and then looked over at Rosa who was staring at him.

"So tell me Charlie," asked Rosa directly, "was coming home everything you thought it would be?"

Her question was leading and she knew it. She liked Chase a lot but she wanted Charlie to win Georgie. She had spent the last few days at Georgie's house and in her company and thought her to be a very caring, generous, intelligent, sensible and beautiful woman.

She made Rosa feel very welcomed, shared her home with her openly and they had a lot of things in common. She hadn't asked Georgie yet about her feelings for Charlie, still testing the waters to make sure she could dive in, but she was certain that Georgie had deeper feelings for Charlie than she did for Chase. Unless she was reading her wrong, Georgie seemed to have a sisterly love towards Chase, hence the teasing and the zingers. But with Charlie, she was slightly demure, as if shy around him or guarded of her feelings. Either way, Rosa knew that Charlie was in love and she wanted Georgie to know. Charlie sat back, pondering her question. He didn't say anything he didn't mean, so he chose his words carefully.

"It has been nothing like I expected and I am pleasantly and completely surprised," he said, quite jovially to her, and raised his beer bottle in toast. "To coming home," he said and the group repeated his cheer, *"To coming home."*

At the bar, Georgie smiled to herself as she kept her head down and worked her numbers. *Amen to that,* she thought.

Chapter 19

Charlie's 50ᵗʰ Birthday Year Begins

The band had toured for 20 years and had traveled across the continental U.S. probably 100 times over. During that time, their loyalty to one another and the band itself was rarely tested. The year leading up to Charlie's 50ᵗʰ birthday was one of those times. Quite simply, he was a complete wreck. He had spent the year exhausting the band with a ridiculous schedule. There were times when one or more of the group were getting pissed off with him and Chase had to talk to them and convince them not to quit. He had managed to isolate himself from everyone at some point or other and they were all ready to walk away. When Chase approached Charlie about it, he just seemed obsessed with keeping on the move, like he was running away from something but Chase had no idea what. He remembered when they were first naming the band and Stilts had liked the name they had chosen because it could be taken for *what is* chasing Charlie? These days it seemed very apropos.

Chase had decided to throw Charlie a sedate little 50ᵗʰ birthday party at a restaurant after the show he had lined up, but he had a hell of a time convincing Charlie to go. Charlie could barely sit still during the get together and he looked as if he was on the verge of heart failure. Chase was really worried about him. He only allowed an hour of celebration and then insisted they were on a tight schedule. Afterward he wanted to go straight to his bus and drive to the next gig. Chase wasn't sure what was behind his behavior but it didn't improve, it only worsened.

By the time a year had gone by and Charlie's 51st birthday approached, Chase was greatly concerned about his big brother and his mental state. Charlie seemed obsessed in making sure that Chase knew everything there was to know about how to run the band, his bus and the books, all of it. As if he was expecting to have Chase take over, but Chase knew that Charlie didn't want to break the band up so *what the fuck?*

Charlie lined up gigs that kept them in California for the winter months from January through to the end of March. After that, he hadn't done a thing. Chase was okay with this thinking; the band could do with a break and if Charlie had something up his sleeve past March, then his hopes were that this bullshit would end and Charlie would go back to being Charlie again. He had always had a sort of serious cloud over him, but lately it consumed him and he wasn't acting like himself. Not to mention he was drinking a lot more lately than he ever had and Chase worried that he was in a decline. If whatever was going to happen was going to happen near the end of March *then bring it on*, thought Chase, *I'll be ready.*

Chapter 20

Charlie's 50ᵗʰ Year Ends

Chasing Charlie was scheduled to play at the Indigo Palace in Carmel California on the night before Charlie's 51ˢᵗ birthday. The band had driven through another crazy week and landed in Carmel at 3:00 am – just enough time to grab some sleep and a shower before getting things set up and doing a sound check. Chase steered clear of Charlie for the most part as he was in another foul mood; he drank too much these days and Chase figured his mood was more so because of a hangover than anything else. Charlie sat quietly at the table as the group ate their ritual meal together, barely touching his food. As each one finished, they left their seat and went about preparing their instrument and getting one last chance at the bathroom. Charlie remained at the table, lost in his thoughts. He had been waiting the whole year and it had been hell. He wished that it was over. *This never knowing was going to be the death of him*, he thought and then laughed at his own pun.

He expected it from the time he hit 50 and it hadn't happened. Surely tonight would be it for him. He knew his time was coming, just like he figured his grandfather George knew it too. He remembered watching his Papa as he tried to perfect his speech enough to say "thank you" confidently to everyone. Charlie believed that George knew it would be his last night and he wanted to say so much more in those two words than just their literal meaning. Now, here was Charlie on the eve of

269

what he believed to be his last night on this earth and he had nothing to show for it.

He had made sure the band was not hugely famous because Charlie didn't want a circus media blitz when he was found dead, or worse yet, to drop dead in front of a massive audience. He was far too private a man for that. Once he was gone, Chase could do whatever he wanted, but he needed to have his privacy knowing it would all be ending very shortly.

He made his way to the bathroom and used the facilities, washed his hands and face and then left to get up on stage. The room was starting to fill up quite quickly and Charlie wondered how much shock everyone would be in when they heard that they had been there to see him play the last night of his life. With that thought, Charlie needed a drink. He made a bee-line for the bar and asked the bartender "Frank" to pour him two fingers of whiskey. The good man complied and handed it to Charlie who downed half of it standing there. As he turned to take the rest up on stage, he met the smiling face of an elderly woman. She was dressed to the nines in her finest swag and her face was lit up as she put her hand out to greet Charlie, who couldn't help but smile at her and accept her extended hand.

"I saw you play many, many years ago," she gushed at him. "It was probably one of your first performances, before you had a group together," she smiled. "I know I'm dating myself but it's wonderful to see you this last time."

Her words immediately hit Charlie hard. *This last time! Did she know? What did she know?* He looked at her intently and studied her face. She seemed slightly familiar to him and yet he couldn't place her. He wondered what she would be doing here and then realized she was probably a lover of jazz and blues from way back and knew that Chasing Charlie spanned 50 years of that genre of music.

As if in answer to his mental question, she parted his hand and replied, "Can't imagine you'll be back here again soon and I'm too old to be coming out like this. Tonight is so very special though – I just couldn't miss it. It's good to see two brothers be so different and yet so close. Each one of you has similar traits but you can tell you aren't cut of the same cloth. And each son follows his father…" and then she added cryptically, "and you're just like him." She smiled and left the bar, walking into the crowd.

Charlie sat there as the whiskey took effect and numbed his brain. Did she just say that he was just like his father? And how the hell would she know that? *He* didn't even know who his father was so how could she possibly know? He spun around to find her again and ask her what she meant. How could he possibly be just like a man he never even knew? He shot back the rest of his whiskey and left the empty glass on the bar. He scanned the room looking for the smartly dressed elderly woman but he couldn't spot her. Not too hard to believe considering the club had close to 350 people packed into it for tonight's performance.

He decided to look for her after the first set and proceeded to the stage to get set up. Within minutes Chase was centre stage quipping with the audience and introducing Charlie "Ladies and Gentlemen, Good Evening… the band's name is Chasing Charlie and I'd like to start off by introducing you to my big brother, Mr. Charlie Spencer Morningstar, who is celebrating his 51st birthday tomorrow." Chase began clapping and stepped away from the mike as the audience led a rendition of "Happy Birthday." Charlie blushed, then bowed, kept his head low and tried not to let them in.

He kept his eyes closed, as usual and played his first hour with ease. At the first break, he took off from the stage like a bolt and looked around the room for the elderly woman. He couldn't find her anywhere which seemed strange to him. He took to the bar to get a drink and maybe a different perspective of the room. She had met him there; perhaps she would be there again. He grabbed a stool and pulled it under him motioning to "Frank" two fingers. Frank understood, poured him the whiskey again and placed it in front of Charlie. As Charlie was about to raise his glass a gentleman approached him. He looked to be in his late sixties, early seventies with a shock of blonde hair cut close to his head, friendly eyes and a huge smile. He was dressed impeccably with a black turtle neck under a black suede jacket and jeans. He looked very polished, confident and healthy. He reached out for Charlie's hand as he approached him and for some reason, instinctively, Charlie shook the man's hand firmly. He tilted his head in question as the man motioned to Frank that Charlie's drink was on him and gave the same two fingered order identical to Charlie's. Frank placed the glass of whiskey in front of the man and took the $20 bill that he placed on the bar waving away any change. The man raised the glass to Charlie who did the same, they clinked their glasses and each took a swig from their drink and placed the remainder on the bar at the same time.

"Do you believe in coincidences, Mr. Morningstar?" he asked Charlie.

It always put him at a disadvantage that people knew his name but he didn't know theirs. He had become used to it over the years, but it was a part of the gig that Charlie didn't much care for.

"Coincidences?" Charlie gave this some thought. Before he could answer, the man interrupted his ponderings and said, "...or, do you believe in fate? Predestined lives, already mapped out and beyond our control." His words were freaking Charlie out. First the old lady talks about *the last time* and now this guy mentions predestined lives with things that were beyond our control. *What the fuck?*. Is this how it was going to be – a series of cryptic conversations that would prepare him for his final journey? Was this what his mother and George had experienced?

"I'm not sure what the hell to believe in anymore," Charlie said to himself as the drink helped calm him just a little.

"I wonder if you'll allow me to tell you a story. One that is of consequence to you, let me make that perfectly clear," he said as he raised his finger. There was something strangely familiar about him and Charlie watched him like a hawk, studying his every move, wondering what the hell it was about this distinguished old gentlemen that intrigued Charlie so.

"Many years ago I had a very lovely and brief relationship with a beautiful young woman which was considered taboo at that time. My mother found out about it and had me shipped off thinking she would nip it in the bud because, you see, she was not my mother's first choice for a mate for me and she did everything she could to manipulate mine and my sister's life back then." He sipped his whiskey and continued.

"So, I was shipped off to Europe after only being with this lovely lady one night but she remained in my heart the whole time. I wasn't able to get word to her of what had happened and hoped that by the time I got back I could reunite with her and explain everything. When I came back to America several months later, she was gone, nowhere to be found. I asked around, I waited out near where she lived but I wasn't able to spot her. I finally gave up, thinking that she had done the same with me." He paused to drink again and let this much of the story sink in for Charlie.

"My sister, Vicky came to me one day a few months later and told me she had overheard a conversation my mother had with a friend of hers regarding the orchestration of sending me away, and that the girl I had fallen for had become pregnant. Vicky said that my mother aided in having the girl sent to a place in Chicago to have the baby and then to give it up for adoption. I was young at the time and when I found this out I blew up at my mother because I loved the girl very much. But she wouldn't hear of it and made it such that I couldn't do anything about it until I became my own man. When I did, it was a quest of my own personal time and money to find my love and my child."

"She once told me a story that her wealthy grandparents had disowned her father because of whom he had fallen in love with. When the parents died tragically, the son was completely left out of the will, leaving all their money to the law firm her grandfather was working for. He had them name the firm after him. I knew of the firm and in time I earned enough money to buy out its shareholders and have the place audited from one end to the other…" As he started saying this, the hair on the back of Charlie's neck stood up. He knew this story, *he knew it well!* It was the same story that was told in the letter Charlie had secretly kept. It was the genesis of all of Charlie's fears.

"See, the firm he owned and all his estate was left to its shareholders. So I had the whole thing investigated and found a 12 minute loop hole. I then had a separate firm seek out my lady love and had them send her

273

a check that I hoped would help her out in her life along with a letter explaining everything, except my involvement and identity," he said slowly, watching Charlie's face turn towards him and look him directly in the eyes.

He reached into his suit pocket and produced a duplicate of the letter that Celia had received that day and showed it to Charlie. Charlie reached into his own breast pocket and produced his wallet. Inside it, he pulled out a very old and worn piece of paper that, when unfolded, was identical to the one the man was holding.

Understanding overcame his face and, after a pause, Charlie asked him "Who are you, sir?" The man hesitated a moment too long – long enough for Charlie to make a connection.

"Are we related?" he asked the distinguished gentleman.

"My name is Bradley *Spencer* Dumont," emphasizing the "Spencer" part of his name. As he shook Charlie's hand firmly again, he added, "…and I do believe I'm your father."

Chapter 21

Present Day: Georgie's Houseguest

As Rosa and Georgie made their way to Georgie's house that night the two were silent, not typical for the usually chatty women. They had spent three days together and talked endlessly about everything, making them fast friends, but now they walked in silence the few blocks to Georgie's house, each having something heavy on their mind.

Knowing that Georgie had spent her childhood watching Charlie become a man and then being there from the moment Chase was born to see him raised, made Georgie a wealth of untapped knowledge into what made each man tick, especially Charlie.

"It must be nice to have Chase and Charlie back here in town again. Had you ever seen them perform before?" she asked innocently. She wanted to bring them into the conversation so that she could ask more direct questions about Charlie Morningstar.

"No... remember, I was too young when Charlie performed the first time for his mom – I babysat Chase that night. The next time we were together again was at Celia's and my father's funeral. I haven't seen him since," she said, like she'd had this conversation with Rosa before.

"Right," Rosa bluffed, "that's right," realizing the importance of tonight for Georgie. "So that means that *tonight*," she emphasized the word by pointing downwards with her finger, "was the *first* time you've seen Chasing Charlie?" she said incredulously and then asked, "So? It must be *very* interesting to finally be able to see the boys on stage. What do you think?" she asked Georgie, her face full on in front of her with her eyebrows raised and an expectant look on her face.

Georgie thought Rosa was a sweetheart and enjoyed her company very much. She had brought laughter to her house which had been quiet for too long after Hailey left. Georgie liked having someone at home.

"I think they are both incredibly talented in their own way. I used to watch Charlie as a teen as he played Meg in his room and made such great music then. Of course, at the time, I didn't appreciate what I was seeing but I knew enough to know he was extremely gifted. His fingers would move like lightening. And I remember hearing my father tell my mother about his ability with a guitar and how amazing he was. If my father thought a lot of him, then you can rest assured he was excellent because my father didn't say that about just anybody," Georgie said with passion, holding her finger out to bring home her point. It made Rosa aware that she spoke as passionately about Charlie as she did of her father. Rosa was a very observant woman.

"Charlie hides his emotion so much but sometimes you get glimpses of it through his face when he plays. I saw that tonight. He closes his eyes and he thinks he's closed off to the audience, but I can see through it. He used to sing and I remember he sang at his mother's funeral. It was unbelievably lovely. I can only imagine he'd be as wonderful if he ever took the mike but I understand he's given that up completely and handed it over to Chase, who," she carried on breathlessly, "is obviously born to be in front of an audience and knows exactly how to work them. I honestly have never seen such stage presence in all the years I've been working a club. Not even during my years in New York did I ever see someone who shines so bright as Chase Morningstar," she said and then stopped.

She looked at Rosa who had a surprised look on her face and the two women broke out laughing. They got inside Georgie's home, put their things away and met back in the kitchen with a glass of vino blanc and a platter of cheese, crackers and grapes to demolish. So what if it was past 2:00 am? It was nice for both women to have the other to bond with. As the girls chatted around the issue, Rosa suddenly put it right back on the hot plate and boldly asked Georgie as she sipped her white wine, "So, of the two Morningstar boys, who do you love more?"

Chapter 22

Like Father, Like Son

Bradley Spencer Dumont stared at his look-a-like son with amusement in his eyes. He knew his news would blow Charlie's mind and he had yet to tell him of how he came to be in this place this very night, of all nights.

"You think you're my father?" Charlie asked incredulously as he gaped at the man standing before him. He scoffed for a moment and looked about the bar to see if anyone else was witness to this.

"I'm sure this is all very hard for you to understand but Celia was the lady that I speak of and she and I were together for only one night. Through my investigations I found out that she went to Manning House in Chicago and instead of adopting out our child, a son she named Charlie, she *kept* the baby. Are you aware of any of this?" he asked. Charlie had known none of this of course, as neither Celia nor Papa George had shared anything negative relating to him being in their lives. He was always treated as if the sun and the moon rose and set on him. He started to realize how hard it must have been for a young teenage Celia and how much she must have struggled to keep him. He wasn't sure if she had George's support from the very beginning or not, but in the end, he had been a wonderful, loving grandfather who cherished and adored his grandson. Had there been ill feelings, to their credit, Charlie was never aware of them.

"Your name… Charlie Spencer Morningstar. I had no idea she had named you that until tonight when your brother said your full name to wish you a happy birthday. My middle name is also…" and as he said the word "Spencer" Charlie mouthed it right along with him. "It's my mother's maiden name, you see," he said smiling.

And there it was – the tie that binds. Celia devised it so that she had the last laugh over Beverly Spencer Dumont. Giving Charlie her family name as a middle name was a great way to link Charlie with Bradley and a sure fire way to piss off Beverly had she ever found out!

"But the most astonishing piece about this whole thing is the way I came to be here tonight," Brad continued, looking at his son in earnest. "After I had the lawyers locate your mother there was little else I could do. I married a few years previous and was in no position to offer up my love or any kind of relationship to her. I hoped the money would help and left it at that. For years I have carried a duplicate of the letter in my brief case should I ever come across an opportunity of searching you out, but until this very afternoon, I believed the letter lost somewhere along my travels. I have seen the world at least three times over for business and pleasure. My late wife and I were avid travelers, so after not seeing the letter for a quite a few years, I assumed it was lost… until this afternoon. I came into town to try and help a business deal that was tanking and after meeting the clientele for lunch, I went back to my hotel room to look over some papers. I decided I needed to get rid of some of the excess papers I had been carrying and found *this* letter," he shook it at Charlie, "in amongst all of the things I had been carrying. It had been there all along. Anyway, when I read it again it reminded me of Celia and I became melancholy and came out to find a club to sit in and have a drink. See, Celia sang this beautiful song for me once that was sad and bluesy but she sang like such an angel, I'll never forget it. And so, every time I think about her, I find a blues bar I can sit in and drown my sorrows in. Tonight, it was *this* bar, of *all* the bars in town," he said and he made his point to Charlie. "Don't you see, it was meant to be that we should meet? Do you realize how many things had to be in play for us to meet up here of all places? If I hadn't found this letter today, or if you had booked another night, our paths would never have crossed. So you see, we were meant to meet up," he said confidently,

Charlie gave this some thought. He was blown away with every sentence that Bradley spoke and yet, he found it hard not to believe the man. As well, it truly was like looking in a mirror. It was obvious that they were closely related; even Charlie could see that now. He sipped his whiskey and asked his father with a slight grin on his face, "So tell me, is my manipulative grandmother still alive?" knowing she'd probably hate to know that he called her that.

"No," Bradley said, shaking his head. "Sadly she passed a few years back. But my dad, your grandfather is still going strong at 89! You come from a very long line of centenarians, Charlie. My father's father, my great grandfather and your great-great grandfather, he lived to be 106 and his father lived until 108!" he said proudly and raised his glass to his fine lineage. "Yup," he said, patting his son on the back and then raising his glass to him, "I know we've lost a few years but by my reckoning, Charlie, we have a good twenty or thirty to go to make up for it."

Chapter 23

Present Day: Rosa Plants a Seed

Georgie's face froze as Rosa looked at her questioningly. Either the wine was getting to her or she was starting to feel very sleepy because she no longer had the desire to sit up and chat with Rosa any longer. Rosa saw it in Georgie's face right away but wouldn't back down.

"Oh no... oh no you don't, girl," she said firmly. "You are not going to close that door on me. Even Stevie Wonder isn't that blind. I have watched you watch both Chase and Charlie. I've seen how you look at them and I've listened while you gush over them. Now, you can sit here until the break of freakin' dawn and tell me till you're blue in the face that you don't have those kind of feelings for either one of them and I would say you are bullshittin' me! I have been around those two men long enough and watched dozens of women fall in love with them and I *know* that look. Thing is, now, I have *never* seen them have the same look back, *except with you*," she pointed her red-tipped finger at Georgie, who stared straight ahead at her glass of wine.

"Now 'fess up here, Georgie. It's just me and you here now. You can be completely honest with me. Do you love one more than the other?" she asked point blank.

Georgie looked into Rosa's face. Even though they had been bonding very quickly, Georgie couldn't help but feel that she had only just met this woman. Why was she sharing these feelings with her, especially when Georgie was only just trying to sort them out within herself? When she walked into Wade's office three days ago, it was as if she had the wind knocked out of her. Never in a million years did she expect to walk in and see Charlie-friggin-Morningstar standing in the middle of the office on a Tuesday mid-morning. But there he was and it took her right back to being the young girl, teenage crush, young adult woman-under-duress, that she was when Charlie had been in her life. All the old feelings came rushing back to her, all the old desires of wishing he acknowledged her as more than just a little sister type friend. But unlike Chase, Charlie never once gave her the impression of anything more than that. Unlike Chase, Charlie had such a serious side to him that she tried hard to figure out and understand and… unlike Chase, she had strong feelings for Charlie.

Chase would always be a little brother to her. They had shared so many different things together and she had played an older role model to him. That would never change even though now he was a handsome, mature man who was showing a definite attraction to her. She could only ever look at him as her "little man" even if, physically, he wasn't any more. And now Georgie wondered if Charlie felt much the same way about her and it frightened her to think that he might.

Chapter 24

What's Going to Happen Tonight, Charlie?

Charlie made his way back on stage after the break. His mind was reeling and he was in a complete state of shock. Chase caught the look on his brother's face and went over to him and whispered, "Hey there, Charlie buddy, ya might want to lay off the nectar, ya know at least until after the gig, okay?" He patted Charlie on the back and smiled at him as he stepped away and grabbed the mike. "Hey, it's Chasing Charlie and we're back for our last set of the night!" he announced to the crowd who cheered and whistled their approval loudly. "And one more round of applause for my big brother's 51st birthday," he yelled out as once again the crowd started singing "Happy Birthday" to Charlie. It was so surreal to Charlie. He heard the rendition, the lilting sing-song, but it faded to the background while another voice came through loud and clear. The voice of an elderly woman whom he had seen a number of times throughout his life. Sometimes at the most troubling times, as he recollected. Like tonight, when he believed he was facing his own impending mortality, she had been here. And she said things to him that were very specific at the time, but they didn't mean anything to him then, only now, in context of all that had happened.

In the record store she said, *"It's up to you to pass his memory onto those that didn't know him, be they stranger or kin!"* and that was just after his grandfather died, almost as if she knew Chase was coming along later on. And then when she asked about George's name and he told her, she replied, "...*especially the Morning Star! It shines so brightly for such a short time but while it does, it outshines all others*." Charlie thought she was talking about him, but she was really talking about George. He now remembered she was also there at the cemetery the day he and Chase left Chicago all those years ago and she consoled him over their loss once again and said to him, "...*such a shame to die so young. I do hope his memory lives long with you*." Lives long with you! And now tonight when she was at the bar she told him that, "*each son follows his father... and you're just like him*." Then shortly after he meets her, he meets his father for the first time who tells him that his paternal lineage is one that has a long line of centenarians amongst it! Who was this woman who passed these messages to him? She was someone who had guided Charlie throughout his life, he had come to realize, but not like he had originally thought. At first he believed that she was foretelling his death, like his mother, grandfather and great grandfather before him. Instead, she was letting him know that he would be the one to outlive them all and that their memories would be his to pass along. It was up to him to ensure that the world knew of the Morningstars that came before him and entertained the world with their love of jazz and blues.

As these thoughts settled into Charlie's mind, he felt a great weight lift off of his shoulders and that nagging feeling he'd carried in the pit of his stomach for all these years finally released. For the first time in many years, Charlie had hope! He had reason to feel happy and something to look forward to, whatever that was. He played through the next set quickly, periodically checking to make sure Brad still stood at the bar where he left him. His father waved at him and gave him the thumbs up half way through and it made Charlie smile to himself. *His father!* He was here and seeing him perform with his band. If Charlie had a million guesses, he would have not have come up with this as the answer to, "*What's going to happen tonight, Charlie?*"

He spent the past year thinking he would not rise tomorrow and now he believed he just might and many more after that! With the last song played and the audience spent, the band took their bows and Charlie made his way straight to the bar to see Brad again. As he approached his father, Brad stepped forward and took him by the arm.

"Look son," he said, "I really hate to cut short this reunion but this old bird is catching an early flight out first thing in the morning," he explained. "Here's my card and all my contact information is on it. I sure would like this conversation to continue. Give me a call if you would as well."

"I'd like that a lot, uh… uh… Brad." He stumbled over what to call this man, his father, but Brad only smiled. He understood Charlie's dilemma.

"Do you have any other children that might have a problem with this?" Charlie asked, thinking quickly.

Brad shook his head and looked at Charlie. "My late wife was unable to have children. We tried for years. By the time we thought about adoption we were both past the age of having the energy, I'm afraid. I always knew you were out there but never told her. So you see? You're the only child I have, Son," he said as he shook Charlie's hand again. Charlie pulled the man into a strong embrace and Brad held his son in his arms for the very first time.

As he pulled away he said to Charlie, "Your mother did such a fine job raising you." He took out a Kleenex and wiped his eyes and nose as he spoke. "You're an incredibly gifted guitar player and have a wonderfully generous heart to be so kind to me," he said shakily. "I'm proud to know you as my son, Charlie." He gave Charlie a strained smile as he held back his full emotions. "I'm in Peoria. Please look me up when you come back home." Charlie simply smiled at his father and watched as Brad turned and made his way out of the bar.

Chapter 25

Present Day: Two Women,
One Man and a little nudge

Georgie decided that giving up everything too quickly wasn't a good idea. Especially when she wasn't so sure that Rosa wouldn't tell Charlie everything she had said. Figuring Rosa's loyalty sat with Charlie, she played it safe.

"I don't really know what to feel, Rosa. Those boys are so like family to me it's hard to think that there would be a romantic feeling amongst us at all," she lied, shaking her head slowly.

Rosa knew what Georgie was doing and couldn't really blame her. Rosa downed her glass, popped a grape into her mouth and got up from her kitchen chair speaking as she chewed it down quickly. "Well, when you figure it out you need to inform them both of where your heart is at 'cause I'm sure one of them is going to be elated and one of them is going to be heartbroken. I'm done," she said and kissed Georgie on the top of her head. "G'night, sweetie," she said endearingly. "We'd better get some sleep or we are going to feel like shit for tomorrow."

Rosa walked out of the kitchen and left Georgie sitting there with her last sentence still fresh in Georgie's mind. "…*one of them is going to be elated and one of them is going to be heartbroken.*" Georgie sighed heavily.

She thought about Charlie tonight and reflected back on his performance. She had watched him more closely than anyone else on stage. When most eyes were drawn to Chase and his energetic style, she couldn't take her eyes off of Charlie. He was such an enigma to her and she wished she had the key to figuring out what he held so closely to him. She noticed him smiling more than she remembered and he had seemed sincere in his answer to Rosa's question about his coming home expectations. In the past, Georgie remembered that Charlie always seemed tense when he was home, almost as if he looked over his shoulder the whole time he was here. But his homecoming this time was different somehow. He had shown a desire to stop touring, not something the Charlie Morningstar she had known was ever interested in doing. Perhaps something had changed to make him want to settle, but what? She had no way of knowing and Charlie wasn't giving out his reasons just yet. She took her glass of wine with her as she went off to bed. She needed to be able to sleep without thinking about Charlie Morningstar and the wine would help.

. . .

Rosa lay in bed thinking about Charlie too. She had been touring with him for 20 years and still didn't think she knew him very well. Until, that is, they came back to his home town and then it all made sense. Rosa believed that the dark cloud that Charlie carried for all these years was because the woman he loved had married someone else and he thought she was lost to him. Now, after coming home and finding her here and available, Rosa believed that Charlie was ready to make his move. She had no way of knowing about his belief that death was just around the corner of his 50th year – Charlie told no one of his fear. So when Charlie's mood seemed to lift soon after their gig at the Indigo Palace in Carmel and he decided to come home, Rosa figured he had been surprised to find Georgie here and he decided to finally do something about it. *Maybe it was hitting 50 that did it*, she thought, a *mid-life crisis*? She was now single again at 48 years old. Having tried marriage twice she came to learn that no man wanted to play second to her love to perform and tour with Chasing Charlie. She knew excellence when she performed with it and Chase and Charlie Morningstar were not only excellence personified, but they brought that out in their band mates as well. Rosa's chemistry with Chase on stage was electric, but off stage they were truly just friends. After she divorced her second husband, she vowed that she would never marry again unless and until she had toured for the last time. She hadn't come to that point yet. More importantly, she just hadn't found anyone worth giving all that up for.

It occurred to Rosa that perhaps Charlie and Georgie needed a little hand to help push them towards one another. She smiled to herself thinking she could provide that push, just a little nudge really but she had to be ingenious about it. She had to let some time pass and see how things played out first and if it didn't come to what she knew was its natural conclusion, she would definitely be nudging one towards the other. She may not be able to manage her own love life very well but she had a very good feeling about Georgie and Charlie. She closed her eyes and drifted off to sleep feeling that there was going to be a real shake up in the next little while. She had no idea how right she was!

Chapter 26

Party On The Bus!

Chasing Charlie sat around the table in the Indigo Palace with a few of the staff and the owner, all enjoying a celebration for the evening's performance and for Charlie's 51st birthday. They toasted him numerous times and Charlie, sitting back and relaxing for the first time in a long time, enjoyed and joined in on their antics. When the bottle of Jägermeister was brought out, Charlie was given three shots one right after the other which resulted in the group chanting, "Char-lie! Char-lie! Char-lie!" while he shot the three back in succession. When he slammed the last shot glass onto the table, they erupted in cheers and applause. Chase left for a moment and came back with a cake and the numbers "51" in candles lit on top and put it in front of Charlie while the group sang "Happy Birthday" to him once again. He blew out the candles and smiled at the group. He could feel the effect of the Jägermeister and allowed it to have its way. *What the hell!* he thought, *you only turn 51 once!* A blonde waitress with a very pretty smile came over to him, kissed him on the cheek and brought a seat over to sit next to him. She flirted with him endlessly for the next hour and when the group decided to continue the party on the bus, she followed along with her arm through Charlie's arm.

"Happy birthday to me," he sung to himself, his eyes glued to her ass as he followed behind her up the bus steps. The party raged for another hour with the best of the blues being played loud as can be from the bus's excellent sound system and Charlie sitting on the couch feeling no pain as everyone celebrated him. Food was brought out, pizza was ordered and munchies of every kind were found after Chase rifled through the kitchen and small pantry.

At one point the bartender, Frank, who also joined the group, sat down beside Charlie. They nodded to each other and Frank clapped his back and shouted over the music, "Many happy returns, Charlie." Charlie nodded his head and smiled at him, drunk. Frank got closer to his ear so he didn't have to shout and said clearly, "Nice to see your dad out enjoying the show too." He pulled back and smiled, nodding at him.

In his drunken state, Charlie reacted quizzically to Frank's comment until he remembered his conversation with Brad and slowly nodded to Frank. *Hmmmm… even the bartender could tell he was my dad*, he thought, *holy shit!* He smiled to himself and raised his glass in silent honor of his new found father and drained it. A diminutive hand took the glass from his and pulled him up off the couch. The blonde with the pretty smile danced as she held his hand and continued to dance him down the hallway towards his bedroom. *Oh, I'm going to be sorry tomorrow!* Charlie thought happily as he closed the door.

Chapter 27

Present Day: Two Brothers,
One Woman and a Red Trunk

Chasing Charlie's second night at Black and Blue was also a huge success. Charlie felt more comfortable on stage than he ever had and was more animated than usual, playing off some of Chase's antics and quipping with him more than once. Even Chase did a double-take when he was given a zinger by Charlie at the end of the first set, but he loved it. Charlie was better than ever!

It was at their round table drinks after the show that Charlie told the group, "I want you all to know that I'm very grateful for your patience with me in the last year or so. I've been..." he paused, choosing his words carefully, "dealing with some demons and ..." he hesitated "... and believe that they're truly behind me now," he explained. Raising his glass to the group, he mouthed "thank you" to them all and made eye contact with each one of his band mates, his brother, Wade and then Georgie. Their eyes locked and she could feel her heart quicken. The group sat, jaw dropped, at Charlie's admission. This was more than he'd expressed to anyone in 20 years' time. Each and every person around that table knew that something had changed inside Charlie Morningstar at that moment and they all had their own suspicions as to what it was.

"Oh, come on now..." he said, laughing. "You don't all have to look so shocked at me. Nothing wrong with a man admitting he's got demons.

I've just come to learn in the last little while that mine aren't what I thought they were," he explained. The group sat silent for a moment and thought about what he had said. Wade watched him closely and made a mental note. Chase finally broke the silence when he raised his glass and said, "May we all learn by your example, big brother."

The table toasted Charlie's evolution and the group fell silent again. It had been an exhausting few days, a hell of a lot longer for the band and now they had three days off before they played again. Charlie had told the group they were headlining at the Black and Blue for a few weeks and, just as Wade predicted, that was just fine for the musicians. Besides, they hadn't had any downtime for quite a while and it was long overdue.

Conversation picked back up again and before long the night was ending. Chase remained at the table while most everyone else started packing up. As Georgie walked past, he grabbed her hand gently and pulled her down to whisper in her ear.

"Wanna stay and have a drink with me? We can get to know each other as adults," he tried, hoping Georgie would be open to the idea. She smiled at him, not wanting to hurt his feelings. He really was a lady killer with his unbelievable smile and his charm. If she hadn't grown up with him, like she had, she'd probably have already been swayed by him. But in her heart, she wished the request came from someone else. *Wrong brother*, she thought as she looked at him. She knelt down in front of him as he sat in the chair.

"I'm sorry Chase, I can't tonight," she said trying to let him down easily. "Maybe we can have a drink before the show on Tuesday. I'm really wiped now and need to get home. Besides, Rosa's staying with me," she said, gesturing to Rosa who stood waiting for Georgie with her bag slung over her shoulder and her hands full. "But thanks," she said kindly.

It wasn't really saying a firm "no" to him but it wasn't misleading him either, *was it?* She squeezed his hand as he continued to hold hers and then rose to depart, letting his hand drop as she walked away.

As Charlie cleared his things from the stage, he kept the entire exchange within his field of vision. He couldn't hear what they said but they looked intently at one another, much the same way that Charlie had looked at her at one time or other these past few days. For him it was trying to come to terms with his feelings for Georgie. He had suppressed them for so many years, first, because of her age, then because of the circumstances. Now, he had no reason to suppress them except he wasn't sure about two things; her feelings or Chase's feelings, both of which were very important to him. Would Georgie ever be able to love him and if so, how could he be with the woman that his brother had loved for years?

While she knelt by his chair, she looked at Chase in such a way that Charlie wasn't able to read it. It could easily be read as "passionate." He knew Chase had a thing for Georgie, he always had. But a schoolboy crush was not the same thing as a grown man's love for a woman and Charlie wasn't sure which his little brother was feeling. *Could Chase see her after all these years and instantly be in love with her?* Charlie wondered. *Well, why the hell not, you are! You fool!* he admitted to himself, but he realized that neither he nor Chase had *instantly* fallen, they had *always* been in love with her and if that was the case then they both had the right to fight for her. Charlie figured he had nothing to lose by trying. He had wasted the last 20 years not having anything, not wanting anything permanent because he wasn't going to live long to enjoy it. Now, he didn't want to waste anymore time. If it was between him and Chase then Georgie would have to choose. Perhaps she'd choose neither one of them, wanting a more familial relationship with them both. He wouldn't like that, but if that's the only way he could have Georgie in his life, then so be it. Perhaps she'd choose Chase, an outcome Charlie would have to learn to live with because he loved them both. He hoped that Chase would feel the same way should he be the lucky one but he'd have to cross that bridge when the time came. As long as Georgie was still an available woman and Charlie had breath in his body, he wasn't going to let her go without trying. He wasn't prepared just yet to declare his love, feeling vulnerable in his new found awakening, but he sure as hell was going to let her know that Chase wasn't the only one who had charm and charisma and a heart with her name on it. He'd just do it in his own way. As he methodically packed Meg away, Charlie started making a plan.

...

After three days off, Rosa entered the bar feeling excited about the night's gig. It had been a long time since the band had any amount of time off like that, where they were settled in a town and could just relax. No traveling, packing or unpacking or checking into or out of a hotel/motel room. Rosa had become quite settled at Georgie's house and spent the 3 days exploring Chicago and taking in some of its highlights — but mostly, she just relaxed.

Georgie spent only a couple of hours each day making sure the club had everything in order but with no show being held Sunday through Tuesday, the girls were free to do as they pleased. It had been a while since either had a close female to chum around with and both enjoyed the other's company. Usually, Rosa would do whatever the guys were doing but Chicago offered her not only a friend's home, but also a friend. She was really starting to like Chicago.

Rosa made her way to a table nearest the stage to drop her things on and sort through whatever costumes pieces she would use for the night. Depending on the song, Rosa had a few things that she would adorn to give it a touch of fun, be it a hat or a feather boa. She always liked to spice up the song. As she sorted through her items she had no idea that a pair of eyes were glued to her every move. Watching from the kitchen was Marlon, a 50 year old cook with a strong Hispanic background who came up to Chicago following a dream of opening his own restaurant, but the money fell through. When Wade found him, he was days from being flat broke. Both felt it was a stroke of luck that the other had come along at the time and their relationship grew into a deep respect and understanding of one another. Marlon wasn't just a cook in a bar. He was a masterful chef who had a way of creating the best of something out of nothing and serving it up at $14 per plate! He had made Wade a very wealthy man just in his food alone, but when the bands starting being of a certain caliber, Black and Blue became somewhat of a hot spot for the city of Chicago.

For Marlon, it was all about having creative freedom in his kitchen, and Wade offered that. He didn't want to serve his patrons "bar food" when such incredible music was being offered. He insisted that his food be as good as the music and because of Marlon, it was. He had worked at the Black and Blue for nearly 10 years and was off on a few days when Chasing Charlie came to town. He had not yet met the band and had no idea who Rosa was; he just knew that she was the most beautiful woman he had ever seen. He couldn't take his eyes off of her as she rooted through her large canvas bag, pulling out different clothing accessories and getting them ready for tonight's show. He peered around the corner for a moment more and then hid again as she turned her head and faced the kitchen area. Rosa thought she'd seen someone in the kitchen and wandered back there to see who was in. She had become pretty friendly with the kitchen staff as was her way; Rosa loved to cook. Whenever she got the chance, her fellow band mates were treated to some incredible dishes thanks to Charlie's small kitchen on his bus and her handy work with food, spices and all things Latin cooking.

"Hello?" she called out as she fixed the feathers on her red boa and made them lay straight. "Is that you Isaac?" she asked.

Marlon stepped around the corner and smiled as he stood there. Rosa looked up expecting to see Isaac, a 20-something college student who was filling in while the regular cook was away. Instead, there stood Marlon. He was 5' 11", a husky man with deep brown eyes, a bushy mustache, and bushy eyebrows that framed his face in such a way that he looked like he was constantly surprised. He was a solid man – legs and arms that had some power to them, but a very soft heart. His face always had a smile on it and as he looked at Rosa, he couldn't help but beam at her. She was just beautiful!

His smile was contagious and she instantly smiled back. She figured he was the regular cook and walked towards him to introduce herself. She always made friends with the kitchen staff, that way she'd be allowed in the kitchen if she felt like watching or sometimes, even teaching a dish or two.

"Hi, I'm Rosa," she said with her hand outstretched as she approached. "I sing backup for Chasing Charlie," she explained. Marlon blushed immediately which Rosa found incredibly endearing. *How lovely*, she thought.

"Pleasure's all mine," he said as he looked directly at her and shook her hand, holding it firmly in his hand. He wasn't sure if she felt the electric jolt that passed between them, but he sure did. "I'm Marlon. I'm the head cook here," he explained. God, his heart was racing.

"Oh hey, Marlon," she said innocently. "Everyone here speaks of you like you're a god or something," she smiled as she told him. "I can't wait to try one of your signature dishes. It's very rare that you get great blues or jazz *and* great food too and I've been touring for many years," she said, nodding her head at him. Isaac, Wade and Georgie had told her about Marlon's ability in the kitchen and all had said that she was in for a real treat when he returned. They stood holding hands for a moment before Rosa let go, embarrassed. *Oh dear God*, she thought, *I know this feeling*. Rosa had an intuition about Marlon that was strong and she became very aware of the electricity between them, it was so palpable.

"Uh… so," she said, clearing her throat, "What's on the menu for tonight? Now that your back, I am told to expect great things," she said.

"I can only hope my reputation precedes me, my lady," he said, gallantly backing away.

It took Rosa's breath away. *He was a romantic! Oh my*, she thought dreamily. Marlon blushed again as he went back to his work. He wanted to make a dinner especially for her, before she went on stage. He created a chicken and vegetable soup with chickpeas, carrot, green beans, chopped avocado, white cheese, and a chipotle chile pepper called caldo tlalpeño. Marlon believed the way to a true Latino woman's heart was through her stomach, much like a man's.

When the band had all arrived for their ritual pre-gig meal, Rosa's meal was placed before her without so much as her asking. The smell alone was intoxicating and all those around the table were wondering why their dinner hadn't arrived as quickly. The moment Rosa put the spoon into her mouth she knew. This man was a fabulous cook!

After the show, she and Marlon sat at a table in the far corner enjoying a platter of cheese, crackers, grapes and selected cold meats with a stellar pino noir as they talked the night away. When Georgie motioned to Rosa that she was leaving, Rosa gave her an "o.k." signal and sent Georgie on her way. Georgie knew Marlon would have the experience and also the keys to be able to close the club up. From the look of things, Marlon would either be bringing her home tonight by car, or tomorrow in time for her gig. Regardless, Georgie was going home alone.

. . .

Chasing Charlie had been playing as the "special house band" at Black and Blue for six weeks. Rosa and Marlon were now seeing each other exclusively and she had practically moved into his small apartment over the last two weeks. Georgie had not seen her at home in a while and whenever they were at the club, they joined at the hip in the kitchen until Chasing Charlie took the stage. The patrons were the true benefactors of their relationship but Marlon and Rosa would deny it, both feeling as though they had found the love of their lives.

Although Georgie was incredibly happy for Rosa and Marlon, she couldn't deny that she missed her house guest and started feeling lonely. She was spending more time at the club enjoying the energy of the Chasing Charlie band mates and also, in hopes that she could see Charlie more often. The shows had been very successful and the band changed things up from one night to the next so you never knew which songs they were going to play. Some nights were simply improvised and those were the nights Georgie loved the best! Chasing Charlie had perfected their bluesy, jazzy sound and Chase always had the crowd begging for more. So, six weeks in and they were still drawing large crowds into the club. Everyone was thrilled, except Chase.

When Chase thought back to his brother's mood over the last year he could definitely tell something was up. Charlie hadn't made any plans past March so naturally Chase kept thinking if he was going to break the band up or do something big then. Chase had prepared for it, convincing himself that he could carry the business end of it if Charlie felt like he needed to take a break from doing it. That was what Chase had expected. Then, when Charlie said they were going home to help Wade, and his brother's mood seemed to lighten, Chase figured that after a few weeks, they'd be moving south again, going back on the road – that whatever it was that was eating at him had resolved itself. But Charlie wasn't talking about moving on. Twice Chase had asked him when they were going to head out and make more bookings and both times Charlie had no answer for him. He seemed quite happy playing the club each night and going home to his bus parked in the back lot. Rosa had all but moved in with Marlon, and Stilts and Simon were renting an apartment above the Chinese food place four blocks down. Even though he and Wade had plenty of room at the McGrath family house, this whole setup was starting to piss Chase off. As much as he understood Charlie's sense of guilt over not staying in contact with Wade after so many years touring together, Chase didn't have that relationship with Wade and didn't feel he owed him anything. In some ways, he resented Wade for taking Charlie out of his life when he was younger. As a grown man he understood it better now, although it still burned him that he now had to put his life on hold to help Wade out. He was stagnating here, always playing to the same crowd. He needed to be out there, in the clubs, different clubs each night. They were in Chicago for Christ's sake, where there was a blues/jazz club on every corner. Why did they stay at the Black and Blue?

Chase had put some feelers out from Illinois going east to New York and received a hell of a lot of interest. Chasing Charlie hadn't really spent a lot of time touring the North East and this was a perfect way for Chase to make himself known nationwide, and then maybe Georgie would see him as more than her "little man." Oh, Chase had a plan!

. . .

Georgie sat down on a stool on the inside of the bar, with her laptop open. As she sat there waiting, resting her elbow on her knee, she looked around to see who had made their way in and then wondered what delicious feast Marlon was fixing up for them tonight. It was about 40 minutes until dinnertime with the band, which had become a ritual that now included Wade, Georgie and Marlon. His culinary creations were something that the group very much looked forward to each night and he never disappointed. Some nights, he and Rosa would cook together and some nights he alone would prepare the feast. Every night, their shared meal was delicious and they always gave the chef their highest praise for his impressive work.

On nights when the club was closed, they would all gather at Wade's home. He still had the family dining table that sat 12 comfortably (with the leaves in) and was found to be in need once again after so many years of a single diner. They became another makeshift family in their weeks together and Georgie smiled thinking of how she and the boys had continued the patchwork family tradition. She had hoped that within these last weeks, she and Charlie would make some headway romantically, but other than some intense staring and knowing smiles, he continued to play it cool and she had given up believing that he could see her as anything but his little sister. What was she to expect? After all, she felt the same way about Chase, didn't she? She hated it but had learned to accept it, thinking that she would enjoy him while he was here and once he left, she'd regroup and go from there. *Stay in the present*, she thought.

"Hey Mom!" Hailey's voice broke through her daydream and suddenly Georgie was staring at the "Skyped" vision of her daughter, thousands of miles away but near enough to touch.

"Oh, honey!" she said, tears instantly welling up in her eyes. "It's so good to see you." They hadn't Skyped for a few weeks and Hailey hadn't been home in almost two years. Georgie held her hands to her face while she gazed upon her daughter's face, who was also crying at this point.

"God, honey, I miss you so much," Georgie gushed to her daughter. Wiping her tears with her hands and laughing at the same time, she asked Hailey, "How did the show go? Were you a hit? Are your classes going well?" in rapid fire. Hailey laughed at her mother. It was the same routine every time they Skyped. Georgie would cry, which would make Hailey cry and then Georgie would fire off questions for the next little while wanting to know everything about Hailey's life. She really needed to contact her mom more often but her schedule was crazy busy between theater classes, rehearsals or performances for whatever show they were working on at the time and holding down a part time job at as a tour guide at the Guggenheim.

"The show went well, really good reviews. I'll send you the link. I got some good reviews personally and one not-so-good review from this bastard who needs to be shot and pissed on. And, my classes are okay. I'll be happy to see this year done, though. It hasn't been a favorite one for me," she admitted to her mother.

"I know you said that this semester was the worst. It didn't get any better then, I assume?" Georgie asked, slightly concerned. As her mom, she always wanted to make sure things went perfectly well for Hailey, but she also knew that was unrealistic.

"No, it sure didn't. I'm actually studying right now for an exam about "Theater in the Jacobean Period" amongst other things. You can't imagine how friggin' boring it all is. I don't get why I have to learn all of this stuff when I want to understudy for "Oklahoma," she quipped, rolling her eyes and then pretending to hang herself with an invisible rope. Hailey had a hilarious way of seeing her world and the theatrical influence only enhanced it. She made her mother laugh every time they were in contact.

"Hailey, the language," she admonished her daughter as she suppressed her laughter. Hailey really could do no wrong in her mother's eyes.

"Whatever, Mom!" she said in a thick New York accent. "If you don't thrive, you won't survive," she said as if quoting a mantra.

"Agreed!" her mother said, raising a glass of water and lime to her daughter.

"And what about you? Are you doing well? How's it been for you with the whole Chase and Charlie being back in town thing?" Hailey asked her. Georgie had confided in her daughter that the boys were back for a rare extended visit and how confused she was feeling. Georgie looked around, not seeing anyone about and then answered her honestly, "Oh, you know, same old same old. Nothing's changed, I'm afraid," she said with a heavy sigh.

"Well, you gotta make it work, Mom. You gotta take that chance!" she encouraged her mother.

Hailey brought her face closer to the screen and Georgie marveled at the fact that she was as old as she was. It seemed like only yesterday that she was toddling around her house, learning how to read in the wingback chair in the den, cuddled up with her mom. The old McGrath red steamer trunk Georgie had used for her own dolls and then for Hailey's toys had become a nice centre piece for Georgie's den until Hailey left for New York and convinced her mom to let her take it with her. Hailey now used it as a table with storage to hold her clothing and other things. The trunk could be seen whenever Hailey put her laptop down on her bed. Georgie would look for it in Hailey's apartment and commented on it as if it were a treasured item, now lost.

. . .

Wade and Charlie sat opposite one another in the office upstairs from the bar, having their own conversation. It had been discussed that Wade wanted Charlie to consider staying a while longer and maybe even permanently. Charlie could take over the hiring of the musical talent and, if the band wished, they could continue playing as the house band.

"I don't know Wade, I think Chasing Charlie is gonna grow old on people," Charlie admitted to his long time friend. "I hear what you're saying but I'm not sure we could fulfill the audience all the time," Charlie said honestly.

"Well, of course not you fool!" Wade admonished jokingly. "You bring in singular acts like Walter Trout or Nina Storey to play or perform. It'd be a sellout, see? That's exactly what *we* used to do and made a fine living off of it for almost 20 years!" he explained to Charlie. He needed Charlie to understand that this was all going to work out and he could have exactly what he wanted but there were difficulties, some sacrifices must be made. The only way for it to work successfully was if a) Chase was willing to share the stage or b) if he wasn't the front man at all. Wade knew that too many times the "guest artist" liked to take centre stage and not play off of some other central performer; especially someone like Chase Morningstar. Wade also knew that Chase didn't like to share centre stage. Charlie and Wade locked eyes for a brief moment and Wade knew instinctively what Charlie was thinking.

"I know," Wade said nodding his head. "It wouldn't work with Chase out front," he said with a tilted head and his hands held up in exasperation. It would be a hard pill to swallow but Charlie needed to realize that in order for he and the rest of Chasing Charlie to stay at the Black and Blue permanently, Chase needed to move on and allow his band mates to play alongside the other artists that might grace the stage. Very few would try and stand next to Chase Morningstar; they knew they wouldn't shine as bright. Rosa, Stilts and Simon were now considered talented artists and veterans at what they did, not to mention Charlie who had his own following and any performer out there would feel privileged to play or sing alongside any of the four remaining group members. But Chase's on stage antics and his reputation plus a solid following, would make any great artist not want to stand beside him for a whole gig.

Charlie had known for a while that Chase wasn't happy staying at the Black and Blue and that he certainly didn't intend to stay for an extended period of time. Charlie was torn between wanting to take root for his own sake or go back out on the road and finally give into Chase's constant requests to try New York and the recording industry. A part of him felt as though he owed Chase that, even though that wasn't the deal they made all those years ago. Charlie's plan was to ensure that Chase's future was soaring, regardless of whether he was a part of it professionally or not.

"I get it, Wade," Charlie said getting up from his chair. "I'm thinking Chase will be getting more on my case about how long we've stayed and that we should be making tracks sooner rather than later. I'll try talking to him and get a feel of where his head is at," Charlie said as he patted the back of the chair.

"Thing is, Charlie," Wade warned him, "He isn't going to be happy staying and…going means without you, doesn't it?" he asked Charlie, testing the waters with him. Charlie stared at him for a moment and then shrugged his shoulders. "Aw hell, Wade, I'm just trying hard to give everyone what they want here, including myself. Chase has been really great for all these years to just be happy with whatever I wanted. Now, I feel I owe it to him… you know, to become the superstar he's meant to be. It's me that's held him back all these years and we both know it. I just feel… I don't know, like it's time I gave him his way. I just don't know what that means yet," Charlie said honestly.

He was struggling so hard with what to do where Chase was concerned. He'd felt so sure of himself weeks ago but lately he had started second guessing his own decisions, vacillating between Chase's demands and what his heart was telling him. He and Georgie were no further along. Part of his plan was to let some time pass, although he hadn't intended on it going on this long without some sort of gesture being made on his part. He just hadn't found the opportunity. Rosa was living with her until 2 weeks ago and he really didn't want to approach her at the club. He had been racking his brain to try and figure out a way of letting her know his feelings for her but no real chances or epiphanies had come forth. With Chase and Georgie both on his mind, he knew he couldn't give Wade a commitment one way or the other yet.

"I'll think on it some and get back to you. It's all in the approach, you know?" Charlie said. He nodded to Wade and waved his hand in a goodbye gesture as he left the office and carried on down the hallway towards the bar.

Wade sat staring at the open doorway, thinking. This was too difficult a decision for Charlie to make. Wade knew he had to make the decision for him. He grabbed his phone and punched in a number, leaned way back in his chair and waited for his call to go through.

"Kramer, Kligman and Stein," the voice answered.

"Roger Stein, please. Tell him it's Wade McGrath."

"Certainly Mr. McGrath," the receptionist replied and transferred the call. After only 2 rings, it was answered again.

"Roger Stein," the voice said confidently.

"Roger, its Wade. I need to meet with you really quickly. Some last minute changes that I need you to make. You'll understand when we meet," he told Roger very quickly.

"Sure thing, Wade. I'll see you in a half hour then?" Roger said, understanding Wade's sense of urgency.

"Excellent, see you then." With that Wade hung up the phone.

As he leaned forward towards his desk he grimaced and his hand flew to his stomach. His breath caught and the color drained from his face as he waited for the pain to pass. It generally did but lately he'd been experiencing more prolonged pain. He remembered that George Morningstar had taught him that breathing in a four beat pace was the best remedy to suffer through bad pain, so he tried it. It worked for a while but he knew that this kind of pain wasn't going to be taken care of with a good breathing exercise. He was glad Roger was willing to see him this quickly. This would help everything for everyone. Wade was sure of it.

• • •

As Charlie left Wade's office he thought about the man he had just left. At 77 Wade was looking his age. He seemed thinner over the last few weeks, perhaps that was to be expected, but Charlie wondered if longevity ran in the McGrath family tree. He'd like to be able for Wade to be a part of his life right up until both of them were old as hell. He was the closest thing to a father Charlie had since his grandfather had passed and the years that he and Wade spent touring up until the fire had been incredible. They had bonded, shared space for months on end and argued over everything from apple sauce to the state of "Zen."

He was a very stable force in an otherwise chaotic lifestyle and Charlie loved him more than he had ever expressed. His silence over the last 20 years was disrespectful and Charlie knew it. He owed Wade so much more than that and one day he was going to tell him about his fear that death was waiting for him. He'd tell Wade all of it and then maybe Wade would understand his distance. Charlie owed him that.

. . .

Georgie and Hailey had been chatting for some time. They covered every topic from school to fashion and even some of the award shows that had taken place in the past weeks since they chatted. Hailey was full of the latest gossip and even gave her mom the latest scoop on her ex-husband's life.

"I swear I almost died when I saw him!" Hailey was saying as Charlie entered the room. He could see Georgie at the bar with her back to him and the laptop sitting on the bar. Technology always intrigued Charlie and he couldn't believe that someone could talk to another person thousands of miles away over a computer! It was a little mind boggling to him, not being that computer savvy.

"Oh my God. Did you say anything to him?" Georgie asked, her voice sounding shocked as she stared at the girl on the computer.

The girl laughed and it sounded just like Georgie's laugh. *The apple and the tree were only inches apart*, he thought. As Charlie drew closer he could see Hailey more clearly and realized that she was a close run to her mother's image. She actually reminded Charlie of the same girl who came to his mother's funeral all those years ago and showed such strength and resilience at such a time of loss for herself as well. He decided to enter into the bar area and make himself a drink. Trying not to be conspicuous, he poured himself a beer.

"No, nothing at all," replied Hailey. "But I had a good look at him. I, like, stared at him for about 10 minutes straight. I swear I thought he was going to sense it but he didn't turn my way once. I have his chin," she said all at once. She spoke so fast that Charlie could barely understand her but then, there seemed to be a lot of excitement in her voice. Maybe that was the reason. As he stood pondering that very thought his reverie was broken by Georgie's voice.

"Charlie, come and say hello to my daughter, Hailey," Georgie said, waving him over with her hand. He came to stand beside Georgie and looked into the computer screen. At this distance she was nearly an exact replica of her mother, except her hair was shorter and, as she said, she didn't have Georgie's chin.

"Hello, Mr. Morningstar." Hailey waved as she smiled into the computer's camera.

"Hey, Hailey, nice to er… meet you?" he said, unsure if this was considered meeting via internet. He wasn't really up on the vernacular of the times.

"Yeah, nice to meet you too," she nodded. "Mom's talked about Chase and Charlie Morningstar for years. It's nice to finally put a face to the name." Just as she said this, a buzzing sound interrupted them and Hailey's head turned to the right abruptly.

"Oh, hang on guys, I have to get the door. I think its Laura Lee." She jostled the laptop for a moment and placed it on her bed so that the visual was now on the rest of her room. As Charlie and Georgie looked on trying to orient themselves to the picture in front of them, Charlie realized what he was looking at.

"Isn't that the red trunk from your room, with all your dolls?" he asked, pointing to the image on the computer screen. The trunk was now off to the left of Hailey's bed. At present it had a small lamp on it, some books and a diet soda.

"Yes," Georgie said, forlornly, as she leaned into the screen to look at it better. "I miss that thing so much. It's such a connection for me to my mom and my childhood and now to my child. Hailey kept all her toys in it too. I hated to part with it but I can't say "no" to her, so I let her take it to New York. I haven't found anything to replace it yet so there's

310

this gaping hole in my den," *not unlike my life*, she added in her head. She wasn't completely sure if she was referring to Hailey's absence or something more.

Charlie also leaned in and took a good long look. He remembered the trunk from all those years ago... and, a then 10 year old girl dancing and twirling about and wanting to help with the preparations for his new baby brother. He remembered her as a kind hearted child and was happy to see she kept that trait. He was very grateful she offered up housing to Rosa while they headlined at the club and the two women seemed to have become very good friends – something Charlie was surprised to see Rosa do. She generally stayed close to the guys, finding most women a pain in the ass to be around.

As both Charlie and Georgie were lost in their thoughts, looking at the blank room on the screen, Hailey suddenly appeared back on the screen and waved again. It was uncanny how much she reminded Charlie of Georgie. They were like twins!

"Okay, so, Laura Lee is here and we have only 15 minutes to catch the bus or else we wait another 40 minutes. Loosely translated, I gotta go," Hailey said apologetically.

She pulled a face looking rather sheepish and her mother broke out laughing which made Charlie laugh too. It was a nice moment between them and both Charlie and Georgie made a mental note of it, with neither the other knowing. Hailey seemed like such a character – even the way she talked had such animation. Charlie immediately liked her. Georgie was obviously her number one fan and her daughter felt the same way about her. It was so nice to see the two of them have such a great relationship. She did a good job, Charlie reasoned. But then, in his mind, if she was anything like Georgie, she was golden.

. . .

Within an hour of his phone call, Wade McGrath sat in Roger Stein's office signing legal documents with witnesses present. It was a bold move but Wade felt as if Jean, Celia and George were on his side and giving him positive vibes. He signed his name to the last page with flourish and dropped the pen beside the documents. The witnesses then signed and dated the documents and it was all handed over to Mr. Stein.

"Now, you make sure that supersedes all others, you understand?" he asked Roger directly.

Roger nodded and answered him with confidence. "It will be the only document of its kind in your portfolio, I assure you," he said nodding his head. He stepped forward and reached his hand out to Wade. Wade handed him an envelope and said, "Should things not go well, give it a month and then give this to her," he told the lawyer.

The lawyer took the envelope, nodded his head and shook his hand. Roger was concerned at his client's appearance. Wade McGrath looked very unwell. Roger knew not to ask any questions; Wade had fully discussed everything with him previously, All Roger could do was carry out Wade's requests.

"It's been a pleasure once again, Wade," he said with fondness towards him.

"Pleasure's been mine, Roger," Wade answered, giving his hand an extra squeeze.

...

Chase and Charlie rarely spent time alone together in the weeks since they hit town. When they did, Chase was always asking about being on the move. Charlie had diverted him so far but knew that the time would come when he'd have to make a decision. These thoughts were on his mind when he offered to go on a product run for Wade. Every so often, Wade required a replacement of dishes and glasses that he bought from a wholesaler on the outskirts of town. It was even cheaper if they were picked up – something Wade usually took care of but lately he had stopped doing these kinds of things, asking Charlie to pick it up instead. Charlie had Wade's truck practically full time when Wade was in the bar, or not using it. This made it easier for him to get about, rather than navigating a tour bus through the streets of Chicago!

Seeing this as a great opportunity to have Chase alone and be able to talk with him, Charlie asked him to come along for the ride. Chase was also eager for the time alone with Charlie. He had spent some time on the phone with Karl Craven who owned a record label called Lapis Labels, meant for its correlation to blue tones. Lapis Labels worked exclusively with artists in the jazz, blues and gospel genre. Karl was interested in making Chasing Charlie, or even more so, Chase Morningstar, a household name! He had been encouraging Chase to come to New York and spend some time wining and dining with some of the label's other artists. Chase Morningstar would be a coup for any label and Karl knew by Chase's tone over their conversations that he was leaning towards going out on his own. If he got him to New York and showed him how great his world could be, he just knew that Chase would sign with him, and he'd make both of them unbelievably rich.

Chase and Charlie headed out on their road trip with a coffee for each and a few morning doughnuts. After a bit of light talk and humor between them, Chase broke the ice.

"So, 'fess up, Charlie. How long do you think Wade will need our help for?" he asked matter-of-factly. He didn't want to beat around the bush with this anymore. He wanted answers… today. Charlie took a heavy sigh and stared out the wind shield with his hand resting on the steering wheel.

"Well, I'm not sure on that Chase. I know you're antsy to get out of here and get on with being back on the road, but I want to make sure Wade and Georgie are doing alright, you know?" he explained as he looked straight ahead. They were doing just fine as a business, but Charlie wasn't 100% sure they were each doing so well individually, at least, he wasn't so sure about Wade which meant it could be rough for Georgie. Charlie didn't share all of that with Chase though. He had his reasons.

"Seriously?" Chase asked incredulously. He was totally fed up with this whole situation. He had kept himself in check for weeks now but having this chance to tell Charlie how he felt made him reach his boiling point sooner and the next thing he knew he was saying it as it was, with no holds barred.

"I cannot fucking believe you, man! How selfish of a dude are you?" his voice rising in frustration. "I've spent the last 20 years putting off my own career so that you can be happy hiding in the shadows. And now, when I think you're finally ready to make some kind of move you do the polar opposite and become stagnant in some bar, playing to the very same people night after night. And you're happy with that? And you expect me to be happy with that?"

Chase paused, staring at Charlie with red hot temper in his eyes. This was at least 12 years in the making and Chase wasn't holding back. "It is so obvious to me that we have different DNA to some degree, because I would have never asked you to make this kind of sacrifice for me for this long and if you think I'm going to stay and play at the Black and Blue for the rest of my life out of some sense of guilt or loyalty, you got another thing coming."

By this time Chase's finger was pointed straight and he was turned towards Charlie and not paying attention to his surroundings at all. But Charlie was. He hit the brakes so hard that Chase's body flew forward and if not for his seat belt, he would have hit his head on the dashboard of the truck. The dust off the road picked up around them, as Charlie pulled the vehicle off to the side and onto the laneway of a farmhouse, with Chase still trying to figure out what had happened.

"What the fuck...?" he snapped as he looked to Charlie for explanation. But Charlie was already jumping out of the truck and calling over his shoulder to Chase.

"Hang on a second, Chase. I need to talk to this guy," Charlie said as he walked toward the farm. Chase watched in exasperation as an old man walked out of the barn and towards Charlie, wiping his hands on a rag of some sort. He saw Charlie gesture towards a grouping of boxes and articles over to the side of the barn with a "for sale" sign hanging nearby. The two were nodding and chatting up a storm as Chase's phone went off. He let out a heavy sigh, completely frustrated with Charlie as he looked at the call display and saw that it was Karl.

"Hey buddy," Chase answered, good-naturedly, checking his temper.

"Hey Superstar," Karl drawled, always the schmooze. He had started calling him Chase Superstar, hoping Chase would drink the Kool-Aid and be on board.

"Are you gonna come to New York or what, my friend?" Karl asked him. He really wanted to sign this guy before Chase realized that many labels would sign him up in an instant if they knew he was on the hunt.

"Yeah, I'm working on it, buddy," he said anxiously. "I can't just up and leave and if I do come up, I can only be gone for a short time or so," he told Karl.

He knew they were pretty slim parameters but that was all he could offer right now. He desperately hoped Karl would work with him on this. It could be his only chance to make his move and he didn't want to blow it. After all, there was so much more than just his career hinging on it.

"Listen, I can arrange for you to meet all the right people whenever you want. You just give me a days notice and I'll make it happen, alright bro?," he told Chase. If he let him know he had his back right away, Chase would trust him enough and he might just sign the deal with Lapis Labels.

Just as Chase was about to answer in the affirmative, a loud thump landed in the back of the truck and Chase was jolted in surprise. He turned to try and see what had been loaded up, but it was covered with a large moving blanket and shoved right up against the back of the cab. Chase couldn't make it out for certain.

"Yeah, a days notice," Chase said absent-mindedly. "I'll call as soon as I know my flight info, how's that?" he assured Karl.

"Excellent," said Karl and hung up the phone. Chase too had closed his phone off just as Charlie entered the cab.

"What the hell was that?" asked Chase, pointing his thumb into the bed of the truck.

"Oh," Charlie said casually. "Just some much needed storage."

He didn't go any further and Chase watched him for a moment before replying, "I suppose after years of living on a bus, you'd want to expand, huh?" rather sarcastically, to which both men smiled and continued on their road trip. Chase wasn't about to let their previous subject go and with Karl's phone conversation still on his mind, he approached the subject one more time.

"You know, we've had a lot of offers over the years, Charlie, and we've said no to every one. I have never argued with you, you know that. But I really thought you were going to leave the band at the end of March and let us go on to whatever destiny has in store, but instead, you get all comfy cozy here and now we haven't toured in months! I mean, I know you drove us hard there for a while, but seriously? After 20 years together, you can't just unilaterally make this kind of a decision for the band, Charlie," explained Chase, holding back his temper as much as possible.

"And does that go the same for you too?" he asked Chase. Chase looked at him as if he didn't understand the question. "Have you talked to Rosa or Stilts or Simon about how they feel? Thing is, Chase, as much as I appreciate your position and I can't argue with what you've said, the fact remains that you are the only one of the whole group that has come to me to ask when we're leaving," Charlie said to Chase, seeing the revelation in his brother's eyes. "C'mon, Chase, think about it. Rosa and Marlon are practically inseparable. You've seen her through two marriages. When have you ever seen her fall for a guy this quickly before? And he really is a perfect match to her, and their cooking..." Charlie rolled his eyes in appreciation. "And Stilts," he continued, "is thinking about taking some summer courses at the local college. He wants to eventually buy an old house and fix it up. He and Simon are renting a place for now but that won't continue if Simon's lady friend comes up from Atlanta. If she follows, he'll be looking for a place with her here." Charlie gave a heavy sigh. "I don't know, Chase, it doesn't look to me like the rest of the group is wanting to pull up stakes. Looks like whatever's been "Chasing Charlie" has stopped," he chuckled to himself at his inside joke. As he talked it all out with Chase it became more and more clear to Charlie that it was Chase that needed to move on. The band would be fine settling in but Chase's eyes burned for the spotlight.

"I can't believe all of you!" Chase threw up his hands in frustration. "You'd all rather spend 20 years on the road slugging our asses from gig to gig with absolutely nothing to show for it, than head to New York and finally sign with a fucking label?" Chase was in absolute shock. If the whole band felt that way, he most certainly would have to leave them behind.

"Well, I can't honestly speak for the rest of the group, you know that. But you should put the question to them and see what they say," Charlie advised. Chances were, he knew he was right and Chase could then make his own decision based on everyone's input. Charlie figured that he could predict what would happen, but he was dead wrong.

That night, when all had finished their ritual meal and had separated to get their gear together and prepare for the night's entertainment, Charlie stopped Georgie behind the bar.

"I have something I'd like to drop off for you tomorrow, if you'll be home," he said to her softly, as he held her arm. Any opportunity at all to touch her was a bonus as far as he was concerned.

She could barely concentrate on his words with him in such close proximity, but she heard enough to agree that she'd be home tomorrow and he could drop by, for what reason, she had no idea.

. . .

Wade walked back to his office after barely eating any dinner, the pain in his stomach getting worse. The medication and pain killers that he had been given weren't working and he knew he didn't have much longer before he had some serious decisions to make about his health and his ability to maintain an active role in the workings of the Black and Blue club. He sat in his office chair and tired to relax while the pain in his stomach increased. He was feeling a pressure in his chest he hadn't felt before and his breathing was tighter. After resting for a moment, his symptoms lessened and he felt a bit better but he knew it was only a matter of time. Hopefully, he had done the right thing and all would fall into place.

. . .

Georgie sat in her soft, grey pajama bottoms, white tank top and grey cashmere cardigan, sipping hot, sweet, black Columbian coffee as the voice of Ray Charles permeated through her small house. She was cross legged in her large wing backed chair, flipping through decorating magazines, enjoying a peaceful and sunny Sunday morning. Windows lined the side of the room and she languished as the morning slowly progressed. Last night had been yet another successful and raucous night at Black and Blue. A stellar crowd, Chase was on fire and the band seemed exceptionally in sync, all in all a great night. She arrived home a little after 1:30 am and slept until 8:00 am, having awoken to the sounds of the birds and the smell of the pre-set coffee maker enticing her into the kitchen.

She was settling into her third cup of coffee when Wade's truck pulled into her driveway with Charlie behind the wheel. She rose from her chair, putting her magazine and her coffee down at the same time. The truck pulled up into the side and followed around to the back as Georgie did the same, watching the truck's progression as she also made her way to the back of the house. She came out through the back door standing on the porch as Charlie got out of the truck. He had a huge smile on his face as he looked up to her on the porch. She self-consciously closed her cardigan over her tank top and secretly wished she had chosen that morning to shower first before she had gone for a cup of coffee. She stepped down the five steps to be on level ground with Charlie.

"Hey, good morning," he said to her, not looking the least bit tired. He'd only come off stage from a grueling night's performance not 6 hours ago, yet he was showered and shaved and fresh. He was unlike any musician she had ever met before.

"Hey. Nice to see you looking so bright-eyed and bushy-tailed this morning," she acknowledged. "Hard to believe you're a musician with the hours you keep." Most were night owls and you couldn't expect to see them before three or four in the afternoon.

"I know," he said, dipping his head and blushing slightly. "It helps when you don't spend the night drinking," he admitted to her. "Besides, I really enjoy the morning. It's the only chance I ever get to see my namesake," he said, having his own little joke. She didn't understand his meaning, but smiled anyway. He was so damned handsome! His blonde hair still thick and shiny and those green eyes! His smile made her feel light-headed and she needed to keep herself in check whenever he came in close contact with her. His touch on her arm at the bar last night was electric and she could still feel where his fingers had been.

He wore dark blue jeans and a grey cotton T-shirt that clung to his upper torso quite nicely. She took a moment to appreciate the whole picture before realizing the sight she must be, having come straight from bed to kitchen to den, without so much as a tooth brush or hair brush passing her by. Thank God she'd grabbed a cardigan.

"So, what's going on?" she questioned. The quicker she could get inside and get to the toothpaste, the better she would feel.

"Uh, well, I… uh… have something for you," he explained as he walked around to the back of the truck, dropped the tailgate and climbed up onto the bed. He walked to the back where a large blue moving blanket was covering something up against the cab.

"Now, close your eyes first," Charlie said, with a mischievous grin. She hesitated for a moment and then closed her eyes and covered them with her hands. Charlie quickly pulled the blanket off of the hidden treasure and told her, "Now… open your eyes."

319

She did as she was told immediately, expecting a joke of some kind. Instead, as her eyesight focused on the object he was standing next to she realized what he had brought her. Beside him was a large red steamer trunk, almost identical to the one that had been handed down in the McGrath family. She covered her hands over her mouth as she stood staring at the trunk. She didn't know what to say to him, it was unbelievable that he had found another so like the original one that now resided in New York.

"Are you kidding me?" she asked incredulously, opening her hands up and pausing them in mid air. She stood where she was, afraid to move. Charlie wasn't sure if she was unable to get up onto the truck bed or didn't want to try alone so he made his way to the edge and held out his hand to help her up. She instinctively reached out to grab his hand and as they grasped hands another jolt passed through them. It paused both of them for a moment, each wondering if the other had felt it. Charlie brought her towards the cab to inspect the trunk.

"It's an authentic piece, I only wiped it down. And look here, it's got the leather strappings at the sides and the brass grommets too," he said proudly. He couldn't believe his luck having spotted it amongst a grouping of things a farmer had put out for sale at the side of his barn as they were driving out to Wade's crockery and glassware wholesaler. He had damn near put Chase through the windshield when he hit the brakes, stopping to be sure not to miss the laneway, but what a find! He just had to have it no matter what the cost. It was exactly the gesture he was looking for to make towards Georgie. Not over, but meaningful.

Georgie was blown away. She knelt down trailing her hand across the front of the trunk. The locks were all still working and she could see that, although the paint had chipped away in some areas, it was in great shape. It had been sitting for a long time, gathering dust. Charlie had wiped off the painted part but the leather strappings still had some of the dust buildup on them. She lifted the lock and opened it up. The tray inside that sat up top of the main trunk was intact and had been carefully lined with mactac although the backing had never been removed. The main trunk had been lined as well but this time the mactac had been applied. It had a bit of a musty smell to it, with an odor of moth balls as well. It was in fantastic shape and Georgie couldn't believe that he found this and so quickly after they had seen it on her Skyped visit with Hailey. She turned to him standing in the back of the truck and gave him a huge hug and then kissed his cheek seven or eight times as she squealed to him, "Oh my God, I cannot believe it! Thank you so much, Charlie!"

He laughed and brought his hand around her waist to hold her in the hug, enjoying the feeling of her in his arms. She smelled wonderful and felt even better. His heart quickened as he stood there in the embrace and then reluctantly let her go. She stepped back and they glanced at one another before Charlie looked away blushing. *Damn it!* he thought. *What the fuck! I'm 51 years old and I can't give a gift to a woman without blushing like a 15 year old. No wonder I'm still single.*

"Oh," it suddenly occurred to Georgie – perhaps she should seem demure rather than accepting it so greedily. "I don't know if I could accept this. It such a huge gift, Charlie," she said, hoping he'd understand.

"Shit!" he swore softly. He paused a moment and thought about it. "Look," he said to her in a pleading tone, hanging his head forlornly. "You have to take it. I can't keep it. I live on a *bus* for Christ's sake," he explained, and smiled with a boyish grin. She busted out laughing at his response and knew he was right. Besides, it would fit perfectly into the void in her den.

. . .

Wade arrived home just before 2:00 am. His stomach felt like hell and he was having a hard time breathing again. Charlie had used the truck for the shipment of dishes and got Stilts to drive Wade home so that he could deliver the trunk to Georgie in the morning. Even Stilts was concerned as Wade left his car, walking with obvious discomfort to the front door of his family home.

"Hey, Wade, you okay there ol' buddy?" Stilts called out as Wade reached the door. Wade only waved him on, smiled and turned to let

321

himself in. Stiles sat there a minute making sure that Wade got through the door and then drove off to his own bed.

Wade got inside and went straight to the kitchen for a glass of water. He then pulled a pill bottle from his pocket and popped the cap and took one pill. Hopefully, it would kick in soon, he thought. He made his way into the living room and sat on the couch hoping to rest a little until the pill took effect and he tried climbing the stairs. He took off his jacket and unbuttoned his shirt to try and get some more air but his breathing continued to become difficult until after a short time he was breathing in short puffs. As he sat there he wondered what he should do. Should he try and call an ambulance? Should he wait and see if the pill settled things down? Should he call Georgie or Charlie to come and take him to the hospital? He wasn't thinking very clearly and his head felt dizzy. He was so grateful that he was on the couch, otherwise he could have fallen and really done some damage, especially to his old bones riddled with cancer. *Oh Lord*, he thought as he drifted out of consciousness, *I hope they don't find me like this.*

. . .

Charlie and Georgie moved the trunk together into the very spot the original had held. As she stood back to appreciate the gift, she was overcome and tears sprang to her eyes. She laughed at herself as she said to Charlie, "It's amazing what the site of an old rusty trunk can do, huh?" as she wiped her eyes. "So many people, so many memories from just this one thing even though I know it isn't the actual one, I feel better having it back in my house," she said as she gestured towards it, more tears flowing by now. Charlie moved towards her and hugged her briefly, rubbing her back as he did. He didn't want to overstep but he couldn't help but want to console her and understand what she was saying. Besides, she was so damned adorable in her pajamas and bed slept hair.

"Okay, well you've definitely earned a typical McGrath-Pelos Sunday morning breakfast for this!" she announced as she turned and left the den. "How do you like your eggs and how many?" she asked Charlie as she walked towards her kitchen and starred immediately lifting out the frying pan. Charlie, not one to over look a free meal, especially a breakfast, called back "Uh… over easy please and just two, thanks," he said as he looked around the den, not too sure if he should follow her into the kitchen or stay put. He eyed the room over, listening to Ray Charles belt out a great live version of "Georgia On My mind." The audience was calling out to him as he sang it and Charlie listened as he sang with his whole heart in the words. He understood that kind of an entertainer, his depth of a song when he performed. Charlie appreciated Ray's soul and passion and decided it was yet another reason to love the woman whose house Ray Charles was singing loud and clear through on this sunny Sunday morning.

"Here," she said as she reappeared in the den and handed him a large mug of coffee. "I poured you one while you wait."

"Oh, thanks," he said, taking it from her and smelling the rich aroma of the hot java. He blew it off first before taking a sip. "Ray Charles, huh? I didn't know you were a fan of his," he said, thinking about what this revealed about the dark haired beauty before him.

"Oh, yes, well that's my mother's influence, you see. Now, I'll give up any day of the week to God, but my Sunday mornings belong to Ray Charles," she said dreamily as "Unchain My Heart" began to play.

Charlie looked at her as she listened to the music, her eyes and face filled with peace as she enjoyed the lyrics. He could stand there looking forever. Georgie had grown into such a lovely woman; he couldn't help but feel the way he did. He just had to win her over and make Chase realize where his heart really was.

Chapter 28

Goodbye Wade, Hello New York

A half hour later Georgie and Charlie sat at her small kitchen table enjoying a breakfast feast of pancakes, bacon, sausage, eggs, toast with jam and each other. They shared a pot of coffee as they told the other stories of their lives while they had lived separately. Her life in New York, his life touring; essentially the last 20 years all rolled up into a quick synopsis that the other sat in wonder at.

Charlie was amazed that Georgie has raised Hailey from the age of one until she left home for college at 18 completely on her own and that Hailey's father was really nowhere in the scene. Georgie had listened in awe as Charlie relayed his and Chase's work throughout the Southern states and confessed that he felt now that he had really held Chase back from a potentially skyrocketing career.

"Hey," Georgie said with hands held so that her palms faced him, "he's a grown man now Charlie. He can only blame you for so long and then he can only blame himself. Chase hasn't found his own mark yet in order to break away and be his own person out there. It's like he blames you for holding him back when really, it's himself. I think he's afraid. He's always had you backing him and if he goes out on his own you won't be there anymore," she said honestly, almost predicting what Charlie hoped would happen.

She rested her head on her knee as she held her coffee mug and finished her meal, enjoying the chatter between them. This was the first time that she and Charlie had shared a moment like this and she was savoring it as the sun rose higher into the morning and the day grew later. As Charlie was about to comment on how intuitive it was of her to pick up on all of that, his words were stopped by the call on her cell phone. She looked at it and cocked her head in question.

"Hello?" she answered as she looked to the ground.

"Is this Georgie Pelos?" the voiced asked. Georgie had returned to her maiden name when Hailey turned 18. She figured it was her choice and since the Banting name had many offspring to carry it on and Pelos would die out in her area of America with her, she decided to change back to it.

"Yes, this is Georgie," she said hesitantly.

"This is Dr. Fryer at Chicago's East General. We have your Uncle, Mr. Wade McGrath in here and you're listed as next of kin?" he asked her.

Her heart froze and she went pale with the news. Charlie was watching her closely and leaned into the table wondering what was going on. He could tell she was hearing something bad.

"Your Uncle is in our palliative care ward here and is asking for you and a man by the name of Charlie Morningstar. Are you able to contact him?" the doctor asked Georgie.

She looked directly at the very man in question and said with a scared voice. "Uh, yes. I believe I can. Can you give me an idea of what's going on doctor?" she asked hesitantly, her eyes growing wide.

"He's extremely ill Ms. Pelos. I think you should come and see him as soon as you can," he said. The line cut off and Georgie closed her phone, looking at Charlie with fear in her eyes.

"It's Wade," she said. "He's sick and in hospital," she said, not saying anymore than that. They'd find the rest out when they got to the hospital. And just like that, their moment together, 20 years in the making, was gone.

. . .

Wade lay with his eyes closed, hooked up to several machines, one keeping track of his heart, one keeping track of his oxygen and one watching his blood oxygen. He was breathing easier now, but had a nose line of pure oxygen feeding into his nostrils. He still felt like shit but at least he knew he was in the right place, especially if he was going to die. Outside of his room Charlie and Georgie were discussing his health with Dr. Fryer and his colleague Dr. Lange. Both men concurred that Wade had cancer that had metastasized to his liver and lungs and probably throughout his body. Over the last few months, they had tried to convince him that he had a slight chance with a strong regimen of radiation and chemotherapy but he refused treatment of any kind, opting for pain killers only. He had requested a DNR just this morning upon entry into the hospital and both doctors felt he didn't have very long at all. His breathing was shallow and his heart rate was low. Dr. Fryer told the two that he was still able to talk at this point and that they should go in and visit with him while he was still conscious.

Charlie led Georgie into the room with his hand on her back. She was holding her true emotions in check as she gently touched Wade's arm and looked into his grey face. He didn't seem ill to her beforehand, but she had missed all the signs. Who could blame her? She and Wade worked together every day and put their heart and soul into the Black and Blue. Only someone from the outside looking in would have seen the difference in Wade, and Charlie saw it as soon as he arrived, and he feared it.

"Wade?" Georgie asked softly. "You awake?"

She was keeping her sentences short because she was afraid to break down mid-sentence in front of him. He didn't need that. Upon hearing her voice, his eyes fluttered and opened. He turned his head towards her and smiled weakly.

"Hey Gina," he said, still using the name that reminded him of his sister Jean. His voice was light from weakness and the Doctors put him on powerful painkillers, as was his only request. He moved slowly and spoke even slower but he was able to talk for a bit.

"I didn't want to die there, alone in my house," he said to her, as if explaining why he was here.

"Who found you... how did you get here?" she asked, wondering at the turn of events.

"Chase," he said simply.

"Is there anything we should do or take care of for you, honey?" Georgie asked him, pulling his bedcovers up closer over his chest.

Georgie looked at Charlie and they both knew that Chase must have come home to Wade's at some point this morning and found him and either brought him to the hospital or called an ambulance. But where was Chase? They had been with the doctor for more than a few minutes finding out his condition and had not seen or heard from Chase the entire time. Charlie would have to ask Chase about the circumstances.

"Insurance information filled out... in my wallet," he said. It took effort for him to speak but he knew that there were things he wanted said before he couldn't say them anymore. His breathing made it difficult for him to speak full sentences. After Georgie located his wallet and found the information inside, he motioned her over towards his bedside. As she approached, he took her hand and raised it to his lips, kissing it before placing it back on the bed, still holding it. He then smiled weakly at her. "Lovely niece... excellent business partner... treasured friend." He said and took a pause and a breath before saying to her, "I want you happy!" His eyes were directly focused on her emphasizing his words. "That's why I did it," he told her. He then settled back into his bed and rested for a moment, exhausted from his efforts.

"Shhhh…" she said to Wade. "Don't get yourself all anxious about it. I understand why you didn't tell me, Wade. You were just trying to protect me." She choked up and starting fussing over his pillow and bedcovers again so that he wouldn't notice her emotion. "Now you let me go and get the paperwork sorted out so I can get back here and visit, okay?" She kissed his cheek and softly rested her face to his. "I love you, Wade," she said, hoping that she'd have the time to say more. Georgie hurried out of the room without looking back at Wade or Charlie who remained standing on the other side of Wade's bedside.

"She doesn't understand…" Wade murmured as he kept his head turned from Charlie.

"What's that you say?" Charlie asked, not thinking he heard Wade properly. Wade seemed startled as if he didn't know Charlie was there and slowly turned his head towards him, again smiling weakly.

"Charlie-boy," he said endearingly as Charlie also smiled and took his hand and held it.

"I have confessions," Wade said to his friend. Charlie tilted his head and leaned in close to better hear Wade's thoughts.

"Celia," he held up a shaking finger, "…only woman I ever loved," he said carefully. Charlie knew it. He had traveled with Wade for all those years and only once or twice did he remember Wade having a lady around him. Mostly he kept his watch on Charlie, as his dear Celia had asked him to.

"She knew it too, buddy," Charlie told him. "Maybe you'll meet up again and be able to have what you couldn't have here," he told the dying man, wanting him to not fear what was coming. Charlie understood the fear – he thought of little else in the last 20 years. But now having released that fear since his birthday, he was able to look at it with a fresh pair of eyes.

His grandfather's death was devastating for him and yet, when he thought back, George had seemed so peaceful and tranquil when he went. His body had failed him but his spirit was ready to move on. It gave Charlie such peace of mind to have that belief that he now saw death as the next step in the natural progression of life and, although incredibly sad for those who are left behind, to the one who is passing, it's a new adventure. It was quite an awakening for him.

"You are a good friend," Wade told Charlie as he lightly squeezed his hand. "Please take care of all I love," he asked of Charlie, closing his eyes.

"I will," Charlie said, gently squeezing his hand back. He could feel the lump in his throat and had to keep himself in check for Wade's sake, but he didn't want Wade to end this way. He wanted him to go out in a blaze of glory, one last performance, like George had. *It would be a fitting thing if all musicians died like that*, he thought, *having given their last performance.*

As if reading Charlie's mind, Wade spoke up while his eyes were still closed. "I wanted to help you make your decision, Charlie. And I did it for her too." Charlie looked at him quizzically. He wasn't too sure if Wade was talking about his health or something else. He quieted the man and told him to rest, but Wade didn't want to sleep, he wanted Charlie to talk to him.

"Tell me why," he said to Charlie, pausing a moment. "What's been chasing after you, Charlie-boy?" he asked in an almost whisper, hoping Charlie would tell him after all these years. He had his suspicions but he wanted to know the truth behind Charlie. Charlie smiled and laughed a little. Oh, it was a story that Wade was going to love! He pulled up a chair next to Wade's bedside and took a seat before he started talking. He began with George's death, and then into the letter that Celia had received. He then added Celia's death just after her 50th birthday and the two different meetings with an elderly woman who he believed was the same elderly woman years apart and how it all got tangled up in his mind to make him think his own death was imminent or was to occur shortly after his 50th birthday. All the while Wade's eyes remained closed but he smiled at certain parts of Charlie's story and frowned when he mentioned Celia's death so Charlie knew he could hear him and was listening. He then began telling him about playing at the Indigo Palace and the encounter he had with that same elderly woman once again and that she had mentioned his father. Wade's eyes popped open when he heard that.

"You know your father?" Wade asked, seeming more alert and aware than before.

"Yes, I actually met him that night. He told me that my paternal lineage was quite long. Very long, in fact. So I guess I realized that I had more in me than just my mother's DNA and it made all the difference to me," Charlie explained.

"You like him… your father?" Wade asked Charlie directly.

"Yes, he seems like a really nice guy. He told me his story and it sounds as though he tried very hard to find my mom and then to help her anonymously once he did. Can't fault the guy for that," Charlie said gently, as Wade's eyes began to close again.

"Good," was all Wade said.

He seemed satisfied with Charlie's story and the answer to the question he wondered about for years. It would have done no good for him to have told Wade before now; Wade never knew who Charlie's dad was. It was before his time. Wade then said something that confused Charlie.

"Campbell," he said with his eyes closed. "Probably dead," he trailed off.

"Campbell?" Charlie repeated. "Sorry, Wade, I don't know what you mean, who is Campbell?" he asked his old friend.

"Chase's… father," Wade said. "Piano player."

He slowly shrugged his shoulders as if to say, *that's all I know*. He then settled into his rest and didn't say anything more to Charlie. Wade let the pain killers take hold of him happy that he had told all of his confessions. Now he only wanted to rest.

Charlie sat by his friend, wondering if Chase would be able to find a piano player named "Campbell" with no other information to go on — and did he hear Wade say that the guy was *probably dead*? He should tell Chase but only when the time was right. At the same time he would also tell him about finding his own father. As he sat looking at Wade's resting form, it occurred to Charlie that he would soon be without all the male role models he had grown up with; first George, then Marco and now lastly Wade. It made Charlie realize there was something important he had to do. He had gone 20 years without speaking a word to Wade and was grateful for having come home in these last few months to see him again. Looking back he realized that from the start Wade was hiding his declining health when he was showing him the ropes, and how his side of the business was run. Charlie figured at first that with his advancing age, Wade was expecting to retire, hoping to leave things in capable hands until Georgie could manage both. Wade must have known he was dying the whole time Charlie had been home.

As Charlie thought back through the many things he and Wade had discussed, Georgie came into the room, holding a bunch of papers. She looked to Wade and panicked, then looked to Charlie who eased her mind when he shook his head "He's just resting," he assured her. She nodded her head and looked back to the face of her Uncle. Wade was such a dear man to her. She had him to thank for helping when her father had died in the fire and then again when she came running home from New York with a baby in tow and finally when her mother's cancer took her life. Now, when he was facing his own death from cancer and he knew what Georgie had gone through with Jean; all the appointments, the treatments and all the hours Georgie had sat nursing her mother's health until finally Jean had succumbed. Wade had decided he just couldn't do that to her. It was hell on Georgie and she understood that he didn't want her to have to do that for him. His doctors had told her that he had asked how long he would be considered palliative, probably in hopes that it wouldn't drag on.

"I got all of the insurance paperwork finished. I didn't realize that he'd been paying on a health insurance policy for just this reason, I guess. He must have done it after my mom died," she whispered to Charlie.

She handed him the forms to look over but he stood, offering her the chair and quickly lifted a chair from the other side of the room and placed it next to her. He then sat and read over some of the forms. Wade had full insurance for any time in the hospital and should he want any palliative care at home that was also an option. He didn't seem to want to go home though; he seemed settled to be here so Georgie wasn't going to fight him.

"Has he said anything to you?" she asked Charlie. He smiled when he remembered and said, "He confessed to always having loved my mother," he said, nodding his head knowingly.

Georgie did the same and smiled too. "Yes," she said sighing heavily. "My mom would do everything she could to encourage him to approach Celia but he never did," she said with melancholy, remembering the conversations she had overheard numerous times between Jean and Wade. She wondered how things would have differed if Wade had married Celia. She would then be related through marriage to Chase and Charlie. *Oh, wouldn't that have been a mess*, she thought.

"He also worries about you," he said tenderly.

This broke her heart. She loved this man dearly, more so than just any uncle. He had been in her life longer than her own father had and the two of them made a fantastic business together. She looked into Charlie's face and the flood gates opened. Her head fell into his chest as his arms went protectively around her, holding her as she cried.

"How could I have missed it?" she sobbed quietly. "How did I not know? I watched my mom battle her cancer for years, and now when I look at him, I see all the signs, but before, I had no idea!" she cried. Charlie reached over to the table next to Wade's bed and grabbed several Kleenex, giving them to her before speaking.

"You can't blame yourself, honey. He told you himself that he did it to protect you – he didn't want you to know. He purposefully hid it from both of us," Charlie told her gently as he rocked her and rubbed her back.

She just couldn't believe that these were her uncle's final hours and that he had been suffering through this alone for so long right in front of her.

"Did you know, Charlie?" she asked him honestly. "Could you see it?" She pulled away and looked into his face.

"I didn't think he looked well when I first arrived, a lot thinner than I remember. But I didn't go there either – I mean he's 77 now. I figured he'd just aged," he told her.

Part of that was true, but the other part was that he had seen Wade grimace once or twice over the pain in his stomach and he'd go pale and break out into a sweat, so Charlie knew he was dealing with a great deal of pain. He popped pills like candy sometimes, but Charlie didn't ask. Maybe both of them had turned a blind eye on something that was there in plain sight. They sat huddled together, Georgie quietly crying while Charlie held her for a while, the machines humming and buzzing, keeping track of Wade's slow decline. After about an hour, Dr. Fryer stepped into the room to look things over.

"When is the last time you spoke to him and he answered you," he asked the couple.

Charlie cleared his throat and thought back, "About an hour or so," he said to the doctor who was flashing a light into Wade's eyes.

"He's slipped into a coma, I'm afraid," he told them. Georgie again started crying and Charlie held her as he asked the doctor, "Do you have any idea how long, Dr. Fryer?" He didn't want Wade to linger any longer. Wade wanted to be on his way. Charlie was sure Wade would be anxious to meet up with Celia and George, Jean and Marco again.

"There's really no way of knowing," he said honestly, with his hand turned up. "I can remove the oxygen and turn off the machines and we can just let him slip away. He has a DNR listing so there isn't anything much we can do but keep him out of pain, and with him going into a coma, we know that's the case," the doctor explained.

"He wouldn't want to live in this state and we know he's not going to survive this, is he?" Georgie said tearfully.

"No, he definitely isn't," the doctor said reassuringly.

She looked into Charlie's face and could see that he was agreeing with her decision. She got up out of the chair and went to Wade's pillow.

"Honey," she said softly to his ear. "I want you to go to sleep now and go onto your next gig. Find your ladylove Celia and your ol' buddy George and my mom and dad…" she smiled through her tears, "and you rest now. I love you, Uncle Wade. Give my love to all of them", she said as her tears ran freely down her face.

Charlie stood on the other side, leaned in close and said into Wade's ear, "Thanks for everything, Wade. Thanks for taking care of me all those years. I promise to do the same for you – I'll take care of everything," he said.

As the doctor removed the oxygen and he quietly removed all the machines that sat beside Wade's bed, Georgie and Charlie stood flanking his pillow, holding each of his hands and waiting for his breath to stop. He slipped peacefully away 10 minutes later as they watched him end his days on earth.

. . .

Chase sat in the darkened sports bar nursing his third double double shot of whiskey. He'd had the world's worst day and was fed up. He had lived in Charlie's shadow for long enough and now this. He just knew that what he came home to find this morning would be all the reason Charlie would need to once again put off moving ahead and Chase could read the writing on the wall. He was 36 years old, nearly 37, and it was time he started making decisions for himself.

Fuck Charlie! Fuck the band! Fuck this! he thought, in his drunken state. He had tried all his best moves on Georgie by this time and knew if Georgie hadn't given him a serious thought since he arrived,

335

then he needed to be better than just a front man in a "bar band." He had to make his mark! If he hooked up with Kyle he could record, do interviews, get his name out in the mainstream media as a serious artist and go huge and then he would come home to Georgie, who would certainly then be impressed! *She didn't want someone who played in her bar*, he thought to himself, *she wanted someone who would play to the world!*

He reached for his phone and hit the button for Kyle's number. As he pressed the call button he smiled to himself. *Wonder how Charlie will like having his life fucked with?* he thought. Kyle's voice answered the phone and Chase just started giggling.

...

Rosa and Marlon came through the hospital doors together, making quite the unintentional entrance. Both Charlie and Georgie looked up at the same time as the couple walked over to them.

Rosa immediately knelt before Georgie in her chair and hugged her saying, "Oh my dear, I am so sorry. We're in shock, absolute shock."

She pulled back to look at Georgie's face, swollen from crying. Rosa too had swollen eyes and her mascara had blurred underneath. Her look of concern made Georgie's eyes well up again and together the girls had a good cry. Rosa continued to kneel in front of Georgie's chair and soon, Marlon came over to rub Rosa's back and comfort her as she comforted Georgie. It was such a tender thing for him to do, it made Charlie take notice. He could see that Marlon was a different kind of man for Rosa and not that he required it at all, but Marlon had Charlie's approval.

The four sat waiting in a small room off the main floor, for all the paperwork to be completed so that Wade's body could be released to the funeral home. Once that was done, they could leave the hospital. Georgie had never wanted to leave a place so badly in her life. It had been different when her mother died. Jean had struggled for a number of years and the last few months just reduced her to a shadow of her former self. When Jean finally passed, it was actually a relief for her

Georgie and Wade. Marco's passing had been so tragic but she had her mother's mental state to worry about. That took priority over grieving or having her own moment to lose it. With both passing's, she was either preoccupied or too exhausted to really feel the emotion at that moment. But Wade's passing was so sudden, so unexpected. Even though she could now see that all the signs were there, she still had not expected him to die so suddenly and she realized that it left her without family nearby. She felt alone and very sad. Dr. Fryer knocked twice and entered the room as four sets of eyes all looked upon him. He handed Georgie a piece of paper and then his card.

"If you need anything else, please let me know," he said softly.

She shook his hand and thanked him with a nod of her head. Charlie stood and shook the man's hand firmly. He walked the doctor to the door as he spoke to him.

"Thanks so much for everything," he said quietly. "I appreciate all that you did for Wade. I know he was a proud man and he wouldn't have wanted a lot of fuss. I'm sure it must have been difficult for you to let him waive treatments."

"Mr. McGrath made it very clear from the get-go that he had lived a long and full life and didn't want to burden his niece with an illness that he'd still end up dying from. We could only offer him a few months more..." Dr. Fryer said, shrugging his shoulders, displaying his defeat. "It's probably one of the most selfless things I think I've seen in a long time," the doctor admitted, nodding his head.

"Thanks again doctor," Charlie said as the two men acknowledged one another and Dr. Fryer left the room.

Georgie had remained seated. She held Wade's death certificate and was staring at it trying to make sense of the day. It started so wonderfully with Ray Charles singing to her as she admired the warm sun and dawn of a new day, an extraordinary gift from Charlie and a lovely breakfast. And now, long after dusk, she sat in a hospital waiting room holding the last remaining document that linked her to Wade McGrath, her beloved uncle and as far as she knew, her only remaining elder. She felt slightly weak and realized she wanted to splash water on her face.

"I need to use the bathroom before we leave," she said as she got up from her seat. Rosa put her arm around her and led her to the door.

"Gentlemen, we'll be back in a moment. My girlfriend here is going to use the facilities and I'm going too," she said to Marlon and Charlie, who sat back down waiting for them to return. Rosa walked down the hallway, her arm still around Georgie's shoulders, and led her straight into the bathroom.

"Girl, you read my mind," said Rosa. "I have wanted to pee for the last hour or so and only just realized how long I left it," she said as she raced into a stall quickly. Georgie managed a smile as Rosa's antics played out. She, herself, made use of the stall two over from Rosa and when she was finished, she came from the stall and went to wash her hands at the sink. She was joined by an elderly woman, probably in her mid 80's. She had apples for cheeks and bright eyes that twinkled. She wasn't very tall but was dressed beautifully, as if she'd been somewhere very posh. *In a hospital?* Georgie wondered.

She and Georgie reached for the same soap dispenser at the same time, touched hands briefly, caught eyes in the mirror and smiled at one another. She allowed the elderly woman to soap her hands first and then she did the same. *It feels surreal that I should be doing something so mundane as washing my hands when Wade's just died,* she thought. As if reading her mind, the elderly woman said to her.

"It's all part of life my dear. Death brings birth or sometimes rebirth. A passing can only mean to make room for something else." After a brief pause, she tilted her head down sadly and said "There, there..." soothingly to Georgie, who stood mesmerized by her. "It will all be well, you'll see. Trust in those you know," she advised as she raised a finger to make her point.

Georgie continued staring at her for a moment as she still soaped her hands. When she looked down to rinse them off, the words the woman said ran through her mind again, *"A passing can only mean to make room for something else... Trust in those you know."* She didn't understand what the elderly woman meant and when she looked up in the mirror to ask her, the woman wasn't there. It made Georgie turn around quickly to look about the bathroom, but the mirror ran the full length of the wall so all stalls were visible to her. As she turned back to look into the mirror, Rosa came out from the stall she had occupied, and as she adjusted her top, looked up to find a very perplexed Georgie staring at her in the mirror.

"What?" Rosa said as she stood stock still immediately, her palms to the air. She waited a moment while Georgie remained staring. "WHAT?" she repeated louder, her eyes wide at Georgie.

"Did you see her?" Georgie asked as Rosa came to the sink next to her and started to wash her hands.

"Did I see who?" Rosa asked, wanting to get her friend home and get a meal into her. She probably hadn't eaten all day.

"The old woman who was here talking to me. Didn't you *hear* her?" Georgie asked, raising her voice as she pointed to the stall Rosa just emerged from.

Oh Boy! Rosa thought. *She's starting to hallucinate! She needs to get out of here and given a good meal.* "C'mon, honey. I need to get you home and feed you. I'll get Marlon to stop by the house and grab some things we've got ready to go. It's been a terrible day. Let's get out of here," she said soothingly. Again, she led Georgie out of the room with her arm around her friend.

...

As Georgie and Rosa stepped away, Charlie excused himself from the room and went into a hallway where no one was around. His heart was heavy and he needed to make a phone call he meant to make weeks before. He slipped his phone from his pocket and searched through the contacts until he found the one he wanted. When he saw it, he pressed "call" and waited for the call to go through. It rang a number of times before a male voice answered.

"Hello?" the voice said. Charlie hesitated a moment and then said softly, "Dad?" his voice cracking. He cleared his throat and caught his breath.

"Charlie... is that you son?" Brad asked. He could barely hear him and wasn't sure if he'd heard "dad" correctly.

"Yeah," Charlie said, speaking more clearly. "Yeah, it's me, Charlie."

"Hey, Charlie how you doing? I hoped you'd call me," he told Charlie, which made him smile.

"Uh... I'm sorry I haven't called before now, we've had a hell of a couple of weeks and I just lost a very dear friend of mine today. We didn't know he was... he uh... was sick for a while and we didn't know" he explained. There was silence for a moment as Charlie composed himself. "But... uh... I wonder if you'd be interested in coming to Chicago for a few days, maybe sometime next week? I'd like to see you and have you meet some friends of mine up here. Are you up for that?" Charlie asked, hoping his father would agree.

"Well sure, I'd like that a lot," his father replied.

"Good but... uh, I've just realized," he said to Brad as he rubbed his eyes, "I may have to make arrangements for you. See, I live on a bus," he said with a little embarrassment. He had said that more with disdain lately rather than the pride he used to feel.

"Oh that's just fine, Charlie. I can set up accommodations. I know quite a few people in Chicago. When do you want me to come?" he asked Charlie.

"The bar opens back up next week and we're doing a memorial tribute to Wade that night. It'll be a good show and you can meet everyone and stay a few days, sound okay?" Charlie asked him.

"Sounds excellent, Charlie. I'm really looking forward to seeing you and spending more time with you," his father said to him. Charlie nodded and closed his eyes as he stood in the hallway.

"Yeah… me too," Charlie agreed. "Come to the Black and Blue for 7:30 and we'll have dinner with the group – it's kind of a thing we do."

"I'll be there, son. Thanks for calling, Charlie. See you on Tuesday," he said and hung up.

Charlie closed his phone and leaned against the wall for a moment, thinking about his father. It's a shame that Wade and Brad would never meet. But he was so very grateful that he knew about Brad and he needed to remember to tell Chase about his possible lineage. Charlie pushed himself off the wall and went back towards the room where he and the rest of the group had been waiting.

. . .

Georgie and Charlie called the remaining band members of Chasing Charlie to inform them of Wade's passing. Chase and Charlie had a brief conversation about what had happened and Chase told Charlie that he came home to find Wade passed out on the couch, near death. He called an ambulance and waited until they had him in transport before he left. He gave Charlie no explanation as to why he hadn't called Charlie or Georgie right away or where he had been for the rest of the day, and Charlie didn't push the issue. Obviously, Chase had an opinion about the whole thing and Charlie wasn't ready to deal with it just yet.

Georgie put an obituary in the local paper as well as a notice on the door of Black and Blue which read, *"Dear Valued Black and Blue Patrons, We have lost our dear Wade. Please allow us to mourn. Out of respect, the Black and Blue will stay dark for a week and reopen next week, Tuesday, with a memorial to our beloved Uncle and friend."*

Georgie, the staff and even the band members received an outpouring of love from the community for the sudden loss of Wade. Within a day of his passing, Roger Stein was contacting Georgie at home letting her know that Wade had left his last wishes with him and that he would deliver the documents to her that night. He also informed her that the reading of Mr. McGrath's Will would take place at the Black and Blue, following his funeral, as was his request.

Charlie and Georgie sat with the funeral director the next morning with Wade's requests in hand and made all the arrangements. He had wanted cremation and his ashes scattered over Celia's grave. Very fitting indeed, thought Charlie. He requested the darkening of the club, only so Georgie would have time to gather herself before having to get back to work. He knew she wasn't expecting this and that it would possibly rock her foundation, if only for a while. A week would give her time to get his passing and ceremony over with, a few days to care for herself, and then he knew she'd be driven back to work again. He also knew if he hadn't requested it, she wouldn't have done it – she'd have kept the bar open if only to lose herself in it.

Wade had also requested that Charlie give his eulogy. And so, on a bright May morning, Charlie, dressed in a black silk shirt, black tie with a matching black suit wearing dark sunglasses, stood before a gathering of blues musicians he had known and worked with over the span of 30 odd years, his family, made up of Chase and Georgie, Rosa, Stilts and Simon and a few who were either friends or fans, and many others who were there to mourn the uncle, dear friend, club owner and amazing trumpet player. As he stood before the crowd he looked out on the number of people who had been touched by Wade McGrath's life. The church was full to overflowing. Those in attendance were all shocked and saddened by the sudden loss of such a gifted trumpet player as Wade McGrath and many shared stories of years past when Wade played the clubs with Marco and then his more than 10 years touring with Charlie.

Of course, most remembered Wade as the "Blue" side of "Black and Blue." Georgie always wore black, Wade represented the Blue. Even though the name was established long before Wade and Georgie came along, it fit them more so than it had for any other owners, Jean included. There was also a little joke between Georgie and Wade about the name, but they kept it to themselves. Charlie cleared his throat and, like any good musician, tested the mike before he began which brought a small round of appreciative laughter from the audience.

"Uh… hello, good day and welcome…" He had prepared a speech that he unfolded but when he looked out upon the crowd – the faces that had known Wade the best and the longest, former band mates and Georgie – he couldn't read; he just wanted to speak from the heart. Charlie kept his sunglasses on and leaned against the altar, his heart heavy. He hung his head a moment to gather himself and looked to Georgie for strength, then spoke into the mike.

"Wade McGrath sacrificed all he could for the happiness of others," Charlie stated honestly. "Wade loved my mother Celia," he held his hand to his heart, "I swear he told me on his deathbed," he assured the crowd causing a gentle laughter to roll through, "and for her love he dragged my ass around the southern part of the states for near 11 years, trying his best to make me famous, to my utter chagrin and reluctance," Charlie admitted, still speaking directly to the crowd. "When Wade's brother-in-law Marco was killed in a tragic fire, Wade told me he needed to be with Jean and help her through that tough time and he did – he stayed with Jean. Wade gave up life on the road as a musician for life in suburbia!" He punctuated the sentence with his fist and got an enormous laugh. He held off proceeding until the crowd had settled once again.

"When Jean took ill, he and Georgie helped one another through that tough time and he then gave Georgie the business side of Black and Blue, knowing it would help her in the loss of her mom. That's just the way Wade operated. The last selfless act he made was seeing to it that his friends and loved ones didn't watch him suffer through endless treatments and clinic days like he experienced with his sister." Charlie looked to Georgie directly, although with his shades on it wasn't that apparent.

"He may not have made decisions based on what pleased everyone else when it came to the way he died, but he sure lived his life based on others' needs," he said to her. "In my view, he deserved that," Charlie said, nodding his head. "If, at the end of our days, all we have left is to control the amount of dignity we have when we die, then we should hold onto that. And that's just what Wade did." He paused a moment for thought and then said, "Wade McGrath was a dear kind soul, who cared more about others than he did himself and who died long before we were ready to let him go. He will forever remain with me as a role model and a very dear friend and I will miss him and mourn him and remember him each day of my life." Charlie's voice cracked as he hung his head in a moment of silence and then left the stage.

In the front row of the church sat Georgie, moved to tears by Charlie's unguarded speech and his moment of exposed vulnerability; Rosa and Marlon, both in tears, holding each other's hand tightly and Chase, who sat wondering how much longer this shit was going to go on 'cause he really needed to get hold of some pain killers and get his ass to the airport and on the next plane to New York. Ever since he found Wade on the couch, Chase had spent the time drinking and in a foul mood. Charlie didn't have a chance to find out what the issue was with him. All he knew was that Chase was making a complete ass of himself at the most difficult time for Georgie, for everyone around. *If he loved her he wouldn't be acting like this at all,* Charlie thought.

The funeral ended, a ceremony was held at the graveside of George and Celia and Wade's ashes were scattered across the area. The group then went back to the Black and Blue for the reading of the will. Before they got down to any business, Mr. Stein stated that he wanted the employees of Black and Blue, the band of Chasing Charlie and his niece to all do a shot of whiskey in Wade's honor. The group of about 20 complied with this request. Each person, including Roger Stein was given a shot glass filled with whiskey. They stood in a circle just in front of the stage and raised their glasses.

"To Wade," Charlie said.

"To Wade," the group repeated.

They all raised their glass once and then shot back the whiskey. Some gasps were heard by those who weren't used to the amber nectar. Hands were shaken and backs were clapped all in Wade's honor. When the crowd had settled some, Roger addressed them all.

"Wade's will is to be read in the company of Georgie and Charlie. The rest of you please wait here."

Roger turned and walked up the hallway towards Wade's and Georgie's office. The two followed him along. It surprised Charlie slightly that he was requested to be present. He figured Roger and Georgie would go to her office and sign the paperwork changing the ownership of the club and his house to her. His presence wasn't necessary for that to happen. He was still pondering these thoughts as Roger began speaking.

"Wade wanted you both to know that everything he did, he did out a strong sense of love for both of you. He wanted that stressed clearly before we begin," he explained, his hands folded in front of him on top of his will. He cleared his throat and then asked, "Shall we begin?" They nodded and he began reading.

"I, Wade McGrath, being of sound mind and body do hereby name the executor of my will, my lawyer, Mr. Roger Stein dated this 22nd of May, 2013."

"That was just days before he died," Georgie said out loud. "Did he change his will just beforehand?" she asked Roger.

"I do believe he did," Roger answered, matter-of-factly. He waited a moment for a response from Georgie but one was not forth coming and he continued. "To my niece, Georgina Pelos, I leave my house, located at 3226 Birchwood Lane, Chicago, Illinois and all things within." Roger stopped speaking and paused a moment. Neither Charlie nor Georgie said a word, expecting there would be more.

Roger continued, "To my friend, Charlie Spencer Morningstar, I leave my pickup truck," Roger paused and Charlie smiled.

Thank God Wade had left him a decent vehicle, Charlie chuckled to himself. It was just like Wade to make sure that Charlie had what he needed to survive. That's how it had been when they toured those many years ago. He was lost in thoughts of Wade's antics when Roger's voice broke in.

"I also leave my full half of the Black and Blue club to Charlie," Roger stated. He looked to Georgie's face and saw the shock that he and Wade both knew she'd feel. No one spoke a word until Charlie finally broke the silence.

"Sorry... what did you just say?" he asked incredulously. He sat ahead in his chair, almost to the edge. He couldn't see Georgie's face at all so he had no idea what she was feeling or how this had hit her.

"Wade has left his half of the club... to you," Roger said slowly. His face showed no expression, deadpan. Charlie scoffed.

"Are you kidding me? C'mon, he wouldn't do that," he said in disbelief.

He sat back in his chair and stared at Roger who simply stared back. *What the fuck...?* he thought. He brought both hands up to his head and pulled them through his hair as he drew his breath in and then out, in and then out in a four beat pace. What the fuck, indeed!

. . .

While the will was being read, the remaining group of employees and band members were treated to a smorgasbord of wonderful dishes that Marlon and Rosa had created for them. It was their way of helping those closest to Wade remember him and enjoy breaking bread in his memory. Simon and his girlfriend Linz (short for Lindsey) had climbed into a booth with two other kitchen staff and were digging into an incredible meal, chatting away. Stilts was eating from a full plate of goodies as he sat at the bar with the bartender. Rosa and Marlon, completely inseparable, sat alone at a larger table, next to one another enjoying their own culinary delights. Marlon told Rosa stories of when he first started working with Wade and how he had inspired Marlon to try different things and gave him full run of the kitchen.

Chase grabbed a plate of food and threw himself into a booth. His ate with his head hung over the plate, picking at the meal with his hands, using no utensils whatsoever. He didn't even have a napkin and kept wiping his hands on his pants. He had immediately grabbed a beer after the shot in honor of Wade and was now nursing it as he ate his meal almost alienating himself from the rest of the group. He had discarded his suit jacket which he crunched into the corner of the booth, pulled apart his tie and rolled up his shirt sleeves. His hair, in bad need of a cut, hung down over his face and covered his left eye. It was a rough look for the usually vain man but even then Chase could turn on his million watt smile and the world was his oyster. He wasn't smiling today, however.

Today was the day for him. He almost thought he should play the lottery because he could predict exactly what was going to happen today and he was just there to play his role in the drama that would play out when Charlie came back into the bar. He was going to confront Charlie here and now about staying or going, and his decision would be based on Charlie's decision, but he already knew what Charlie's decision would be. He looked about the room from under his hair and eyed his fellow band mates. Rosa certainly was *with* Marlon. She was happier than he had ever seen her. Chase could see that Rosa had changed in the time they had been in Chicago. She had settled and Chase couldn't remember a time that Rosa had ever settled – not like this. And Marlon followed her around like a lovelorn puppy. Having not known the man beforehand, all Chase could do was be happy for him that he had found love after age 50. *You better take good care of her*, he thought as he watched them. He then looked over to Simon and Linz – a long blonde-haired girl with a tall thin body. Another "meant for each other" couple, who had been seriously committed to a long distance relationship for over four years now. Once the band had stayed more than a few weeks in Chicago, Simon called Linz to come up. When she arrived, he quickly located an apartment and Linz started looking for work. Chase was glad she'd come for Simon's sake. She really seemed to make him happy but her voice got on Chase's nerves.

Stilts and the bartender were engrossed in a CNN report and were watching the TV that hung above the bar. His plate, once filled to over flowing, was now completely empty. Stilts still had the most unbelievable

347

appetite that Chase had ever seen. He and Stilts had a great relationship, but Chase wasn't sure if it was strong enough to divide loyalties. He had to face facts that he was probably going to be alienating himself even more than he had in the past few days with his mood and behavior. He had, in fact, made up his mind about this whole situation days previous and was only going through the motions.

He sat back having finished picking at his plate and leaned his back against the side wall of the booth and brought his legs up to rest on the booth seat. He had a clear view of the entire bar and could see all of the room as he watched closely and drained his beer.

As the crowd chatted easily and returned periodically to the smorgasbord, suddenly the room heard clearly raised voices and a door slammed from the upstairs area. They could hear the click of the high heel boots as they hit each step with force and continued their rhythmic sound as Georgie marched across the room and straight out the doors. The entire group stood immobilized, all looking at the door the dark haired beauty went through and then all turned at once as Charlie came running down the stairs calling her name.

"Georgie… Georgie… hang on a sec… wait now and let's talk…" he called pleadingly as all eyes followed him across the room on the same path as Georgie. Everyone held their gaze on the door as Charlie went through in pursuit of her, trying to comprehend what just happened. Roger Stein came down from the offices then entered the bar area and went straight over to the food.

Grabbing a plate and looking over the smorgasbord, he turned to the jaw-dropped group and said rather casually, "Hell of spread for a hell of a show. Wade would be impressed!" as he popped sesame breaded shrimp into his mouth and smiled.

. . .

Roger Stein sat at Wade's desk, as per his instructions, and told Georgie and Charlie of Wade's intention to leave his share of the club to Charlie, lock, stock and barrel. The tension in the room was suddenly palpable as Georgie rose slowly from her chair and turned to the bewildered Charlie. She was silent for a while, just staring at him her head tilted. Her eyes were wide and her usually beautiful full-lipped mouth was suddenly drawn and severe, her brows practically curled as she looked at Charlie, fury in temporary check.

"Is that what this has all been about then?" she asked, her voice rising. She waited a moment. Charlie stared at her in disbelief, unable to find his voice, or even an understanding of what had happened. "You came back here just in time to talk Wade out of leaving me what's rightfully mine, only so you can have some nice little nest egg to retire on? You've been working on this for some time, haven't you Charlie?" she asked, her eyes piercing into his.

"What?" he exclaimed, astounded at her accusations. "No!" he insisted. "It wasn't like that at all! I had no idea that he was going to do this, none at all," he kept insisting, his hands held out to her.

"I get it now, I *so* get it now," she said, raising her voice loudly as her temper flared, shaking her head and gathering her things. "What a fool I've been," she said, almost to herself. "I foolishly thought that your coming home was going to be healing for you and maybe we could… " she stopped herself short from continuing the thought, "but I had no idea what you had planned. I really didn't see this coming, Charlie," she said as she threw her bag over her shoulder, turned on her heels and left the room slamming the door behind her.

She could hear Charlie's voice calling after her but had no idea what he was saying, nor did she care. She felt like such a fool, as though she and Wade had been set up. She wondered how long Charlie had played upon both of their emotions. She had visions of all the times that Charlie and Wade were holed up in the office deep in conversation and realized he must have been plotting this from the very beginning. She did not believe that Wade would be capable of doing this of his own accord. He knew that Georgie had put her heart and soul into this club, giving her spare time and basically anything close to a social or private life in order to keep it going as smoothly as it did from the business end. He had no reason to leave it to anyone else but her and she was livid that Charlie now had 50% of the shares in a business that she had worked to build for the past 15 years.

In reality, neither Wade nor Charlie was capable of such duplicity. Georgie, still reeling from the sudden loss of her uncle and business partner, wasn't able to see things clearly; her broken heart making most of her decisions and muddling her thinking. Charlie had tried chasing after her but there was no catching up to her, high heels or not. He had followed her out of the door watching, defeated, as she walked like fury towards her home and away from him. Even in her wildest temper, with her back retreating from him in furious anger, Charlie marveled at how beautiful she looked.

...

When the bar door opened again, Charlie entered to face a stunned, silent audience. As if in a spotlight, Charlie froze as he came into the room, knowing that he was being watched intently. At first he smiled shyly and hung his head, but then he spotted Chase in the booth, lounging with his legs spread out in front of him, enjoying the show. Charlie made a bee line for the seat opposite him and climbed in.

"Did you pay full price at the door?" Charlie asked sarcastically, trying to be funny and also poking fun at Chase's obvious pleasure at the present situation.

"Hey, if she's not that flaming mad at me, that's good thing," he said as he smiled. He was feeling the buzz from the shot and the beer he had quickly drank. He really wanted another beer but wanted to use this opportunity to corner Charlie.

"So, can I assume that all is not well then?" Chase asked, as he faced forward, still stretching his legs out. He felt in a position of power and sat up straight as Charlie slumped in the booth. Charlie sighed heavily and took almost the same position as his younger brother only with one leg on the floor and his head lying back with his eyes closed, his arms raised above and resting on his head. Again he did his four pace breathing exercise and waited until his mind and racing heart had slowed. "Wade left me his share of the club," Charlie admitted.

Chase turned to look at him, jaw dropped and then whistled loud. He truly believed that he could read the writing on the wall. Wade would will Georgie his half of the bar and she would be so overwhelmed and such a damsel in distress, Charlie would find yet another reason (better than ever) to stay even longer, if not permanently, to help Georgie manage things. Chase could also see where the rest of the band members would fall in line with Charlie, using Georgie's distress as a reason to hang on rather than move ahead. He had in no way anticipated Wade's decision to make Charlie and Georgie partners in the club. This could be the best possible situation for Chase yet.

Regardless, he believed that it was his lack of fame and financial position that held him back from Georgie. If he could take the bar off of her hands financially, she wouldn't have to manage this place anymore. They could leave it to someone who they'd pay to keep it running while they were traveling across the world with Chase, promoting his latest CD. Chase had big ideas and Georgie could be a part of them, once he broke free of his trappings. He needed to get to New York and meet up with Kyle and get things going. In order to do that, he needed Charlie to give him the ultimatum.

"No wonder she left the bar in such a fury. Wouldn't want to be you, brother," admitted Chase, laughing. He continued to smile as Charlie started softly banging his head against the wooden backing of the side wall of the booth and groaned.

"What just happened?" he asked as he stopped his head banging. "One minute we were having breakfast and the next she's blaming me for coercion and business sabotage and walking out without giving me a chance," he said innocently. "How does that happen in less than five days?" he asked, stunned by the outcome of the meeting with Roger Stein.

"So, naturally, you're going to stay and figure this out," Chase said predictably, not bothering to listen to Charlie or catching the *having breakfast* comment.

Charlie didn't pick up on his mood or the tone with which he asked his question. "Well, of course I'm going to stay and figure this out, Chase. I'm not five years old, I don't run away from my problems," he said, almost defensively.

"Oh! Apart from the last 20 years...! Naturally," Chase mimicked.

This Charlie picked up on. He opened his eyes and turned his head immediately, looking at Chase. In an instant they were reduced to 19 and 4 years old. Once again the difference in their ages came out only this time, Chase stood his ground.

"I've had enough of this shit, Charlie! How much more do you expect me to take?" he asked, as he raised his voice and launched himself from the booth and made it to the bar in seconds flat. He motioned to the bartender to give him another beer and another shot and then turned to face his brother. *Bring it on, Charlie,* he thought. *I'm so ready to do this.*

"What the hell is your damage, Chase?" Charlie asked as he remained in the booth. Their voices were raised enough that most of those gathered about had stopped what they were doing to watch the continuing entertainment that was provided.

"You are!" Chase yelled at him as he pointed his finger directly at him. "You're my fucking damage... my problem" he spat, "and I regret ever making that deal with you all those years ago. You've held me back from doing want I want to do and now that you're ready to settle your old ass down, you've stuck me here. You took advantage of me Charlie!" He took a swig of his beer and wiped his mouth. "There's no way in hell I'm staying here to headline at a fucking club when I've got people calling me to come to New York." He waited for Charlie's reaction and was delighted to see his eyebrows lift at Chase's mention of New York.

"That's right, Charlie. They aren't interested in you, they want me. Kyle Craven has me scheduled on a flight outta O'Hare for 3:00 pm this afternoon and I am so on it." He sat back down at the bar, his back to Stilts and the bartender. As he faced Charlie, he felt empowered.

"You're leaving today?" Charlie asked.

"…on jet plane," Chase sang as he laughed at the use of the song to make his statement. He felt so good. He should have done this years ago.

"Look Chase, I hear you about wanting to go to New York, but we have the memorial for Wade on Tuesday. Leave straight after that but don't leave before. We need you, man" Charlie said trying to reason with him. Not only had Charlie come to the bar but so had Rosa and Simon when they caught on to what Chase was saying.

"You're leaving town, Chase?" Stilts asked him directly.

"Damn straight. I'm sick of this place and I'm tired of having Charlie rule over what I can and cannot do. I'm a grown man and I start making decisions for Chase Morningstar right now," Chase said indignantly, pointing to his chest with the same hand he held his beer, which he promptly drained and placed the bottle with a thump on the bar. He was starting to feel more affected by the booze and it was giving him some courage. Rosa stepped forward hoping to lighten the situation and talk some sense into Chase. "Look Chase, I know it's been hard for you to settle for a bit. But we've been going like nuts for years now. We all just needed a break, I guess. But you're now talking of breaking up Chasing Charlie. If you go to New York, is that what you intend to do – leave the band?" she asked him as she came and took the stool next to him. He had his elbows resting on the bar facing into the group. He had a sneering grin on his face and she knew he didn't give a shit about anything but himself. She could see it in his eyes.

"I don't know what's going to happen. If I get there and given an offer to work with the music industries big guns then, yeah, I'm probably going to be moving on," he argued to Rosa. She hung her head and thought about what she could say to him, but he already knew her thinking.

"Listen Doll, it isn't a personal thing. I've waited for years to get out there and explode onto the music scene and New York is definitely the place to do it. You know any one of you can come with me," he said, offering looks to Simon and Stilts as well. They just continued to stand around in a group, eyes looking downwards.

"Yeah," Chase scoffed, "that's what I figured. None of you want to make it big. You're all just happy staying here and stagnating. Not even a small amount of desire to play to larger crowds, huh?" Chase asked in a condescending tone.

"It's not about the size of the crowds, Chase, it's about the music we all make together," Simon said.

"Oh fuck, not you too, Si," Chase groaned. "You sound like you've been brainwashed too!" he said as he turned on his stool and motioned for another beer. "You're wrong buddy. No one looks at us and thinks, ...*what a great band, been touring for years!* No... they look at us and think what a bunch of fuckin' idiots we are 'cause we've chased Charlie for the last 20 years and got nothing to show for it!" he yelled at them and again pointed directly at Charlie when he finished. "What kind of a band does NOTHING but touring? No interviews, no recordings not even listening when we've been approached by a label?" Chase counted off the last statement with his fingers to emphasize his point. It didn't really need it though – he was most certainly getting his point across.

"Yeah, we all get it Chase, you're frustrated. But that doesn't change the fact that we are doing Wade's memorial in just a few days. You can't bail on us now," Stilts said, trying to reason with him.

"Oh yeah? Watch me," he said with confidence. He didn't need Charlie's ultimatum. It was obvious to him that he was the only one who wanted out. He stood up from his stool, drained his new beer, slammed it down on the bar and walked through the group and out the door. All eyes turned to Charlie who hung his head and came to sit on the stool surrounded by his remaining band mates. He sighed heavily and looked at each of them.

"Well, I guess if any of you feel the same way you'd better speak up now and let's get this all out in the open," Charlie said, hating the confrontation that Chase had now opened up. He had Georgie so centered in his mind, he just wanted to get this done with so he could figure out what the hell he was going to do about that situation. The group all stayed quiet for a moment and then Rosa spoke up.

"I don't feel like Chase does, Charlie," she said shaking her head. "I'm in it for the long haul." She put her arm around him and kissed his cheek.

"Well, there's no way I'm kissing you buddy, but I'm not interested in leaving the band," Stilts said with a crooked smile.

Charlie and Simon laughed and Simon agreed with Stilts, "Yeah, sorry Charlie, no can do on the whole kissing thing either, but I'm happy to do whatever the group decides. As long as we keep playing and getting paid, we're solid," Simon said, shrugging his shoulders. The other band members all nodded their heads and it was agreed, regardless of Chase's decision, Chasing Charlie was still together.

"So, that begs the question…" Rosa said as the other three looked at her, "do we keep the name?" she asked, eyebrows raised. The guys looked at one another and all hesitated to speak.

"I think we should see what Chase's trip brings about," said Charlie wisely. Why go upsetting the apple cart? Chase hadn't even left yet. They didn't know how long he would be gone but Charlie figured if he had to, he could possibly perform a bit and he could start bringing other talent in, just as Wade had suggested. This would certainly solve the whole "other artists and Chase on stage" problem.

"What are we going to do on Tuesday?" asked Stilts. This group had never seen Charlie take centre stage. It was only a few days back that he actually quipped with Chase on stage, after 20 years together.

"Well, let's start pulling together some set ideas, and then see what we need. I can start calling some talent and see if they'll sit in and if not…"

he hesitated, not wanting to speak the words for fear they may come true.

"If not…?" Simon questioned. "If not, what?"

"If not I'll… uh… I'll see what I can do. I guess I should also sit down and think about what Wade would have wanted to hear," he said thoughtfully, almost to himself.

"Can't Georgie help with that?" Rosa asked.

She knew something was up, obviously, by the way Georgie stormed out of there and Charlie raced out after her. Rosa figured something in the will had upset her but she didn't want to press Charlie for information. She hoped her suggestion would mean getting the two of them back in a room together and maybe mending whatever got broken between them. Charlie looked at Rosa in deep thought. If he approached Georgie about this, he may get an opportunity to talk with her and let her know that he had no idea about Wade's revised will, and that coming back home to acquire Wade's half was not his intention at all. Then again, his priority should be to get someone in here who was good enough to fill in for Chase at a moment's notice; otherwise, Charlie Morningstar was going to make his re-emergence into the centre stage spotlight!

"Maybe you can talk with Georgie for me, will you do that Rosa?" he asked. "I really do need to get making some calls."

He didn't wait for Rosa's reply – he just squeezed her arm affectionately and left immediately for the office. Rosa watched Charlie's retreating back and shook her head.

"I swear those two are as stubborn as mules," she said to Stilts and Simon. "Which can only mean one thing…" she continued, seriously, "I think they'll make a perfect couple!" She smiled knowingly at Simon and Stilts and walked away, leaving them both confused as hell.

…

Once Chase left the Black and Blue, he got in a cab, went straight to Wade's house where his bags were packed and waiting. As he grabbed his things and made his way to the door, his eye caught a picture of Wade and Charlie from years ago, taken while they were touring. They both looked so much younger; Wade's mustache extending almost the full length of his face and Charlie's shock of blonde hair and green eyes clearly standing out in the photo. Chase grabbed it and studied it for a moment. Just then, the cabbie honked the horn, breaking Chase's concentration.

He put the picture back in its place and said, "Sorry Wade. I gotta do this."

With that he went through the door, jumped back into the cab and left for the airport. He checked his watch. He would have plenty of time for a few drinks and check in before his flight took off. He had eaten at the smorgasbord after Wade's funeral and wasn't in need of food, but drinking had become a great way to numb his frustrations.

For years he had trusted in Charlie. He had always respected him and looked up to him, even as a grown man. Charlie always had a level head, didn't make rash decisions and was completely responsible, all so Chase didn't really have to be. But in the last year while Charlie had experienced his mid-life crisis or whatever the hell it was, the roles had reversed. Chase had become used to calling some of the shots where business decisions were concerned and now, since Charlie's birthday, things had reverted back to the old way and Chase didn't like it. This flight to New York was a huge blow to the band and Chase knew it but he also knew that if he didn't do it now, it would never happen. Even so, something about it still didn't feel very good in the pit of his stomach. He slouched down in the cab, his decision weighing on him.

But there was more to gain here than just an explosive music career, there was Georgie too. Chase was convinced that his success in New York would make Georgie look at him differently. He was certain that she'd want nothing to do with Charlie now that Wade had overlooked her to give Charlie his half of the bar. It could not have worked out better for Chase. Even if Georgie came around to getting over it and being able to work alongside Charlie, she'd never date him after that – Chase was sure of it. So all Chase had to do was get on that plane and meet up with Kyle. The rest would fall neatly into place.

When the cab pulled up to the unloading area, Chase paid the cabbie and hopped out with his bag. He walked through the airport on a mission to find his check in area and a bar closest to his departure gate. Once checked in and the bar located, he ordered a two finger glass of whiskey and sat at the bar while he waited to board. He thought about Kyle's plans for him. He was going to be introduced to some pretty famous rock, blues and jazz stars. He was going to be petted and stroked to sign a contract and he was going to enjoy every damn minute of it. And then, when he had a contract for his first CD, he was going to come back to Chicago and walk right up to Georgie and show her that he was someone worth being with.

With his mind starting to fuzz from the drinks, he thought back to those days on the couch when they would fall asleep cuddled together. He could still smell her and feel the silkiness of her hair. If only it had stayed that way between them. If only she would cuddle with him now. He smiled to himself with the thought, *it won't be long.*

. . .

It had been two days since Georgie stormed out of the office at the Black and Blue club. Rosa had left her alone that first night and the next day, calling her on the third day and asking to come over and talk. Not trusting her loyalty to Charlie and feeling rather alone and vulnerable, Georgie kept the visit short.

"I wrote out a listing of songs that I thought might be nice," she said, handing Rosa a piece of paper. "You guys can decide if any of them can be worked into the set. Charlie might have an idea about it," she suggested, shrugging her shoulders.

Rosa took the piece of paper and read it over, then looked back to Georgie. She looked like hell and her eyes were very sad. Rosa wanted to drop everything and just hug the poor girl, but Georgie wasn't giving off that vibe acting slightly distant towards Rosa. After the day they spent together when Wade died, she couldn't understand why but Rosa didn't want to push Georgie right now. Obviously she was shaken by her uncle's unexpected death and perhaps just wanted to get this whole memorial thing behind her, Rosa figured.

"I'm sure we can work with this," she said. She smiled at Georgie and they locked eyes. Woman to woman, Rosa knew Georgie was hurting more than just for Wade. She had lost someone even more important to her and, judging by the distance between them, Rosa knew who that was. Maybe if she mentioned Charlie's name, it would help segue into opening up about what happened.

"So… uh… Charlie got Wayne Mack Murray to headline with us on Tuesday and he's actually signed on for a few more gigs after that," she told Georgie, hoping that Charlie's efforts to keep things rolling smoothly would give Georgie reason to pause.

"Oh?" Georgie said, looking at her confused. "How's Chase with that?" she asked, wondering. Obviously, Rosa realized she hadn't been told. That meant that Georgie had not been in contact with anyone at the club. She didn't know about Chase's departure.

"Uh… he's not too concerned considering he flew his ass to New York the day of Wade's funeral to meet up with someone who wants to sign him to a recording contract," Rosa said as she raised one eyebrow and jutted her lips out.

"What?!" Georgie said in disbelief. "What the hell?" she asked Rosa.

"Said he'd finally had enough of Charlie calling the shots and that he'd been having a conversation with some guy in New York and he was leaving to… make it happen, I guess," Rosa said, leaving her hands up in the air.

Holy shit, Georgie thought, *Charlie must be reeling*. "So, what's going to happen?" she asked. "Wade's memorial is so close! I've been working from home and taking some calls and it sounds like we'll be full to capacity," she said anxiously.

Oh! Rose thought, *so she had been in touch, just not with Charlie or the band. Good.* Going back to a sense of normalcy and doing it from home was the best of both worlds for Georgie. *What a smart woman! Except,* thought Rosa, *regardless of why she's distant she will have to come back into the bar and face Charlie tomorrow.* This ought to be interesting!

"And that's why Wayne Mack Murray is headlining with us," Rosa said, with a look of "you get it?"

Georgie acknowledged with a slight nod and briefly smiled as she cast her eyes downwards, taking in the vision of Wayne Mack Murray as the front man for Chasing Charlie.

"Is he here yet?" she asked, wondering how Charlie managed that so fast.

"Oh hell yes! Flew in yesterday. We've rehearsed once and are again this afternoon," she answered, putting Georgie's mind at ease. She was relieved but something in her couldn't help but feel jilted.

"Yes, well, I'm sure Charlie is running things quite smoothly," Georgie said and for a moment Rosa couldn't tell if she detected tone, maybe even sarcasm in her voice. *What the hell?* she wondered. Charlie is making helping her out, why was she being bitchy about it? Maybe Rosa was reading too much into it. Maybe she should just walk away and let them work it out. After all, they're grown adults!

"Okay, well I'm heading out," Rosa said, wanting to leave Georgie to her privacy. "Oh!" she stopped instantly. "I almost completely forgot," Rosa said, tapping her head like she'd lost her mind. "Charlie is making a collage of Wade. He's got some computer tech to come in and set up a picture memorial that'll splash on a screen while we play. It looks great and I keep getting a bit weepy when we rehearse while it plays." She paused, once again letting Charlie's attention to detail for Wade's memorial sink in to Georgie. "He asked me if I would ask for any pictures you might want to have shown," Rosa explained.

"Oh!" Georgie stopped. "Uh… yes, of course. I have a ton of pictures actually, I've pulled them out and have been looking at them a lot lately," she said to Rosa. Her eyes welled up a bit and Rosa gave her a sad face, rubbing her arm.

"C'mon, sweetie. Let's see whatcha' got," Rosa said in a bit of a cheery voice.

She affectionately put her arm around Georgie and they walked into the den. There, Georgie stopped to reach for a photo album while Rosa looked around the room. Georgie took a moment to pull out a handful of loose photos and then grabbed a few framed pictures that lined the book shelves. She handed them all to Rosa who took them from her.

"That's great," she said and she juggled them all until putting them in her oversize handbag slung over her shoulder. She looked once more at Georgie and then around the room. In a complete change of subject, Rosa said, "I like this room," she said offhandedly. "And I love the trunk. I don't remember it being here, is it new?" she asked.

Georgie turned to look at the trunk Charlie had gifted her with just a few days before. "Yes," she answered honestly, thinking back to that morning they had spent together over breakfast, hot coffee and Ray Charles.

"Well, it works beautifully, completes the room nicely and fits perfectly in the space. Excellent taste, my dear," Rosa acknowledged.

Hmpphhff! Georgie scoffed internally, *I thought so too at one time!*

Chapter 29

Wade's Memorial

As the day dawned, Charlie awoke inside the bus and got showered and ready. Tonight was going to be a big night for the Black and Blue club, Chasing Charlie as a band and for Charlie in general. He missed Chase and had tried calling him but had no luck getting through to him directly. He did leave two messages, but didn't bother after that. His messages let Chase know that he wanted to talk with him but he didn't need to nag him. He was certain Chase knew to call when he wanted to talk. Obviously, right now, he needed his space.

Charlie's first order of the day was to pick up the photos of Wade that he'd had enlarged to place around the bar. He'd only done a few of them – one of just Wade, one of Wade and Georgie and the one taken of the entire McGrath, Pelos and Morningstar lot after Chase's seventh birthday dinner. It was enough, but all of them poignant. He then had a haircut and went shopping for a new shirt. Tonight, he was going all out, not just because he wanted to do it for Wade, but he wanted Georgie to see that he didn't take any of this lightly. Once this memorial was behind them he hoped that he and Georgie would be able to sort this all out. Frankly, he had given it some thought and he really didn't want to give back the club to Georgie. He would certainly give her cash for it, if she really pushed the issue, but he wasn't going to let Wade or himself down now. Wade had done this for a reason and it may not be clear to him now but he was willing to give it a chance to see what came of it. He hoped that, in time, Georgie would be able to live with this. Right now, that was all he could hope for; asking for her love would be too much.

By the time Charlie made it to the Black and Blue it was late afternoon. As he entered the bar, the aroma of Marlon's incredible cooking for this evening was simmering or brewing or whatever it was doing. Charlie almost walked straight into the kitchen but managed to waylay that thought for a moment while he focused on the one task he wanted to get done before taking a break. He had borrowed easels from the funeral home and set them up strategically around the bar and placed the pictures into each of them. The picture of Wade and Georgie was taken at the bar at a birthday celebration for her a few years back. Wade was smiling wide, showing all his teeth and looked as though he was enjoying himself immensely. His arm was slung around Georgie's shoulders as she smiled at the camera. Her dark features and red lipped smile captured perfectly as she had been surprised. It was a simply gorgeous picture of the both of them, one of Georgie's that she had given to Rosa from her book shelf and Charlie couldn't help but enlarge it and put it front and centre. She wasn't just his business partner – she and Hailey were the only blood relative Wade had remaining and Georgie deserved to have a special spot with Wade for tonight. Charlie made sure that their picture was the one you saw from every visual vantage point in the bar. Once he placed the large pictures, he made his way to the office. He had figured he'd just take over Wade's desk and had been working at it for the past few days when he wasn't jamming with Wayne and the rest of the band. He placed a call to a florist and requested a large bouquet of fresh flowers be delivered this afternoon. He specifically requested one red rose be placed in the very centre and that it be the highest point. Charlie meant it for Georgie, but he knew that anyone could read into it what they wanted. He also called a photographer so that pictures could be sent to the local paper after the fact. It would be great publicity for the bar and Wayne would like it too!

By the time he made his phone calls and straightened through some papers on his desk, he was starving. The smells coming from the kitchen had him following his nose. He wasn't surprised to find Rosa in there, testing some of the soups, salsas and dips that Marlon had created special for this evening. The massive fridge/freezer in the back of the kitchen had appetizers of cooked shrimp, cheeses from all over the world, grapes, apples, fresh citrus slices of every kind, chunks of kielbasa, chunks of lean roast beef, fresh vegetables such as carrots, celery, snow peas, radish, broccoli and cauliflower; more fruit including strawberries and kiwi with large chunks of dark chocolate stacked to the ceiling on platters; all of these Wade's personal favorites. These would be served throughout the first set. Marlon had planned a second set event that would include steak, salmon, chicken halves or ribs as a main course. With Charlie's approval, he had been preparing and shopping for days and felt that he wanted to do his part to show how much he appreciated and cared for his beloved late boss. He had cooked many special and different meals for Wade over the years. Wade had been his taste tester and he rarely disliked what he tasted. But then, Wade loved all food groups.

The smell that brought Charlie to the kitchen was a jambalaya that Marlon would often make for Wade. It was the one thing he requested most and tonight, Marlon had made enough to easily feed 350 people.

"Hey!" Rosa greeted him with a smile. "Look at you all shit, showered and shaved," she said. Charlie really did consider her his younger sister at times. "Even a new shirt on… looking good Mr. Morningstar. If I didn't know any better…"

She let her sentence trail off and Charlie was glad for it. He knew that Rosa had been paying close attention to him and Georgie and she probably knew something wasn't right – perhaps Georgie had even confided in her. Nonetheless, he was guarded with how much he said. At this point, Chase was the only one Charlie had told about Wade's will and his decision to leave his half of the bar to Charlie. In some ways, Charlie didn't want anyone else knowing yet. Not until he and Georgie could settle it. For now, he was happy if they figured he was just working on Wade's behalf and for Georgie's sake. He'd tell them when the time was right, and the time wasn't right, right now.

. . .

As Georgie stood at the arrivals gate in O'Hare airport, she thought back upon the last years working with Wade. He had confidently taken care of the talent and was incredible in negotiating great acts that would keep the Black and Blue in the top 10 of the best blues and jazz bars in Chicago. She had appreciated his ear for a fine musician and a great band. He had appreciated her knack for numbers and uncanny ability to run the club in the black. It was always their little joke that the "Black" part of the name really referred to their profits each year, not just Georgie's wardrobe!

Georgie and Wade had made a nice little nest egg for themselves. Wade's portion was now distributed between the club he gave to Charlie, the house and Hailey's college expenses, as Roger Stein later told Georgie after she stormed out of the office. He had called to ask a convenient time to come over for some signatures regarding the house and other assets and mentioned that Wade had left Hailey a nice little inheritance. She gave the lawyer Hailey's contact information and then called her as soon as Roger left the house. Hailey knew of her great Uncle's passing and wanted to hurry home to be with her mother, but it hit right as performances of her "Theater as a Natural Art" class was showcasing their top three assignments and Hailey was the lead role in her ensemble. She simply couldn't leave until after the performances wrapped which was past the date for Wade's funeral. She could however, come home for his memorial concert at the club and Georgie was thrilled to have her home. It had been almost two full years since she and her daughter had spent any decent amount of time together and Hailey was coming home for the whole week! Georgie was happy to have some personal support, especially since everyone seemed to be leaning towards Charlie and his new role. She figured the staff had become used to Charlie performing some of Wade's tasks in the past few months, but it seemed that every time Georgie spoke to someone in the last few days they mentioned how they had already been speaking to Charlie and how grateful she must be to have him around at this dreadful time! *Little did they know,* she thought.

Her reverie was interrupted by a nudge to her shoulder. She broke her gaze and looked about to see Hailey smiling and standing before her.

She instinctively beamed back at her and then grasped her into a mother bear hug that had the young woman almost gasping for breath.

"Holy shit, Mom. Easy! I'm only human you know!" Hailey said jokingly.

"I'm so glad to see you, Bunny-bear," a nickname she had called Hailey since birth.

Georgie held onto her child a little longer and tighter, having not been able to do so in two years time. Her daughter, recognizing and appreciating the message, hugged her back and they stood for a moment enjoying the embrace. When Georgie pulled away, she took a good look at her beautiful daughter, holding her face in her hands with tears in her eyes. They didn't need to speak, having an ability to read the other's very thoughts. They were so alike, mother and daughter.

As Georgie looked over her daughter she took stock in her physical well being. Hailey seemed thinner and her features had lost that baby-faced look to them. At 21, she looked much more mature and grown up to Georgie and she longed to have Hailey back near to where she could see her more often.

"What are the chances you'll come home this summer instead of spending it working?" Georgie asked, making a slight reference to Hailey's inheritance.

"Not very good, I'm afraid. I've been asked to play Desdemona for the summer theater's "Shakespeare in the Park" production. The exposure is pretty good. It will be a great addition to my acting resume, not to mention there's a revival of "Othello" starting production off-Broadway in October and if I've spent the summer doing the part, I could easily land it again and pick up another so many weeks of work," she said, laying out her plan.

Georgie loved this about her daughter; she wasn't in it for the money, she truly loved the theatrical actor's life. Hailey seemed to thrive on ridiculously crazy schedules. When most other students would be crying poor and waning from exhaustion trying to balance school and work, Hailey excelled at it. She had never really needed to work as hard as she did because Georgie had been able to fund most of her schooling and some of her living expenses, but Hailey wanted to be an independent New Yorker which meant the grueling schedule. It astonished her mother and only made her abilities to juggle school, guiding tours and doing shows at the same time seem all the more extraordinary. Of course, Georgie was a little biased and Hailey's number one fan.

Georgie put her arm around her daughter and walked her out of the arrivals area. They picked up her baggage at the baggage claim and walked out to where Georgie had parked. As they drove back to Georgie's house, mother and daughter chatted about Wade's sudden passing, the house he left behind and the memorial for him tonight. It wasn't until they were within sight of the club that Hailey finally asked.

"So what's the story?" she asked inquisitively. "You haven't told me a thing and I don't mean to sound greedy but I'm dying to know. Are you now the proud owner of the Black and Blue?" turning her whole body towards her mother with the question as she sat in the passenger seat of the car.

'Nope," Georgie replied firmly, goading Hailey on.

"What?" Hailey asked her, stunned by her response, her mouth gaping open.

"Well... see... Uncle Wade decided to leave his half to Charlie," Georgie said slowly, with a bit of a condescending tone to her voice. Hailey knew it wasn't meant for her, more for the situation Georgie had been put into.

"I can't believe it," said Hailey as they turned into Georgie's driveway. "Why would he do that to you after all these years?" she asked, trying to understand her great uncle's last decision that would have such a huge impact on her mother, his niece and business partner of almost 15 years.

"I honestly don't know," admitted Georgie as they unloaded from the car. "I have a strong suspicion that Charlie Morningstar has a lot to do with it though," she told her daughter.

Hailey, surprised at her mother's admission, gave this some thought. She had only once met Charlie during a Skyped conversation with her mother and he seemed okay at the time. It was more the talk she had heard over her entire lifetime of "Chase and Charlie Morningstar" that had her feeling like she knew them both fairly well. So with this news of her mother's suspicion of Charlie's hand in turning Wade's decision around, Hailey was skeptical. Especially since she saw how Charlie had blushed over her mother's shoulder when they had finally been introduced. He just seemed too sincere and had a genuine affection for her mom. Hailey could see that plain as day and she had thought her mother felt the same. Now she wasn't sure what was going on but clearly her mother blamed Charlie for Wade's choice and had taken a giant step backwards where Charlie Morningstar was concerned. It wasn't exactly the direction Hailey was hoping for.

They entered the house through the back door and Hailey headed straight through the kitchen, onwards to the den on her way upstairs to her old bedroom. As she walked through the den she stopped dead just before the door leading to the stairs and turned around.

"Where did you find *that*?" she asked with her finger pointing towards the red trunk. *Oh God*, Georgie thought, *I don't want to have to explain that.*

"Oh… it was found for me a few days ago," she said, giving nothing away. Hailey eyed her mother closely knowing full well there was more to the story. She didn't let up and finally Georgie broke down.

"Oh for God's sake," she huffed. "Charlie found it out of town and bought it for me. He delivered it last Sunday," she said quickly, hoping that her casual explanation would be the end of it, but of course, it wasn't.

"Charlie found it for you?" Hailey asked, with a stunned look, facing her mother. "How did Charlie know about the trunk?" she asked wanting her mother to cough up the whole story.

"He noticed it when I was Skyping with you the day I introduced you," Georgie tossed back over her shoulder. "He remembered it from when I was a young girl and it had my dolls in it."

Hailey knew by the way her mom was acting that this had meant more to her at the time than she was letting on. She had mentioned to Hailey on more than one occasion how empty the house was now that she was gone and especially the den where Georgie didn't see the McGrath's toy trunk in there on a daily basis. She knew the trunk held a special place in her mother's heart and for Charlie to have picked up on that was really lovely.

"So let me get this straight…" Hailey continued, reluctant to leave it alone. "The man who you believe thwarted you by getting Wade to leave him his part of the club when he died, went out of his way to bring you a trunk that he knew meant a lot to you?" she asked with disbelief in her voice, one eyebrow raised and a quizzical look on her face. "How do you explain that?" she posed to her mother.

"Guilt," was all her mother said as she proceeded to carry Hailey's belongings past her and up the stairs.

. . .

Hailey stood looking at the trunk for a moment longer. It was practically identical. She couldn't believe he had found it. She also didn't believe that Charlie had done anything of the sort by giving it to her out of guilt. Hailey turned to make her way upstairs shaking her head. She couldn't wait to get to the bar and in front of Charlie so she could figure out the situation for herself. Her mom wasn't helping at all.

"The smell through the entire club is unbelievable, Marlon," Charlie said as he walked over to where the cook was sampling guacamole. Marlon offered Charlie a tortilla chip and the dip and Charlie tried a large scoop. He smiled, nodding his head and patting Marlon on the shoulder.

"Best damn cook I've ever been around," he said as he and Marlon shook hands. "Have you got everything you'll need for tonight?" Charlie asked Marlon. The man nodded his head and cast his eyes sideways as if to tell Charlie he wanted to speak privately with him, away from Rosa. Charlie followed his eyes and nodded himself, heading to the back of the kitchen near the fridge/freezer.

Marlon made sure that Rosa was out of sight and preoccupied when he turned to Charlie and said, "I need to ask you something," in a near whisper. He seemed nervous and Charlie could swear that he was sweating, but not from the heat in the kitchen.

"What's the matter buddy," Charlie said concerned. "You feeling alright? Do I need to get you to the hospital?" he asked.

"No… I… no, I'm fine. It's not that at all," he smiled briefly at Charlie. "Look, I realize my timing sucks but I can't help it, it's like I'm possessed or something." he said trying to explain himself.

Charlie looked at him still lost. "So spill it man," he said impatiently.

"I want to ask Rosa to marry me," he said bluntly. "You probably know her best of all. Do you think she'll reject me?" he looked at Charlie with pleading eyes.

So now I get it, he thought. *Marlon was hopelessly in love.* Charlie smiled at the man with whom he had become quite fond of.

"I've known Rosa for twenty years now, Marlon. And I've seen her through two marriages, but she has never met a man with such a fine character and great cooking skills as you." He smiled his million watt smile at Marlon and Marlon smiled and hung his head in humility. "I bet you she would run down that aisle and nearly knock the priest over to marry you," Charlie said confidently.

He didn't think he was overstepping by encouraging him. Marlon was Rosa's equal in most ways and opposite in some. It made for excellent chemistry and mix between them and they really moved as one together. Anyone looking at Marlon knew right away he had lost his heart just by the look in his eyes when she was near. He was a goner. Marlon reached into his pants pocket and retrieved a black velvet ring box. He opened it and showed Charlie, who nearly swallowed his tongue.

"Holy shit, is that thing real?" Charlie asked, nearly blowing their cover. Marlon closed it immediately and put it back in his pocket before someone came looking.

"Yes!" he said proudly. "I've been waiting for this lady to come into my life for more than 30 years. That deserves a ring that size. I have never done this before and I don't intend on doing it again so I'm sparing no expense," he said to Charlie, with his head held high. Charlie smiled and thrust his hand out to Marlon. The two men shook hands with a new found respect for one another.

"So when are you going to do it?" Charlie asked him. "Tonight?" he said enthusiastically.

"I don't know…" Marlon shook his head. "I think it's inappropriate to do it tonight. I was thinking maybe in a few days, while Wayne is still playing. Thought I might go up on stage after a set and propose in front of the crowd. Whaddya think? Would she like that?" he asked, slightly unsure of his plan.

"If I know Rosa, she loves to be the Queen Bee on display. She'd love your plan. But I think you're right, save it for Wayne's last night or something, it'll end the week on a higher note and we could all do with celebrating something happy for a change," Charlie said.

Marlon nodded and they shook hands again with Charlie patting him on his back in a brotherly fashion. *He's a good shit,* they each thought of the other.

. . .

When Hailey came down from getting ready for the memorial, she went to the kitchen. Georgie had laid out a glass of white wine for each of them and a snacks and nibbles tray while they fussed a bit more. Georgie, in her usual all black, accented herself with gold for tonight. She wore a sleeveless black slip dress with embossed roses covering the fabric which could only be seen as the dress moved. It hugged her figure closely and came to just above her knee with a tiny slit on her left thigh. Her watch, rings, bracelets, earrings and necklaces were all gold. She had leg hugging black high heel boots that came to just below her knee. She looked very sleek and elegant and put together. She turned to see Hailey smiling at her again and said, "That's twice you've snuck up on me today," as she surveyed her daughter's attire.

Dark flared jeans with a deep purple tank, lambskin black jacket and all silver accessories. Her hair was up and exposed her beautiful, long neck and the statement earrings she wore that hung from her ears in large diamond shapes. She was a stunning girl and Georgie was almost gushing as she came over to hug her.

"Oh, you look so lovely Hailey," she said, hugging her lightly and stepping away. "Purple is your color color, huh?" she asked as she admired her girl.

"And I see you still favor black despite the fact that the world has a million colors for you to choose from," she replied. In all the years she had worked at the club, Hailey could not remember her mother wearing any other color.

"I go to what I know – what can I say?" she answered, shrugging her shoulders and smiling. She popped a few grapes into her mouth with a piece of cheese and chewed away, smiling, and then finished her wine.

"Ready to go?" she asked Hailey as she put her own empty wine glass down on the table.

"Sure am," she said as she walked towards the back door off the kitchen.

The girls walked arm in arm, slowly, towards the club taking their time and enjoying the late afternoon sun. It was late May in Chicago but the night air was still quite crisp. The girls wore light jackets to keep the chill off for their short walk to the bar. They didn't say much as they got to the club, each lost in thoughts of what to expect for the evening. Georgie hadn't been into the club since the reading of Wade's will days previous, nor had she set eyes on Charlie or anyone else except Rosa. Most would have assumed she was in mourning but only one would really understand her distance.

As they entered the club, Georgie led Hailey to the coat check area and took their jackets off. Hailey came through the hallway first into the bar and stood staring at the picture of her mother and great uncle, large and visible. Beside it was a beautiful floral bouquet with fresh flowers of all kinds springing forth from all over it. In the top centre was the largest red rose Hailey had ever seen. Its bloom was so full and scented you could almost pick it out amongst all the others. The sight of both the photo and the bouquet was breathtaking and Hailey, not having a chance to grieve Wade's passing, got a huge lump in her throat looking at his smiling face, large and in print. She walked over to the photo and studied it closely. It was such a great shot of the two of them, the proud business owners and niece and uncle to boot! She couldn't believe that Wade would have done something in a vicious manner towards her mom in any way. There was definitely a reason for his decision and Hailey was determined to figure it out. As she studied the picture, she heard a gasp behind her and turned to see her mother across the room staring at the picture and the flowers. Georgie's eyes were wide and she held her hand to her mouth.

She knew the photo very well, it was her favorite of all the photos she had of Wade. It was taken on her birthday as Wade surprised her with a party. The picture was snapped just as she had entered the bar for the night's show. It had scared the hell out of her to have a bar full of people yell "surprise" and sing "Happy Birthday" to her and she laughed hard at her own expense. The picture had held a very prominent place in her den on the book shelf and was one offered to Rosa in a frame. She looked around the room and pointed and gasped at the other pictures Charlie had placed about. She absent mindedly walked over to the large group picture taken at Chase's birthday and looked at the size her family once was. Now it was only she and Hailey that were blood relatives. She looked at Chase, her "little man" at the time and reached out to touch the small boy's picture thinking of him and wondering how his trip was going. Even in the picture you could see he was full of energy, beaming at the camera. Charlie was standing to one side of Celia with his blonde hair falling over his eyes, his brow furrowed but with the slightest smile; a moment frozen in time. How different the brothers seemed now.

Georgie looked at herself back then – she was 14, almost 15 when it was taken. She remembered that night well. It began with her seeing Charlie in his underwear running through the living room and ended with them chatting in the same room and him saying that she'd be hounded by all the football guys in school. He couldn't have been more wrong, but it was a lovely thing to say to a young, awkward, teenage girl at the time and she had appreciated his gentleness for years afterward. At her father's funeral it was Charlie who had seen her overwhelmed and offered her a way out and his gift of the red steamer trunk told her he'd been paying attention to what mattered to her. Oh so it seemed. Was it really all just an act?

Hailey came to stand beside her not saying a word. Guessing from the pictures Charlie had chosen, the man cared very much for Wade and Georgie, despite what her mother thought. Having known Wade like Hailey had, she knew that the things he cared about most in the world were in this club tonight, and Charlie had captured them all in the pictures; even his trumpet was seen in the picture of just Wade and Charlie. Hailey's belief that Charlie had some mastermind plan to swindle her mom out of half the club was diminishing. But she still reserved her judgment until she laid eyes on him and studied his character.

As the two women walked to each picture and were quietly discussing them, Charlie entered into the bar area from the office to get a coffee. When he saw Georgie with her daughter he stopped, hoping to be introduced. Georgie turned and they locked eyes for a moment; the moment of truth. Neither looked away and when Georgie spoke she held his gaze, feeling stronger with Hailey there.

"Hailey, this is Charlie Morningstar. You met him over my shoulder during a Skype visit," she said, knowing full well that Hailey remembered who he was. She just didn't want it to seem as though he had been a large topic of conversation between them. The less he knew the better. Hailey smiled her mother's beautiful smile and held her hand out to Charlie who smiled equally as lovely right back.

"Nice to see you again, Mr. Morningstar," she said as she shook his hand firmly.

"Call me Charlie," he answered her, good naturedly. "Glad to see you could make it here for this. I know you being here means a lot to your mom," he gestured towards Georgie who kept her eyes low. He noticed.

"I... uh... was hoping to get a chance to speak with you at some point Georgie," he said, wanting her to know that it was important to him to get this straightened out.

She didn't say anything, only nodded briefly and smiled. Then she took Hailey by the arm and walked towards the kitchen area. When they entered, Charlie heard Marlon's voice raise and laughter come from the kitchen at the obvious joy at seeing Hailey back in town. He could hear the chatter from the voices in there and wished like hell he could break through to Georgie and be in there with them enjoying the reunion. *Patience you fool*, he admonished himself, *patience!*

...

The night was a sellout. Georgie wanted to have it as an invitation only memorial, but Charlie knew that some of his fans would pay a hefty price for tonight's memorial show. He needed to start thinking like a club owner and at least try to make some profit. Basically those that paid for a ticket covered the cost of the food for all. The bar was still a cash bar but with reduced prices for the night. Georgie made sure that people felt like if they had to pay, it was only to cover a slight overhead. Besides, Wade would have approved making sure never to do anything without at least breaking even. Charlie put some of his own money into the stage show, pictures, the bouquet and a few other touches. Wade's trumpet was placed into a glass box with a brass plate underneath telling his story. A photo of him leaned against the beloved instrument. When the night was over, Charlie was going to dedicate it to the club and put it in a place of honor.

Charlie had also taken the time to straighten out the desk area in the upstairs office making it as neat and tidy as Georgie's, so when she and Hailey entered the room she was shocked to see the desk so clean. He had also put a comfy couch off to one side, possibly for late night jam sessions *or if there had been too much drinking*, she thought, scoffing. He had left both lamps on and it cast a warm glow over the office, making it seem welcoming. She liked the glow the lamps gave off and went to her desk to see if there was anything of urgency that required taking care of.

"Well… at least he's a tidy guy. Means he's got standards right?" Hailey asked in a positive manner.

"Yeah," Georgie said sarcastically, "don't forget my dear, the man lives on a bus!"

. . .

Brad entered the bar just after 7:30 pm as Charlie had suggested. He once again made for a very striking sight in his rust calfskin jacket, black turtle neck and black pants. His white hair was thick and slightly wavy and hung a little longer than most men would wear, but he liked it that way. He was a confident man and enjoyed dressing well. He went straight to the bar and ordered a two finger whiskey. He had told Charlie that he would meet him there around this time and as he received his drink and had his first taste, Charlie was behind him and slapping him on the back.

"Hey, it's really good to see you again," he said genuinely and hugged the elder man tightly before ordering the same drink for himself. "How was the drive up?" Charlie asked.

"Oh, no troubles," Brad answered. "Sorry about your loss, Charlie," he said softly. "I hope he's in a better place now," he said as he raised his glass and Charlie did the same. The two men drank from their glasses and each put them down on the bar.

"Me too," Charlie said. "Uh... I wonder if you can advise me on a couple of things, business in nature?" Charlie asked him bringing him into his confidence.

He knew that Brad had been a businessman for over 50 years and was very successful at whatever it was that he did business in. Charlie explained the situation with Wade's bar and also his current and future plans as the elder man listened intently. He agreed with Charlie's decisions, offered him suggestions and said he would contact someone who would get hold of Charlie to help in his future decision makings. He and Charlie shook hands as Charlie thanked him for his advice and his confidence.

"I feel honored that you would tell me this Charlie. I'd love to help in any way I can," he admitted, smiling his near identical smile right back at his son.

They were still lost in conversation when Brad's eye caught Georgie walking into the bar area and greeting those in attendance. A young woman who was Georgie's double hovered nearby, smiling shyly. Brad's face made Charlie turn around and he knew right away that Brad had seen Georgie. She had that effect on men. He smiled as she walked their way although she hadn't seen them yet. When Georgie approached them she caught Brad looking at her and did a double take. It was an uncanny resemblance that he had to Charlie who stood next to him and Georgie wondered who he was. She tilted her head as she cautiously approached the two men, her daughter in behind her seeing the same thing. They were both dressed impeccably well, Charlie wearing a silk navy shirt with dark jeans, the man next to him equally as groomed. Charlie, taking the opportunity to draw her near and perhaps put aside their rift if only for a moment, stepped towards Georgie and touched her arm briefly as he made introductions.

"Georgie Pelos and her daughter Hailey Banting, this is my father, Mr. Bradley DuMont," Charlie said proudly.

The two women jolted backwards as he said the word "father" never expecting it. Brad puffed up proudly and smiled as he held out his hand. Georgie was stunned. She couldn't speak. She didn't know what to say. If she didn't know better she would think this to be a joke on her as another way of humiliating her, except there was no mistaking that this was Charlie's relative in some way. *Damn near identical twin!* She held out her hand, smiling at Brad with astonishment in her eyes.

She studied his face closely for a moment or two and finally said "Pleasure to meet you, Mr. DuMont," hardly keeping the awe from her voice. *Wasn't he just full of surprises,* she thought!

"Oh, I can assure you my dear," he said smoothly, his eyes twinkling, "the pleasure is all mine. Enchanté," he said as he took her hand and kissed it. She blushed slightly and imagined Charlie doing the very same thing, even though she was still so upset with him.

"So how exactly did this come about?" Georgie asked. But Charlie wasn't going to give up too much just yet. He had his hand on his father's arm and squeezed it slightly in an attempt to keep him from answering.

"It happened quite suddenly," Brad said, looking to Charlie for guidance. "I was informed some time ago that I had a son out there." He said no more thinking that this gave enough information and Charlie could add what he wished.

"Brad found me back in Carmel some weeks ago. A letter, a few lawyers and a touch of serendipity was all it took," he said mysteriously. He didn't elaborate past that and Georgie didn't press. She was still trying to fathom the existence of Charlie's father. For years, she wondered if Wade might be his father and when he handed the club over to Charlie, the thought crossed her mind again. But standing before Charlie's perfect elder version, she had no doubt that he was telling the truth.

"And what is it that you do, Mr. DuMont?" she asked, genuinely interested. Her face had lost that stern look and Charlie once again marveled at her beauty as she spoke with his dad.

"I'm a broker in acquisitions" he admitted honestly, taking another sip of his drink. Careful not to spill on his cashmere sweater he wasn't paying attention to Georgie's face as it fell when he mentioned his occupation, but Charlie saw it and he knew what she was thinking. *Oh shit,* he thought, *that's not going to come across very well.*

Georgie stared at Brad for a moment and then looked to his son. She laughed briefly as their eyes locked as if to say "got me good" and then excused herself to the other end of the bar taking Hailey with her.

"Did I say too much?" Brad asked innocently. "I hoped that wouldn't be too much," he added, not wanting to be completely vague with her.

"No," Charlie said heavily, "I don't think anything is going to win her over at this point. She'll probably read too much into everything I do."

He stayed with his father for a few more minutes until he was informed that Wayne had entered the building through the back door and the show was ready to start. He got Brad the table of his choice and made sure a waiter was to check on him personally every 20 minutes or so. He then went to the back of the bar behind the stage where the waiting area for the talent was located. When he knocked on the door, Wayne jerked it open and stood there smiling at him. He had Chase's energy level, that was for sure, but he made a song his own, sometimes for the better and sometimes not so much. Even still, he had a hell of a following and in rehearsals had shown such great chemistry with the remaining Chasing Charlie band members, that tonight's audience was in for a treat.

"Everything ready to go then, buddy?" Wayne asked him as he drank a beer. At almost 55 year of age you could tell he had been on the road a while. He'd played worldwide, was well known in the blues/jazz clubs and festivals and had lived a hard musician's life. He had played with Wade and Charlie many years back and had returned to the Black and Blue plenty of times to headline. He was honored to be doing this gig and Charlie was thrilled that he accepted. Wade would have applauded him proudly!

"We'll be on in about 15 minutes. You feelin' good tonight?" Charlie asked him, feeling a sense of responsibility now as half owner of the club. He had to be doubly sure to please his talent and his audience now. He liked the pressure though; it had been a long while since he felt challenged.

"I'm feelin' excellent, buddy. Ready to do Wade proud," he said and shook Charlie's hand.

It brought a lump to Charlie's throat to think about how proud Wade would be tonight. To know that these people had gathered in his honor to be entertained by the best and listen to his favorite blues and jazz songs being played out for all to enjoy would've made him pleased as punch. Charlie couldn't wait to take the stage. Many years had passed since he felt this anxious for a show to begin.

. . .

The night did not disappoint. Wayne Mack Murray and Chasing Charlie were electric. They played everything from James Brown to Stevie Ray Vaughan and originals of both Chasing Charlie and Wayne's made each set. The food was excellent, everyone was impressed with how the night played out. It was hard to believe that such fine fare and elegant dining could take place inside a blues club in Chicago. It would be a night long talked about and the photographer that was in attendance got pictures that made entry in the following Sunday's Chicago Tribune's Entertainment Edition. Most had not expected to see a different front man for the band other than Chase Morningstar. But Wayne was perfection, understanding Chase's energy and adding his own dollop of fun and cleverness to the set. He had musicality as well as his smooth voice were a nice added touch to Charlie's guitar, Rosa's harmonizing, Simon's piano and Stilts' drums. They had missed Chase but found new energy with Wayne. No matter how excellent though, the band wasn't the same. The night ended with the song "Gifted Hands" and Wayne and the band did a stellar performance causing the audience to rise to their feet.

All inside the Black and Blue that night were left feeling as though they had done honor to Wade's memory. Brad stood at the bar clapping, proud of the son he'd only just begun to know, wanting to help him in his quest to have the life he dreamed of. Hailey applauded the band having thoroughly enjoyed the evening. She had watched her mother closely and made note that her attention had been directed solely towards one person.

Georgie was clapping her hands and watching Charlie intently. He had closed his eyes for almost the whole performance so it was hard to judge his temperament or his thoughts. She loved watching him play and it took her back to a time when she'd watch his reflection in the mirror of his bedroom as he played, concentrating with all his might. She loved him back then and she still did now, even though she didn't believe she could trust him any longer.

Charlie had some visibility from the stage. Lights often helped blur out the crowd but only to a certain point. He could clearly see his father sitting at the table with two blonde ladies and another young couple. He seemed in his element and each time they caught each other's eye, Brad would wink at him. He had thought a lot about finding his father and how much more complete he felt knowing his ancestry. He wanted to tell Chase about Wade's admission to him and the name Campbell but Chase had left before Charlie could say anything to him. Soon, he hoped Chase would return his calls and they could talk about things.

Charlie could also make out Georgie at the back near the bar with Hailey beside her. He tried to not pay her too much attention — she was a big enough distraction as it was — but every once in a while he would steal a glance to see what she was doing. Only once did their eyes meet but she turned away quickly and the look was gone. Mostly, Charlie concentrated and got lost in the night's performance. With his eyes closed he played his heart out to his dear friend. When it was all over, he felt satisfied.

The evening was winding down and once again the band sat around enjoying drinks at the after show party with one another. A few extras were included in tonight's festivities such as Simon's girlfriend Linz,

Hailey, Brad and of course, Wayne. Marlon looked happy and exhausted as he sat next to Rosa holding hands. Charlie introduced the astonished crowd to his father getting used to everyone's jaw hanging open as he did introductions around the room. His father simply smiled at them all, thrilled to be included in the group and was instantly engaged in conversations with both Rosa and Marlon who wanted to know all the details. Other conversations around the table ranged from stories of Wade on the road with Charlie to Wade running the talent side of the business and some of the fun they had. Laughter was heard throughout the emptied bar well into the wee morning hours as all of Wade's family and closest friends remained to toast him and roast him.

"Well… I don't know about you all and meaning no disrespect to Wade and all but I could do with some happiness for a change," Rosa said honestly, yawning and stretching as she said so. "I'm tired of wearing black," she said, pulling at her black skirt. Marlon caught Charlie's eye and the two men held their gaze for a moment, knowing what the other was thinking. They each nodded their agreement to one another. No time like the present! Marlon looked at Rosa for a second, gaining his courage and then stood and dropped to one knee, producing the ring box from his pocket.

"Then how about wearing white?" he asked matter-of-factly. He said his proposal in a quiet but confident voice and the room was dead silent as everyone at first gasped and then hushed to watch it take place.

"Rosa," he began, "you have become the light in my life I have been waiting for. In the last few months you have made my existence glow brighter and seem more meaningful than it ever has. I want to spend my days with you. I want to spend my nights with you and wherever you go I promise to follow. Will you marry me and do me the honor of being my wife?" he asked as he opened the ring box. The group held their breath, all waiting for Rosa's answer.

Georgie's eyes welled up for Rosa because she knew it was a dream come true for both she and Marlon. Everyone in the room leaned in looking at Rosa as she sat there stunned at Marlon, bent down on one knee. Rosa threw her arms open to Marlon and yelled "YES!" to his question. He rose and swept her up into a bear hug, kissing her and swinging her around as he did. The group all cheered and clapped and the moment Rosa's feet hit the floor both were surrounded and congratulated heartily. Once the group had settled Charlie made sure that everyone had their glasses filled as he made a final toast of the night. He raised his glass and said, "To future happiness, to Marlon and Rosa and to Wade who would have approved whole-heartedly."

Cheers! The group replied in response. It was a perfect end to a perfect evening.

Chapter 30

Chasing New York

As soon as Chase's plane hit the ground, Kyle had him well in hand. He was greeted almost before he was through the arrivals gate and was raced into the back of a limo, drinking a beer and being taken to a club in Manhattan. There he would be partying with some of Lapis Labels most famous artists. He was on a natural high but Kyle made sure it stayed there through whatever measure necessary.

Chase was enjoying the ass kissing. He figured he was long overdue for this and reveled in every moment. All manner of women were paraded before him and it was made clear he only had to choose and she would be his for the night. They were all gorgeous woman with bodies that would have kept him humping through the night but he couldn't help but wish he was there with Georgie.

By the end of the week, he was partied out and had to beg off Kyle's request for a late lunch, opting instead for the quiet of his hotel room and a few extra hours rest. He didn't know if this is what he could expect from working with Kyle's label but he'd have to pace himself for certain 'cause this was a much different lifestyle than he'd been used to. Kyle had offered him the chance to sit in on a recording gig taking place that evening. This was amazing — the first time he was going to be in the recording studios and he was pumped for the experience. So far he had met quite a few blues artists that Kyle had signed and all of them spouted his attributes as a producer. Without Kyle and Lapis Labels backing them, each felt they wouldn't be where they were. It all seemed very cut and dry to Chase. Have label, will rocket.

He thought once or twice about the band and Charlie back in Chicago. He was very aware of the fact that Wade's memorial had taken place and wondered how it all went. He requested a copy of the Chicago Tribune at the front desk of his hotel and as he drank his morning coffee, he read about Wayne Mack Murray's stellar performance with the remaining members of Chasing Charlie and the tribute they had played to Wade McGrath.

"...despite the missing front man for "Chasing Charlie", Chase Morningstar, it seems that the only thing chasing Charlie is dollar signs," read the article. It was a blow that Chase had not expected. How did they manage without him? Could he really be so easily replaced? Chase didn't like reading how successful the night had been and when he saw the enlarged picture of Wade and Georgie and his fellow band mates smiling widely beside Wayne in a publicity shot, his gut ached. He threw the paper down and jumped for the in-room mini bar, opening the bottle of whiskey and downing it. He laid on the bed, scrunched up the pillow under his head and tried for some much needed rest but his thoughts lingered on the article. He realized that for the first time ever, Charlie had done publicity! His anger grew instantly and he pushed himself off the bed. He then called Kyle and asked where to meet him. At the other end of the phone, Kyle just smiled.

...

Not in the mood for a meal, Chase convinced Kyle to let him go into the recording studio early. Kyle checked to see who was in studio and gave Chase the go ahead; Kyle would send a car for him and meet him there. Chase was picked up by yet another limo and driven to a high rise on the east side of Manhattan. Kyle had texted him to take the elevators to the 22nd floor and come to suite 2217. When the limo driver pulled up to the building and Chase got out, he automatically looked up to the top of the building – all 86 floors. *Thank God I'm only going up 22 floors,* he thought. He wasn't a big fan of heights.

The building's lobby was all marbled white and grey. Even the lightest of step caused a sound to be heard as people made their way in and out of the busy building. Chase looked about interested in those around him and found his way to the elevators. He stepped aboard; the only occupant of one going up and pressed button 22 which lit up. The doors were almost closed when he heard a voice ask, "Hold the elevator?" and suddenly they stopped closing and began opening. They revealed an elderly woman – Chase figured she was 80 odd years old. She apologized profusely for holding him up and kind of staggered onto the elevator. Chase reached out to help steady her and she grabbed his arm holding it tightly. She had very bright eyes and apple cheeks and Chase couldn't help but smile at her. A familiar feeling came over him as though he knew her well.

"You're so kind to help me. I haven't felt so steady on my feet lately," she explained to him as he made sure she was okay. He smiled and looked at her hoping she'd reassure him that she'd be fine but she kept on talking past his questioning look.

"I used to want independence so much, nearly fought tooth and nail for it and now I realize that it only makes me more vulnerable. We are always strongest with those that we love surrounding us," she said, almost to herself. Then she turned her head towards Chase and spoke directly to him.

"You need to meet your mark before you can move ahead. When you've done that, it'll help you. Meet your mark," she repeated, her crooked finger pointing at him firmly.

Chase stared at her closely. He remembered her in a different setting that he couldn't quite place but had a sense that it was long ago. He knew she had spoken to him before because he recognized her voice. It caused his senses to be on extra alert and he felt as though he was tunneling; only focused on her.

"What do you mean by "meet my mark?" he asked inquisitively. She intrigued him. He was wide awake and yet he felt as though he was caught in a dream. She captivated him in a way that he had never felt before. He watched her very closely and listened when she spoke, analyzing her words. As they held each other's gaze, the elevator doors opened and several people got on chatting and bustling, breaking the spell. Chase's vision came back from a bit of a blur and he looked to find himself surrounded by numerous strangers, none of them an elderly woman. He reoriented himself to where he was and what he was doing there and when the elevator doors opened on floor 22 he got off, welcoming the freedom and shaking his fuzzy head.

He found suite 2217 and entered the door, heading straight to the reception desk. A brunette in her mid thirties sat wearing a headset speaking to someone but motioned for Chase to come forward. She spoke softly into the microphone near her mouth and smiled as she pressed a button on the phone set on her desk.

"Welcome to Lapis Labels, can I help you?" she asked Chase as she looked directly at him.

"Yes… uh… Chase Morningstar to see Kyle Craven, " he said quietly, leaning down to her.

She smiled a brilliant smile at him and nodded. "Please take a seat Mr. Morningstar and Mr. Craven will be right with you," she said as if expecting him.

He thanked her and chose one of many overstuffed leather chairs adorning the reception area. On every table top a copy of the latest "The Blues Revue" was waiting for the next person to pick it up and thumb through it as they waited to meet with one of the labels big wigs. Chase took a seat and scanned the magazine briefly. It helped fuel his fire as he glanced from one article to another about the various blues artist making big news out in the blues world. He shook his head thinking of the years he had wasted touring with Chasing Charlie, never being able to interview on behalf of the band, always having to be satisfied with a mediocre existence when he should be on all the magazine covers. At his age and the amount of work he'd done, most music stars had already hit the charts and he wasn't even known in main stream music, yet he'd been touring for 20 years! *Thanks for nothing Charlie!* Chase thought bitterly. His resentment had been growing for some time and after the past year he'd experienced with Charlie, he now carried a whole hell of a lot of resentment, like a burden.

He threw down the magazine in disgust and sat impatiently waiting for Kyle. Moments later Kyle emerged through the solid glazed glass and stainless steel doors that stood to the right of the receptionist's desk. He walked over to Chase and held his hand out.

"Hey Chase, buddy," he shook Chase's hand vigorously, "Excellent to have you here. Follow me and I'll introduce you around," he said, jerking his head towards the glass doors and then smiling and winking at the receptionist. Off he went with Chase following. They walked on through the open doors to a hallway lined with offices off them. As they passed by, Chase looked into a few of them and saw various people sitting in front of computer screens, most with picturesque windows in front of them talking on the phone, working at their job, doing whatever the hell they do that earns them a living. *Not my job, thank fuck,* he thought. *BORING!*

They continued to walk to the end of the hallway until they reached a door, opened it and descended one flight and went through another door.

"Sorry," Kyle explained. "You can't get to the studio from the 21st floor. We designed it that way so that our artists have the most security and privacy we can offer them." He said proudly.

He had been a big part of the design team when it came to the recording studios and he was happy to impress any and all with his assistance in the clever and unique design. To Chase, it was all magnificent so its cleverness was completely lost on him having nothing to compare it to. Nevertheless, Kyle hoped that Chase's socks were blown off.

Chase couldn't hear the music until they were standing in front of the band separated by glass. A group of three played a clean version of Dave Brubeck's Take Five and Chase stood mesmerized at their precision. It sounded so crisp and clear from where he stood and he was enthralled as he watched the musicians all wearing headphones on the other side of the glass. No other noise, no other influences, just them. The drummer, a hefty guy with a lot of facial hair had a solo and played it down to next to nothing, his sticks barely touching the skins. The piano player was an older guy with a great smile who kept in eyesight of the sax player. The two of them worked off one another and his hands moved across the keys like they were attached to his fingers and guided the guy on sax in whatever direction he went. The sax player was a long-bearded guy who would nearly roll his eyes into the back of his head whenever he played. Chase thought of 'Charlie' affinity to that kind of performance and how it lacked a connection to the audience, but it didn't seem to matter – the music drew you in. They improvised for longer than 10 minutes and Chase was hoping it wouldn't end. He didn't know who any of the artists were but he was sure he had heard their names more than once. It was spellbinding to him, no stage, no lights, just their crisp clear sound. He loved it.

When the music ended the guys all started talking and removed their headsets. The sax player gave thumbs up to the guy sitting at the controls and he gave the same in return. Chase watched the musicians intently and how they interacted. They all seemed to know each other well and the piano player was chatting them up, making them laugh. Chase imagined himself amongst them, even if he only played the guitar on an instrumental piece, he was willing to do whatever it took to start having everyone hear his music and get his name out there. Kyle could not have done anything better than to invite him to this recording. It had really motivated him to get into the studio.

Kyle leaned over the sound board and hit a switch. "Hey guys," he said over the intercom, "I want you to meet Chase," as he pointed to Chase standing to his left.

Chase raised his hand and smiled, feeling kind of awkward. As Kyle was about to speak again his phone rang. He grabbed it with his other hand and looked at the caller. Holding up one finger he said, "Gotta take this, sorry. Just go in and get acquainted and I'll be in right away," he said apologetically to Chase. He pointed towards a door that led into the actual studio and Chase moved towards the door as Kyle took the call turning his back to him.

He couldn't hear the three men talking until he entered the room. The piano player was just ending the punch line to a joke when Chase came in. They were laughing heartily and enjoying the moment as he walked over, a smile on his face.

"Hey… uh… hoping to work with you guys on something. Kyle is trying to get me to sign with Lapis and I… uh… am strongly thinking about it," he continued nervously, as they watched him closely. "Loved your 'Take Five' just then… hell of a cover sound," he said appreciatively.

The piano player eyed him over and then cocked his eyebrow at him. "Your new here aren't you?" he said with smile. "Have you never been in a recording studio before?" he asked, appreciating his enthusiasm.

"No… actually," he replied, almost embarrassed. He didn't want to explain anything more than he had to so he just said. "I've been touring for the most part and Kyle saw me play a night in Phoenix and has been chasing me ever since."

The piano player smiled at him. "Was that a funny you just made?" he asked. "*Chasing* me ever since?" he laughed as if Chase had meant to do it. At first Chase thought he was making fun of him, but then he got his humor and laughed right along with him.

"Well, the recording studio may always have your sound but there's nothing like playing off a real live audience. I did it for many years until I came to New York," said the piano player.

"Did you give it up? Are you in the studio only now?" Chase asked him inquisitively while nodding his head.

"Something like that," answered the piano player. By the time Kyle arrived, Chase had broken the ice with the three and they were chatting all about gigs and songs and everything music. Chase was given a guitar and sat in with the group on a few songs improvising riffs and playing as effortlessly as they were, making the music seem to flow easily from all of them. Kyle stood on the other side of the glass watching them and clicking the end of the pen he was holding continuously, chewing his gum hard. He knew Chase Morningstar was going to make him rich, he just knew it.

Once the impromptu jam session ended, the sax player and drummer left, noting other appointments they needed to make. Chase and the piano player sat talking and sharing their individual musical backgrounds. Kyle watched them together unable to shake an uncanny feeling about them. If he didn't know better he'd think they had known one another from somewhere before and figured they must have played together at one time and not remembered. After all, they were both well traveled musicians in the genre and although one hadn't toured much in the last 20 years he had recorded a ton of music. The other had done the opposite, never having recorded but toured his entire career.

The studio intercom had been turned off and Kyle was interested in what they were so grossly locked in conversation about. Each was as animated as the other and it was like watching a fine dance while the two of them conversed about God only knows what. Kyle did find them engaging though and as he entered the room he made sure not to break into their deep conversation with a jarring door opening. He quietly made his way in to hear Chase saying, "...at an early age. My mother would sing to me as a small boy and I'd just be in heaven at her voice. She was just like Billie Holiday. When I hear her now I think of my mother," Chase ended his sentence.

"Oh, I remember a woman who sang like Billie," said the piano player, reminiscing. "...they don't make women like that anymore," he smiled to himself. "Only knew her for a short time but she plays on my mind to this day. She had an interesting name, as I recall" he said, shaking his head as if remembering a long lost love. Neither said a word for a moment and Kyle chose it as the perfect opportunity to break in.

"Well gentlemen, sorry I didn't make formal introductions earlier," he said apologetically, "...but, better late than never."

Realizing neither had bothered, the piano player held his hand out to Chase and said, "My apologies, I didn't even realize. The name's Mark Hagen," he smiled at Chase showing a dazzling wide smile that lit up his whole face, "…but everyone calls me Campbell."

Chase shook the man's hand vigorously thinking how much he liked the guy and would like Charlie to meet him.

"Chase Morningstar," he said proudly, as he watched the man's face drop instantly.

Chapter 31

Two Favors

Within days of Rosa and Marlon's engagement they had set a date. They wanted to be married on June 29th, less than a month later. Neither wanted to wait any longer than they had to and nothing was stopping them. They filed papers immediately and met with Roger Stein regarding any last minute legal details around Rosa's previous marriages. Rosa started to plan from the get go and had a binder already full of ideas and color swatches as if she were a first time bride.

"It may be my third but it's the first time I'm doing it right," she would tell anyone who would listen and gush as she'd hold out her hand to show off the two carat diamond ring that Marlon presented to her. She had asked Georgie to be her maid of honor and Linz to be a bridesmaid. She had one more person to ask if they would participate and she was very nervous about it. She timidly knocked on Charlie's office door one afternoon as he sat behind the desk. He looked up at her from his papers and smiled immediately, gesturing her to come into the room.

"Come on in," he said smiling at her. "How's the bride-to-be?" She positively beamed and they both took a moment to enjoy the mood.

"I tell you Charlie," she shook her head, "in all my years I have never felt such happiness and peace, you know?" she said hoping he could connect. She wanted everyone to feel the love that she and Marlon

"I can't tell you how happy it makes me to hear you say that, Rosa," Charlie said honestly. "We've been working a long hard road for many years and it's about time that you had some enjoyment and stability and happiness," he said.

He wanted to see her settled as much as he wanted to see himself settled. He was tired of dragging his ass across the country. The more he stayed at the Black and Blue, the more he didn't want to leave at all. Now that he had been running his side of things, he felt even more determined to make this work with Georgie somehow and make a life here. She didn't have to love him; she only had to work cordially with him. He might be able to live with that. He might be able to turn her around. Since Wade's memorial she had softened slightly towards him but gone were the long lingering looks. The red trunk had brought them so close, almost there but she felt betrayed and he knew it. He understood, he just didn't know how to prove that it wasn't what he had planned at all. And although Hailey stayed in town for a few days afterward and really seemed to make an effort to engage him when her mom was near, Georgie was reluctant to be alone him and would often make it so that there was someone else around when they spoke business. Hailey had gone back to New York but not before she had given Charlie a bit of a pep talk.

"Don't give up, Charlie," she said to him in the bar quietly one afternoon. "I know she's hurting and you'll just have to give her time but I honestly think she'll figure it out and when she does…" she left it at that nodding her head. He trusted Hailey but still felt unsure. Hailey trusted Charlie and knew that there was nothing sinister in his actions, Wade had made this decision and judging from what she had seen while she'd been home, she thought she knew why.

shared. She would never again be alone and this marriage would never falter because she knew in her heart that he was the man she was meant to be with. Should the group move on she may not choose to, but if she did, she was confident that Marlon would move with her. That's just how they were, living for one another.

Charlie stared at Rosa as she snapped her fingers in front of his face. "Hello?" she said sarcastically, breaking his daydream. "Wake up now. I need you to be alert." She paused a moment waiting for him to acknowledge her. When he nodded at her she continued. "I have a favor to ask of you. Well… I actually have two favors to ask." She held up two fingers as she emphasized the number. "Number one…" she paused, dropping one finger. "I would be honored if you would… uh… walk me down the aisle" she said shyly, quickly watching his face for a reaction.

He looked stunned at first and then his face broke into his million watt smile. "Absolutely!" he said proudly. He had never imagined he would walk someone down the aisle and now he was going to. Another good reason to never say never!

"And favor number two…" she said sheepishly. "Would you consider letting us have our ceremony *and* reception here at the club? It would mean the need for a dance floor and redesign of the seating for a night… pretty-please?"

She stood before him with her eyes all full of hope, her face full of love and happiness. He couldn't remember ever seeing her like this before. How could he say no?

"I don't see why not," he said holding his palms to the ceiling and shaking his head. "Have you asked Georgie too?" he asked, just to make sure she had been included. Everyone had pretty much started to turn to Charlie when it came to bookings and such and no one had ever asked about whether Georgie was the sole owner, they just assumed it had gone that way and that Charlie was helping per an agreement between them.

"Well, yes, of course I did. She was fine with it as long as you were but she did raise an issue that I didn't quite think of", she said, confessing the snag. "If I'm marrying that night and the whole band will be there partying, we won't want to play."

Charlie saw her point, understanding that they would need to get an entire band in to play for the wedding. "Well, do you have anyone in mind?" he asked her. It didn't bother him if someone else took the stage that night. He had been successful in avoiding the spotlight, yet always managing to find someone who would play the front man or woman to their group of four. Charlie would always be in the background, eyes closed with his guitar, happy to be hidden and he hoped to keep it that way. So someone else coming to play for the night made Charlie very happy.

"I was hoping you, me and Marlon could audition a few bands," she said and he nodded his agreement. "We only have a couple of weeks so we'll have to get on this." He grabbed a large red binder and told her, "Go through this. It's a bible of all the bands Wade booked throughout the years and everything you want to know about them." He handed Rosa the massive binder. She looked at him in disbelief and threw it back on his desk. Sometimes he was such a caveman!

"Holy shit, Charlie. Ever heard of the internet?" she said sarcastically. "How 'bout you and Fred Flintstone get together and take a computer class?" she said jokingly to him. "Never mind about the binder, I've gone through some of the stuff on the web and found three bands I want to see," she explained to him. "Can I get them to come here through this week and we'll audition them?" She asked him again smiling widely.

He swore if he had a little sister, she'd be just like her! "Yes, yes, of course," he said laughing. "You let me know what you need to pull this off and make it the day you dreamed of and I promise it'll happen," he told her.

She came around the side of his desk squealing and gave him a huge hug and a big, red, lipstick kiss on his forehead. She left all chatty and reaching for her phone as she made the first of many calls to organize auditions. He smiled as he watched her go. The wedding had been a blessing to the club, giving them all something to focus on if only for a little while Wade's death had been a difficult time but they were managing. The enlarged pictures remained in the bar as did the bouquet, although Georgie had been keeping it pruned and it was starting to look pretty thin. He wanted to make sure it was replaced every week or so, at least for the next little while.

Slowly everyone associated within the club was starting to heal and things continued along fairly smoothly. Charlie was able to carry on in Wade's footsteps but was finding it hard to continue living on the bus as it sat stationary. It needed to be kept plugged in so that he had hydro and every once in a while he had to drive it to a place where he could clean it out, gas and charge it up. It was becoming a pain in the ass. As fond as he was of it, he realized that it was not a great way to live when you weren't on the move. At Brad's advice, he spoke to Roger Stein about a real estate agent he could hire who would help him find suitable permanent housing. He had an appointment that afternoon to see a place that was set to come up on the market but not yet ready to show. He was anxious to see it and hoped it would have all he wanted in a house. Having never bought one before, he thought of his mother's home growing up and pulled from that memory to help make his decision. It would take some getting used to but he was sure he'd grow accustomed to waking up without wheels underneath him.

. . .

Georgie had stayed distant from Charlie in the weeks following Wade's death. At first he had been preoccupied with the memorial and then shortly after, Rosa's wedding so she was able to pretty much dodge him and carry on without them having to speak much at all. It had taken all her strength to see Roger Stein again and sign over the documentation required for the preparation for the sale of Wade's house and some other things he had for her to address. Mr. Stein was an excellent lawyer and watched Georgie closely as she came in to sign away most of her frustrations.

"We'll put the house to market very soon. Have you cleared the place out of all his personal belongings?" he asked her. Georgie looked up at him in shock. "No!" she said with a heavy sigh. "I suppose I should go over there and see what's in there." She sounded defeated, like she'd been pushed to the edge of her limit. She had not entered into Wade's house since his death and really didn't want to now.

"You know, if the furniture isn't too bad, we might be able to sell it lock, stock and barrel. You'd have to remove his more personal items, clothing, pictures and things you want but there are many times that people buy a house fully furnished," he offered her. He could see how overwhelmed she felt and said gently, "Listen, my brother-in-law sells real estate for a living. I'll give him a call and get him on board and the thing will pretty much sell itself, I'm sure," he said, hoping to help her get back to her old self. She had seemed lost since Wade died and although he figured she was grieving, there was also something else afoot.

"Yes, that sounds good" she said as she prepared to leave the office.

"You know, your uncle loved you very much, Georgie," he said to her, placing his hand on her back as he guided her towards the door. "He would be heartbroken to see how sad you are from all of this," he told her.

"Then he should have anticipated my confusion over his decision and talked to me about it first. It was a punch to the jaw right after the shot to the gut that I really didn't need." She held his gaze firmly and with a pull on the door, walked out leaving Roger Stein standing there. He had always thought she was an incredible beauty and even in such a state of turmoil, she could still take a man's breath away.

Roger turned and went back to his desk. He opened his top desk drawer and took out the sealed envelope that read "Georgina." He hesitated a moment, tapping the one end of it against his fingertips. It had only been a couple of weeks and Wade had made his wishes very clear that it was not to be delivered until at least a month after his death, if at all. Roger was only to deliver the envelope if he saw discord between Charlie and Georgie continuing after a month's time of working together. Wade had figured that once the dust settled, they'd look across and see each other standing there and fall into each other's arms professing their love for one another, the club be damned!

Well, such was not the case and Roger knew that before too long he'd be walking that envelope over to Georgie's house to help try and mend the chasm that was growing between her and Charlie. Wade knew his niece well enough to know that all of this was going to hit her very hard so he prepared a letter for Georgie that explained everything. He had only hoped that Charlie and Georgie would find their way back to one another without any help from beyond.

. . .

After leaving Roger's office, Georgie decided she had better go to Wade's house to see what she could clean out. Most of his personal items like clothing and such could go straight to Goodwill – she certainly didn't need to keep any of it. She could stop and get boxes from the club and grab what she could of his personal things. While at the club she made a phone call to a house cleaning crew and arranged to have them go in to clean this afternoon to get it ready for showing and hopefully selling. With all this in order, she went to Wade's house to sort and remove his personal effects.

She drove along her old street looking at house after house as she thought back all those years ago to life on Birchwood Lane. She passed what used to be Celia's house. For a number of months after the fire it remained a burned out hole in the ground that marred the face of the street like a nasty unhealed wound. The other houses that had been affected by the fire that night were cleaned up shortly after but Charlie had signed over the property to the City of Chicago and it sat as an eyesore for a little while. The City left it as such until the spring of the following year when they came in, tore down the burned mess, and prepared the property for a builder to build another family home in its place. Georgie couldn't drive past it without a feeling of loss. She hadn't been there to witness it all but she remembered her mother's eyes when she had finally managed to get into town. Jean had still seemed stunned by what she had witnessed that night and she had told Georgie about the house collapsing right in front of her eyes knowing that there were people she loved inside and they weren't coming out.

Georgie drove past the old Morningstar lot and could easily spot her own childhood home and Wade's, just doors away. Her house was sold years ago and the family that purchased it had taken loving care of it. It stood out now as the owners had painted it a brighter color and replaced the doors and windows. The house was more fitting with today's times but Georgie still remembered fondly the music and fun that it once had beneath its roof. Just two doors away stood the McGrath family home. Wade's parents, Georgie's maternal grandparents, owned it from the time the street was developed. The McGrath's were one of the first families to populate this street and it held prominence if only for that. Georgie pulled into the driveway and got out, looking at the house from the outside. She could see where it needed a little tender loving care before she listed it and thought about what would need to be done to get this house ready to sell. She really didn't want this to be a long drawn out process so she'd see what the realtor thought and go with that. Hopefully, she could unload it before too long and be done with the whole thing. She held some sentimental value for the home especially of late when Chasing Charlie had come to town and they would meet there for meals on a day off from performing. The house had not seen so many people in quite some time and she was happy for it.

She had always appreciated it's finely appointed details, hardwood floors, wainscoting and deep baseboards. She had thought about renting it out for a bit but then soon realized that would make her a landlord to someone and she had enough of a business to run without doing that. She thought about letting Hailey live in it but Hailey wasn't planning on moving back to Chicago any time soon and Georgie couldn't let it sit without a tenant until Hailey possibly returned. No, much as she hated to, she knew she had to sell it and hoped it would go to a family as wonderful as the McGrath's had been. She made a mental note to ask the realtor to ensure it was by someone who would really cared about the place.

She entered the house finding it pretty much in the same shape as when Chase had walked out the door the afternoon of Wade's funeral. It was stuffy from being closed up for so many weeks and the dust was starting to collect but other than that, Wade had kept things pretty tidy. She began going through some of the personal things he had about – pictures, documents, and photo albums. She filled three boxes full and was just starting on a fourth when a knock came at the door. She answered it, happy to see the cleaning crew had arrived. *Good*, she thought, *they'll get this place in tip top shape in no time.* She gave them some quick instructions and the four girls from the cleaning company set to work right away. As they got busy, Georgie continued up into Wade's bedroom. There she found a lot of things that she just couldn't part with. Wade's gold watch bought for him by Georgie's mother for Christmas many years ago. She put that in her handbag along with some gold cuff links, a gold chain and a single diamond studded earring that Wade had been fond of wearing. She filled her fourth box with more photos and family mementoes and took one more look around his room. She turned towards the door and was going to leave when she noticed something poking out from behind the mirror on his dresser. She walked towards it, looking very closely at it, not sure what it was. It looked to be the corner of a large envelope that had been stashed in between the mirror and the wood. She pulled it from the side but it wouldn't budge. She put the box down on the bed and reaching from over the top of the mirror she managed to straighten the envelope and pull it out straight from the top. It was an extremely large envelope with what looked to be x-rays inside. She pulled them out and held them up to the light. They were labeled, "McGrath, Wade." She had no idea what she was looking at but the date of the x-ray caught her attention – October 15, 2012. She assumed these were x-rays confirming his cancer and, if so, that meant that Wade had known about the cancer long before Charlie's return to town – eight months before! She wasn't too sure if Wade had kept his secret from Charlie until the very end or if he had shared the news with him long beforehand. *That's the $64,000 question*, she thought. Did Wade possibly do this without Charlie's knowledge, keeping his secret and then changing his mind about the will near the end of his life? And did Charlie encourage him to do that or was he just as surprised as she was by the turn of events. He had certainly seemed surprised at the time the will was read but she had stormed out so fast and had not given him any chance to really discuss it with her since. She pondered this for a moment and started feeling badly that she had been so stubborn and distant. Perhaps Charlie is just as innocent in this as she is. Wade was not one to be easily swayed and perhaps he had wanted his old friend to have something of his and the truck just didn't cut it. She was confused about things these days. She wanted to call Hailey and chat with her and tell her of her find. Hailey had been good to confide in while things had gone cold. She seemed to have a clearer perspective than Georgie. However, she also seemed to be leaning in Charlie's direction which also gave Georgie some thought. What could her own daughter see that she couldn't?

Shaking her head, she kept the x-rays and placed them on top of the box she now carried down the stairs. The cleaning crew was scrubbing, vacuuming and washing everything in sight and already the house was beginning to brighten. She had even requested washing all drapes and curtains and the windows too. The house got a fair bit of sun and after being closed up for so long it needed some life brought back into it. She got to the front door, opened it and went out to her car to load up the boxes of Wade's things. On her last trip inside she briefly spoke to the lead supervisor of the cleaning crew making sure they would do a thorough job and be gone before the end of the day. She was assured of this and handed the portly woman $50 as a tip. The woman was extremely grateful and got to work promptly taking down all the drapes in the living room.

Georgie took one last look around the house before she left. The kitchen, visible through the living room was bright and shiny clean now thanks to the crew and a large living area that was now much brighter because of the drapes coming down. She had dreaded doing this and yet found it quite soothing not to mention intriguing. Some of Wade's belongings were things that she had no idea she cared about, but now she was glad to have them in her possession. As she stood there with the door open ready to exit the McGrath's family home for the final time, she was surprised to see the shell of a lived in home that, she imagined, someone could easily picture themselves living in, and fingers crossed that the place sold without having to remove the furniture. That would be a godsend!

...

Rosa had become obsessed with wedding planning and rightly so considering it was to happen in less than five days. She was taking Georgie and Linz with her to pick out a dress, although, she wasn't going for a traditional white dress with a long train so she wasn't panicked. She was hoping to find a long ivory lace dress that would be suitable and off the rack. She wanted Marlon and his groomsmen in black tuxes and Charlie as well.

When the three ladies arrived at the boutique they spread out to try and find something suitable for Rosa to wear. A salesperson by the name of Marlena came over and asked Rosa how she could help. Rosa told the woman of her wishes, her desire to perhaps find something for her ladies to wear as well and their short time frame. Poor Marlena near about had a case of the vapors at the task set before her but she steadied her flawlessly coiffed chignon and marched off in search of the perfect wedding dress for Rosa. She found three dresses for Rosa to try on and Georgie and Linz took a seat while Rosa changed into the first gown with Marlena's help. Both Georgie and Linz had the same thought as they sat looking around the boutique, *I wonder if it will ever be me?*

They heard a door creak open and footsteps as Rosa entered into the viewing room and stepped up onto the pedestal for all to see. The dress was ivory, with lace lining the collar. It came slightly off her shoulders and hung to the floor in wispy soft folds. It was a nice dress but judging by the look on everyone's face, it wasn't a stand out. Back she went into the dressing room to try on dress number two. As she re-entered the viewing room wearing the second dress, Georgie could see that Rosa liked this dress. It was another long ivory dress but with more of a mermaid shape to it, more structure around the middle area and a sweetheart neckline. When Rosa came to stand in front of the mirrors and could see herself in 360 degrees, she turned around and marched right back into the changing room, not giving anyone the option to say anything. She liked how it felt on her but called out to the three women over her shoulder, " …did you see my ass!?" She wasn't wearing anything that made her ass look *that* big! Back to the dressing room!

On her third attempt, Rosa came out beaming. She practically floated into the room wearing a sleeveless satin gown with ivory lace overlay. It hugged her figure in all the right places and made her waist look like it was 24 inches around. She looked breathtaking. Both Linz and Georgie gasped and welled up when they looked at her. She even turned to show off her backside and pointed and nodded her head, "No ass issues", she said proudly. To finish off the look, Marlena chose a long ivory lace veil to drape over Rosa's dark hair and gave her a bouquet of cream roses to hold. She looked absolutely spectacular. She was Marlon's perfect bride and all three women sat staring at her with wide smiles and love in their hearts.

"It would be lovely to find something just like this for Georgie and Linz," Rosa said as she admired her reflection in the mirror, turning and looking from every angle.

"Well, say no more my dear bride. This dress comes in many different colors! You could have them wearing the same dress in the same color or each in a complimentary color, whatever you want," she announced, solving everyone's dilemma.

She shot off to find the matching dress in their sizes and a bunch of colors. Marlena took Linz into the dressing room first and sent her out wearing her dress in black. Both Georgie and Rosa loved it, especially with her long blonde hair. They agreed to the black but wanted to see Linz in other colors. She came back out wearing a soft green and a pale pink but neither did anything for her and the black was decided on as the best color for Linz.

Then it was Georgie's turn. Georgie secretly hoped to be wearing her signature black too. Marlena followed her into the dressing room and helped her into a red dress. Georgie looked around the room for other dresses in other colors and asked Marlena about it when she didn't see any.

"Why do I only have the one dress to try on?" she asked as Marlena turned her to zip her up.

"Trust me, darling," she said confidently. "This is the only color you were meant to wear." With that she opened the dressing room door for Georgie to walk out. When she walked into the viewing area both Linz and Rosa sat jaw-dropped as they watched her approach. She was such a vision of beauty that Rosa had a brief moment of jealousy, but then realized that this could make everything fall into place.

"You look incredible," Rosa gushed as she clapped her hands. "Truly, you'll be a vision." The red dress was more a blue tone red and made Georgie's skin glow. Even without her hair done up fancy, no jewelry and hardly any makeup, Georgie was absolutely stunning in the dress and she herself could see it. The silence in the room was weighing on her as everyone held their breath

"Wait a minute," said Georgie. "I'm not the one getting married, I shouldn't be standing next to you wearing the same dress," she argued, but Rosa wasn't having it.

"You didn't say that when Linz came out of the room and she looked equally as stunning. Face it Georgie, you can't win this one and I'm the bride so whatever I say goes, and I say our dress search is over!" she announced proudly.

. . .

Charlie pulled Wade's truck into the driveway of the house he was to look at. The realtor had worked his magic and managed to get him to have a look just before it listed; *helps when you are friends with a lawyer,* Charlie mused. He walked towards the house and before going inside had a look at it from the outside. The windows had been cleaned and didn't look too old, the brick on the outside was in good shape and the front porch was large. *Excellent for early morning star gazing,* he thought. As he stood there, he took a look up and down the street to survey the neighborhood. The street seemed to be filled with children playing, younger families and a nice atmosphere. The onset of summer was making everything lush and green again. As he stepped up the front steps to the house he took a huge breath and let it out slowly. Fresh air.

The house was nice and tidy, cleaned inside and out. He was happy to see the amount of light it offered and walked around surveying the walls, floors and some of the features. He checked the upstairs out thoroughly and even went into the master bedroom, staying for a few minutes in quiet contemplation. When he came downstairs the agent was sitting at the kitchen table working his numbers. Charlie grabbed a chair and sat with him.

"I want it," he said. The agent's head shot up quickly as he looked at Charlie with a smile on his face.

"Well, that's excellent news, Mr. Morningstar. What price were you thinking we should start the bidding at?" he asked, getting his pen ready.

"The asking price is just fine. No less. I don't wish to haggle over things, I want it just as it is," he told the agent.

"Oh! Uh… do you mean with the furniture and all?" he asked, knowing the house could be sold as is if the buyer wished.

"Yup, that's perfect for me. I'll take it just like this," he said and reached his hand across to the agent to seal the deal.

"Well, it's a pleasure doing business with you, Mr. Morningstar. I'll get everything lined up and have you in to sign the papers as quickly as possible. I'm sure the owner will be happy it sold as quickly. She's had a bit of a rough go lately and really needed this off her list," he confessed to Charlie.

I know she has, thought Charlie, *I know.*

Chapter 32

The Wedding Day

All preparations for the wedding had been made. Flowers lined the stage of the club and along each wall in all the gorgeous summer colors. For effect, Rosa had requested a similar red rose be placed in the centre of each bouquet, just as Wade's bouquet had done. She liked it regardless of whether or not she knew of its true meaning, she probably wouldn't have opposed it anyway. She was a bride on a mission.

Marlon had spent the week going over the recipes he and Rosa had chosen with the catering staff. Luckily, they were to be using Black and Blue's kitchen for their meal preparation and Marlon felt that he needed to oversee it all, which pissed the caterer off to no end. He didn't care – this was his one and only wedding and he and Rosa deserved nothing but the best.

For a surprise, Charlie had rented a limo that would come to pick him up at the club and then drive the two blocks to pick up Rosa, Georgie and Linz, all at Georgie's place, having been chosen as the best place for Rosa and Linz to spend the night before. The limo seemed a bit extravagant but Charlie didn't want Rosa having to walk the distance in her dress – he wanted her and her girls to show up in style. It was his little gift to her, to them all.

Georgie had opened her house up to Rosa and Linz and enjoyed having them around as the excitement of the wedding day built. She made sure that the fridge was well stocked with goodies to eat and some lovely wines for them to sip as they fussed about to prepare the bride and themselves for the wedding. Rosa wanted a hairdresser who would fix all their hairdo's for them but trusted no one when it came to her make-up. She was insistent that she do her own. Georgie was sipping her mimosa and was wearing her long housecoat, not wanting to put her dress on until the final moment. She was also expecting Roger Stein to arrive with documents to sign from the house being sold. She was thrilled that, after a nudging from her realtor, she had allowed the house to be seen prior to listing the very afternoon she had gone to clean it out of Wade's personal effects. What luck was that? And he must be some kind of whiz Realtor because the buyer took the whole lot, all furniture, appliances, everything. She didn't have to go back and empty the house at all. It was really the perfect ending for her except that now the house would no longer be in the family, but she knew she couldn't dwell on that. She got the asking price, no questions asked and she would move on. She was also feeling softer towards Charlie. They had spoken only briefly over the past few weeks but finding Wade's x-rays behind the mirror got Georgie thinking that maybe Wade had kept his secret from everyone and that Charlie really didn't know he was as sick as he was. While sipping her drink and lost in her thoughts, she missed the car pulling into the driveway and before she knew it there was a knock at the back door. She broke from her daydream and went to answer it.

Roger Stein stood poker straight in his business suit with his eyes staring ahead. *Ever efficient little man!* she thought. She opened the door to him and welcomed him in. The house smelled of fresh flowers and perfume and right away Roger was enchanted by it all. She could see him looking around at the wedding effects lying about, the bride's veil in clear plastic near to the door as it would be placed upon her head as she walked out. Her bouquet was left open in its box just so Rosa and the girls could gaze upon it when they were in the room and for its lovely fragrance that filled the air. There was the sound of women's laughter and voices coming from upstairs as she led Roger through the kitchen into the den and sat him down next to the red trunk. He spent a moment admiring the décor and then put his briefcase and gloves down on the seat next to him.

"Preparing for a big celebration I see," he said, not wanting to rush away.

"Rosa and Marlon are marrying this afternoon," Georgie explained as she smiled at him. It was the first he had seen her smile in a long time and he was held by her beauty. She certainly seemed worth it all. *No wonder*, he thought.

"Ms. Pelos, before we get down to signing the legal documents for the sale of the house there is something I need to give to you." He handed over the envelope from Wade. She looked at it stunned and then looked back up to Roger. "Who is this from? It looks like Wade's writing," she said examining the handwriting closely.

"It is," he said, letting his breath out. "He asked me to give it to you at a certain time after his death. I believe now is that time," he said mysteriously. "Go ahead," he encouraged her with his hand gesture. "I think it will help to mend a few misgivings and misunderstandings that have gone on long enough," he said in a slightly patronizing voice.

She turned her head to him, not liking his tone but flipped the envelope around and started to open it up. Instinctively, she stood turning away from the lawyer sitting on her couch, watching her intently. Regardless of what the letter said, she didn't want him being front row centre to her private and personal reaction.

...

Upstairs Rosa pampered her face in the oak vanity in Georgie's bedroom. Georgie's laptop sat open as she anticipated a call from Hailey that morning and had asked to be called when it came in. Rosa had completed her makeup and the hairdresser was just finishing curling the tendrils that hung down around her face when suddenly Hailey's face popped on the screen. It scared Rosa half to death and both women laughed at the reaction.

"Oh my God, you look so beautiful," Hailey said to her as she gushed at the bride's beaming face. "Is that your dress behind you?" Hailey asked, pointing as Rosa turned her head to look. Georgie had hung the dresses from the top of her bedroom closet door so they wouldn't touch the ground. Her dress was the first one in the background and Hailey could see it clearly.

"Yes!" she said shaking her head excitedly. "Isn't it beautiful," she asked the young woman moving out of the way of the camera.

"Oh, it's so stunning!" Hailey gushed more, always a sucker for a wedding.

"I know and wait until you see your mother. Oh my God, Hailey, Charlie is going to lose his mind when he sees her. If this doesn't break the ice between them, nothing will," she admitted to Hailey.

"Well it's about friggin' time, Rosa," Hailey said in frustration. The two women had been plotting about what to do ever since Hailey's return home the week of Wade's memorial. They had exchanged emails and phone calls numerous times in the past few weeks planning this very day. It was Rosa's idea to have Charlie and Georgie in the wedding party hoping that being a part of Rosa's wedding would help spur their own love on. But when Hailey suggested that Rosa dress her in something that Charlie would not be able to resist, Rosa was in! Being fully confident in her own beauty and love that she had found in Marlon, she selflessly welcomed the idea. Rosa knew she was the bride for the day but Georgie really was breathtaking in the red dress.

"Well, I think you're such a sweetheart for doing this for my mom, Rosa. I wish I could be there. I'm so sorry I have such a crazy life!" Hailey said, feeling bad for missing out on another huge occasion. Rosa had invited Hailey as well as Charlie's father to the nuptials in hopes of having all the extended family there. She even phoned Chase and left him a voicemail but he hadn't returned her call so she figured he was off making his name and didn't care.

"Thank you so much – you have no idea what it means to me," Hailey said, heartfelt, referring to how much Rosa had tried to help bring Charlie and Georgie together.

"Hey, it's not just for you sister, it's for the two of them and all of us combined. Today is about love and Charlie and Georgie are damn well going to fall deeply in love today and they are damn well going to like it!" Loud female laughter could be heard all throughout the house.

. . .

Charlie entered the bar and took his guitar case straight to the stage, hiding it in the back near the curtains. No one could find it there and when the time came he wanted to be able to grab it and go. He had nervous butterflies in the pit of his stomach and hoped that he'd be able to settle himself long before the time came. Once Meg was stashed away, he left the stage and went to the bar to pour himself a small drink – just a little something to steady his nerves. He stood sipping his drink as the door opened and the sunshine pouring in illuminated his father's form. He had only met him on three occasions now and yet he could pick him out in a crowd blindfolded. Brad walked casually over to his son and they shook hands. Charlie was not yet dressed in his tux and standing next to Brad, already wearing his suit for the big day, he felt incredibly underdressed. He was proud that his father was such a fine looking man and could see why Celia had loved him all those years. It must have been hard for her to look upon Charlie and not think of Brad time and again. The two men shook hands with genuine affection and began speaking quietly amongst themselves.

"I heard back from the investigators on the information you gave me regarding Chase's father. Now, it could be a long shot but I have a name and a number of a guy living in New York. I'm not sure what you'll find of it but he used to work under the nickname of "Campbell." He's a piano player. They felt pretty confident that it was the same guy but…" he stopped talking, shrugged his shoulders and handed the piece of paper to Charlie.

413

"Mark Hagen." Charlie read the name aloud. It meant nothing to him. He didn't ever remember Celia or Wade saying this name but then, he didn't remember hearing about a "Campbell" either until Wade mentioned it. He looked a moment longer, lost in his thoughts and then put it into his wallet. He still hadn't heard from Chase although he had heard through the grapevine that he was doing it large in New York. At least Charlie knew he was still alive.

"Also," his father continued, "I worked a deal with the realtor and I know that worked out because he told me the deal is closing as we speak," he said, patting his son on the back.

"Yeah… uh… thanks again for moving so quickly on that. I really didn't want it going on the market so I'm grateful I was the very first to see it," Charlie said. His father had pulled a few strings for him in the last little while and Charlie was very grateful.

"Now, enough of business and favors for me. We have a wedding to attend and I have a bride to give away," he said, smiling at his father. "Really glad you're here to share in this… dad," he said rather shyly.

Brad's face lit up and he smiled right back at him. "Pleasure to be here, son," he said proudly.

. . .

May 22, 2013

My Dearest Georgina,

If you're reading this letter then I must first take the opportunity to apologize to you. My cancer diagnosis was given to me last fall and when they told me that I wasn't going to outlive it, I just didn't have the heart to make you go through the same kind of hell that you went through with your mom. I know it must have been one hell of a shock to you, but I hope you know that those were my wishes and I was happy to not have to watch you become my nursemaid to the bitter end.

I'll bet you're also royally pissed at me if not completely confused and Charlie is also probably not in your good books either lately. I want you to know that Charlie had absolutely nothing to do with me making my decision to leave him my share of the club. As a matter of fact, Charlie was considering leaving to go back out, head to New York and give Chase what he wanted and not split up the band. I changed my will in hopes that Charlie would feel he had to stay. It was my own personal choice and decision and one that my lawyer will verify I made in sound mind and without coercion. Roger drew up the will within a half an hour of me writing this letter to you. Charlie was played as much as you. And here's why:

BECAUSE HE LOVES YOU

And you love him. Period. End of sentence. Now, quit being stubborn mules, the pair of you. Go tell that man how you feel about him and make him read this letter. Thank you for all you ever did for me. I loved having you as my niece and business partner.

Have a nice life!

You're welcome.

I love you and Hailey immensely,

Uncle Wade xxx

Georgie took note of the date on the letter again, May 22; three days before he died. Georgie turned to look at Roger with tears in her eyes and a small smile upon her face. He hadn't read the letter but figured Wade had written to help his niece understand his decisions better and it seemed to have worked. He smiled briefly at her and she sat back down across from him still holding the letter in her hand as the tears fell down her cheeks.

"He called me up out of the blue and said he wanted to make some changes to his will. Said that he didn't want you to be left alone to run it and" he mimicked Wade " *...that a damn fool was about to walk out on the best thing that had happened to him in 30 odd years!* " He felt he had no choice but to leave Charlie his share so that Charlie would stay and you and he could make a life together," the lawyer explained. "He seemed adamant that Charlie was deeply in love with you and was ready to stay and profess himself to you but Chase kept chasing him towards New York. So, he took matters into his own hands," he shrugged. "Bit of a matchmaker and also a hopeless romantic," Roger said, laughing at the softness of his old friend.

Georgie nodded, understanding now everything that had happened. When she thought back to the day Wade had died, she remembered he had said, "Lovely niece... excellent business partner... treasured friend... I want you happy... That's why I did it!" and now she understood. She had thought he meant keeping his cancer a secret but he wasn't referring to that at all. He was referring to his decision to change his will, only it hadn't been divulged at that point – Wade was still alive and talking to her then. Everything came into focus now and she starred feeling very badly for how rude and accusatory she had been to Charlie. He didn't know any of this at all; Wade's instructions were for her to let Charlie read the letter as well.

"Thank you so much for giving me this, Roger. It certainly does help to clear up some things. Now, if you'll excuse me..." she rose and made her way to leave quickly but Roger interrupted her.

"Oh, but we aren't done yet, Georgie. There's the sale of Wade's house to sign off on," he reminded her, handing her a pen. She nodded as if to say "oh, of course" and came and sat down again, taking the pen from his hand. He handed her the first of three documents to sign. She read the top portion and froze, her eyes scanning the information several times over.

"Is this true?" she asked Roger, turning the document towards him.

"Yes," he smiled, hoping her reaction would be better rather than worse.

She held still for a moment holding the forms and then smiled and quickly placed them on the red trunk to sign her name. She signed the three documents handed to her and gave them back to him along with his pen. She extended her hand to him and shook it firmly as she rose.

"Thank you, Mr. Stein. It's been a pleasure. You've been a real doll to my uncle with how carefully you took care of his last wishes. You have my highest regard," she said to him as she showed him to the door.

He thanked her, beaming and left the house.

. . .

Rosa was ready and came down the stairs and into the kitchen area, making a grand entrance where Georgie and Linz stood waiting. All three women were now dressed and ready and had just a few moments to go before Charlie was to arrive.

Rosa looked incredibly beautiful. Her skin shone and her eyes were bright and wet with the emotion of the day. Her dress was exquisite and she didn't mind that her two girls were wearing the same dress only in a different color because it looked completely different on each of them. Rosa was shorter, even with heels, but the dress had the style of a long draping flapper dress sans fringe. The material hugged her closely but had such a romantic flow that it made her curves respectful and alluring. Exactly the effect she was going for.

Linz was tall in her black dress and heels. The black only emphasized her porcelain skin and her hair was up in a full chignon. She had diamond shaped crystal earrings, a gift from Rosa for both girls to wear tonight. Rosa wanted them to wear a deep red lipstick, all to match Georgie's dress, especially since Rosa's name meant "red" and it was her favorite color. Thankfully, it looked good on both women. Linz looked very elegant and lovely and Rosa thought of how much Simon would be anxious to get his gorgeous girlfriend home tonight.

Georgie fidgeted with her hair a moment and Rosa gently tapped her hand away. "Leave it alone, you'll screw up the curl," she admonished and all three women laughed. Rosa had noticed Georgie loosen up over the course of the afternoon and wondered if signing the papers off on Wade's house had been a closing relief to Georgie. Something was different; she positively glowed, never mind the dress!

Georgie chose to wear open toed satin high heeled shoes in the exact same red and painted her toes and finger nails all in the matching color. The effect was striking. She wore only the gifted earrings for jewelry and carried a small red clutch completing the effect. It was breathtaking. The dress simply caressed her lovely figure in some areas and clung to her in others. She looked positively stunning. Her hair was up in a half chignon with tendrils cascading down the sides of her face. Rosa had been more specific about how she wanted Georgie to look than with her own appearance it seemed, but not to worry; there was no mistaking who the bride was. The girls had been sharing a mimosa, munching on some of the snacks made available by Georgie and having a few moments before leaving, when a long, black limo pulled into Georgie's driveway and drove its full length straight towards the back of the house. Rosa screamed when she saw it and covered her hand over her mouth running through the house back and forth in excitement.

"Oh my GOD!" she screamed. "I can't believe he did this!" she laughed and cried at the same time.

The three women were giddy as the limo came to a stop. Rosa gathered her thoughts quickly enough to orchestrate how this would go.

"Linz, you will help me get my veil on, and Georgie you go out and take that man's breath away," Rosa said, conniving the whole time.

Georgie looked at her a moment, hesitant at first then broke into a wide smile that dazzled. Rosa blew her a kiss and Georgie turned for the door.

...

Charlie had dressed on the bus and made sure that everything was in place for the big event. He entered the bar through the back door near the ramp and surveyed the room one more time, feeling very satisfied that it was the most beautiful setting for a wedding he had ever seen. It had been completely transformed for the ceremony with tables set up to the side for dinner served immediately afterward. The dancing area had been built to Charlie's specifications so that it was close to the stage. He was thinking of talking to Georgie about keeping it in there but didn't want to think about business tonight. He had other plans!

Happy with how the club looked, he chatted with his father and Marlon and was introduced to Marlon's brother's who were serving as best man and groomsman and the rest of Marlon's family. Charlie continued to watch the door, waiting for the limo to pull up. When it did, he climbed into the back of it and had the driver go down the few blocks to Georgie's house. They were there in no time and Charlie felt the car come to a stop along the back of Georgie's house. The tinted windows made it almost impossible to see anything on the outside and he squinted his eyes and reached for his sunglasses as he left the limo, stepping into the late sunny afternoon. He closed the car door and came around the back end of the limo, intending to jump up the back steps and reach for the door when he suddenly froze.

He saw her first from the feet up. Every square inch of her standing before him, rather five steps above him, like a goddess in red. He couldn't get up the stairs so he just leaned against the bottom railing and removed the newly donned sunglasses as he caught his breath. They didn't speak a word to one another – they just stood there until, finally, Charlie found his voice.

"I... uh... thought there was a rule about outshining the bride on her wedding day. Bad taste and all..." he said as he smiled at her taking her in. Her heart raced ahead a few beats and she had to swallow to answer him. "You haven't seen the bride yet," she said softly.

It was all she could manage, he too being a very handsome sight in his tux. His shock of blonde hair freshly cut but shiny and thick, his green eyes standing out. He nodded at her response but kept his thoughts to himself. He managed to pull himself up the stairs and came to stand before Georgie.

"You're breathtaking," he said honestly. He wanted to kiss her so badly but didn't want to push his luck.

She blushed and pulled at the arm of his tux, "Thank you," she said. "You clean up very nicely yourself, Mr. Morningstar," she said, hoping to keep her head from swimming.

She could feel all her misgivings drain away as she looked at him and almost wanted to talk with him there and then but knew it wasn't the time or place. She managed to reach for the door and open it just as Rosa came out onto the porch for Charlie to see. His face grew into a huge smile the minute he saw her.

"Rosa, darlin', I have never seen you looking so incredibly beautiful," he said as he bent to kiss her cheek.

Her veil had been pinned to the center of her hairdo and fell lightly, full length down her back. It was exquisite and finished the bride's look off nicely. She was truly a vision. Charlie pulled out a camera as Linz came to stand on the porch and the four of them took pictures for a few minutes, even asking the limo driver to take one of the four of them before they left for the bar. When the bridal party arrived at the club and descended from the limo, Georgie took Charlie aside.

"Charlie, I have something for you," she said as she took his hand. She gave him a pair of gold cuff links, Wade's watch, his chain and diamond earring. "I found these in Wade's bedroom recently. I want you to have them and thought it might be nice if you wore them today." She shrugged her shoulders. "I bet Wade would be happy that Marlon and Rosa were marrying and that his things were worn by you when you walked Rosa down the aisle. Marlon and Wade were good friends you know," she said to him. It was more than she had spoken to him in a few weeks and still trying to find his voice from her beauty, he was floored.

"I'd be honored, Georgie," he said, genuinely touched to have Wade's things. "Can you help me put them on before the show starts?" he asked smiling. She smiled back.

...

Chase's flight got in to O'Hare at 5:00 pm. He was hoping to be able to get a cab and get to the Black and Blue before the wedding started for 6:00 pm but it was going to be tight. He still needed to get his bags and he wanted to have a chance to change first. He didn't bother calling anyone to let them know, 'cause he hadn't been sure himself until just this morning. Then it had been a race like all hell to get organized and packed up. Kyle was furious with him but he'd get over it. Besides, Chase was going to make him a very rich man, eventually. He had signed his life away with Kyle and Lapis Labels worth an estimated three million dollars. He spent the last few weeks getting a band behind him and would start recording once he returned. He just needed to do this one thing while he had the chance and before his life overtook him.

He picked up his luggage after a 10 minute wait and found a bathroom where he could get into a decent suit. It was a wedding after all and he didn't want to wear the suit on the flight. He managed to clean himself up and was rather impressed with how well he looked considering. Thankfully, his suit was not smashed into his luggage as usual and it had made the trip with hardly any wrinkles at all. Once dressed appropriately, he went outside the airport to hail a cab. It didn't take long before he was on his way to the Black and Blue, estimated time of arrival 30 minutes tops.

...

The doors to the bar opened to the sounds of Pachelbel's Canon playing over the sound system. It was Marlon's choice for his beautiful Rosa to walk down the aisle to and she loved it the minute she heard it. She had walked to "Here Comes the Bride" twice before and wanted this to feel completely different from the others, and it did. She was happier than the other two times, knowing full well that Marlon and she could balance anything they set their minds to. They were the perfect team.

Linz came down the aisle first on Marlon's middle brother, Manuel's arm, smiling wide, the crowd appreciating how beautiful the couple looked. Next was Georgie on Marlon's younger brother, Leo's arm. A very stunning couple; the eyes of the crowd unable to take their gaze from Georgie. Then came Charlie with Rosa. She walked slowly to the beat of the canon and smiled, looking at her man, Marlon, beaming at her from up on the stage. She had tears in her eyes as Charlie led her up the stairs to stand beside her soon-to-be husband. The minister started the service and the whole time Charlie stared straight ahead. He knew he had one more thing he had to do while he was standing there and he wanted to be sure he concentrated and took care of his last obligation to Rosa.

"Who then gives this woman to be with this man?" asked the minister.

"I do," said Charlie proudly and from the audience, just as fast, both Stilts and Simon stood in unison and said, "So do we," to which those in attendance all broke out laughing.

Charlie took Rosa's hand and placed it then in Marlon's hand and stepped away and down the steps taking a seat at the front where he had a perfect view of Georgie. During the ceremony, all through the vows right to the end when they kissed, Charlie didn't take his eyes off of her. He had wanted her for so long and now he felt as though she might be within reach once again. Half way through the vows, Georgie caught Charlie's look and they held it for a long time. So much was needed to be said between them and she hoped there would be a chance as soon as Rosa was married and off on honeymoon. There wouldn't be a chance to really talk things out thoroughly until then. Even still, she was certainly going to let Charlie know she was sorry and that she wasn't still angry with him. Hopefully, the gift of Wade's jewelry was a good start.

The wedding guests cheered as Marlon and Rosa were wed and he kissed her rather long and deeply, once given permission. She blushed and smiled as she turned to face the crowd and raised her arm in the air and cheered, "Wahoo!" and everyone laughed. It was so lovely to see them married and happy and the crowd gathered around them as they descended the stairs. Once Georgie was able to make it down the stairs she made her way to the back door making sure it was propped opened for air circulation and easy access for the caterers and eventually the band members that would be coming in and out soon after the meal.

She went to organize the setup for the head table on the stage while photos were being taken of just the bride and groom. She and Rosa had discussed the need for Georgie to have a chance to whip everything into shape before she'd be able to stop and take pictures and Rosa was fine with that. She darted back and forth making sure everything worked like clockwork and then went back to the wedding party for dozens of pictures.

When the dinner was ready, the guests took to their seats and dined on a menu that was painstakingly chosen by Marlon and Rosa. Every detail was attended to, making sure that the meal would leave no one wanting. They dined on barbecued duck & wild mushroom quesadillas with a roasted pepper & mango salsa, mojito shrimp on silver spoons with citrus wasabi aioli, conch fritters with chili mango sauce, beef empanadas with mint mojo for the hors d'oeuvres. The entrée's were a choice of grilled lamb lollipops with rosemary & garlic mojo, papaya rum glazed chicken satays, roasted chicken breast stuffed with three cheeses & served with black bean stew, a tamarind glazed pork loin or churrasco beef tenderloins sliced and served with rosemary & garlic mojo.

This was all accompanied by several choices of sides ranging from an antipasto, three different kinds of rice, roasted or mashed potatoes and salad. Marlon had ensured that all of their favorite foods were included. The guests ate like kings and several times during the meal glasses were clinked as the bride and groom stood to kiss and appease their guests. Sweet treats, coffee, espresso and tea were served after dinner with a formal cake cutting ceremony taking place later. Rosa and Marlon also arranged for a smorgasbord to be served at 11:30 pm.

A few short speeches were made by Marlon's brothers and by Marlon himself asking that Georgie and Charlie stand so that all knew who they were and thanking them for the use of the club and for all their help and support. Marlon raised his glass and said "to Georgie and Charlie" as the crowd mimicked and Rosa smiled secretively to herself.

. . .

The wedding party finished their meal and were moved to a table off the stage so that the band could get set up. Rosa, Marlon and Charlie had auditioned three bands and gave the job to a seven piece group called "Midnight Blue" consisting of two guitar players, a piano player, a trumpet player, a saxophonist, a drummer and a female backup singer who sometimes did lead vocals. They had promised to follow certain time frames, making sure that the proper wedding protocols were adhered to and assured the bride, groom and Mr. Morningstar that they would be able to fulfill the dreams of the newly married couple. As the front man took to the microphone and welcomed everyone to Rosa and Marlon's wedding, he asked the crowd to gather around as the couple were to dance their first dance. Rosa and Marlon came and stood in the centre of the dance floor and waited for the band to start playing the music to "At Last" by Etta James. Charlie and Georgie stared at each other from across the dance floor, their desire electric. Their eyes were locked on each other for the whole song and only broke their gaze as it ended.

As the party was about to begin, Georgie noticed the back door closing and went to prop it open again with the chair. As she opened it she was shocked to find Chase standing at the bottom of the small loading ramp with his back leaning against the railing, tapping the full bloom of a very long-stemmed red rose against his black shoe. He was dressed in a black suit with a white shirt and black tie. She presumed he had tried to make it in time for the wedding but missed out and didn't want to barge in at an importune moment. Either that or he just couldn't face coming in.

"Hey!", she said, completely surprised to see him. He looked up and she saw his face hold as he took in the full sight of her. He was without words for a few moments as she stood there looking at him, waiting for some sort of explanation. Finally she asked him, "What's going on? Are you here for the wedding?"

He looked down to where the rose was tapping his shoe and shook his head. He had come in through the front doors hoping to get in before the ceremony ended. He knew he was late and thought he might just make it in time to see them kiss. He put his luggage on the inside of the doorway and stepped into the bar hoping to see Rosa and Marlon.

Instead, his scan of the room immediately caught sight of Charlie and Georgie staring at one another from across the dance floor. He watched them watching each other, never moving their eyes. His stomach lurched and he turned right around and stood before the doors wondering what he should do. He spotted the red rose in the centre of the bouquet near the doorway and grabbed it as he went back outside the doors around to the back of the bar. How was he going to convince Georgie that it was him she should be with? He hoped to gallantly present her with the rose and was contemplating his speech to her when Georgie found him.

"I missed it, I think," he said, keeping his head down.

She wondered what was wrong with him. Maybe he was drunk or something.

"It was a beautiful ceremony," she said. "Rosa will be thrilled that you came at all." She moved closer to him and came to lean beside him on the railing. As she waited to see if he would say anything to her Georgie noticed the dark sky and impending rain that would soon start; she could smell it in the air. She causally wondered if Chase had brought the rain with him, his mood seeming as such. When he didn't say anything for a moment she asked him honestly and openly, "Why didn't you say goodbye when you left, Chase?"

It had bothered her that he hadn't given anyone else a thought when he took off, he just left. She didn't remember him being so selfish as a younger boy; far from it. But he had changed over the years. He was far more moody and self-centered.

"Oh, I don't know Georgie," he said, shaking his head, still keeping it down. "I had to get out of here, I was losing my mind, you know? I just felt like I had to break free. And now I have," he said, turning to her and looking her straight in the face. *God, she's so beautiful,* he thought. He raised the rose so that it was between them, offering it to her as they spoke.

"And did you find what you were looking for in New York?" she asked him, ignoring the rose. He nodded his head and bit into his lip. "Yup,"

425

he said proudly. "I signed a three million dollar contract and I'm going to make records." In the distance the two heard a low rumble of thunder.

He was smiling proudly, continuing to nod his head affirming his success, but recognizing the obvious snub of the offered rose, he dropped it and continued to tap its bloom against his shoe.

"Good for you, Chase," she said rubbing his arm. "You finally got what you always wanted," she said to him.

"Not quite," he said, looking directly at her, stopping the tapping. "I've waited for this my whole life but it would mean so much more to me if you were with me, Georgie," he confessed. It nearly took his breath away to say it but it was now or never. Seeing her standing there before him in her gorgeous red dress all fancy and beautiful, he couldn't help himself. He hoped that his success would make her see him now as the grown man he was and successful artist he had always promised her he would grow up to become. Now it was all within his reach and Georgie could complete his dream.

"I want you to come back to New York with me. That's why I'm here. Fuck the wedding. I came back for you. Come to New York with me and I'll make you the happiest woman ever," he said, urging her to decide. "I promise I'll take good care of you and make sure you have everything you need." After a brief pause he added, "Your daughter could even come and stay for a while," hoping that would seal the deal for her.

She didn't know what to say to him. She said nothing at first but it was her eyes that told him everything she couldn't vocalize at the moment. He read her face and looked back down to his shoe, again tapping the rose's bloom against it. In the background she could hear the band playing and the excitement of the crowd as they played "Mess Around" for the audience with another low rumble of thunder as if forewarning them of the coming rain. She stood with Chase for a moment waiting for him to say something more. She didn't want to leave him standing there.

"Rosa will be thrilled to see you here, Chase," she said, hoping to comfort him but not knowing what to say.

"But not you, huh?" he said, sounding defeated.

She looked him in the eyes and shook her head disagreeing with him. "Chase, I am thrilled to see you. I just can't go back to New York with you," she said honestly.

He waited a beat, nodded his head and said, "Wrong time?"

Nope! she thought again, *just the wrong brother*, as she took Chase by the arm and led him indoors.

. . .

The band had played just a few songs when the front man came to the mike and spoke to the crowd.

"Ladies and gentlemen, we have a very special treat for you tonight. We have with us here, as I am sure you're all aware, Mr. Charlie Morningstar who has…" the audience applauded heartily. He quieted them down with his hands "…who has asked if he could take the mike for a minute, so please put your hands together for Mr. Charlie Morningstar."

The audience applauded even louder and some sharp whistles were heard. Charlie came up the steps, still in his tux with his jacket removed and his collar loosened. He looked so handsome. He moved to get something just behind the curtain and brought out his guitar case containing his beautiful Meg. The audience held their breath collectively wondering what was about to happen.

Just as Charlie was being introduced, Georgie was bringing Chase through the back door and into the bar. She came and stood to the side of the bar visible from the stage and to Charlie. He cleared his throat, got Meg in position and stepped to the mike.

427

" Uh… hello." His face broke into a million sunbursts as he smiled and dropped his head, still shy after all these years. "I… uh… I'd like to congratulate Rosa and Marlon and wish them many years of happy wedded bliss." He paused, letting the audience applaud and cheer for the couple.

"I want you all to know that I have the bride's complete permission to do this." He gave another pause, cleared his throat and then said, "I've been told I am a man of few words and that may be so, but I will say this… Rosa and Marlon, your love has truly inspired me…" waiting a beat, "and what I say, I mean. And this… I mean," he said and then he began to play.

Georgie was transfixed on him. She instantly recognized the song he played as one Ray Charles wrote called, "You Don't Know Me." She knew it was meant for a woman who didn't know that someone she thought was only a friend, was truly in love with her. She listened as Charlie's deep, rich, bluesy, beautiful voice sang the words and she realized that Charlie was staring directly at her, singing the song to her rather than to the audience. His eyes never left hers and rather than closing them in his usual fashion, he kept them open and focused and never once broke his gaze. It was everything he couldn't say to her before now and she felt the song wash over her. She hadn't known – how could she? He had played it so close. Had he really loved her all this time? The song was finishing and she couldn't take her eyes off of him.

…I watched you walk away beside the lucky guy.
Oh, you'll never ever know
The one who loved you so.
Well, you don't know me.

When he finished, the audience waited a heartbeat, then applauded and cheered as they all looked towards Georgie. Rosa stood holding her hands in front of her heart and gushed as she smiled and her eyes welled up. All her hard work had paid off and she got a lovely wedding out of it to boot! *Worth every damn second of planning,* she thought.

Charlie removed Meg from around his shoulders and as the audience still applauded below him, he placed her safely away, closed and locked the case and carried it down off the stage and to the bar coming to stand before Georgie. The crowd behind them waited a moment and feeling slightly intrusive, collectively turned and started chatting and moving about, letting the couple have a private moment. As soon as it was only the two of them, Georgie looked at Charlie and smiled, her eyes nearly full, having difficulty catching her breath.

"Why didn't you ever tell me Charlie?" was the only thing she could think of, shaking her head to him.

"I think I just did," he said, deadpan, as he motioned for a quick drink. When he got it, he shot it back quickly and returned the glass to the bar. He then took Georgie by the arm and moved her gently towards the back doorway. He wanted to take her outside and talk to her just as Chase had, leaning on the railing. He had seen them as they stood there talking and he heard what Chase was offering her and as much as he loved his brother, he couldn't let Georgie go without telling her exactly how he felt. Chase didn't use the words "I love you" – he only made Georgie an offer, a change in geography, really. No mention of love, only an offer of being taken care of. Charlie had planned to sing something at Rosa's request, but the more he had thought about it, the more he wanted to make it about Georgie. He had asked Rosa if she was okay with this and she agreed whole heartedly. Rosa had filled Hailey in completely during her Skype chat while getting ready and it passed Hailey's approval with flying colors.

As they reached the doorway to step outside, rain started to fall and kept them from going any further, instead choosing to stand on the inside of the doorway as it came down in torrents outside. A rose had been tossed down onto the ground and its beautiful bloom was being smashed into the pavement with the weight of the heavy rain; its petals breaking free and littering the ground just outside near the ramp.

Briefly, they stared at one another. Georgie was about to apologize to him for her behavior since Wade's death but Charlie couldn't wait another minute and put his hand around her waist, pulling her to him as he bent his head to kiss her. He had waited to do this for more years than he could remember and it was such electricity that he broke from her a moment and stared at her before kissing her again and this time he held her in a lock tight grip while he finally kissed the woman he loved. The rain thundered down as they stood just out of its reach, kissing each other, Charlie's hands caressing through her hair and holding her head, stroking her sides and feeling her curves and taking her all in as he finally wrapped his arms around her and held her tight. When their mouths broke apart, they rested foreheads together feeling at long last, peace. There was no mistaking how they felt about one another and both were grateful the other finally knew.

"I love you, Charlie Morningstar," Georgie admitted to him softly.

"I love you, too," Charlie said to her. "I always have and I always will. I hope very soon to make you Mrs. Morningstar. I want you to be my wife and work together making this club a success and I promise you I will love you for as long I take breath and I have it on pretty good authority that it could be a very long time," he said to her, holding her head in his hands. He told her directly so that she had no questions about his intentions.

She stared at him and then broke into a huge smile. "You call that a marriage proposal?" she asked, joking with him and raising an eyebrow.

"Oh… no," he said. "I have a much more elaborate plan in mind for that, but I think it's in poor taste to get engaged at a wedding where you're the maid of honor and your fiancé gave the bride away," he replied, laughing with her.

...

While Charlie was on stage serenading Georgie, Chase watched for only a moment and then left the building through the back door tossing the rose away in disgust. He now stood watching their entire interaction inside the doorway from the other side of the parking lot. The rain poured down on him, soaking him, as he watched his older brother accepting kisses that should be meant for him. He wanted to go over and challenge Charlie but what the hell would he do, beat the crap out of his older brother? And who's to say he could? He loved them both very much and as he stood watching them rejoice in their own awakening, he couldn't help but feel conflicted. He was happy for them but he really thought Georgie would see him differently once he had something to show her. He realized at that moment that he never really stood a chance with Georgie. She had been Charlie's all along, even if Charlie didn't know it. He thought back over the years the three had known one another and saw that if he'd only opened his eyes, he'd have seen it for himself. He now understood that feeling in his gut he'd had for so long. He wanted to hate Charlie but he'd never really seen him so happy. In all the years they performed together, Charlie never once sang with his eyes open. It was just a given… except tonight, when he made his point well known to Georgie. Charlie had changed a lot in the past year and he had wished for that change the entire time they were together touring. Charlie was now being the Charlie that Chase had always wished for and yet Chase now wished he would go the hell away.

Huh, he scoffed, what was that his mother always said? *"Be careful what you wish for."* Well he got it in spades, didn't he? How could he have been so blind for so long? He would have to learn to live with it because he couldn't argue the point anymore; it was always in front of him – he just chose to ignore it. He stopped watching the couple and walked towards the front door, leaving them to their privacy and the moment they shared, his mind reeling from the emotions running through him. At least he still had his three million dollar contract. That would keep him warm at night.

. . .

Georgie and Charlie were still in the doorway when she remembered the letter from her uncle. "Come with me" she said to him, taking her hand and leading him up the stairs to the office.

"Right on," he said, thinking something else completely. He practically bounded up the steps two at a time before she stopped him with her hand.

"That's not what's going to happen here, Romeo, so just hang on there," she said, half joking to him. She walked into the office searching for her clutch. When she found it on her desk, she opened it and took Wade's letter from it and handed it to Charlie.

"Something else of Wade's that I want to give you tonight," she said.

He took the paper from her but held her gaze, opening it up slowly. He turned his attention to the handwriting, focusing intently on his old friend's written word and then he smiled wide when he got to the large lettering at the bottom. He shook his head gently and folded the paper back up.

"Wise old dog," he said.

"You're not mad at him for manipulating you?" she asked him gently.

"About as much as you are," he answered her and then pulled her into him for another deep kiss. "God, Georgie, I feel like I've wasted so much time running away from things that weren't real," he confessed. He had a lot of things to explain to her and in time, and plenty of Sunday mornings with Ray Charles, he would tell her all of it. For now, he just wanted to kiss her.

"Oh, and uh... I signed the papers over to Wade's house this afternoon." She paused. "Congratulations," she said smiling at him. He looked at her for a moment and said, "I think I'll make it a wedding gift to Rosa and Marlon. After all, I'm not going to need it... am I?" he asked her as he picked her up and kissed her.

"No," she responded. "I'm just glad you gave up the bus!"

...

The first person to greet them after they came from the office was Brad, smiling like the Cheshire cat. He held his arms out to Georgie and took her into his embrace.

"He has exquisite taste, I must say," he said fondly. She blushed wondering how much he had shared with his new found father, although she couldn't help but feel thrilled by his acceptance. Hopefully, they would be seeing more of Brad in the months and years to come. Things had only just started between Charlie and his father and it would be interesting to watch them find out about one another.

"I'd love to hear about how you found each other," Georgie said to them both as they stood before her.

"How about you two chat for a bit while I try and find Chase," Charlie suggested to them.

Georgie nodded and led Brad over to his table, chatting away, already shooting him rapid fire questions. Charlie smiled to himself as he watched them move through the crowd. He saw people nodding to them and then do a double take. He was such a dead ringer for his dad. Amazing!

. . .

Chase stepped out of the rain and entered the bar from the front doors. He grabbed the handle on his luggage and dragged it into the men's washroom where he picked it up and put it on the counter. He had to try and find something decent to put on and get out of his wet clothes. His felt defeated and didn't feel like staying for anyone's wedding now. What was the point? Georgie had had chosen Charlie and it hurt like a bitch. He was just removing his wet clothes and stuffing them into the garbage when Charlie walked in.

"There you are. I've been looking all over for you," he said as he saw Chase. "Uh… thinking of doing a strip tease for the bride?" he asked, hoping to lighten the mood. Although Chase had his back to him, Charlie could see his face in the mirror and knew that Chase was not happy.

"I'm changing into something dry and then I'm leaving, back to New York," Chase said angrily, his back still turned to his brother.

"Leaving, huh?" Charlie said, walking towards him and leaning against the counter so they were side by side now.

"Yup, everything I want is back in New York," Chase said, rummaging through his things for a clean shirt and pulling it on as he spoke.

"Except everyone who loves you, Chase," Charlie said softly as he watched his brother tear apart his luggage in anger. "I'm sure New York has a lot to offer and I don't want to stop you from going back but I want you to always remember that your family is here and always hoping you'll come home," Charlie said, trying to get through to him.

Chase just got angrier and let it overtake him. He started slamming his things back into the luggage until he spun around to look Charlie directly in the face.

"Bullshit!" he spat out at Charlie. "The one person I loved the most wants nothing to do with me and the other person I love took her from me. Does that sound like I'm fucking loved to you?" Chase asked him.

"I didn't take her from you, Chase. I simply told her that I loved her and I always have," Charlie explained gently with compassion to Chase's feelings. He wouldn't want to be in Chase's shoes. "She loves me too. You know she couldn't love both of us that way, don'tcha?" Charlie asked patiently, keeping his tone calm.

Chase dropped his head, leaned his arms against the counter and closed his eyes. For a moment Charlie wondered what was wrong with him and then he realized Chase was crying. Charlie immediately walked across the room and locked the door. *Okay*, he thought, *if we're going to do this in here then I'm giving us some guaranteed privacy.*

When he walked back towards Chase he could see that he had covered his face with his hands and was sobbing. He got back to his brother and touched him on the shoulder. Chase dissolved even more. Charlie's heart broke for his little brother and the two men embraced for a moment. Charlie pulled away first.

"I'm sorry, Chase. I didn't want you to feel so hurt. This whole thing, coming home, has been more emotional for me than I thought it would," he explained. "Finding Georgie here was a complete surprise and then with Wade's death and the club handed to me, I guess I just wanted to make it all complete. To me, that meant Georgie needed to be part of my life," he tried explaining to Chase.

Chase had turned his back to the mirror and still keeping his head down wiped his eyes while Charlie tried to make him understand.

"What the fuck, Charlie? I don't get it," Chase said confused. "For 20 years you do everything in your power to NOT come home, to NOT make a huge musical career for yourself, or anyone else and I can't remember you even caring about having a permanent woman in your life. What changed?" he asked honestly.

Chase wanted to know the truth from Charlie about his actions of the past year and why he had made Chase believe that something big was going to happen.

"Well, I envisioned this happening more at the bar with a couple of drinks in front of us, but I guess this is as good a place as any," he said more to himself.

His comment caused Chase to look up and around at the surroundings and he smiled briefly. "I never said I was a stickler for fine décor when it comes to hashing out life's dramas," Chase joked through his tears.

It was progress and Charlie was grateful for the humor. One thing could always be said about Chase, he could always make you laugh. Charlie nodded his head and smiled at his younger brother.

"I hear ya there, Chase," he said as he tried to figure out where to start. He decided the best thing to do was start with the letter.

"The day you were born, mom got a letter in the mail from a law firm that basically gave her the inheritance from Papa George's mother's estate, our great-grandmother," he explained. "The letter outlined our

435

little family tree going back to our great-grandparents and it listed their birthdates and the day they all died. When I read the letter I became obsessed with the fact that all of them, our great-grandparents and Papa George all died by their 50th birthday. That's why when Mom's 50th birthday came 'round, I was constantly calling home and insisted that we come home and be with her. I guess I thought I could protect her. I even insisted that she have a house party because the others had all been out on the night of their 50th birthday and died while they were out. When it didn't happen then, I spent a few weeks hovering nearer to home and then I relaxed. The fire happened a few months after that and again, within a year of her turning 50." He stopped for a moment to see if Chase was taking this all in. His tears had dried; he had pulled on a pair of dry jeans and was leaning barefoot with his shirt still open, his head hung down listening intently. Recognizing that he held his attention, Charlie continued.

"The fire only added to my fears and I just believed that death was chasing after me. I totally believed I would hit 50 and drop dead on stage with a full audience. I pictured seeing a People Magazine with my smiling face and the headline, "Blues artist dies at 50 on stage." He said this as he pointed out the imaginary headline with his hands, "It started making me nuts and by the time I became 50 and through that year, I was certain that I was going to drop dead at any moment," he said, confessing it all to Chase.

Chase nodded his head remembering Charlie's antics in the past year. A lot of this made sense to him.

"So how did you finally realize that you weren't going to die?" Chase asked, truly interested. Charlie was grateful that Chase had calmed enough to listen and seemed to understand the fear he'd lived with for many years.

"Well, at the show in Carmel, remember at the Indigo Place?" Charlie asked Chase and he nodded his head. "I met someone that night who told me something that changed everything," he said hoping Chase would bite… and he did.

"Who was it?" Chase asked, looking at him now, still leaning against the counter.

"I met my father," Charlie said and stopped.

Chase's head snapped back in disbelief. He stared at Charlie, mouth wide open. Charlie nodded his head at Chase knowing full well his shock.

"How the hell…?" Chase asked him.

Charlie told him the story of Bradley DuMont, their mother and how he came to be that night at the Indigo Palace. When Charlie finished Chase just shook his head.

"Unbelievable," Chase said, trying to figure out some reasonable explanation as to why it had all happened. "Did you do a paternity test or something to prove it?" he asked his brother.

Charlie just shook his head, "Didn't need to – you'll understand why when you meet him," Charlie said confidently.

Chase nodded at him believing he knew what he was talking about. "So you went running for all those years, never wanting to make it big, never wanting to make yourself known because you were certain you were going to die… at 50?" Chase asked him, showing Charlie that he now understood the fear he had lived with for the past 20 years, maybe more. When Charlie nodded his head in agreement, Chase just whistled.

"I can see how that would fuck with you something fierce, Charlie," Chase said softly, with compassion.

"So, when I wake up on my 51st birthday, still alive, despite the hangover I had…" Chase smiled at his brother for that, Charlie continued, "I just wanted to come home, you know? I was bone tired of the road and running away and I just hoped I could come home and settle. When I found Georgie here too, it was more than I expected." Charlie ended hoping that gave Chase enough information to help him understand.

Chase stayed quiet for a bit, still leaning against the bathroom counter, his head still hanging down.

The two brothers stayed there for a moment until Chase asked him, "What's your father like?"

"He's actually here tonight. Rosa invited him," Charlie said. "I'll introduce you to him," he offered. "I've wanted you to meet him for a while now," he said.

"I'd like that a lot," he said sounding conciliatory. Charlie stood for a moment looking at Chase. He thought a change in subject might help things along even more.

"So, why don't we get out of the shitter, get us a drink and go and sit with my father and you can tell me all about New York?" he asked Chase, hoping he was ready to leave the bathroom.

"I'd like *that* a lot, too," Chase said smiling. "Anyway, if we stay in here much longer with the door locked there is either going to be a revolt or a much juicier People Magazine headline about the Morningstar brothers and you know how you shy from publicity!" Chase said with a brighter smile and he and Charlie laughed together as they grabbed Chase's luggage and unlocked the door.

· · ·

Georgie and Brad were deep in conversation as Charlie and Chase approached the table. When Georgie caught Chase's eye she looked cautiously at him.

"Georgie, it's okay," he said to her. "I'm going to have to get used to this if I visit for birthdays, Thanksgiving or Christmas, right? Besides, at least it keeps you in the family," he said good naturedly to her and he bent in and kissed her head. "Believe it or not... I'm happy for you, Georgie," he said sincerely.

Georgie wasn't sure what had gone on in the bathroom but somehow Charlie had managed to make Chase understand things better and he seemed resolved to the outcome. Georgie smiled at him, mouthed "thank you".

"Bradley DuMont, I'd like you to meet my younger brother, Chase Morningstar. Chase, this is Bradley Spencer Dumont, my father," Charlie said as he introduced the two men.

Chase's head turned quickly to Charlie at the name "Spencer" and back to Brad as he held out his hand and Brad rose to accept it. The two men shook hands firmly, both smiling. Chase could not get over the uncanny resemblance and stared at the elder man for a bit before saying, "Christ, you so cheap you couldn't have paid for my brother to have his own face?" to which the whole table dissolved into laughter. Leave it to Chase; it was a good ice breaker.

. . .

As the wedding guests partied around them, the four sat huddled in deep conversation. Chase told them of his New York trip, how successful it had been and the contract he had signed.

"Kyle figures we'll be recording within a month, now that we've got a band backing me. Oh and speaking of which, I met a real character who thinks he once performed with mom," Chase said, directing the conversation to Charlie.

"Oh!" Charlie said interested. He had only heard of her performances through Wade having never really been to one himself. "What did he think?" asked Charlie.

"He thought she was just like Billie Holiday!" Chase answered proudly. "He's the piano player that Kyle knows. He's been recording with some pretty famous people and I sat in on a jam session with him and few other guys. It was excellent. The guy's name is Mark but everyone calls him Campbell. Funny as hell – kept me laughing the whole time," Chase said nonchalantly.

Charlie and Brad exchanged glances. Could it be? Had serendipity played a hand with the Morningstars yet again? Georgie and Chase could see that the father and son knew something about Chase's piano player and Chase asked the question, "What?" looking from Brad to Charlie and back again.

Charlie smiled at his younger brother and said simply, "Brother, I think we've finally put all the pieces of the puzzle together," and he left it at that. He would show Chase the information Brad had found regarding Campbell later, when they were alone. If Chase wished to go any further with it was his prerogative.

• • •

It wasn't until Rosa had gone past the table twice as the front end of a conga line that she spotted Chase sitting with Charlie, Georgie and Brad. She squealed with delight as she came over and practically knocked him out of his chair.

"Oh, Chase, you made it!" she screamed as she hugged him around the neck and rocked him back and forth. "I knew you'd come, I just knew you'd come," she repeated as she embraced with him.

"Hey," he said smiling. "Of course, I'd come, I wouldn't miss seeing you finally marry the right guy!" he said as she kissed near his ear and was swept off again by the conga line she had left.

The whole table smiled as Rosa, Marlon and the rest of the guests conga'd past the four sitting at the table. To Rosa, the day was complete.

• • •

Most of the guests had left, the bar looked good and thoroughly used and the dance floor was deserted. Midnight Blue had packed up and left more than a half hour ago. Rosa and Marlon remained, their honeymoon flight not leaving until 4:00 pm the next day. The rest of the group – Simon, Linz, Stilts, Brad, Georgie, Charlie and Chase, sat around a table enjoying one last drink between them for the night.

Chase had been grilled about New York and he told all of them about his recording contract, what famous musicians he had met and how much he had worked in the past month.

"Haven't sung on a single stage, but I've seen the recording studio a few times. Nothing of my own yet though. Haven't had a chance to write much. I'm hoping that'll happen soon," he said as they all sat around listening to him.

"I think you're going to miss performing to a live audience Chase," said Stilts, leaning back in his chair and drumming on his leg. "If you do ever miss it, it's not like you don't know anyone with a club where you could come and play," he hinted to Chase. The group chuckled at his not so subtle remark.

"Who is playing next, Charlie?" asked Simon. "Are we even going to bother? I mean with Rosa in England for two weeks and no Chase, are we just going to be known as "the Guys?" He shrugged his shoulders at Charlie. Charlie smiled at him and whispered something in Georgie's ear. She nodded in agreement and Charlie coughed and asked the group for their attention.

"Uh… you should all be aware that uh… Georgie and I are now…" Charlie waited and smiled at the group who were expecting him to say something else, which Charlie had anticipated, "…equal owners of the Black and Blue."

The group all gasped and collectively said, "What?" All except Chase who held his smile as he looked down.

"Wade willed his share of the club to me," Charlie admitted humbly. The group was in an obvious state of shock and all eyes looked to Georgie for guidance.

She smiled at all of them. "Seems my Uncle knows what's better for me than I do myself", she said as she squeezed Charlie's hand tightly and smiled wide to the rest of them. "Oh, don't think he's so lucky because I'm going to make him work like a slave," she joked, thrusting her thumb in Charlie's direction and they all laughed with her. The voices chatted around the table all openly wondering how that must have worked out and why he did it.

Finally, Charlie interrupted with, "...and Wade left one last thing." He reached into this pants pocket and pulled out keys. Georgie spotted them and smiled. This was a good thing. "He left these keys to his house and I believe they have Rosa and Marlon's name on them," he said, handing them to Marlon. "Congratulations," he said to them.

The couple looked at Charlie in disbelief. Marlon took the keys into his hand and turned to show them to Rosa. They both looked down at the keys and then up to Charlie.

"Seriously?" Rosa asked him incredulously.

"Seriously," Charlie answered.

He and Georgie shared a laugh and Chase looked over at them. He caught the moment between them and saw that they were holding hands and looked away. He knew that it was going to take more than just an afternoon to get over losing her. *It could take me a lifetime to accept it. Can't wait to go back to New York away from this,* he sat thinking. Almost as though she were reading his thoughts, Rosa asked him

"So, do you plan on staying in New York permanently?" her eyebrows raised and a hand on her newly married husband's leg possessively. Chase looked down as if contemplating his answer, but he didn't have to think about it. His heart couldn't stay around here, not now.

"For the unforeseeable future, yes," he answered honestly. He nodded and looked around at the band members. They were all nodding back at him as if in agreement; it was time he moved on.

"So," Rosa said, "It begs the question... do we keep the name Chasing Charlie? After all..." she pointed out cleverly, "there *is* no more Chase in Charlie, in more ways than one," she said, smiling and feeling pleased with herself.

"I think we should call ourselves "the house band" and leave it at that," suggested Stilts as grumbles and moans disagreed.

"What about just Charlie's Band?" Simon asked but he was booed by the table. They all sat thinking for a moment before Charlie broke the silence.

"Seems to me," said Charlie reflectively, "that the name "Chasing Charlie" was more about what *was* chasing Charlie and now that I'm home and no longer running from anything…" he paused and looked to Georgie for a moment, "I think we should be called "Chillin' Charlie."

The table started laughing and saying the name amongst them, but the more Charlie thought about it, the more he thought it was perfect. Regardless of what they voted, it was going to be his new mantra. He raised his glass, "here's to Chillin' Charlie" he said and the rest of the table repeated his toast.

Epilogue

The hustle and bustle of the kitchen was staggering. It was a big day for the nursing home and the staff was all very busy ensuring that everything was in order. The newspapers were to be there as well as local Channel 5 News. After all, it isn't everyday that a resident turns 102!

When he awoke that morning he did so with a smile. He took his time getting ready, making sure that his once blonde hair, now a shock of pure white, was combed and sat properly on his head. Lately it seemed to have a mind of its own! He stared at his reflection in the mirror and saw the face of his father from many years ago staring back at him. Even though he'd been gone some 18 years now, he had kept his promise and lived well over a hundred years, and now, so had his son. He took one last look, remembering a time long ago when his Papa looked at himself in a mirror before his time too. He looked deeply into his own eyes seeing the layers of family before him. George and Celia, both had gone lifetimes ago now. Together they didn't reach the age that he had. Interesting.

Before he left the room he reached down under his bed and pulled out the case. He hadn't opened it in years, but today he wanted her on display. She deserved that much at least. He unlocked the case and threw the lid open exposing the beautiful guitar, his Meg. He ran his fingers up and down the length of her neck, feeling the frets as his fingers gently plucked at the strings. It had been so many years since she had sung for him. He missed her greatly too. Leaving the lid open

445

and the case on the bed, he made his way out of his room and down to the main banquet hall. Today, he was BIG MAN ON CAMPUS and the notoriety didn't bother him in the least.

He walked with slow determination towards his destination making sure that everyone who passed was greeted with a cheery, "Hello!" He heard many happy birthday wishes along his route and he thanked the person each time.

When he entered the hall a loud "Surprise" was yelled out at him and he smiled his million watt smile at them as they led him to a wing backed chair decorated with balloons and "Happy Birthday" signs stuck all over it. He got seated and looked around the room. There weren't too many faces that he knew from years before. Many of the faces he saw were new to him, having only been in the nursing home for a few months since his beloved Georgie's death in January, half way through her 94th year.

Their marriage spanned 50 years despite their late starr. They were never apart, having owned and operated an extremely successful blues club, renamed The Morning Star, up until they sold it when Charlie was 89. He had played for a few years with the band, then stepped back and worked behind the scenes, hiring the talent and keeping the show running. Charlie had lived up to his obligation (as the elderly woman had told him) and filled the club with pictures of George and Celia during their lifetime of performances. He told anyone who would listen about the Morningstar family. About how musically gifted they were. His grandfather's natural talent passed down through to his daughter and her onto her two sons. He also loved to embellish on the fact that he and Chase escaped death by luckily having fathers with some longevity, and someone watching over them. The Morning Star became a beacon in the city for blues and jazz and Charlie and Georgie had to face facts that at age 89 and just over 81 they had to walk away from it. They just couldn't manage it anymore. They retired to their home just two blocks away and continued to come to the club for the fine food and music right up until near the end. Days before her death, Charlie had sat outside with Georgie on the back porch bundled up one last time to watch the rise of the morning star. It was something they had done together for years – something he had shared with her that she too had loved to do. He missed her greatly.

One of the staff came to his side and congratulated him on his birthday. He thanked the kind woman and nodded as she showed him a cone shaped Happy Birthday hat and gestured to him to allow her to put it on him. He nodded in agreement and once fitted, no one could mistake whose birthday it was today.

Charlie sat smiling as the crowd fussed about him. He had lived 51 years past when he last had a celebration of this magnitude, only today he was hoping for a different outcome. He had lived a good long life. Much longer than he had ever thought he would. Thanks to his DuMont genes, Charlie was indeed a centenarian. He had lived long enough that he had watched all those he loved and treasure die before him. Most of the Chasing Charlie band members were dead and gone many years.

Chase was 87, a long ago music star with an illustrious listing of Grammy's, CD's, fans and people who did everything for him. Everything. He'd had his share of trials and tribulations, good and bad publicity and paid a great price for some very bad decisions, but Chase lived up to his name and chased the hell out of his life. His story didn't go exactly like Charlie's after reuniting with his father. He may have had the scars to prove it but he was still alive and was living in Boca Raton with his much younger wife, number 3. Over the years they'd communicated a lot but hadn't seen each other much. Chase's schedule was always so hectic. He had managed to come for Georgie's funeral and looked very tired then. Charlie had held him tightly knowing full well that it would be the last time the brothers would be able to see each other. He and Dana had sent Charlie a card for his birthday and a single large red rose. It brought a tear to Charlie's eye when he saw it.

Cameras were snapping pictures of him and a microphone was thrust in front of his face and someone asked him, "What's the secret for your longevity, Mr. Morningstar?"

Charlie thought for a moment and then smiled answering, "I didn't let death chase me into an early grave, I loved only one woman my whole life and I had good family genes," he said matter-of-factly. It was all true after all.

The crowd began singing "Happy Birthday" as a huge cake was wheeled in and set before him. "Make a wish, Charlie," one of the staff encouraged him. "Go ahead and make a wish and blow the hell out of those candles," she said to him while steadying a camera to get the best picture.

Charlie thought about it for a moment. He had spent his first 51 years running away from death. Not anymore. His last 51 years he had spent living and loving and enjoying life. He was satisfied. Charlie knew what he had to do. He tilted his head back and closed his eyes and for the first time in 51 years he made his final birthday wish of his life. *Please take me home*, he wished in his head.

As he opened his eyes and blew out the candles a round of cheers and applause lit up the room, but the sound seemed to fade to Charlie as his vision became focused on one soul standing at the back of the room, quietly. She was a black elderly woman with apples for cheeks and bright eyes. She was impeccably dressed and Charlie felt he knew her from somewhere. She held Charlie's gaze steadily and continued smiling at him as all else seemed to fade away around him. Charlie knew there and then and prepared himself, ready to go home.

It is said that if you die on your birthday, you have lived a full life.

His epitaph read: Rest in peace Mr. Morningstar, may you always shine brightly.

THE END

DJ Sherratt is passionate about many things. A great story is one of them; she loves getting consumed by great narrative. Having worked in the healthcare industry for many years, she's been engaged in countless stories, many of which have enriched her life beyond words. Others prompted her to discover a creative outlet to provide balance to her heart and soul. Sherratt's father was the greatest storyteller she knew and she has fond memories of listening to his fables and tales. After years of participating in amateur theatre, raising a family and doting over her loving husband, this self-proclaimed "bargain fashionista" began to write. The idea for Chasing Charlie was born after a long drive to her home in London, Ontario one winter afternoon, while accompanied by Ray Charles. This is Sherratt's first novel.

CPSIA information can be obtained
at www.ICGtesting.com
Printed in the USA
BVHW042352201020
591453BV00026B/217

9 781496 921055